INVENTORY 98

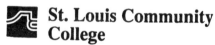 **St. Louis Community College**

Forest Park
Florissant Valley
Meramec

Instructional Resources
St. Louis, Missouri

GAYLORD

Christmas
in the
Good Old Days

Other Books by the Author

A Blessing

God bless the master of this house,
　　the mistress, also,
And all the little children
　　that round the table go:
And all your kin and kinsfolk,
　　that dwell both far and near;
I wish you a Merry Christmas,
　　and a Happy New Year.

The BABE, the SON,
The Holy ONE of
Mary.

CHRISTMAS IN THE GOOD OLD DAYS

A Victorian Album of
Stories, Poems, and Pictures of the Personalities
Who Rediscovered Christmas

Edited by DANIEL J. FOLEY

Illustrated with Sketches by CHARLOTTE
EDMANDS BOWDEN, Photographs by PAUL
E. GENEREUX, and a Portfolio of Christ-
mas Decorations Drawn by LUCY ELLEN
MERRILL in the Nineteenth Century

CHILTON COMPANY · BOOK DIVISION
Publishers
PHILADELPHIA AND NEW YORK

Republished by Omnigraphics ● Penobscot Building ● Detroit ● 1994

Designed by William E. Lickfield

Library of Congress Cataloging-in-Publication Data

Christmas in the good old days : a victorian album of stories,poems,
and pictures of the personalities who rediscovered Christmas /
edited by Daniel J. Foley.
p. cm.
Originally published: Philadelphia : Chilton, 1961.
Includes bibliographical references and index.
ISBN 0-7808-0003-6 (lib. bdg. : alk. paper)
1. Christmas—Literary collections. I. Foley, Daniel J.
PN6071.C6C527 1993
810.8'033—dc20   93-28202
                                                      CIP

Printed in the United States of America

FOR

*Priscilla
Sawyer
Lord*

1961

In Appreciation

To my MOTHER and MARGARET who have endured no end of inconvenience for the past year as the material for this book was being assembled.

To PRISCILLA SAWYER LORD who dreamed up the idea for "Christmas in the Good Old Days" and guided me in the selection of the stories and poems.

To Mrs. FRANK HAYWARD SAWYER, ELEANOR and ELIZABETH BROADHEAD, and C. SALLY LOW for permission to reproduce illustrations from their Victorian scrapbooks.

To DOROTHY S. GARFIELD for typing the manuscript and handling the infinite number of details associated with the preparation of this book.

To CHARLOTTE EDMANDS BOWDEN who made the sketches of the authors, as well as numerous drawings, and assembled the entire collection of illustrations for publication with the assistance of C. SALLY LOW and PAUL HUBBARD.

To PAUL E. GENEREUX for the photographs of the drawings of Miss Lucy Ellen Merrill and the Christmas decorations adapted from them.

To the HISTORICAL SOCIETY OF OLD NEWBURY for permission to use the pen-and-ink drawings of Lucy Ellen Merrill and especially to Mrs. C. W. BULLARD, who with the Members of the Society re-created the Spirit of a Victorian Christmas in December 1958, as portrayed in the Portfolio for Holiday Decorations.

To ABBOT MEMORIAL LIBRARY;
Miss LILLY ABBOTT;
Mrs. JULIA BARROWS;
THE BAY COLONY BOOKSHOP;
The Staff of the BOSTON ATHENAEUM;
BOSTON PUBLIC LIBRARY;
Miss MARGARET BRINE;
Mr. CHARLES H. P. COPELAND;
Mr. & Mrs. RALPH E. ERICSON;
Mr. DEAN A. FALES, Jr.;
Mr. RICHARD FLOYD;
Miss WINNIFRED FOLEY;
Mrs. W. W. K. FREEMAN;
Mr. EDWARD GARFIELD;
Mr. LEONARD GARFIELD;
Mrs. WARDER I. HIGGINS;
Miss MARGARET JEFFERSON;
Dr. G. L. LAVERTY;
Miss KATHERINE VAN ETTEN LYFORD;
Mr. FRANCIS J. LYNCH;
LYNN PUBLIC LIBRARY;
Mrs. BRUCE McLAUGHLIN;
Mrs. CHARLES A. POTTER;
Mrs. AMELIA McSWIGGIN RAWDING;
Mrs. FRANCES DIANNE ROBOTTI;
Staff of the SALEM PUBLIC LIBRARY;
Dr. ALFRED SHOEMAKER;
SWAMPSCOTT PUBLIC LIBRARY;
Rev. FRANCIS X. WEISER, S.J.;
Mrs. RICHARD L. WIGGIN, and
WOBURN PUBLIC LIBRARY who have contributed generously by lending books and providing technical assistance and sharing the fruits of their research.

I am grateful to the following authors, their representatives and publishers, for permission to include the selections indicated:

The TRUSTEES OF BERWICK ACADEMY for *An Empty Purse,* by Sarah Orne Jewett.

DOUBLEDAY & CO., INC., for *The Gift of the Magi,* from *The Four Million,* by O. Henry.

THE REILLY & LEE CO. for selections from *The Real Diary of a Real Boy,* by Henry A. Shute.

HOUGHTON, MIFFLIN COMPANY for *The Peterkins' Christmas Tree* from *The Peterkin Papers,* by Lucretia P. Hale, and *The Birds' Christmas Carol,* by Kate Douglas Wiggin.

THE MACMILLAN COMPANY for *Merry Christmas in the Tenements,* by Jacob A. Riis.

DANIEL J. FOLEY

Introduction

CHRISTMAS in the good old days, as recorded by the warm-hearted Victorians who wrote with faith, hope and love, fills the pages of this holiday book. The good old days means many things to many people, but more than anything else this phrase brings to mind a feeling of nostalgia. And, at no season of the year does this mood engulf our hearts with warmer emotion than at Christmas. The ever-inspiring message of "Peace on Earth to Men of Good Will" and "Joy to the World" flows with an evergreen freshness through the writings of a great galaxy of writers, spearheaded by Charles Dickens.

In the Victorian era, when emotion and sentiment dominated the hearts of men, Dickens won acclaim as the man who rediscovered Christmas. As the new architect of the most festive of seasons, he inspired the novelists, the poets, and the storytellers of his own day, and for decades to follow. He came to America on two occasions to spread the news, and in the words of Miss Elizabeth Wormely of Beacon Hill, "a fierce light shone upon every deed and word of the popular idol." The result was a romantic, heart-warming flood of pleasant reading, blended with tears and laughter, beginning with his own *Christmas Carol* and ending with Kate Douglas Wiggin's *The Birds' Christmas Carol,* nearly fifty years later. So all-embracing was Dickens' influence on both sides of the Atlantic that he was referred to as Father Christmas. When he died in 1870, a ragged girl in Drury Lane was heard to exclaim, "Dickens dead? Then will Father Christmas die, too?" In reply to this query, Theodore Watts wrote a little poem entitled "Dickens Returns on Christmas Day."

> "Dickens is dead." Beneath that grievous cry
> London seemed shivering in the summer heat:
> Strangers took up the tale like friends that meet:
> "Dickens is dead," said they, and hurried by;
> Street children stopped their games—they knew not why,
> But some new night seemed darkening down the street;
> A girl in rags, staying her way-worn feet,
> Cried, "Dickens dead? Will Father Christmas die?"
> City he loved, take courage on thy way
> He loves thee still in all thy joys and fears:
> Though he whose smiles made bright thine eyes of gray—
> Whose brave sweet voice, uttering thy tongueless years,
> Made laughters bubble through thy sea of tears—
> Is gone, Dickens returns on Christmas Day.

It was in the 19th century that St. Nicholas was transformed into a jolly, fat character known as Santa Claus. Decorated trees sprang up all over the land. The various states declared Christmas a legal holiday, and the age-old customs of carol singing and decking the halls with holly were revived with great gusto and enthusiasm. The elegant era of Christmas cards was launched with all the brilliance that the new color process of the time could produce.

In those golden days, faith and feeling burned with new brightness in cottages and mansions across the land as children and grownups read hundreds of stories and poems dramatizing the joy, the hope, and the love we know in a very special way at Christmas.

As one forgotten writer of the nineteenth century expressed it, "Before the Christmas fire that for two thousand years has sunk into embers to blaze again into a great light at the end of the twelfth month, men are not only reunited in the unbroken continuity of their fortunes, but in the wholeness of their life; in their power of vision as well as of sight, in their power of feeling as well as of thought, in their power of love as well as of action."

This "Album of Stories, Poems, and Pictures" is based on an attempt to present each selection with a picture of its author, sketched from existing portraits, together with a brief biography and some of the details relating to the stories and poems to set the stage for a full enjoyment of these personalities who rediscovered Christmas in the gilded era.

It is a nostalgic book, including such old favorites as Clement Moore's "A Visit from Saint Nicholas," Washington Irving's "Reminiscences of Christmas in England," selections from Henry A. Shute's "Real Diary of a Real Boy," Louisa May Alcott's "A Hospital Christmas," and Hans Christian Andersen's unforgettable tales. Kate Douglas Wiggin, Lucretia Peabody Hale, Frank Stockton, Herman Melville, Francis Bret Harte, Will Carleton, Henry Wadsworth Longfellow, John Fox, Jr., Irwin Russell, famous for his "Christmas Night in the Quarters," Horatio Alger, Jacob Riis, Phillips Brooks, and many others—are all here to recall and recapture the spirit of Christmas as it was lived and loved in Victorian days.

The rest of the story is told in woodcuts, steel engravings, pen-and-ink drawings and those wonderful lithographs which are as much fun to collect today as they were when they were printed in the good old days.

DANIEL J. FOLEY

Salem, Massachusetts

Contents

CHRISTMAS

In the Good Old Days

A PICTORIAL ALBUM

(Reproductions of Authentic Nineteenth Century
Christmas Collectors' Items)

A merry Christmas

A JOYFUL CHRISTMAS TO THEE

A merry Christmas
and a happy New Year.

With hope for our anchor
We've nothing to fear
So wish you bright Christmas
And happy New Year!

Copyright.

"Christmas
for
Ever!"

Wishing you   A Happy New Year.

Christmas in the Civil War Years

Recaptured in Diaries, Letters, Journals and Verse

"It was a clear, frosty Christmas Eve. Need I mention the date, when I say that Father Christmas came upon us with a deep gloom over his usually cheerful old features; that he made a mourning wreath instead of his holly and mistletoe; and that the nation was borne down by a grief so deep and so universal, that it was rather a time of national sorrow than of our great festival? The wound is yet too deep to necessitate reminding my readers of the troubled times through which we have just passed." This was the opening paragraph of "A Story About a Goose," which appeared in *Godey's Lady's Book* for December 1862. The story was unsigned and may have been Sarah Josepha Hale's subtle and genteel way of referring to the Great Conflict. The previous Christmas had also been overshadowed with gloom, but the festive seasons of 1863 and 1864 were truly dark with despair, want, and suffering.

Curiously enough, between 1861 and 1865 thirteen states declared Christmas a legal holiday. The movement for official observance of the day began in 1836 with Alabama, followed in 1838 by Louisiana and Arkansas. During the following twenty years, fifteen states followed suit. It is a singular fact that the District of Columbia did not give Christmas legal recognition until 1870. For those folk who had always celebrated according to their own heritage, it was not merely a day but a season for rejoicing in an era when the hearth and the home were the center of togetherness to a marked degree. Traditions and customs rooted in the Old World, particularly those of England, Germany, France, Holland, Scotland, and Ireland, were revived as memories of bygone Christmases came to mind. It was as it had always been, a nostalgic season in which tears and laughter were part of the outward expression of the day. The legal establishment of Christmas as a holiday merely provided more leisure for the enjoyment of the feast day that had been kept in the heart even when outward manifestations were frowned upon. Even a civil war that tore at the very fiber of a new nation, not yet a century old, could not obliterate the observance of Christmas in some special way.

Of all things, Christmas meant homecoming, with the attendant excitement of family reunions, but all was changed now. The black shadow of war hung heavily over the land. Families were separated, soldiers were ill-clad and food was scarce. Locked in the heart of every woman in the land was a feeling of despair, but the outward evidence of this deep feeling was not apparent. Bolstered by the philosophy and the courage which the anonymous poet expressed in the Christmas week issue of *Harper's Weekly,* wives and mothers and sisters could take courage in this kind of verse, and they did.

> For the peace of Christ hath millions
>   Accepted the battle trust;
> And yet, till His peace is perfect,
>   Shall war for the right be just;
>
> War for the right unshaken,
>   To partake not of a sin;
> War with its outward horrors,
>   And the heavenly peace within.
>
> The right is the peace eternal:—
>   And thus is this Christmas morn
> Rich in that day's fruition
>   When the Prince of Peace was born.

In countless letters and diaries written in those trying years are to be found vivid word pictures of how Christmas was spent. Mary Boykin Chesnut, in her "Diary from Dixie," has left us a picture of the sumptuous dinner she enjoyed at Christmas, 1863, with her friends on a plantation near Camden, South Carolina. Her husband was the first Southerner to resign from the U.S. Senate, and served on the staff of Jefferson Davis. This extraordinary woman set down more than 400,000 words in forty-eight little books. She had always kept a diary, and when on December 6, 1861, she began her account of the War, she wrote: "From today forward, I will tell the story in my own way." Even though oranges were five dollars apiece, if you could get them, there was no shortage of food on the elegantly set table which she described: "We dined at the Prestons'. I wore one of my handsomest Paris dresses." (From Paris before the war . . .) "We had for dinner oyster soup—soup à la reine; it has so many good things in it—besides boiled mutton, ham, boned turkey, wild ducks, partridges, plum pudding, sauterne, burgundy, sherry and Madeira. There is life in the old land yet!"

Recording the everyday events of the same year, J. B. Jones painted a more dismal picture of life in the Confederate capital at Richmond as he remarked that turkeys, which had sold for $11.00 apiece in 1862, were priced off the market for him, and men's shoes cost $25.00 a pair. Relying on his war clerk's salary, and a small royalty received for a book he had written, he was beginning to feel the pinch in the winter of 1863, but it was nothing compared to the conditions that were to follow. This and many other shrewd observations which appeared in *A Rebel War Clerk's Diary,* published in two volumes in Philadelphia in 1866, have made Jones's *Diary* fascinating reading ever since it was published. "It is a sad Christmas; cold and threatening snow. My two youngest children, however, have decked the parlor with evergreens, crosses, stars, etc. They have a cedar Christmas tree, but it is not burdened. Candy is held at $8. per pound."

Lewis Tibbals, with a shop at 512 Broadway in New York City, was advertising "Patent Spring Rocking Horses" for healthy exercise. In a two-inch advertisement in *Harper's Weekly* readers were informed of this wonderful toy for "Children of both sexes from 1½ to 12 years of age. Teaches the child to sit erect and expands the chest. Is a certain cure for round shoulders." There was no mention of price, for it was necessary to send stamps for an illustrated circular. Not everybody was feeling the drastic effects of war.

The household edition of the *Works of Charles Dickens,* published in 1863, brought this comment from the *New York Times,* December 19, of that year: "It is consoling to find in these evil days of rebellion that literature is not particularly suffering with the times. Indeed, so far from this being the case, we have noticed, within the last year or two, a growing improvement—a higher standard adopted by our publishers. There may be fewer books issued, but they are of more value; and they are certainly better presented in print and paper. If something more is charged for them, the purchaser gets more in proportion for his money.

". . . Beside the good heart in sending forth so luxurious an edition as this of Dickens at this time, the holiday season of the year, is particularly appropriate for a recognition of his genius. No author of modern times has so much of the good cheer of Christmas about him, or brings such a full flavor of the jolly Saint Nicholas into company. . . . Dickens brings the old Christmas into the present out of bygone centuries and remote manor-houses, into the living homes of the very poor of to-day."

Mrs. Roger Pryor was the wife of one of the "fire-eaters" of the South who championed slavery and deeply resented the war, calling it the "irrepressible conflict." She traveled with her husband throughout his varied career before, during, and after the war, and knew first-hand all the tragedy of the times. Roger was a prisoner in a Washington jail when she was trying to keep her family together during the dreadful "winter of want" in 1864. The dinner she prepared was in marked contrast to the fare she had been accustomed to, and with only faithful John, the colored servant, to help her. In *Reminiscences of Peace and War,* she wrote: "I resolved to give my family a Christmas dinner. John invented a method of making a perfectly satisfactory pie out of sorghum molasses, thickened with a little flour, mixed with walnut meats, and baked in a 'raised' crust. He prepared a number of these. I bought a piece of corned beef for fifty dollars. This was boiled with peas. But just as we were about to gather around the table, we saw a forlorn company of soldiers passing the door. They had gone out on some raid a week before. The snow was falling fast, the soldiers walked wearily, with dejected countenances. 'Boys,' I said, 'are you willing to send the dish of beef and peas out to them?' They agreed, if only they might carry it; and the bold little fellows liked the pleasure they gave more than they would have enjoyed the dinner. They were full of it for days afterward."

1864 marked the fourth Christmas of the great upheaval. The weariness of war, the great loss of life, the privation, the scarcity of food, the destruction—in short, a feeling of utter chaos and desperation—shook the land. Again an anonymous poet wrote a Christmas verse which appeared in *Harper's Weekly*. The last two quatrains express with proper Victorian feeling the hope which both sides held out for peace.

> Let harsh oppression pass away,
> And want and sin from off the earth,
>   And ever sacred be the day
>   That gave the blessed Saviour birth;
>
> Let black-winged pestilence disappear
> And war with all its horrors cease,
>   And may we in the tempest hear,
>   The solemn voice of Christ say "Peace!"

The chances are that Sarah Rice Pryor did not read these lines. Nor did the distraught soldier's wife in Nancemond County, Virginia, whose opening words in a letter to her husband, who was serving with General Pickett, were "things is worse and worse." Her concern was not with lofty thoughts, but rather with food for her four ragged, starving children. She wrote on December 17, 1864: "Christmus is most here again . . . I have got my last kalica frock on, and that's patched. Everything me and the children's got is patched. Both of them is in bed now covered up with comforters and old pieces of karpet to keep them warm, while I went 'long out to try and get some wood for their feet's on the ground and they have got no clothes, neither: and I am not able to cut the wood, and me and the children have broken up all the rails 'roun' the yard and picked up all the chips there is. We haven't got nothing in the house to eat but a little bit o' meal. The last pound of meet you got from Mr. G— is all eat up, and so is the chickens we raised. I don't want you to stop fighten them yankees till you kill the last one of them, but try and get off and come home and fix us all up some and then you can go back and fight them a heep harder than you ever fought them before. We can't none of us hold out much longer down here. One of General Mahone's skauts promised me on his word to carry this letter through the lines to you, but, my dear, if you put off acomin' 'twon't be no use to come, for we'll all hands of us be out there in the garden in the old graveyard with your ma and mine."

After he received the letter, the worried soldier went home without seeking a furlough and upon his return to camp was arrested as a deserter, found guilty and sentenced to be hanged. He appealed to General Pickett's wife, who interceded with her husband. The execution was postponed, and three days later an order came from the Confederate capital at Richmond reprieving all deserters.

Judith Brackenbrough McGuire was described by a contemporary as "a thoughtful, refined, eminently Christian matron." In her *Diary of a Southern Refugee, During the War,* which was published immediately after the war, she reveals the sad state of affairs as observed by the wife of an Episcopal minister. "Dec. 26th, 1864 . . . The sad Christmas has passed away . . . The Church services in the morning were sweet and comforting. St. Paul's was dressed most elaborately and beautifully with evergreens; all looked as usual; but there is much sadness on account of the failure of the South to keep Sherman back. When we got home our family circle was small, but pleasant. The Christmas turkey and ham were not. We had aspired to a turkey, but finding the prices range from $50 to $100 in the market on Saturday, we contented ourselves with roast-beef and the various little dishes which Confederate times have made us believe are tolerable substitutes for the viands of better days. At night I treated our little party to tea and ginger cakes—two very rare indulgences; and but for the sorghum, grown in our own fields, the cakes would be an impossible indulgence. Nothing but the well-ascertained fact that Christmas comes but once a year would make such extravagance at all excusable."

From the great array of Civil War diaries that were published in the Reconstruction Era, and others that appeared decades later, can be drawn the substance for many a true story of Christmas. The diversion which the contents of an old black chest provided for his family during the gloomy Christmas of 1864 is recounted by J. B. Jones in his *Rebel War Clerk's Diary.* The chest, containing "odds and ends of housekeeping," had been brought to Richmond from Burlington, New Jersey, when he and his family had come there four years earlier. The chest had never been opened, since the key was lost. Several attempts with keys and wire having brought no results, Jones pried it open with a poker while his family was attending Christmas services. A casual glance at the top layer revealed only "odds and ends," as far as he observed. His entry for December 26 gave the following account: "I closed it, replaced the striped cover, and put cage with the parrot on it, where it usually remains. The day, and the expressed objection of my wife to have the lock broken or injured, have, until to-day, restrained me from revealing to the family what I had done. But now I shall assemble them, and by a sort of Christmas story, endeavor to mollify my wife's anticipated displeasure. The examination of the contents will be a delightful diversion for the children, old and young.

"My impromptu Christmas tale of the old Black Chest interested the family, and my wife was not angry. Immediately after its conclusion, the old chest was surrounded and opened, and among an infinite variety of rubbish were some articles of value, viz., of chemises (greatly needed), several pairs of stockings, 1 Marseilles petticoat, lace collars, several pretty baskets, 4 pair ladies' slippers (nearly new), and several books . . . There were also many toys and keepsakes presented Mrs J. when she was an infant, forty years ago, and many given our children when they were infants, besides various articles of infants' clothing, etc., both of intrinsic value, and prized as reminiscences. The available articles, though once considered rubbish, would sell, and could not be bought here for less than $500.

"This examination occupied the family the remainder of the day and night—all content with this Christmas diversion—and oblivious of the calamities which have befallen the country. It was a providential distraction."

"I beg to present to you as a Christmas gift the city of Savannah." These were the words contained in General Sherman's telegram, sent to President Lincoln on Sunday, December 25, 1864. The news spread quickly, and both capitals were buzzing with excitement. On New Year's Day, 1865, the jubilant spirits of the revelers in Washington and the impenetrable gloom of the croakers kindled within the hearts of many the hope that they had witnessed the last of the grim war Christmases. And they had.

No truly great writing emerged from these dark days, but several poems express the sadness of heart felt on both sides. William Gordon McCabe, the young University of Virginia student, wrote "Christmas Night of '62" at Yorktown. The following year Henry Wadsworth Longfellow poured out his heart in "Christmas, 1863." Louisa May Alcott painted a graphic picture of hospital life in Washington in her book, *Hospital Sketches,* which appeared in 1863. Seven years later "A Hospital Christmas," one of her early stories, brought back Christmas memories of those eventful days. In later years, Frank A. Burr reminisced in his colorful account, "Christmas in Libby Prison." A sizable volume could be compiled to tell a more complete story. The selections included in this anthology are but a sampling.

Washington Irving

A POLISHED writer who was also a good-humored satirist, with a flair for vivid description, Washington Irving made for himself an enviable place in American literature. One of his great gifts was his ability to create legends. The *Sketch Book,* with its fabulous stories of "Rip Van Winkle" and "The Legend of Sleepy Hollow," was produced during his seventeen-year residence in England. This book brought him great fame as the first American writer to be recognized in Europe.

Irving was born in 1783 and died in 1859. Life for him became an extraordinarily cosmopolitan venture. On his first trip to Europe, pirates attacked the ship in which he was traveling. As a talented writer he came to know nearly every literary personality of stature in his day. He was on friendly terms with six American presidents, and shared a rare friendship with many of the crowned heads of Europe. In the 1840's he rendered valuable service as our Minister to Spain.

During his long residence at his beautiful estate, Sunnyside-on-the-Hudson, in New York State, Irving wrote several notable biographies, among them a life of Washington. His style, his knowledge of history, the warmth of his writing, and his amazing versatility in the literary world made him greatly loved and widely read.

When the *Sketch Book* appeared, issued in several parts in 1819-20, it was warmly received both in England and America. The essays and stories were read and reread and many of them have been reprinted frequently in a variety of editions for nearly a century and a half. Three devoted to English Christmas have that kind of perennial charm that is as traditional as holly and mistletoe. Dickens greatly admired Irving's writings and knew them intimately.

CHRISTMAS IN ENGLAND

THERE is nothing in England that exercises a more delightful spell over my imagination than the lingerings of the holiday customs and rural games of former times. They recall the pictures my fancy used to draw in the May morning of life when as yet I only knew the world through books, and believed it to be all that poets had painted it; and they bring with them the flavour of those honest days of yore, in which, perhaps with equal fallacy, I am apt to think the world was more homebred, social, and joyous than at present. I regret to say that they are daily growing more and more faint, being gradually worn away by time, but still more obliterated by modern fashion. They resemble those picturesque morsels of Gothic architecture which we see crumbling in various parts of the country, partly dilapidated by the waste of ages, and partly lost in the additions and alterations of latter days. Poetry, however, clings with cherishing fondness about the rural game and holiday revel, from which it has derived so many of its themes—as the ivy winds its rich foliage about the Gothic arch and mouldering tower, gratefully repaying their support by clasping together their tottering remains, and, as it were, embalming them in verdure.

Of all the old festivals, however, that of Christmas awakens the strongest and most heartfelt associations. There is a tone of solemn and sacred feeling that blends with our conviviality, and lifts the spirit to a state of hallowed and elevated enjoyment. The services of the church about this season are extremely tender and inspiring. They dwell on the beautiful story of the origin of our faith, and the pastoral scenes that accompanied its announcement. They gradually increase in fervour and pathos during the season of Advent, until they break forth in jubilee on the morning that brought peace and good-will to men. I do not know a grander effect of music on the moral feelings than to hear the full choir and the pealing organ performing a Christmas anthem in a cathedral, and filling every part of the vast pile with triumphant harmony.

It is a beautiful arrangement, also derived from days of yore, that this festival, which commemorates the announcement of the religion of peace and love, has been made the season for gathering together of family connections, and drawing closer again those bonds of kindred hearts which the cares and pleasures and sorrows of the world are continually operating to cast loose; of calling back the children of a family who have launched forth in life, and wandered widely asunder, once more to assemble about the paternal hearth, that rallying-place of the affections, there to grow young and loving again among the endearing mementoes of childhood.

There is something in the very season of the year that gives a charm to the festivity of Christmas. At other times we derive a great portion of our pleasures from the mere beauties of nature.

*   *   *   *   *   *

In the course of a December tour in Yorkshire, I rode for some distance in one of the public coaches, on the day preceding Christmas. The coach was crowded, both inside and out, with passengers, who, by their talk, seemed principally bound to the mansions of relations and friends to eat the Christmas dinner. It was loaded also with hampers of game, and baskets and boxes of delicacies and hares hung dangling their long ears about the coachman's box—presents from distant friends for the impending feasts. I had three fine rosy-cheeked schoolboys for my fellow-passengers inside, full of the buxom health and manly spirits which I have observed in the children of this country. They were returning home for the holidays in high glee, and promising themselves a world of enjoyment. It was delightful to hear the gigantic plans of pleasure of the little rogues, and the impracticable feats they were to perform during their six weeks' emancipation from the abhorred thraldom of book, birch, and pedagogue. They were full of anticipations of the meeting with the family and household, down to the very cat and dog; and of the joy they were to give their little sisters by the presents with which their pockets were crammed; but the meeting to which they seemed to look forward with the greatest impatience was with Bantam, which I found to be a pony, and, according to their talk, possessed of more virtues than any steed since the days of Bucephalus. How he could trot! how he could run! and then such leaps as he would take—there was not a hedge in the whole country that he could not clear.

They were under the particular guardianship of the coachman, to whom, whenever an opportunity presented, they addressed a host of questions, and pronounced him one of the best fellows in the whole world. Indeed, I could not but notice the more than ordinary air of bustle and importance of the coachman, who wore his hat a little on one side, and had a large bunch of Christmas greens stuck in the buttonhole of his coat. He is always a personage full of mighty care and business, and he is particularly so during this season, having so many commissions to execute in consequence of the great interchange of presents.

* * * * * * *

Perhaps the impending holiday might have given a more than usual animation to the country, for it seemed to me as if everybody was in good looks and good spirits. Game, poultry, and other luxuries of the table, were in brisk circulation in the villages; the grocers', butchers', and fruiterers' shops were thronged with customers. The housewives were stirring briskly about, putting their dwellings in order; and the glossy branches of holly, with their bright red berries, began to appear at the windows. The scene brought to mind an old writer's account of Christmas preparations: —"Now capons and hens, besides turkeys, geese, and ducks, with beef and mutton—must all die; for in twelve days a multitude of people will not be fed with a little. Now plums and spice, sugar and honey, square it among pies and broth. Now or never must music be in tune, for the youth must dance and sing to get them a heat, while the aged sit by the fire. The country maid leaves half her market, and must be sent again, if she forgets a pack of cards on Christmas eve. Great is the contention of Holly and Ivy, whether master or dame wears the breeches. Dice and cards benefit the butler; and if the cook do not lack wit, he will sweetly lick his fingers."

Clement C. Moore

In 1821, the year before Dr. Clement C. Moore wrote "A Visit from St. Nicholas" for the amusement of his children, a small juvenile was published in New York called *The Children's Friend*. It was a simple book with eight small color plates and an equal number of verses about "Santeclaus," who was shown riding in a sleigh drawn by a single reindeer. This is believed to be the first mention of Santa's reindeer and sleigh as we know them today.

Washington Irving had told the story of St. Nicholas and Santa Claus in his *Knickerbocker History,* which was first published in 1809. Undoubtedly Dr. Moore had read Irving's book, for it became popular at a time when there were few American writers. He may have been familiar with *The Children's Friend.* At any rate, he wrote one of the best loved and most widely quoted poems ever produced in America. Yet, at the time, he thought it of little merit. To a scholar of Hebrew who was working on a dictionary in that language, a man who was also a distinguished Episcopal preacher and the son of the Bishop of New York, it probably seemed like doggerel. It was simply a bit of verse to delight his own children, and the story was based on his own family and their surroundings.

Clement Moore's St. Nicholas was no austere saint, such as was portrayed in the old-world Dutch tradition or by Washington Irving. Rather, he was a jolly fat man, typical of the prosperous Dutchman who had settled New York nearly two centuries earlier. In fact, this inimitable characterization may well have been inspired by a real person whose name was Jan Duyckinck. He was the caretaker at the Moore home in New York, and it is claimed that he was "fat, jolly and bewhiskered" and that he smoked "a stump of a pipe." Dr. Moore's St. Nicholas had eight reindeer, each with a name, to enable him to get around in his wonderful sleigh.

"The Night Before Christmas," as the poem is fondly referred to, would surely have been forgotten or lost had it not been for Miss Harriet Butler, the daughter of a clergyman from Troy, New York, who was visiting the Moores that Christmas and heard the clergyman read his poem. She got permission to copy it in her album and, the following year, it appeared anonymously in *The Troy Sentinel* just before Christmas. However, it was not until 1837, when it appeared with a collection of local poetry in book form, that Dr. Moore acknowledged that he was the author. Curiously enough, that same year Robert W. Weir, professor of art at West Point, painted a portrait of Santa Claus, fat and jolly, about to go up a chimney after filling the stockings he found there.

The story of Santa's phenomenal rise to fame in the years that followed, and his versatility in meeting the requests of children all over the world, has been told in scores of books. However, there is more to the story of this wonderful poem. During the latter years of his life, Dr. Moore lived in a large, rambling farmhouse in Newport, Rhode Island—which is still standing. Each year at Christmas since 1954, James Van Alen, a native of this historic community, has presented a dramatic reading of "A Visit from St. Nicholas," assisted by his wife and four children from the neighborhood. Dressed in costumes of the period, the group assembles in front of the fireplace of the Newport house for the reading of the poem. Then it is re-enacted in the yard under floodlights for the pleasure of the neighbors, followed by carol singing. Later, gifts from the sleigh, which arrives on a float, are distributed to a local children's home. Jimmy Van Alen, as he is popularly known, has organized the House of Santa Claus Society, and hopes to be able to raise enough funds to make the Moore house a historic shrine and Christmas Museum. This enthusiastic champion of Dr. Moore believes that no American has provided more joy for young and old. Mr. Van Alen has written a sequel of seventeen couplets to the poem, because as a child he thought the poem ended too soon, and he wanted "to make the fun last longer." In an interview with Charles D. Rice, he added, "I used to worry about Father standing there by the open window as the poem closes. I was afraid he might catch cold, so now I've tucked him safely into bed. I hope Dr. Moore isn't cross at me."

A VISIT FROM ST. NICHOLAS

'Twas the night before Christmas, when all through the house
Not a creature was stirring, not even a mouse;
The stockings were hung by the chimney with care,
In hopes that ST. NICHOLAS soon would be there;

The children were nestled all snug in their beds,
While visions of sugar-plums danced through their heads;
And Mamma in her 'kerchief, and I in my cap,
Had just settled our brains for a long winter's nap,—

When out on the lawn there arose such a
clatter,
I sprang from my bed to see what was the
matter;
Away to the window I flew like a flash,
Tore open the shutters and threw up the
sash.

The moon on the breast of the new-fallen
snow
Gave the lustre of midday to objects below;
When, what to my wondering eyes should
appear,
But a miniature sleigh, and eight tiny
reindeer,

With a little old driver, so lively and
quick,
I knew in a moment it must be SAINT
NICK.
More rapid than eagles his coursers they
came,
And he whistled, and shouted, and called
them by name:

"Now, *Dasher!* now, *Dancer!* now, *Prancer*
and *Vixen!*
On, *Comet!* on, *Cupid!* on, *Donder* and
Blitzen!
To the top of the porch! to the top of the
wall!
Now, dash away! dash away! dash away
all!"

As dry leaves that before the wild hurricane
fly,
When they meet with an obstacle, mount
to the sky,
So up to the house-top the coursers they
flew,
With a sleigh full of toys—and ST. NICH-
OLAS too!

And then, in a twinkling, I heard on the
roof,
The prancing and pawing of each little
hoof.
As I drew in my head, and was turning
around,
Down the chimney ST. NICHOLAS came
with a bound.

He was dressed all in fur, from his head
to his foot,
And his clothes were all tarnished with
ashes and soot!
A bundle of toys he had flung on his
back,
And he looked like a pedlar just opening
his pack;

His eyes—how they twinkled! his dimples,
how merry!
His cheeks were like roses, his nose like a
cherry!
His droll little mouth was drawn up like
a bow,
And the beard of his chin was as white
as the snow.

The stump of a pipe he held tight in his
teeth,
And the smoke, it encircled his head like
a wreath.
He had a broad face, and a little round
belly,
That shook, when he laugh'd, like a bowlful of jelly.

He was chubby and plump; a right jolly
old elf;
And I laughed, when I saw him, in spite
of myself.
A wink of his eye, and a twist of his head,
Soon gave me to know I had nothing to
dread.

He spoke not a word, but went straight
to his work,
And filled all the stockings—then turned
with a jerk,
And laying his finger aside of his nose,
And giving a nod, up the chimney he
rose.

He sprang to his sleigh, to his team gave
a whistle,
And away they all flew, like the down off
a thistle.
But I heard him exclaim, ere he drove out
of sight,
*"Happy Christmas to all! and to all a
good night!"*

Charles Dickens

WHEN Charles Dickens made his first trip to America in 1842, he arrived in Boston at 5:00 P.M. on the 22nd of January. Accompanied by his wife and daughter, he was met by a flock of newspapermen who set the tone of his exciting visit. Immediately he was hailed in the *Boston Daily Mail* as "the unrivaled delineator of human life, the author of mirth-provoking 'Pickwick,' the kind-hearted friend of poor 'Oliver' and 'Nicholas' and sweet little 'Nelly.' The solace of the lonely, the companion of the gay, the beloved and admired of all ages and classes, wherever the English language is spoken."

Although the young author was only twenty-nine years old, he was already widely known. He was no sooner settled at the Tremont House than a sculptor, a painter, hundreds of autograph seekers, and the ever-present reporters descended upon him, together with a host of distinguished visitors. Dickens had been in Boston for only six hectic days when an envoy from New York arrived bearing invitations for his reception in the great metropolis. Before leaving Boston, he was honored at a great dinner at which Josiah Quincy, President of Harvard University, paid him lofty tribute in company with all the leading social and literary men of the city. No public reception to any literary man in America could compare with the hospitality and the display of affection that were tendered him. He visited many other American cities as well, but Boston always held a warm spot in his heart.

In December 1843, *A Christmas Carol,* the most fabulous Christmas story ever written, was published by Bradbury and Evans in London, and behind its appearance was the tale of its author and his own personal struggle for survival. With a wife, a sister-in-law, and a growing family to support, Dickens had more than the usual financial worries of a young writer. For nearly a year monthly installments of "Martin Chuzzlewit" had occupied his time, but sales were not spectacular. Living expenses were mounting with the passing of each day, and he was soon to become the father of a fifth child. A trip to Italy where the cost of living was low might solve his problems, but it did not materialize. It was during these desperate October days that he dreamed up the idea for a Christmas story and he tackled it with zest. As he wrote later, he "wept, and laughed, and wept again, and excited himself in the most extraordinary manner in the composition, and thinking thereof he walked about the black streets of London, fifteen or twenty miles, many a night when all the sober folks had gone to bed." The story was finished in a little more than a month. "A Christmas Carol in Prose, Being a Ghost Story of Christmas" appeared on the stands just six days before Christmas. The first edition of 6,000 copies sold out the first day and letters of praise began to pour in from all parts of England.

The stimulation resulting from his trip to America the previous year was mild compared with the jubilation in the Dickens household that Christmas. "Such dinings, such dancings, such conjurings, such blind-man's buffings, such theatergoings, such kissings-out of old years and kissings-in of new ones, never took place in these parts before." But the royalty statement which came in February was a jolt. The book had sold about 15,000 copies but the production costs had been high and royalties did not measure up to expectations. However, the Scrooge production continued to sell throughout his lifetime and to this day holds its place in popularity and sales as one of the greatest little books in the world.

The "Christmas Carol" earned for Dickens the title of "Father Christmas." He was considered the spirit of "Christmas incarnate" and a kind of incarnation of this festive season. So prevalent was this feeling in England that when he died many simple folk thought that there would be no more Christmases. As William A. Watt has written, "The persistence of this assumption is a tribute to the magic of Dickens's pen." And he adds, "If Dickens was Father Christmas himself, he was a father who became as dejected over Christmas bills as he was elated over Christmas wassail."

When Dickens wrote his masterpiece in the "hungry forties," England was in the midst of an economic upheaval. The tragedy of poverty cut deeply into his social consciousness. In 1853 when he gave his first public reading of the "Christmas Carol," he demanded that seats be set aside for working men and their families at prices they could pay. Aside from his warm humanitarianism, he inspired the plain people of his homeland and of America also to become avid readers. His feelings and his mode of expression gave them hope and courage.

In his public readings, Dickens charmed and captivated his audiences. He made them laugh and cry and held them suspended in animation. Like a magician, he used his voice, his expression, the movements of his hands and his own distinguished appearance to hold his listeners in the palm of his hand. Dickens became a professional entertainer as he literally breathed for his characters, and the heartbeat of Tiny Tim could be heard in the audience. Success was the keynote of all his lecture tours. Dickens was lionized and overwhelmed by his listeners and he loved every minute of it, but the experience took its toll on his health.

For a century the critics have had their day commenting and theorizing about the implications of the "Christmas Carol." But the author's own statement about his Christmas books, stated with simple modesty, simplicity and sincerity, tells more than all the critics' theories. "My purpose was, in a whimsical kind of mask which the good humor of the season justified, to awake some loving and forebearing thoughts, never out of season in a Christian land."

Every Dickens enthusiast recalls with pleasure the titles of his hero's writings on Christmas. He had first expressed himself in "Sketches by Boz," then in the Dingley Dell scenes in "Pickwick Papers," before the "Carol" was written. In the years that followed, he wrote "The Chimes," "The Cricket on the Hearth," "The Battle of Life," and "The Haunted Man." Shorter pieces, twenty in number, appeared in "Household Words" and "All the Year Round." However, "A Christmas Carol" topped them all.

On his second visit to America in 1868, only two years before his death, he wrote, "I have got to know the 'Carol' so well that I can't remember it, and occasionally go dodging about in the wildest manner, to pick up lost pieces. They took it so tremendously last night that I was stopped every five minutes. One poor girl in mourning burst into a passion of grief about Tiny Tim and was taken out." Such was the spirit of Christmas which Dickens imparted, and the imprint has left its mark.

A CHRISTMAS CAROL
In Four Staves

Stave One: Marley's Ghost

MARLEY was dead, to begin with. There is no doubt whatever about that. The register of his burial was signed by the clergyman, the clerk, the undertaker, and the chief mourner. Scrooge signed it. And Scrooge's name was good upon 'Change for anything he chose to put his hand to.

Old Marley was as dead as a door-nail.

Scrooge knew he was dead? Of course he did. How could it be otherwise? Scrooge and he were partners for I don't know how many years. Scrooge was his sole executor, his sole administrator, his sole assign, his sole residuary legatee, his sole friend, his sole mourner.

Scrooge never painted out old Marley's name, however. There it yet stood, years afterwards, above the warehouse door—

Scrooge and Marley. The firm was known as Scrooge and Marley. Sometimes people new to the business called Scrooge Scrooge, and sometimes Marley. He answered to both names. It was all the same to him.

Oh! But he was a tight-fisted hand at the grindstone, was Scrooge! a squeezing, wrenching, grasping, scraping, clutching, covetous old sinner! External heat and cold had little influence on him. No warmth could warm, no cold could chill him. No wind that blew was bitterer than he, no falling snow was more intent upon its purpose, no pelting rain less open to entreaty. Foul weather didn't know where to have him. The heaviest rain and snow and hail and sleet could boast of the advantage over him in only one respect,—they often "came down" handsomely, and Scrooge never did.

Nobody ever stopped him in the street to say, with gladsome looks, "My dear Scrooge, how are you? When will you come to see me?" No beggars implored him to bestow a trifle, no children asked him what it was o'clock, no man or woman ever once in all his life inquired the way to such and such a place, of Scrooge. Even the blind men's dogs appeared to know him, and when they saw him coming on, would tug their owners into doorways and up courts; and then would wag their tails as though they said, "No eyes at all is better than an evil eye, dark master!"

But what did Scrooge care! It was the very thing he liked. To edge his way along the crowded paths of life, warning all human sympathy to keep its distance, was what the knowing ones call "nuts" to Scrooge.

Once upon a time—of all the good days in the year, upon a Christmas eve—old Scrooge sat busy in his counting-house. It was cold, bleak, biting, foggy weather; and the city clocks had only just gone three, but it was quite dark already.

The door of Scrooge's counting-house was open, that he might keep his eye upon his clerk, who, in a dismal little cell beyond, a sort of tank, was copying letters. Scrooge had a very small fire, but the clerk's fire was so very much smaller that it looked like one coal. But he couldn't replenish it, for Scrooge kept the coal-box in his own room; and so surely as the clerk came in with the shovel, the master predicted that it would be necessary for them to part. Wherefore the clerk put on his white comforter, and tried to warm himself at the candle; in which effort, not being a man of a strong imagination, he failed.

"A Merry Christmas, uncle! God save you!" cried a cheerful voice. It was the voice of Scrooge's nephew, who came upon him so quickly that this was the first intimation Scrooge had of his approach.

"Bah!" said Scrooge; "humbug!"

"Christmas a humbug, uncle! You don't mean that, I am sure?"

"I do. Out upon merry Christmas! What's Christmas time to you but a time for paying bills without money; a time for finding yourself a year older, and not an hour richer; a time for balancing your books and having every item in 'em through a round dozen of months presented dead against you? If I had my will, every idiot who goes about with 'Merry Christmas' on his lips should be boiled with his own pudding, and buried with a stake of holly through his heart. He should!"

"Uncle!"

"Nephew, keep Christmas in your own way, and let me keep it in mine."

"Keep it! But you don't keep it."

"Let me leave it alone, then. Much good may it do you! Much good it has ever done you!"

"There are many things from which I might have derived good, by which I have not profited, I dare say, Christmas among the rest. But I am sure I have always thought of Christmas time, when it has come round—apart from the veneration due to its sacred origin, if anything belonging to it can be apart from that—as a good time; a kind, forgiving, charitable, pleasant time; the only time I know of, in the long calendar of the year, when men and women seem by one consent to open their shut-up hearts freely, and to think of people below them as if they really were fellow-travellers to the grave, and not another race of creatures bound on other journeys. And therefore, uncle, though it has never put a scrap of gold or silver in my pocket, I believe that it *has* done me good, and *will* do me good; and I say, God bless it!"

The clerk in the tank involuntarily applauded.

"Let me hear another sound from you," said Scrooge, "and you'll keep your Christmas by losing your situation! You're quite a powerful speaker, sir," he added, turning to his nephew. "I wonder you don't go into Parliament."

"Don't be angry, uncle. Come! Dine with us to-morrow."

Scrooge said that he would see him—yes, indeed he did. He went the whole length of the expression, and said that he would see him in that extremity first.

"But why?" cried Scrooge's nephew. "Why?"

"Why did you get married?"

"Because I fell in love."

"Because you fell in love!" growled Scrooge, as if that were the only one thing in the world more ridiculous than a merry Christmas. "Good afternoon!"

"Nay, uncle, but you never came to see me before that happened. Why give it as a reason for not coming now?"

"Good afternoon."

"I want nothing from you; I ask nothing of you; why cannot we be friends?"

"Good afternoon."

"I am sorry, with all my heart, to find you so resolute. We have never had any quarrel, to which I have been a party. But I have made the trial in homage to Christmas, and I'll keep my Christmas humour to the last. So A Merry Christmas, uncle!"

"Good afternoon!"

"And A Happy New-Year!"

"Good afternoon!"

His nephew left the room without an angry word, notwithstanding. The clerk, in letting Scrooge's nephew out, had let two other people in. They were portly gentlemen, pleasant to behold, and now stood, with their hats off, in Scrooge's office. They had books and papers in their hands, and bowed to him.

"Scrooge and Marley's, I believe," said one of the gentlemen, referring to his list. "Have I the pleasure of addressing Mr. Scrooge or Mr. Marley?"

"Mr. Marley has been dead these seven years. He died seven years ago, this very night."

"At this festive season of the year, Mr. Scrooge," said the gentleman, taking up a pen, "it is more than usually desirable that we should make some slight provision for the poor and destitute, who suffer greatly at the present time. Many thousands are in want of common necessaries; hundreds of thousands are in want of common comforts, sir."

"Are there no prisons?"

"Plenty of prisons. But under the impression that they scarcely furnish Christian cheer of mind or body to the unoffending multitude, a few of us are endeavouring to raise a fund to buy the poor some meat and drink, and means of warmth. We choose this time, because it is a time, of all others, when Want is keenly felt, and Abundance rejoices. What shall I put you down for?"

"Nothing!"

"You wish to be anonymous?"

"I wish to be left alone. Since you ask me what I wish, gentlemen, that is my answer. I don't make merry myself at Christmas, and I can't afford to make idle people merry. I help to support the prisons and the workhouses,—they cost enough,—and those who are badly off must go there."

"Many can't go there; and many would rather die."

"If they would rather die, they had better do it, and decrease the surplus population."

At length the hour of shutting up the counting-house arrived. With an ill-will Scrooge, dismounting from his stool, tacitly admitted the fact to the expectant clerk in the tank, who instantly snuffed his candle out, and put on his hat.

"You want all day to-morrow, I suppose?"

"If quite convenient, sir."

"It's not convenient, and it's not fair. If I was to stop half a crown for it, you'd think yourself mightily ill-used, I'll be bound?"

"Yes, sir."

"And yet you don't think me ill-used, when I pay a day's wages for no work."

"It's only once a year, sir."

"A poor excuse for picking a man's pocket every twenty-fifth of December! But I suppose you must have the whole day. Be here all the earlier next morning."

The clerk promised that he would, and

Scrooge walked out with a growl. The office was closed in a twinkling, and the clerk, with the long ends of his white comforter dangling below his waist (for he boasted no great-coat), went down a slide, at the end of a lane of boys, twenty times, in honour of its being Christmas eve, and then ran home as hard as he could pelt, to play at blindman's buff.

Scrooge took his melancholy dinner in his usual melancholy tavern; and having read all the newspapers, and beguiled the rest of the evening with his banker's book, went home to bed. He lived in chambers which had once belonged to his deceased partner. They were a gloomy suite of rooms, in a lowering pile of building up a yard. The building was old enough now, and dreary enough, for nobody lived in it but Scrooge, the other rooms being all let out as offices.

Now it is a fact, that there was nothing at all particular about the knocker on the door of this house, except that it was very large; also, that Scrooge had seen it, night and morning, during his whole residence in that place; also, that Scrooge had as little of what is called fancy about him as any man in the city of London. And yet Scrooge, having his key in the lock of the door, saw in the knocker, without its undergoing any intermediate process of change, not a knocker, but Marley's face.

Marley's face, with a dismal light about it, like a bad lobster in a dark cellar. It was not angry or ferocious, but it looked at Scrooge as Marley used to look,—ghostly spectacles turned up upon its ghostly forehead.

As Scrooge looked fixedly at this phenomenon, it was a knocker again. He said, "Pooh, pooh!" and closed the door with a bang.

The sound resounded through the house like thunder. Every room above, and every cask in the wine-merchant's cellars below, appeared to have a separate peal of echoes of its own. Scrooge was not a man to be frightened by echoes. He fastened the door, and walked across the hall, and up the stairs. Slowly too, trimming his candle as he went.

Up Scrooge went, not caring a button for its being very dark. Darkness is cheap, and Scrooge liked it. But before he shut his heavy door, he walked through his rooms to see that all was right. He had just enough recollection of the face to desire to do that.

Sitting-room, bedroom, lumber-room, all as they should be. Nobody under the table, nobody under the sofa; a small fire in the grate; spoon and basin ready; and the little saucepan of gruel (Scrooge had a cold in his head) upon the hob. Nobody under the bed; nobody in the closet; nobody in his dressing-gown, which was hanging up in a suspicious attitude against the wall. Lumber-room as usual. Old fire-guards, old shoes, two fish-baskets, washing-stand on three legs, and a poker.

Quite satisfied, he closed his door, and locked himself in; double-locked himself in, which was not his custom. Thus secured against surprise, he took off his cravat, put on his dressing-gown and slippers and his nightcap, and sat down before the very low fire to take his gruel.

As he threw his head back in the chair, his glance happened to rest upon a bell, a disused bell, that hung in the room, and communicated, for some purpose now forgotten, with a chamber in the highest story of the building. It was with great astonishment, and with a strange, inexplicable dread, that, as he looked, he saw this bell begin to swing. Soon it rang out loudly, and so did every bell in the house.

This was succeeded by a clanking noise, deep down below as if some person were dragging a heavy chain over the casks in the wine-merchant's cellar.

Then he heard the noise much louder, on the floors below; then coming up the stairs; then coming straight towards his door.

It came on through the heavy door, and a spectre passed into the room before his eyes. And upon its coming in, the dying flame leaped up, as though it cried, "I know him! Marley's ghost!"

The same face, the very same. Marley in his pigtail, usual waistcoat, tights, and boots. His body was transparent; so that Scrooge, observing him, and looking through his waistcoat, could see the two buttons on his coat behind.

Scrooge had often heard it said that Marley had no bowels, but he had never believed it until now.

No, nor did he believe it even now. Though he looked the phantom through and through, and saw it standing before him,—though he felt the chilling influence of its death-cold eyes, and noticed the very texture of the folded kerchief bound about its head and chin,—he was still incredulous.

"How now!" said Scrooge, caustic and cold as ever. "What do you want with me?"

"Much!"—Marley's voice, no doubt about it.

"Who are you?"

"Ask me who I was."

"Who were you then?"

"In life I was your partner, Jacob Marley."

"Can you—can you sit down?"

"I can."

"Do it, then."

Scrooge asked the question, because he didn't know whether a ghost so transparent might find himself in a condition to take a chair; and felt that, in the event of its being impossible, it might involve the necessity of an embarrassing explanation. But the ghost sat down on the opposite side of the fireplace, as if he were quite used to it.

"You don't believe in me."

"I don't."

"What evidence would you have of my reality beyond that of your senses?"

"I don't know."

"Why do you doubt your senses?"

"Because a little thing affects them. A slight disorder of the stomach makes them cheats. You may be an undigested bit of beef, a blot of mustard, a crumb of cheese, a fragment of an underdone potato. There's more of gravy than of grave about you, whatever you are!"

Scrooge was not much in the habit of cracking jokes, nor did he feel in his heart by any means waggish then. The truth is, that he tried to be smart, as a means of distracting his own attention, and keeping down his horror.

But how much greater was his horror when, the phantom taking off the bandage round its head, as if it were too warm to wear indoors, its lower jaw dropped down upon its breast!

"Mercy!" Dreadful apparition, why do you trouble me? Why do spirits walk the earth, and why do they come to me?"

"It is required of every man that the spirit within him should walk abroad among his fellow-men, and travel far and wide; and if that spirit goes not forth in life, it is condemned to do so after death. I cannot tell you all I would. A very little more is permitted to me. I cannot rest, I cannot stay, I cannot linger anywhere. My spirit never walked beyond our counting-house—mark me!—in life my spirit never roved beyond the narrow limits of our money-changing hole; and weary journeys lie before me!"

"Seven years dead. And travelling all the time? You travel fast?"

"On the wings of the wind."

"You might have got over a great quantity of ground in seven years."

"O blind man, blind man! not to know that ages of incessant labour by immortal creatures for this earth must pass into eternity before the good of which it is susceptible is all developed. Not to know that any Christian spirit working kindly in its little sphere, whatever it may be, will find its mortal life too short for its vast means of usefulness. Not to know that no space of regret can make amends for one life's opportunities misused! Yet I was like this man; I once was like this man!"

"But you were always a good man of business, Jacob," faltered Scrooge, who now began to apply this to himself.

"Business!" cried the Ghost, wringing

its hands again. "Mankind was my business. The common welfare was my business; charity, mercy, forbearance, benevolence, were all my business. The dealings of my trade were but a drop of water in the comprehensive ocean of my business!"

Scrooge was very much dismayed to hear the spectre going on at this rate, and began to quake exceedingly.

"Hear me! My time is nearly gone."

"I will. But don't be hard upon me! Don't be flowery, Jacob! Pray!"

"I am here to-night to warn you that you have yet a chance and hope of escaping my fate. A chance and hope of my procuring, Ebenezer."

"You were always a good friend to me. Thank'ee!"

"You will be haunted by Three Spirits."

"Is that the chance and hope you mentioned, Jacob? I—I think I'd rather not."

"Without their visits, you cannot hope to shun the path I tread. Expect the first to-morrow night, when the bell tolls One.

Expect the second on the next night at the same hour. The third, upon the next night, when the last stroke of Twelve has ceased to vibrate. Look to see me no more; and look that, for your own sake, you remember what has passed between us!"

It walked backward from him, and at every step it took, the window raised itself a little, so that, when the apparition reached it, it was wide open.

Scrooge closed the window, and examined the door by which the Ghost had entered. It was double-locked, as he had locked it with his own hands, and the bolts were undisturbed. Scrooge tried to say, "Humbug!" but stopped at the first syllable. And being, from the emotion he had undergone, or the fatigues of the day, or his glimpse of the invisible world, or the dull conversation of the Ghost, or the lateness of the hour, much in need of repose, he went straight to bed, without undressing, and fell asleep on the instant.

Stave Two: The First of the Three Spirits

When Scrooge awoke, it was so dark, that, looking out of bed, he could scarcely distinguish the transparent window from the opaque walls of his chamber, until suddenly the church clock tolled a deep, dull, hollow, melancholy ONE.

Light flashed up in the room upon the instant, and the curtains of his bed were drawn aside by a strange figure,—like a child; yet not so like a child as like an old man, viewed through some supernatural medium, which gave him the appearance of having receded from the view, and being diminished to a child's proportions. Its hair, which hung about its neck and down its back, was white as if with age; and yet the face had not a wrinkle in it, and the tenderest bloom was on the skin. It held a branch of fresh green holly in its hand; and, in singular contradiction of that wintry emblem, had its dress trimmed with summer flowers. But the strangest thing about it was, that from

the crown of its head there sprung a bright clear jet of light, by which all this was visible; and which was doubtless the occasion of its using, in its duller moments, a great extinguisher for a cap, which it now held under its arm.

"Are you the Spirit, sir, whose coming was foretold to me?"

"I am!"

"Who and what are you?"

"I am the Ghost of Christmas Past."

"Long Past?"

"No. Your past. The things that you will see with me are shadows of the things that have been; they will have no consciousness of us."

Scrooge then made bold to inquire what business brought him there.

"Your welfare. Rise and walk with me!"

It would have been in vain for Scrooge to plead that the weather and the hour were not adapted to pedestrian purposes; that bed was warm, and the thermometer a long way below freezing; that he was clad but lightly in his slippers, dressing-gown, and night-cap; and that he had a cold upon him at that time. The grasp, though gentle as a woman's hand, was not to be resisted. He rose; but finding that the Spirit made towards the window, clasped its robe in supplication.

"I am a mortal, and liable to fall."

"Bear but a touch of my hand *there*," said the Spirit, laying it upon his heart, "and you shall be upheld in more than this!"

As the words were spoken, they passed through the wall, and stood in the busy thoroughfares of a city. It was made plain enough by the dressing of the shops that here, too, it was Christmas time. The Ghost stopped at a certain warehouse door, and asked Scrooge if he knew it.

"Know it! I was apprenticed here!"

They went in. At sight of an old gentleman in a Welsh wig, sitting behind such a high desk that, if he had been two inches taller, he must have knocked his head against the ceiling, Scrooge cried in great excitement: "Why, it's old Fezziwig! Bless his heart, it's Fezziwig, alive again!"

Old Fezziwig laid down his pen, and looked up at the clock, which pointed to the hour of seven. He rubbed his hands; adjusted his capacious waistcoat; laughed all over himself, from his shoes to his organ of benevolence; and called out in a comfortable, oily, rich, fat, jovial voice: "Yo ho, there! Ebenezer! Dick!"

A living and moving picture of Scrooge's former self, a young man, came briskly in, accompanied by his fellow-apprentice.

"Dick Wilkins, to be sure!" said Scrooge to the Ghost. "My old fellow-prentice, bless me, yes. There he is. He was very much attached to me, was Dick. Poor Dick! Dear, dear!"

"Yo ho, my boys!" said Fezziwig. "No more work to-night. Christmas eve, Dick. Christmas, Ebenezer! Let's have the shutters up, before a man can say Jack Robinson! Clear away, my lads, and let's have lots of room here!"

Clear away! There was nothing they wouldn't have cleared away, or couldn't have cleared away, with old Fezziwig looking on. It was done in a minute. Every movable was packed off, as if it were dismissed from public life for evermore; the floor was swept and watered, the lamps were trimmed, fuel was heaped upon the fire; and the warehouse was as snug and warm and dry and bright a ballroom as you would desire to see on a winter's night.

In came a fiddler with a music-book, and went up to the lofty desk, and made an orchestra of it, and tuned like fifty stomach-aches. In came Mrs. Fezziwig, one vast substantial smile. In came the three Miss Fezziwigs, beaming and lovable. In came the six young followers whose hearts they broke. In came all the young men and women employed in the business. In came the housemaid, with her cousin the baker. In came the cook, with her brother's particular friend the milkman. In they all came one after another; some shyly, some boldly, some gracefully, some awkwardly, some pushing, some pulling; in they all came, anyhow and everyhow. Away they all went, twenty couples at once; hands half round and back again the other way; down the middle and up again; round and round in various stages of affectionate grouping; old top couple always turning up in the wrong place; new top couple starting off again, as soon as they got there; all top couples at last, and not a bottom one to help them. When this result was brought about, old Fezziwig, clapping his hands to stop the dance, cried out, "Well done"; and the fiddler plunged his hot face into a pot of porter especially provided for that purpose.

There were more dances, and there were forfeits, and more dances, and there was cake, and there was negus, and there was a great piece of Cold Roast, and there was a great piece of Cold Boiled, and there were mince-pies, and plenty of beer. But the great effect of the evening came after the Roast and Boiled, when the fiddler struck up "Sir Roger de Coverley." Then old Fezziwig stood out to dance with Mrs. Fezziwig. Top couple, too; with a good stiff piece of work cut out for them; three or four and twenty pair of partners; people who were not to be trifled with; people who would dance, and had no notion of walking.

But if they had been twice as many— four times—old Fezziwig would have been a match for them, and so would Mrs. Fezziwig. As to her, she was worthy to be his partner in every sense of the term. A positive light appeared to issue from Fezziwig's calves. They shone in every part of the dance. You couldn't have predicted, at any given time, what would become of 'em next. And when old Fezziwig and Mrs. Fezziwig had gone all through the dance,—advance and retire, turn your partner, bow and courtesy, corkscrew, thread the needle, and back again to your place, —Fezziwig "cut,"—cut so deftly, that he appeared to wink with his legs.

When the clock struck eleven this domestic ball broke up. Mr. and Mrs. Fezziwig took their stations, one on either side the door, and, shaking hands with every person individually as he or she went out, wished him or her a Merry Christmas. When everybody had retired but the two 'prentices, they did the same to them; and thus the cheerful voices died away, and the lads were left to their beds, which were under a counter in the back shop.

"A small matter," said the Ghost, "to make these silly folks so full of gratitude. He has spent but a few pounds of your mortal money,—three or four perhaps. Is that so much that he deserves this praise?"

"It isn't that," said Scrooge, heated by the remark, and speaking unconsciously like his former, not his latter self,—"it isn't that, Spirit. He has the power to render us happy or unhappy; to make our service light or burdensome; a pleasure or a toil. Say that his power lies in words and looks; in things so slight and insignificant that it is impossible to add and count 'em up: what then? The happiness he gives is quite as great as if it cost a fortune."

He felt the Spirit's glance, and stopped.

"What is the matter?"

"Nothing particular."

"Something, I think?"

"No, no. I should like to be able to say a word or two to my clerk just now. That's all."

"My time grows short," observed the Spirit. "Quick!"

This was not addressed to Scrooge, or to any one whom he could see, but it produced an immediate effect. For again he saw himself. He was older now; a man in the prime of life.

He was not alone, but sat by the side of a fair young girl in a black dress, in whose eyes there were tears.

"It matters little," she said softly to Scrooge's former self. "To you very little. Another idol has displaced me; and if it can comfort you in time to come, as I would have tried to do, I have no just cause to grieve."

"What idol has displaced you?"

"A golden one. You fear the world too much. I have seen your nobler aspirations fall off one by one, until the master-passion, Gain, engrosses you. Have I not?"

"What then? Even if I have grown so much wiser, what then? I am not changed towards you. Have I ever sought release from our engagement?"

"In words, no. Noever."

"In what, then?"

"In a changed nature; in an altered spirit; in another atmosphere of life; another Hope as its great end. If you were free to-day, to-morrow, yesterday, can even I believe that you would choose a dowerless girl; or, choosing her, do I not know that your repentance and regret would surely follow: I do; and I release you. With a full heart, for the love of him you once were."

"Spirit! Remove me from this place."

"I told you these were shadows of the things that have been," said the Ghost. "That they are what they are, do not blame me!"

"Remove me!" Scrooge exclaimed. "I

cannot bear it! Leave me! Take me back. Haunt me no longer!"

As he struggled with the Spirit he was conscious of being exhausted, and over-come by an irresistible drowsiness; and, further, of being in his own bedroom. He had barely time to reel to bed before he sank into a heavy sleep.

Stave Three: The Second of the Three Spirits

Scrooge awoke in his own bedroom. There was no doubt about that. But it and his own adjoining sitting-room, into which he shuffled in his slippers, attracted by a great light there, had undergone a surprising transformation. The walls and ceiling were so hung with living green, that it looked a perfect grove. The leaves of holly, mistletoe, and ivy reflected back the light, as if so many little mirrors had been scattered there; and such a mighty blaze went roaring up the chimney, as that petrifaction of a hearth had never known in Scrooge's time, or Marley's, or for many and many a winter season gone. Heaped upon the floor, to form a kind of throne, were turkeys, geese, game, brawn, great joints of meat, sucking pigs, long wreaths of sausages, mince-pies, plum-puddings, barrels of oysters, red-hot chestnuts, cherry-cheeked apples, juicy oranges, luscious pears, immense twelfth-cakes, and great bowls of punch. In easy state upon this couch there sat a Giant glorious to see; who bore a glowing torch, in shape not unlike Plenty's horn, and who raised it high to shed its light on Scrooge, as he came peeping round the door.

"Come in,—come in! and know me better, man! I am the Ghost of Christmas Present. Look upon me! You have never seen the like of me before."

"Never."

"Have never walked forth with the younger members of my family; meaning (for I am very young) my elder brothers born in these later years?" pursued the Phantom.

"I don't think I have, I am afraid I have not. Have you had many brothers, Spirit?"

"More than eighteen hundred."

"A tremendous family to provide for! Spirit, conduct me where you will. I went forth last night on compulsion, and I learnt a lesson which is working now. To-night, if you have aught to teach me, let me profit by it."

"Touch my robe!"

Scrooge did as he was told, and held it fast.

The room and its contents all vanished instantly, and they stood in the city streets upon a snowy Christmas morning.

Scrooge and the Ghost passed on, invisible, straight to Scrooge's clerk's; and on the threshold of the door the Spirit smiled, and stopped to bless Bob Cratchit's dwelling with the sprinklings of his torch. Think of that! Bob had but fifteen "bob" a week himself; he pocketed on Saturdays but fifteen copies of his Christian name; and yet the Ghost of Christmas Present blessed his four-roomed house!

Then up rose Mrs. Cratchit, Cratchit's wife, dressed out but poorly in a twice-turned gown, but brave in ribbons, which are cheap and make a goodly show for sixpence; and she laid the cloth, assisted by Belinda Cratchit, second of her daughters, also brave in ribbons; while Master Peter Cratchit plunged a fork into the saucepan of potatoes, and, getting the corners of his monstrous shirt-collar (Bob's private property, conferred upon his son and heir in honour of the day) into his mouth, rejoiced to find himself so gallantly attired, and yearned to show his linen in the fashionable Parks. And now two smaller Cratchits, boy and girl, came tearing in, screaming that outside the baker's they had smelt the goose, and known it for their own; and, basking in luxurious thoughts of sage and onion, these young Cratchits danced about the table, and exalted Master Peter Cratchit to the skies, while he (not proud, although his collars nearly choked him) blew the fire, until the slow potatoes, bubbling up, knocked loudly at the saucepan-lid to be let out and peeled.

"What has ever got your precious father then?" said Mrs. Cratchit. "And your brother Tiny Tim! And Martha warn't as late last Christmas day by half an hour!"

"Here's Martha, mother!" said a girl, appearing as she spoke.

"Here's Martha, mother!" cried the two young Cratchits. "Hurrah! There's such a goose, Martha!"

"Why, bless your heart alive, my dear, how late you are!" said Mrs. Cratchit, kissing her a dozen times, and taking off her shawl and bonnet for her.

"We'd a deal of work to finish up last night," replied the girl, "and had to clear away this morning, mother!"

"Well! Never mind so long as you are come," said Mrs. Cratchit. "Sit ye down before the fire, my dear, and have a warm, Lord bless ye!"

"No, no! There's father coming," cried the two young Cratchits, who were everywhere at once. "Hide, Martha, hide!"

So Martha hid herself, and in came little Bob, the father, with at least three feet of comforter, exclusive of the fringe, hanging down before him; and his threadbare clothes darned up and brushed, to look seasonable; and Tiny Tim upon his shoulder. Alas for Tiny Tim, he bore a little crutch, and had his limbs supported by an iron frame!

"Why, where's our Martha?" cried Bob Cratchit, looking round.

"Not coming," said Mrs. Cratchit.

"Not coming!" said Bob, with a sudden declension in his high spirits; for he had been Tim's blood-horse all the way from church, and had come home rampant,—"not coming upon Christmas day!"

Martha didn't like to see him disappointed, if it were only in joke; so she came out prematurely from behind the closet door, and ran into his arms, while the two young Cratchits hustled Tiny Tim, and bore him off into the wash-house, that he might hear the pudding singing in the copper.

"And how did little Tim behave?" asked Mrs. Cratchit, when she had rallied Bob on his credulity, and Bob had hugged his daughter to his heart's content.

"As good as gold," said Bob, "and better. Somehow he gets thoughtful, sitting by himself so much, and thinks the strangest things you ever heard. He told me, coming home, that he hoped the people saw him in the church, because he was a cripple, and it might be pleasant to them to remember, upon Christmas day, who made lame beggars walk and blind men see."

Bob's voice was tremulous when he told them this, and trembled more when he said that Tiny Tim was growing strong and hearty.

His active little crutch was heard upon the floor, and back came Tiny Tim before another word was spoken, escorted by his brother and sister to his stool beside the fire; and while Bob, turning up his cuffs,—as if, poor fellow, they were capable of being made more shabby,—compounded some hot mixture in a jug with gin and lemons, and stirred it round and round, and put it on the hob to simmer, Master Peter and the two ubiquitous young Cratchits went to fetch the goose, with which they soon returned in high procession.

Mrs. Cratchit made the gravy (ready beforehand in a little saucepan) hissing hot; Master Peter mashed the potatoes with incredible vigour; Miss Belinda sweetened up the apple-sauce; Martha dusted the hot plates; Bob took Tiny Tim beside him in a tiny corner at the table; the two young Cratchits set chairs for everybody, not forgetting themselves, and mounting guard upon their posts, crammed spoons into their mouths, lest they should shriek for goose before their turn came to be helped. At last the dishes were set on, and grace was said. It was succeeded by a breathless pause, as Mrs. Cratchit, looking slowly all along the carving-knife, prepared to plunge it in the breast; but when she did, and when the long-expected gush of stuffing issued forth, one murmur of delight arose all round the board, and even Tiny Tim, excited by the two young Cratchits, beat on the table with the handle of his knife, and feebly cried, Hurrah!

There never was such a goose. Bob said he didn't believe there ever was such a goose cooked. Its tenderness and flavour, size and cheapness, were the themes of universal admiration. Eked out by apple-sauce and mashed potatoes, it was a sufficient dinner for the whole family; indeed, as Mrs. Cratchit said with great delight (surveying one small atom of a bone upon the dish) they hadn't ate it all at last! Yet every one had had enough, and the youngest Cratchits in particular were steeped in sage and onion to the eyebrows! But now, the plates being changed by Miss Belinda, Mrs. Cratchit left the room alone, —too nervous to bear witnesses,—to take the pudding up, and bring it in.

Suppose it should not be done enough! Suppose it should break in turning out! Suppose somebody should have got over the wall of the back yard, and stolen it, while they were merry with the goose,—a supposition at which the two young Cratchits became livid! All sorts of horrors were supposed.

Hallo! A great deal of steam! The pudding was out of the copper. A smell like a washing-day! That was the cloth. A smell like an eating-house and a pastry-cook's next door to each other, with a laundress's next door to that! That was the pudding! In half a minute Mrs. Cratchit entered,— flushed but smiling proudly,—with the pudding, like a speckled cannon-ball, so hard and firm, blazing in half of half a quartern of ignited brandy, and bedight with Christmas holly stuck into the top.

Oh, what a wonderful pudding! Bob Cratchit said, and calmly too, that he regarded it as the greatest success achieved by Mrs. Cratchit since their marriage. Mrs. Cratchit said that now the weight was off

her mind, she would confess she had had her doubts about the quantity of flour. Everybody had something to say about it, but nobody said or thought it was at all a small pudding for a large family. Any Cratchit would have blushed to hint at such a thing.

At last the dinner was all done, the cloth was cleared, the hearth swept, and the fire made up. The compound in the jug being tasted, and considered perfect, apples and oranges were put upon the table, and a shovelful of chestnuts on the fire.

Then all the Cratchit family drew round the hearth, in what Bob Cratchit called a circle, and at Bob Cratchit's elbow stood the family display of glass,—two tumblers, and a custard-cup without a handle.

These held the hot stuff from the jug, however, as well as golden goblets would have done; and Bob served it out with beaming looks, while the chestnuts on the fire spluttered and crackled noisily. Then Bob proposed:—

"A Merry Christmas to us all, my dears. God bless us!"

Which all the family re-echoed.

"God bless us every *one!*" said Tiny Tim, the last of all.

He sat very close to his father's side, upon his little stool. Bob held his withered little hand in his, as if he loved the child, and wished to keep him by his side, and dreaded that he might be taken from him.

Scrooge raised his head speedily, on hearing his own name.

"Mr. Scrooge!" said Bob; "I'll give you Mr. Scrooge, the Founder of the Feast!"

"The Founder of the Feast indeed!" cried Mrs. Cratchit, reddening. "I wish I had him here. I'd give him a piece of my mind to feast upon, and I hope he'd have a good appetite for it."

"My dear," said Bob, "the children! Christmas day."

"It should be Christmas day, I am sure," said she, "on which one drinks the health of such an odious, stingy, hard, unfeeling man as Mr. Scrooge. You know he is,

Robert! Nobody knows it better than you do, poor fellow!"

"My dear," was Bob's mild answer, "Christmas day."

"I'll drink his health for your sake and the day's," said Mrs. Cratchit, "not for his. Long life to him! A merry Christmas and a happy New Year! He'll be very merry and very happy, I have no doubt!"

The children drank the toast after her. It was the first of their proceedings which had no heartiness in it. Tiny Tim drank it last of all, but he didn't care twopence for it. Scrooge was the Ogre of the family. The mention of his name cast a dark shadow on the party, which was not dispelled for full five minutes.

After it had passed away, they were ten times merrier than before, from the mere relief of Scrooge the Baleful being done with. Bob Cratchit told them how he had a situation in his eye for Master Peter, which would bring him, if obtained, full five and sixpence weekly. The two young Cratchits laughed tremendously at the idea of Peter's being a man of business; and Peter himself looked thoughtfully at the fire from between his collars, as if he were deliberating what particular investments he should favour when he came into the receipt of that bewildering income. Martha, who was a poor apprentice at a milliner's, then told them what kind of work she had to do, and how many hours she worked at a stretch, and how she meant to lie abed to-morrow morning for a good long rest; to-morrow being a holiday she passed at home. Also how she had seen a countess and a lord some days before, and how the lord "was much about as tall as Peter;" at which Peter pulled up his collars so high that you couldn't have seen his head if you had been there. All this time the chestnuts and the jug went round and round; and by and by they had a song, about a lost child travelling in the snow, from Tiny Tim, who had a plaintive little voice, and sang it very well indeed.

There was nothing of high mark in this. They were not a handsome family; they were not well dressed; their shoes were far from being waterproof; their clothes were scanty; and Peter might have known, and very likely did, the inside of a pawnbroker's. But they were happy, grateful, pleased with one another, and contented with the time; and when they faded, and looked happier yet in the bright sprinklings of the Spirit's torch at parting, Scrooge had his eye upon them, and especially on Tiny Tim, until the last.

It was a great surprise to Scrooge, as this scene vanished, to hear a hearty laugh. It was a much greater surprise to Scrooge to recognize it as his own nephew's, and to find himself in a bright, dry, gleaming room, with the Spirit standing smiling by his side, and looking at that same nephew.

It is a fair, even-handed, noble adjustment of things, that while there is infection in disease and sorrow, there is nothing in the world so irresistibly contagious as laughter and good-humour. When Scrooge's nephew laughed, Scrooge's niece by marriage laughed as heartily as he. And their assembled friends, being not a bit behind-hand, laughed out lustily.

"He said that Christmas was a humbug, as I live!" cried Scrooge's nephew. "He believed it too!"

"More shame for him, Fred!" said Scrooge's niece, indignantly. Bless those women! They never do anything by halves. They are always in earnest.

She was very pretty; exceedingly pretty. With a dimpled, surprised-looking, capital face; a ripe little mouth that seemed made to be kissed,—as no doubt it was; all kinds of good little dots about her chin, that melted into one another when she laughed; and the sunniest pair of eyes you ever saw in any little creature's head. Altogether she was what you would have called provoking, but satisfactory, too. Oh, perfectly satisfactory.

"He's a comical old fellow," said Scrooge's nephew, "that's the truth; and not so pleasant as he might be. However, his offences carry their own punishment, and I have nothing to say against him.

Who suffers by his ill whims? Himself always. Here he takes it into his head to dislike us, and he won't come and dine with us. What's the consequence? He don't lose much of a dinner."

"Indeed, I think he loses a very good dinner," interrupted Scrooge's niece. Everybody else said the same, and they must be allowed to have been competent judges, because they had just had dinner; and, with the dessert upon the table, were clustered round the fire, by lamplight.

"Well, I am very glad to hear it," said Scrooge's nephew, "because I haven't any great faith in these young housekeepers. What do you say, Topper?"

Topper clearly had his eye on one of Scrooge's niece's sisters, for he answered that a bachelor was a wretched outcast, who had no right to express an opinion on the subject. Whereat Scrooge's niece's sister —the plump one with the lace tucker; not the one with the roses—blushed.

After tea they had some music. For they were a musical family, and knew what they were about, when they sung a Glee or Catch, I can assure you,—especially Topper, who could growl away in the bass like a good one, and never swell the large veins in his forehead, or get red in the face over it.

But they didn't devote the whole evening to music. After a while they played at forfeits; for it is good to be children sometimes, and never better than at Christmas, when its mighty Founder was a child himself. There was first a game at blindman's buff though. And I no more believe Topper was really blinded than I believe he had eyes in his boots. Because the way in which he went after that plump sister in the lace tucker was an outrage on the credulity of human nature. Knocking down the fire-irons, tumbling over the chairs, bumping up against the piano, smothering himself among the curtains, wherever she went there went he! He always knew where the plump sister was. He wouldn't catch anybody else. If you had fallen up against him, as some of them did, and stood there, he would have made

a feint of endeavouring to seize you, which would have been an affront to your understanding, and would instantly have sidled off in the direction of the plump sister.

"Here is a new game," said Scrooge. "One half-hour, Spirit, only one!"

It was a Game called Yes and No, where Scrooge's nephew had to think of something, and the rest must find out what; he only answering to their questions yes or no, as the case was. The fire of questioning to which he was exposed elicited from him that he was thinking of an animal, a live animal, rather a disagreeable animal, a savage animal, an animal that growled and grunted sometimes, and talked sometimes, and lived in London, and walked about the streets, and wasn't made a show of, and wasn't led by anybody, and didn't live in a menagerie, and was never killed in a market, and was not a horse, or an ass, or a cow, or a bull, or a tiger, or a dog, or a pig, or a cat, or a bear. At every new question put to him, this nephew burst into a fresh roar of laughter; and was so inexpressibly tickled, that he was obliged to get up off the sofa and stamp. At last the plump sister cried out:—

"I have found it out! I know what it is, Fred! I know what it is!"

"What is it?" cried Fred.

"It's your uncle Scro-o-o-oge!"

Which it certainly was. Admiration was the universal sentiment, though some objected that the reply to "Is it a bear?" ought to have been "Yes."

Uncle Scrooge had imperceptibly become so gay and light of heart, that he would have drank to the unconscious company in an inaudible speech. But the whole scene passed off in the breath of the last word spoken by his nephew; and he and the Spirit were again upon their travels.

Much they saw, and far they went, and many homes they visited, but always with a happy end. The Spirit stood beside sickbeds, and they were cheerful; on foreign lands, and they were close at home; by struggling men, and they were patient in their greater hope; by poverty, and it was rich. In almshouse, hospital, and jail, in misery's every refuge, where vain man in his little brief authority had not made fast the door, and barred the Spirit out, he left his blessing, and taught Scrooge his precepts. Suddenly, as they stood together in an open place, the bell struck twelve.

Scrooge looked about him for the Ghost, and saw it no more. As the last stroke ceased to vibrate, he remembered the prediction of old Jacob Marley, and, lifting up his eyes, beheld a solemn Phantom, draped and hooded, coming like a mist along the ground towards him.

Stave Four: The Last of the Spirits

The Phantom slowly, gravely, silently approached. When it came near him, Scrooge bent down upon his knee; for in the air through which this Spirit moved it seemed to scatter gloom and mystery.

It was shrouded in a deep black garment, which concealed its head, its face, its form, and left nothing of it visible save one out-stretched hand. He knew no more, for the Spirit neither spoke nor moved.

"I am in the presence of the Ghost of Christmas Yet to Come? Ghost of the Future! I fear you more than any spectre I have seen. But as I know your purpose is to do me good, and as I hope to live to be another man from what I was, I am prepared to bear you company, and do it with a thankful heart. Will you not speak to me?"

It gave him no reply. The hand was pointed straight before them.

"Lead on! Lead on! The night is waning fast, and it is precious time to me, I know. Lead on, Spirit!"

They scarcely seemed to enter the city; for the city rather seemed to spring up about them. But there they were in the heart of it; on 'Change, amongst the merchants.

The Spirit stopped beside one little knot of business men. Observing that the hand was pointed to them, Scrooge advanced to listen to their talk.

"No," said a great fat man with a monstrous chin. "I don't know much about it either way. I only know he's dead."

"When did he die?" inquired another.

"Last night, I believe."

"Why, what was the matter with him? I thought he'd never die."

"God knows," said the first, with a yawn.

"What has he done with his money?" asked a red-faced gentleman.

"I haven't heard," said the man with the large chin. "Company, perhaps. He hasn't left it to me. That's all I know. By, by."

Scrooge was at first inclined to be surprised that the Spirit should attach importance to conversation apparently so trivial; but feeling assured that it must have some hidden purpose, he set himself to consider what it was likely to be. It could scarcely be supposed to have any bearing on the death of Jacob, his old partner, for that was Past, and this Ghost's province was the Future.

He looked about in that very place for his own image; but another man stood in his accustomed corner, and though the clock pointed to his usual time of day for being there, he saw no likeness of himself amongst the multitudes that poured in through the Porch. It gave him little surprise, however; for he had been revolving in his mind a change of life, and he thought and hoped he saw his newborn resolutions carried out in this.

They left this busy scene, and went into an obscure part of the town, to a low shop where iron, old rags, bottles, bones, and greasy offal were bought. A grey-haired rascal, of great age, sat smoking his pipe. Scrooge and the Phantom came into the presence of this man, just as a woman with a heavy bundle slunk into the shop. But she had scarcely entered, when another woman, similarly laden, came in too; and she was closely followed by a man in faded black. After a short period of blank astonishment, in which the old man with the pipe had joined them, they all three burst into a laugh.

"Let the charwoman alone to be the first!" cried she who had entered first. "Let the laundress alone to be the second; and let the undertaker's man alone to be the third. Look here, old Joe, here's a chance! If we haven't all three met here without meaning it!"

"You couldn't have met in a better place. You were made free of it long ago, you know; and the other two ain't strangers. What have you got to sell? What have you got to sell?"

"Half a minute's patience, Joe, and you shall see."

"What odds then! What odds, Mrs. Dilber?" said the woman. "Every person has a right to take care of themselves. *He* always did! Who's the worse for the loss of a few things like these? Not a dead man, I suppose."

Mrs. Dilber, whose manner was remarkable for general propitiation, said, "No, indeed, ma'am."

"If he wanted to keep 'em after he was dead, a wicked old screw, why wasn't he natural in his lifetime? If he had been, he'd have had somebody to look after him when he was struck with Death, instead of lying gasping out his last there, alone by himself."

"It's the truest word that ever was spoke, it's a judgment on him."

"I wish it was a little heavier judgment, and it should have been, you may depend upon it, if I could have laid my hands on anything else. Open that bundle, old Joe, and let me know the value of it. Speak out plain. I'm not afraid to be the first, nor afraid for them to see it."

Joe went down on his knees for the greater convenience of opening the bundle, and dragged out a large and heavy roll of some dark stuff.

"What do you call this? Bed-curtains!"

"Ah! Bed-curtains! Don't drop that oil upon the blankets, now."

"*His* blankets?"

"Whose else's do you think? He isn't likely to take cold without 'em, I dare say. Ah! You may look through that shirt till your eyes ache; but you won't find a hole in it, nor a threadbare place. It's the best he had, and a fine one too. They'd have wasted it by dressing him up in it, if it hadn't been for me."

Scrooge listened to this dialogue in horror.

"Spirit! I see, I see. The case of this unhappy man might be my own. My life tends that way, now. Merciful Heaven, what is this!"

The scene had changed, and now he almost touched a bare, uncurtained bed. A pale light, rising in the outer air, fell straight upon this bed; and on it, unwatched, unwept, uncared for, was the body of this plundered unknown man.

"Spirit, let me see some tenderness connected with a death, or this dark chamber, Spirit, will be for ever present to me."

The Ghost conducted him to poor Bob Cratchit's house,—the dwelling he had visited before,—and found the mother and the children seated round the fire.

Quiet. Very quiet. The noisy little Cratchits were as still as statues in one corner, and sat looking up at Peter, who had a book before him. The mother and her daughters were engaged in needlework. But surely they were very quiet!

"'And he took a child, and set him in the midst of them.'"

Where had Scrooge heard those words? He had not dreamed them. The boy must have read them out, as he and the Spirit crossed the threshold. Why did he not go on?

The mother laid her work upon the table, and put her hand up to her face. "The colour hurts my eyes," she said.

The colour? Ah, poor Tiny Tim!

"They're better now again. It makes them weak by candlelight; and I wouldn't show weak eyes to your father when he comes home, for the world. It must be near his time."

"Past it rather," Peter answered, shutting

up his book. "But I think he has walked a little slower than he used, these few last evenings, mother."

"I have known him walk with—I have known him walk with Tiny Tim upon his shoulder, very fast indeed."

"And so have I," cried Peter. "Often."

"And so have I," exclaimed another. So had all.

"But he was very light to carry, and his father loved him so, that it was no trouble, —no trouble. And there is your father at the door!"

She hurried out to meet him; and little Bob in his comforter—he had need of it, poor fellow—came in. His tea was ready for him on the hob, and they all tried who should help him to it most. Then the two young Cratchits got upon his knees and laid, each child, a little cheek against his face, as if they said, "Don't mind it, father. Don't be grieved!"

Bob was very cheerful with them, and spoke pleasantly to all the family. He looked at the work upon the table, and praised the industry and speed of Mrs. Cratchit and the girls. They would be done long before Sunday, he said.

"Sunday! You went to-day, then, Robert?"

"Yes, my dear," returned Bob. "I wish you could have gone. It would have done you good to see how green a place it is. But you'll see it often. I promised him that I would walk there on a Sunday. My little, little child! My little child!"

He broke down all at once. He couldn't help it. If he could have helped it, he and his child would have been farther apart, perhaps, than they were.

"Spectre," said Scrooge, "something informs me that our parting moment is at hand. I know it, but I know not how. Tell me what man that was, with the covered face, whom we saw lying dead?"

The Ghost of Christmas Yet to Come conveyed him to a dismal, wretched, ruinous churchyard.

The Spirit stood amongst the graves, and pointed down to One.

"Before I draw nearer to that stone to which you point, answer me one question. Are these the shadows of the things that Will be, or are they shadows of the things that May be only?"

Still the Ghost pointed downward to the grave by which it stood.

"Men's courses will foreshadow certain ends, to which, if persevered in, they must lead. But if the courses be departed from, the ends will change. Say it is thus with what you show me!"

The Spirit was immovable as ever.

Scrooge crept towards it, trembling as he went; and, following the finger, read upon the stone of the neglected grave his own name—EBENEZER SCROOGE.

"Am *I* that man who lay upon the bed? No, Spirit! Oh no, no! Spirit! hear me! I am not the man I was. I will not be the man I must have been but for this intercourse. Why show me this, if I am past all hope? Assure me that I yet may change these shadows you have shown me by an altered life."

For the first time the kind hand faltered.

"I will honour Christmas in my heart, and try to keep it all the year. I will live in the Past, the Present, and the Future. The Spirits of all three shall strive within me. I will not shut out the lessons that they teach. Oh, tell me I may sponge away the writing on this stone!"

Holding up his hands in one last prayer to have his fate reversed, he saw an alteration in the Phantom's hood and dress. It shrunk, collapsed, and dwindled down into a bedpost.

Yes, and the bedpost was his own. The bed was his own, the room was his own. Best and happiest of all, the Time before him was his own, to make amends in!

He was checked in his transports by the churches ringing out the lustiest peals he had ever heard.

Running to the window, he opened it, and put out his head. No fog, no mist, no night; clear, bright, stirring, golden day.

"What's to-day?" cried Scrooge, calling downward to a boy in Sunday clothes, who

perhaps had loitered in to look about him.
"Eh?"

"What's to-day, my fine fellow?"

"To-day! Why *Christmas* day."

"It's Christmas day! I haven't missed it.
Hallo, my fine fellow!"

"Hallo!"

"Do you know the Poulterer's, in the
next street but one, at the corner?"

"I should hope I did."

"An intelligent boy! A remarkable boy!
Do you know whether they've sold the
prize Turkey that was hanging up there?
Not the little prize Turkey,—the big one?"

"What, the one as big as me?"

"What a delightful boy! It's a pleasure
to talk to him. Yes, my buck!"

"It's hanging there now."

"Is it? Go and buy it."

"Walk-*er!*" exclaimed the boy.

"No, no, I am in earnest. Go and buy it,
and tell 'em to bring it here, that I may
give them the direction where to take it.
Come back with the man, and I'll give you
a shilling. Come back with him in less than
five minutes, and I'll give you half a
crown!"

The boy was off like a shot.

"I'll send it to Bob Cratchit's. He sha'n't
know who sends it. It's twice the size of
Tiny Tim. Joe Miller never made such a
joke as sending it to Bob's will be!"

The hand in which he wrote the address
was not a steady one; but write it he did,
somehow, and went down stairs to open
the street door, ready for the coming of
the poulterer's man.

It *was* a Turkey! He never could have
stood upon his legs, that bird. He would
have snapped 'em short off in a minute,
like sticks of sealing-wax.

Scrooge dressed himself "all in his best,"
and at last got out into the streets. The
people were by this time pouring forth, as
he had seen them with the Ghost of
Christmas Present; and, walking with his
hands behind him, Scrooge regarded every
one with a delighted smile. He looked so
irresistibly pleasant, in a word, that three or
four good-humoured fellows said, "Good

morning, sir! A merry Christmas to you!"
And Scrooge said often afterwards, that,
of all the blithe sounds he had ever heard,
those were the blithest in his ears.

In the afternoon, he turned his steps
towards his nephew's house.

He passed the door a dozen times, before he had the courage to go up and knock.
But he made a dash, and did it.

"Is your master at home, my dear?"
said Scrooge to the girl. Nice girl! Very.

"Yes, sir."

"Where is he, my love?"

"He's in the dining-room, sir, along with
mistress."

"He knows me," said Scrooge, with his
hand already on the dining-room lock. "I'll
go in here, my dear."

"Fred!"

"Why, bless my soul!" cried Fred, "who's
that?"

"It's I. Your uncle Scrooge. I have come
to dinner. Will you let me in, Fred?"

Let him in! It is a mercy he didn't
shake his arm off. He was at home in five
minutes. Nothing could be heartier. His
niece looked just the same. So did Topper
when *he* came. So did the plump sister
when *she* came. So did every one when
they came. Wonderful party, wonderful
games, wonderful unanimity, won-derful
happiness!

But he was early at the office next morning. Oh, he was early there. If he could
only be there first, and catch Bob Cratchit
coming late! That was the thing he had
set his heart upon.

And he did it. The clock struck nine.
No Bob. A quarter past. No Bob. Bob was
full eighteen minutes and a half behind his
time. Scrooge sat with his door wide open,
that he might see him come into the tank.

Bob's hat was off before he opened the
door; his comforter too. He was on his
stool in a jiffy; driving away with his pen,
as if he were trying to overtake nine o'clock.

"Hallo!" growled Scrooge, in his accustomed voice, as near as he could feign
it. "What do you mean by coming here
at this time of day?"

"I am very sorry, sir. I *am* behind my time."

"You are? Yes. I think you are. Step this way if you please."

"It's only once a year, sir. It shall not be repeated. I was making rather merry yesterday, sir."

"Now, I'll tell you what, my friend. I am not going to stand this sort of thing any longer. And therefore," Scrooge continued, leaping from his stool, and giving Bob such a dig in the waistcoat that he staggered back into the tank again,—"and therefore I am about to raise your salary!"

Bob trembled, and got a little nearer to the ruler.

"A merry Christmas, Bob!" said Scrooge, with an earnestness that could not be mistaken, as he clapped him on the back. "A merrier Christmas, Bob, my good fellow, than I have given you for many a year! I'll raise your salary, and endeavour to assist your struggling family, and we will discuss your affairs this very afternoon, over a Christmas bowl of smoking bishop, Bob! Make up the fires, and buy a second coal-scuttle before you dot another *i*, Bob Cratchit!"

Scrooge was better than his word. He did it all, and infinitely more; and to Tiny Tim, who did NOT die, he was a second father. He became as good a friend, as good a master, and as good a man as the good old city knew, or any other good old city, town, or borough in the good old world. Some people laughed to see the alteration in him; but his own heart laughed, and that was quite enough for him.

He had no further intercourse with Spirits, but lived in that respect upon the Total Abstinence Principle ever afterwards; and it was always said of him that he knew how to keep Christmas well, if any man alive possessed the knowledge. May that be truly said of us, and all of us! And so, as Tiny Tim observed, God Bless Us, Every One!

WHAT CHRISTMAS IS AS WE GROW OLDER

TIME was, with most of us, when Christmas Day encircling all our limited world like a magic ring, left nothing out for us to miss or seek; bound together all our home enjoyments, affections, and hopes; grouped everything and every one around the Christmas fire; and made the little picture shining in our bright young eyes, complete.

Time came perhaps, all too soon, when our thoughts overleaped that narrow boundary; when there was some one (very dear, we thought then, very beautiful, and absolutely perfect) wanting to the fulness of our happiness; when we were wanting too (or we thought so, which did just as well) at the Christmas hearth by which that some one sat; and when we intertwined with every wreath and garland of our life that some one's name.

That was the time for the bright visionary Christmases which have long arisen from us to show faintly, after summer rain in the palest edges of the rainbow! That was the time for the beatified enjoyment of the things that were to be, and never were, and yet the things that were so real in our resolute hope that it would be hard to say, now, what realities achieved since, have been stronger!

What! Did that Christmas never really come when we and the priceless pearl who was our young choice were received, after the happiest of totally impossible marriages, by the two united families previously at daggers-drawn on our account? When brothers and sisters-in-law who had always been rather cool to us before our relationship was effected, perfectly doted on us, and when fathers and mothers overwhelmed us with unlimited incomes? Was that Christmas dinner never really eaten, after which we arose, and generously and eloquently rendered honour to our late rival, present in the company, then and there exchanging friendship and forgiveness, and founding an attachment, not to be surpassed in Greek or Roman story, which subsisted until death? Has that same rival long ceased to care for that same priceless pearl, and married for money, and become usurious? Above all, do we really know, now, that we should probably have been miserable if we had won and worn the pearl, and that we are better without her?

That Christmas when we had recently achieved so much fame; when we had been carried in triumph somewhere, for doing something great and good; when we had won an honoured and ennobled name, and arrived and were received at home in a shower of tears of joy; is it possible that *that* Christmas has not come yet?

And is our life here, at the best, so constituted that, pausing as we advance at such a noticeable milestone in the track as this great birthday, we look back on the things that never were, as naturally and full as gravely as on the things that have been and are gone, or have been and still are? If it be so, and so it seems to be, must we come to the conclusion that life is little better than a dream, and little worth the loves and strivings that we crowd into it?

No! Far be such miscalled philosophy from us, dear Reader, on Christmas Day! Nearer and closer to our hearts be the Christmas spirit, which is the spirit of active usefulness, perseverance, cheerful discharge of duty, kindness, and forbearance! It is in the last virtues especially, that we are, or should be, strengthened by the unaccomplished visions of our youth; for, who shall say that they are not our teachers to deal gently even with the impalpable nothings of the earth!

Therefore, as we grow older, let us be more thankful that the circle of our Christmas associations and of the lessons that they bring, expands! Let us welcome every one of them, and summon them to take their places by the Christmas hearth.

Welcome, old aspirations, glittering creatures of an ardent fancy, to your shelter underneath the holly! We know you, and have not outlived you yet. Welcome, old projects and 'old loves, however fleeting, to your nooks among the steadier lights that burn around us. Welcome, all that was ever real to our hearts; and for the earnestness that made you real, thanks to Heaven! Do we build no Christmas castles in the clouds now? Let our thoughts, fluttering like butterflies among these flowers of children, bear witness! Before this boy, there stretches out a Future, brighter than we ever looked on in our old romantic time, but bright with honour and with truth. Around this little head on which the sunny curls lie heaped, the graces sport, as prettily, as airily, as when there was no scythe within the reach of Time to shear away the curls of our first-love. Upon another girl's face near it—placider but smiling bright—a quiet and contented little face, we see Home fairly written. Shining from the word, as rays shine from a star, we see how, when our graves are old, other hopes than ours' are young, other hearts than ours are moved; how other ways are smoothed; how other happiness blooms, ripens, and decays—no, not decays, for other homes and other bands of children, not yet in being nor for ages yet to be, arise, and bloom and ripen to the end of all!

Welcome, everything! Welcome, alike what has been, and what never was, and what we hope may be, to your shelter underneath the holly, to your places round the Christmas fire, where what is sits openhearted! In yonder shadows, do we see obtruding furtively upon the blaze, an enemy's face? By Christmas Day we do forgive him! If the injury he has done us may admit of such companionship, let him come here and take his place. If otherwise, unhappily, let him go hence, assured that we will never injure nor accuse him.

On this day we shut out Nothing!

"Pause," says a low voice. "Nothing? Think!"

"On Christmas Day, we will shut out from our fireside, Nothing."

"Not the shadow of a vast City where the withered leaves are lying deep?" the voice replies. "Not the shadow that darkens the whole globe? Not the shadow of the City of the Dead?"

Not even that. Of all days in the year, we will turn our faces towards that City upon Christmas Day, and from its silent hosts bring those we loved, among us. City of the Dead, in the blessed name wherein we are gathered together at this time, and in the Presence that is here among us according to the promise, we will receive, and not dismiss, thy people who are dear to us! Yes. We can look upon these children angels that alight, so solemnly, so beautifully among the living children by the fire, and can bear to think how they departed from us. Entertaining angels unawares, as the Patriarchs did, the playful children are unconscious of their guests; but we can see them—can see a radiant arm around one favourite neck, as if there were a tempting of that child away. Among the celestial figures there is one, a poor misshapen boy on earth, of a glorious beauty now, of whom this dying mother said it grieved her much to leave him here, alone, for so many years as it was likely would elapse before he came to her—being such a little child. But he went quickly, and was laid upon her breast, and in her hand she leads him.

There was a gallant boy, who fell, far away, upon a burning sand beneath a burning sun, and said, "Tell them at home, with my last love, how much I could have wished to kiss them once, but that I died contented and had done my duty!" Or there was another, over whom they read the words, "Therefore we commit his body to the deep," and so consigned him to the lonely ocean and sailed on. Or there was another, who lay down to his rest in the dark shadow of great forests, and, on earth, awoke no more. Oh, shall they not, from sand and sea and forest, be brought home at such a time?

There was a dear girl—almost a woman —never to be one—who made a mourning Christmas in a house of joy, and went her trackless way to the silent City. Do we recollect her, worn out, faintly whispering what could not be heard, and falling into that last sleep for weariness? Oh, look upon her now! Oh, look upon her beauty, her serenity, her changeless youth, her happiness! The daughter of Jairus was recalled to life, to die; but she, more blest, has heard the same voice, saying unto her, "Arise for ever!"

We had a friend who was our friend from early days, with whom we often pictured the changes that were to come upon our lives, and merrily imagined how we would speak, and walk, and think, and talk, when we came to be old. His destined habitation in the City of the Dead received him in his prime. Shall he be shut out from our Christmas remembrance? Would his love have so excluded us? Lost friend, lost child, lost parent, sister, brother, husband, wife, we will not so discard you! You shall hold your cherished places in our Christmas hearts, and by our Christmas fires; and in the season of immortal hope, and on the birthday of immortal mercy, we will shut out Nothing!

The winter sun goes down over town and village; on the sea it makes a rosy path, as if the Sacred tread were fresh upon the water. A few more moments, and it sinks, and night comes on, and lights begin to sparkle in the prospect. On the hill-side beyond the shapelessly diffused town, and in the quiet keeping of the trees that gird the village-steeple, remembrances are cut in stone, planted in common flowers, growing in grass, entwined with lowly brambles around many a mound of earth. In town and village, there are doors and windows closed against the weather, there are flaming logs heaped high, there are joyful faces, there is healthy music of voices. Be all ungentleness and harm excluded from the temples of the Household Gods, but be those remembrances admitted with tender encouragement! They are of the time and all its comforting and peaceful reassurances; and of the history that reunited even upon earth the living and the dead; and of the broad beneficence and goodness that too many men have tried to tear to narrow shreds.

Hans Christian Andersen

TALES of wonder and enchantment, told with that kind of directness which children understand and enjoy, made Hans Christian Andersen universally loved when his stories were first translated more than a century ago. From a childhood of dire poverty, he fashioned a life that was even more full of wonder than his most wonderful tale. The fabulous storyteller, born in 1805, left fatherless at an early age, was as strange as he was fascinating. His high-strung temperament revealed itself in his extremely sensitive nature, particularly where criticism of any kind was concerned. In his own mind, he felt that he was far more important in the field of literature than a mere teller of fairy tales for children. He also wrote plays, poems, and novels, and his autobiographical writings provide a fascinating field for present-day researchers and critics.

Hans Andersen succeeded in expressing "the very essence of the Danish spirit—its kindly, simple realism, its humor, its directness and homeliness, no less than its lyrical and gentle fantasy," as Stephen Clissold reminds us in his delightful book, *Denmark, the Land of Hans Andersen*. He has become a greatly revered figure in his homeland, and the little low-roofed house in Odense where he spent his childhood is now a museum. It is filled with the most fascinating objects imaginable. "His top hat is there, still well spun and glossy, reposing on its box of battered leather, the top boots which once encased his spindly legs, his traveling trunks, his umbrella and the coil of rope which he carried with him for fear of being trapped by fire in some strange bedroom."

The reverence for him in Denmark is sometimes difficult for others to realize, but it is the reflection of a nation's love for a great writer who furnished the whole atmosphere and charm of the country they loved. It is truly Hans Andersen land.

He loved Christmas and all its symbolism. In his letters to friends, in his autobiography and in his stories, some of which were written especially for this joyous season, the spirit of Christmas comes to life with this storyteller's gift of simple realism and gentle fantasy. "The Little Match Girl" was based on a story his mother told him, and he clothed it in language that has made it live. The idea for "The Fir-Tree" came to him while attending the opera *Don Juan* in 1846. As was his custom, he went home and wrote it immediately.

At Christmas 1829 a little collection of Andersen's poems appeared and, in the years that followed, collections of his stories appeared during the Christmas season. In all, he wrote 168 tales, and most of these were published during his lifetime. Honors were heaped on him by his own country, by Sweden, Germany, and Mexico. In 1867, the people of Copenhagen tendered him a great reception and banquet, complete with a torchlight procession and a bonfire, and the children sang "In Denmark I Was Born," the hymn he had written for his beloved country. This was but one tribute. At the time, and for years to follow, children in many lands paid him silent homage as they read and reread his stories. Adults enjoyed them, too. Today in England and America Andersen remains a kind of faraway myth, more real in his stories than he ever was in life. In Copenhagen, his statue in the King's Garden stands in eloquent tribute to the prince of storytellers, whose books have remained a never-ending source of delight for more than a century to children the world over.

THE FIR-TREE

OUT in the woods stood a nice little Fir-tree. The place he had was a very good one: the sun shone on him: as to fresh air, there was enough of that, and round him grew many large-sized comrades, pines as well as firs. But the little Fir wanted so very much to be a grown up tree.

He did not think of the warm sun and of the fresh air; he did not care for the little cottage children that ran about and prattled when they were in the woods looking for wild-strawberries. The children often came with a whole pitcher full of berries, or a long row of them threaded on a straw, and sat down near the young tree and said, "Oh, how pretty he is! what a nice little fir!" But this was what the tree could not bear to hear.

At the end of a year he had shot up a good deal, and after another year he was another long bit taller; for with fir-trees one can always tell by the shoots how many years old they are.

"Oh! were I but such a high tree as the others are," sighed he. "Then I should be able to spread out my branches, and with the tops to look into the wide world! Then would the birds build nests among my branches: and when there was a breeze, I could bend with as much stateliness as the others!"

Neither the sunbeams, nor the birds, nor the red clouds which morning and evening sailed above him, gave the little tree any pleasure.

In winter, when the snow lay glittering on the ground, a hare would often come leaping along, and jump right over the little tree. Oh, that made him so angry! But two winters were past, and in the third the tree was so large that the hare was obliged to go round it. "To grow and grow, to get older and be tall," thought the Tree, "that, after all, is the most delightful thing in the world!"

In autumn the wood-cutters always came and felled some of the largest trees. This happened every year; and the young Fir-tree, that had now grown to a very comely size, trembled at the sight; for the magnificent great trees fell to the earth with noise and cracking, the branches were lopped off, and the trees looked long and bare; they were hardly to be recognised; and then they were laid in carts, and the horses dragged them out of the wood. Where did they go to? What became of them?

In spring, when the swallows and the storks came, the Tree asked them, "Don't you know where they have been taken? Have you not met them any where?"

The swallows did not know any thing about it; but the Stork looked musing, nodded his head, and said, "Yes; I think I know; I met many ships as I was flying hither from Egypt; on the ships were magnificent masts, and I venture to assert that it was they that smelt so of fir. I may congratulate you, for they lifted themselves on high most majestically!"

"Oh, were I but old enough to fly across the sea! But how does the sea look in reality? What is it like?"

"That would take a long time to explain," said the Stork, and with these words off he went.

"Rejoice in thy growth!" said the Sunbeams, "rejoice in thy vigorous growth, and in the fresh life that moveth within thee!"

And the Wind kissed the Tree, and the Dew wept tears over him; but the Fir understood it not.

When Christmas came, quite young trees were cut down: trees which often were not even as large or of the same age as this Fir-tree, who could never rest, but always wanted to be off. These young trees, and they were always the finest looking, retained their branches; they were laid on carts, and the horses drew them out of the wood.

"Where are they going to?" asked the Fir. "They are not taller than I; there was one indeed that was considerably shorter; and why do they retain all their branches? Whither are they taken?"

"We know! we know!" chirped the Sparrows. "We have peeped in at the windows in the town below! We know whither they are taken! The greatest splendor and the greatest magnificence one can imagine await them. We peeped through the windows, and saw them planted in the middle of the warm room and ornamented with the most splendid things, with gilded apples, with gingerbread, with toys, and many hundred lights!"

"And then?" asked the Fir-tree, trembling in every bough. "And then? What happens then?"

"We did not see any thing more: it was incomparably beautiful."

"I would fain know if I am destined for so glorious a career." cried the Tree, rejoicing. "That is still better than to cross the sea! What a longing do I suffer! Were Christmas but come! I am now tall, and my branches spread like the others that were carried off last year! Oh! were I but already on the cart! Were I in the warm room with all the splendor and magnificence! Yes; then something better, something still grander, will surely follow, or wherefore should they thus ornament me? Something better, something still grander *must* follow—but what? Oh, how I long, how I suffer! I do not know myself what is the matter with me!"

"Rejoice in our presence!" said the Air and the Sunlight; "rejoice in thy own fresh youth!"

But the Tree did not rejoice at all; he grew and grew, and was green both winter and summer. People that saw him said, "What a fine tree!" and towards Christmas he was one of the first that was cut down. The axe struck deep into the very pith; the tree fell to the earth with a sigh; he felt a pang—it was like a swoon; he could not think of happiness, for he was sorrowful at being separated from his home, from the place where he had sprung up. He well knew that he should never see his dear old comrades, the little bushes and flowers around him, any more; perhaps not even the birds! The departure was not at all agreeable.

The Tree only came to himself when he was unloaded in a courtyard with the other trees, and heard a man say, "That one is splendid! we don't want the others." Then two servants came in rich livery and carried the Fir-tree into a large and splendid drawing-room. Portraits were hanging on the walls, and near the white porcelain stove stood two large Chinese vases with lions on the covers. There, too, were large easy-chairs, silken sofas, large tables full of picture-books and full of toys, worth hundreds and hundreds of crowns—at least the children said so. And the Fir-tree was stuck upright in a cask that was filled with sand; but no one could see that it was a cask, for green cloth was hung all round it, and it stood on a large gaily-colored carpet. Oh! how the Tree quivered! What was to happen? the servants, as well as the young ladies, decorated it. On one branch there hung little nets cut out of colored paper, and each net was filled with sugar-plums; and among the other boughs gilded apples and walnuts were suspended, looking as though they had grown there, and little blue and white tapers were placed among the leaves. Dolls that looked for all the world like men—the Tree had never beheld such before—were seen among the foliage, and at the very top a large star of gold tinsel was fixed. It was really splendid —beyond description splendid.

"This evening!" said they all, "how it will shine this evening!"

"Oh!" thought the Tree, "if the evening were but come! If the tapers were but lighted! And then I wonder what will happen! Perhaps the other trees from the forest will come to look at me! Perhaps the sparrows will beat against the window-panes! I wonder if I shall take root here, and winter and summer stand covered with ornaments!"

He knew very much about the matter!—but he was so impatient that for sheer longing he got a pain in his back, and this with trees is the same thing as a headache with us.

The candles were now lighted— What brightness! What splendor! The Tree trembled so in every bough that one of the tapers set fire to the foliage. It blazed up famously.

"Help! help!" cried the young ladies, and they quickly put out the fire.

Now the tree did not even dare tremble. What a state he was in! He was so uneasy lest he should lose something of his splendor, that he was quite bewildered amidst the glare and brightness; when suddenly both folding-doors opened and a troop of children rushed in as if they would upset the Tree. The older persons followed quietly; the little ones stood quite still. But it was only for a moment; then they shouted that the whole place re-echoed with their rejoicing; they danced round the Tree, and one present after the other was pulled off.

"What are they about?" thought the Tree. "What is to happen now!" And the lights burned down to the very branches, and as they burned down they were put out one after the other, and then the children had permission to plunder the Tree. So they fell upon it with such violence that all its branches cracked; if it had not been fixed firmly in the ground, it would certainly have tumbled down.

The children danced about with their beautiful play-things; no one looked at the Tree except the old nurse, who peeped between the branches; but it was only to see if there was a fig or an apple left that had been forgotten.

"A story! a story!" cried the children, drawing a little fat man towards the Tree. He seated himself under it and said, "Now we are in the shade, and the Tree can listen too. But I shall tell only one story. Now which will you have; that about Ivedy-Avedy, or about Humpy-Dumpy, who tumbled down stairs, and yet after all came to the throne and married the princess?"

"Ivedy-Avedy," cried some; "Humpy-Dumpy," cried the others. There was such a bawling and screaming!—the Fir-tree alone was silent, and he thought to him-

self, "Am I not to bawl with the rest?—
am I to do nothing whatever?" for he was
one of the company, and had done what he
had to do.

And the man told about Humpy-Dumpy
that tumbled down, who notwithstanding
came to the throne, and at last married
the princess. And the children clapped their
hands, and cried. "Oh, go on! Do go on!"
They wanted to hear about Ivedy-Avedy
too, but the little man only told them
about Humpy-Dumpy. The Fir-tree stood
quite still and absorbed in thought; the
birds in the wood had never related the
like of this. "Humpy-Dumpy fell down
stairs, and yet he married the princess! Yes,
yes! that's the way of the world!" thought
the Fir-tree, and believed it all, because the
man who told the story was so good-look-
ing. "Well, well! who knows, perhaps I
may fall down stairs, too, and get a princess
as wife!" And he looked forward with joy to
the morrow, when he hoped to be decked
out again with lights, play-things, fruits,
and tinsel.

"I won't tremble to-morrow!" thought
the Fir-tree. "I will enjoy to the full all
my splendor! To-morrow I shall hear again
the story of Humpy-Dumpy, and perhaps
that of Ivedy-Avedy too." And the whole
night the Tree stood still and in deep
thought.

In the morning the servant and the
house-maid came in.

"Now then the splendor will begin
again," thought the Fir. But they dragged
him out of the room, and up the stairs into
the loft: and here, in a dark corner, where
no daylight could enter, they left him.
"What's the meaning of this?" thought the
Tree. "What am I to do here? What shall
I hear now, I wonder?" And he leaned
against the wall lost in reverie. Time enough
had he too for his reflections; for days and
nights passed on, and nobody came up;
and when at last somebody did come, it
was only to put some great trunks in a corner, out of the way. There stood the Tree
quite hidden; it seemed as if he had been
entirely forgotten.

" 'T is now winter out of doors!" thought
the Tree. "The earth is hard and covered
with snow; men cannot plant me now,
and therefore I have been put up here
under shelter till the spring-time comes!
How thoughtful that is! How kind man
is, after all! If it only were not so dark
here, and so terribly lonely! Not even a
hare!—And out in the woods it was so
pleasant, when the snow was on the
ground, and the hare leaped by; yes—even
when he jumped over me; but I did not
like it then! It is really terribly lonely here!"

"Squeak! squeak!" said a little Mouse,
at the same moment, peeping out of his
hole. And then another little one came.
They snuffed about the Fir-tree, and
rustled among the branches.

"It is dreadfully cold," said the Mouse.
"But for that, it would be delightful here,
old Fir, wouldn't it?"

"I am by no means old," said the Fir-
tree. "There's many a one considerably
older than I am."

"Where do you come from," asked the
Mice; "and what can you do?" They were
so extremely curious. "Tell us about the
most beautiful spot on the earth. Have you
never been there? Were you never in the
larder, where cheeses lie on the shelves, and
hams hang from above; where one dances
about on tallow candles: that place where
one enters lean, and comes out again fat
and portly?"

"I know no such place," said the Tree.
"But I know the wood, where the sun shines
and where the little birds sing." And then
he told all about his youth; and the little
Mice had never heard the like before; and
they listened and said,

"Well, to be sure! How much you have
seen! How happy you must have been!"

"I!" said the Fir-tree, thinking over what
he had himself related. "Yes, in reality
those were happy times." And then he
told about Christmas-eve, when he was
decked out with cakes and candles.

"Oh," said the little Mice, "how fortunate you have been, old Fir-tree!"

"I am by no means old," said he. "I came

from the wood this winter; I am in my prime, and am only rather short for my age."

"What delightful stories you know!" said the Mice: and the next night they came with four other little Mice, who were to hear what the Tree recounted: and the more he related, the more he remembered himself; and it appeared as if those times had really been happy times. "But they may still come—they may still come! Humpy-Dumpy fell down stairs, and yet he got a princess!" and he thought at the moment of a nice little Birch tree growing out in the woods: to the Fir that would be a real charming princess.

"Who is Humpy-Dumpy?" asked the Mice. So then the Fir-tree told the whole fairy tale, for he could remember every single word of it; and the little Mice jumped for joy up to the very top of the Tree. Next night two more Mice came, and on Sunday two Rats even; but they said the stories were not interesting, which vexed the little Mice; and they, too, now began to think them not so very amusing either.

"Do you know only one story?" asked the Rats.

"Only that one," answered the Tree. "I heard it on my happiest evening; but I did not then know how happy I was."

"It is a very stupid story! Don't you know one about bacon and tallow candles? Can't you tell any larder stories?"

"No," said the Tree.

"Then good-bye," said the Rats; and they went home.

At last the little Mice stayed away also; and the Tree sighed: "After all, it was very pleasant when the sleek little Mice sat round me, and listened to what I told them. Now that too is over. But I will take good care to enjoy myself when I am brought out again."

But when was that to be? Why, one morning there came a quantity of people and set to work in the loft. The trunks were moved, the tree was pulled out and thrown,—rather hard, it is true,—down on the floor, but a man drew him towards the stairs, where the daylight shone.

"Now a merry life will begin again," thought the Tree. He felt the fresh air, the first sunbeam,—and now he was out in the courtyard. All passed so quickly, there was so much going on around him, the Tree quite forgot to look to himself. The court adjoined a garden, and all was in flower; the roses hung so fresh and odorous over the balustrade, the lindens were in blossom, the Swallows flew by, and said, "Quirre-vit! my husband is come!" but it was not the Fir-tree that they meant.

"Now, then, I shall really enjoy life," said he exultingly, and spread out his branches; but, alas! they were all withered and yellow. It was in a corner that he lay, among weeds and nettles. The golden star of tinsel was still on the top of the Tree, and glittered in the sunshine.

In the court-yard some of the merry children were playing who had danced at Christmas round the Fir-tree, and were so glad at the sight of him. One of the youngest ran and tore off the golden star.

"Only look what is still on the ugly old Christmas tree!" said he, trampling on the branches, so that they all cracked

And the Tree beheld all the beauty of the flowers, and the freshness in the garden; he beheld himself, and wished he had remained in his dark corner in the loft; he thought of his first youth in the wood, of the merry Christmas-eve, and of the little Mice who had listened with so much pleasure to the story of Humpy-Dumpy.

" 'T is over—'t is past!" said the poor Tree. "Had I but rejoiced when I had reason to do so! But now 't is past, 't is past!"

And the gardener's boy chopped the Tree into small pieces; there was a whole heap lying there. The wood flamed up splendidly under the large brewing copper, and it sighed so deeply! Each sigh was like a shot.

The boys played about in the court, and the youngest wore the gold star on his breast which the Tree had had on the happiest evening of his life. However, that was over now—the Tree gone, the story at an end. All, all was over;—every tale must end at last.

THE LITTLE MATCH GIRL

IT WAS terribly cold; it snowed and was already almost dark, and evening came on, the last evening of the year. In the cold and gloom a poor little girl, bare-headed and bare-foot, was walking through the streets. When she left her own house she certainly had had slippers on; but of what use were they? They were very big slippers, and her mother had used them till then, so big were they. The little maid lost them as she slipped across the road, where two carriages were rattling by terribly fast. One slipper was not to be found again, and a boy had seized the other, and run away with it. He thought he could use it very well as a cradle, some day when he had children of his own. So now the little girl went with her little naked feet, which were quite red and blue with the cold. In an old apron she carried a number of matches, and a bundle of them in her hand. No one had bought anything of her all day, and no one had given her a farthing.

Shivering with cold and hunger she crept along, a picture of misery, poor little girl! The snow-flakes covered her long fair hair, which fell in pretty curls over her neck; but she did not think of that now. In all the windows lights were shining, and there was a glorious smell of roast goose, for it was New Year's Eve. Yes, she thought of that!

In a corner formed by two houses, one of which projected beyond the other, she sat down, cowering. She had drawn up her little feet, but she was still colder, and she did not dare to go home, for she had sold no matches, and did not bring a farthing of money. From her father she would certainly receive a beating, and besides, it was cold at home, for they had nothing over them but a roof through which the wind whistled, though the largest rents had been stopped with straw and rags.

Her little hands were almost benumbed with the cold. Ah! a match might do her good, if she could only draw one from the bundle, and rub it against the wall, and warm her hands at it. She drew one out. R-r-atch! how it sputtered and burned! It was a warm bright flame, like a little candle, when she held her hands over it; it was a wonderful little light! It really seemed to the little girl as if she sat before a great polished stove, with bright brass feet and a brass cover. How the fire burned! how comfortable it was! but the little flame went out, the stove vanished, and she had only the remains of the burned match in her hand.

A second was rubbed against the wall. It burned up, and when the light fell upon the wall it became transparent like a thin veil, and she could see through it into the room. On the table a snow-white cloth was spread; upon it stood a shining dinner service; the roast goose smoked gloriously, stuffed with apples and dried plums. And what was still more splendid to behold, the goose hopped down from the dish, and waddled along the floor, with a knife and fork in its breast, to the little girl. Then the match went out, and only the thick, damp, cold wall was before her. She lighted another match. Then she was sitting under a beautiful Christmas tree; it was greater and more ornamented than the one she had seen through the glass door at the rich merchant's. Thousands of candles burned upon the green branches, and colored pictures like those in the print shops looked down upon them. The little girl stretched forth her hand toward them; then the match went out. The Christmas lights mounted higher. She saw them now as stars in the sky: one of them fell down, forming a long line of fire.

"Now some one is dying," thought the little girl, for her old grandmother, the only person who had loved her, and who was now dead, had told her that when a star fell down a soul mounted up to God. She rubbed another match against the wall; it became bright again, and in the brightness the old grandmother stood clear and shining, mild and lovely.

"Grandmother!" cried the child, "O! take me with you! I know you will go when the match is burned out. You will vanish like the warm fire, the warm food, and the great, glorious Christmas tree!"

And she hastily rubbed the whole bundle of matches, for she wished to hold her grandmother fast. And the matches burned with such a glow that it became brighter than in the middle of the day; grandmother had never been so large or so beautiful. She took the little girl in her arms, and both flew in brightness and joy above the earth, very, very high, and up there was neither cold, nor hunger, nor care—they were with God.

But in the corner, leaning against the wall, sat the poor girl with red cheeks and smiling mouth, frozen to death on the last evening of the Old Year. The New Year's sun rose upon a little corpse! The child sat there, stiff and cold, with the matches, of which one bundle was burned. "She wanted to warm herself," the people said. No one imagined what a beautiful thing she had seen, and in what glory she had gone in with her grandmother to the New Year's Day.

Herman Melville

BECAUSE of his deep interest in the South Pacific, we hardly think of Herman Melville as a writer who would contribute to the literature of Christmas. He was born in 1819 and died in 1891. His greatest novel, *Moby Dick,* published in 1851, was dedicated to Hawthorne. At the time, both men were living in western Massachusetts and saw each other frequently.

His popularity waned greatly during his lifetime because of his book, *Pierre,* which offended the accepted conventional standards of the Victorian era. Nearly thirty years after his death, serious readers and literary scholars turned their attention to this forgotten writer, for such had been his fate even before his death. *Moby Dick* became the source of extensive study. Was it a parable of man's struggle against nature, fate, or God? Many theories have been advanced. Melville has been widely acclaimed for his rhythmic prose, his imagery and his symbolism, and new groups of readers are continuously attracted to his books. In describing the *Pequod* as it sailed out of Nantucket in search of Moby Dick, he wrote. "It was a short, cold Christmas; and as the short northern day merged into night, we found ourselves almost broad upon the wintry ocean, whose freezing spray cased us in ice, as in polished armor. The long rows of teeth on the bulwarks glistened in the moonlight; and like the white ivory tusks of some huge elephant, vast curving icicles depended from the bows."

MERRY CHRISTMAS

AT LENGTH, towards noon, upon the final dismissal of the ship's riggers, and after the *Pequod* had been hauled out from the wharf, and after the ever-thoughtful Char- ity had come off in a whale-boat, with her last gift—a night-cap for Stubb, the second mate, her brother-in-law, and a spare Bible for the steward—after all this, the two

Captains, Peleg and Bildad, issued from the cabin, and turning to the chief mate, Peleg said:

"Now, Mr. Starbuck, are you sure everything is right? Captain Ahab is all ready—just spoke to him—nothing more to be got from shore, eh? Well, call all hands, then. Muster 'em aft here—blast 'em!"

"No need of profane words, however great the hurry, Peleg," said Bildad, "but away with thee, friend Starbuck, and do our bidding."

How now! Here upon the very point of starting for the voyage, Captain Peleg and Captain Bildad were going it with a high hand on the quarter-deck, just as if they were to be joint-commanders at sea, as well as to all appearances in port. And, as for Captain Ahab, no sign of him was yet to be seen; only, they said he was in the cabin. But then, the idea was, that his presence was by no means necessary in getting the ship under weigh, and steering her well out to sea. Indeed, as that was not at all his proper business, but the pilot's; and as he was not yet completely recovered—so they said—therefore, Captain Ahab stayed below. And all this seemed natural enough; especially as in the merchant service many captains never show themselves on deck for a considerable time after heaving up the anchor, but remain over the cabin table, having a farewell merry-making with their shore friends, before they quit the ship for good with the pilot.

But there was not much chance to think over the matter, for Captain Peleg was now all alive. He seemed to do most of the talking and commanding, and not Bildad.

"Aft here, ye sons of bachelors," he cried, as the sailors lingered at the main-mast. "Mr. Starbuck, drive 'em aft."

"Strike the tent there!"—was the next order. As I hinted before, this whalebone marquee was never pitched except in port; and on board the *Pequod,* for thirty years, the order to strike the tent was well known to be the next thing to heaving up the anchor.

"Man the capstan! Blood and thunder!—jump!"—was the next command, and the crew sprang for the handspikes.

Now in getting under weigh, the station generally occupied by the pilot is the forward part of the ship. And here Bildad, who, with Peleg, be it known, in addition to his other offices, was one of the licensed pilots of the port—he being suspected to have got himself made a pilot in order to save the Nantucket pilot-fee to all the ships he was concerned in, for he never piloted any other craft—Bildad, I say, might now be seen actively engaged in looking over the bows for the approaching anchor, and at intervals singing what seemed a dismal stave of psalmody, to cheer the hands at the windlass, who roared forth some sort of chorus about the girls in Booble Alley, with hearty good will. Nevertheless, not three days previous, Bildad had told them that no profane songs would be allowed on board the *Pequod,* particularly in getting under weigh; and Charity, his sister, had placed a small choice copy of Watts in each seaman's berth.

Meantime, overseeing the other part of the ship, Captain Peleg ripped and swore astern in the most frightful manner. I almost thought he would sink the ship before the anchor could be got up. Involuntarily I paused on my handspike, and told Queequeg to do the same, thinking of the perils we both ran, in starting on the voyage with such a devil for a pilot. I was comforting myself, however, with the thought that in pious Bildad might be found some salvation, spite of his seven hundred and seventy-seventh lay; when I felt a sudden sharp poke in my rear, and turning round, was horrified at the apparition of Captain Peleg in the act of withdrawing his leg from my immediate vicinity. That was my first kick.

"Is that the way they heave in the marchant service?" he roared. "Spring, thou sheep-head; spring, and break thy backbone! Why don't ye spring, I say, all of ye—spring! Quohog! spring, thou chap with the red whiskers; spring there, Scotch-cap; spring, thou green pants. Spring, I say, all of ye, and spring your eyes out!" And so saying, he moved along the windlass, here and there using his leg very freely, while imperturbable Bildad kept leading off with his psalmody. Thinks I, Captain Peleg must have been drinking something to-day.

At last the anchor was up, the sails were set, and off we glided: It was a short, cold Christmas; and as the short northern day merged into night, we found ourselves almost broad upon the wintry ocean, whose freezing spray cased us in ice, as in polished armor. The long rows of teeth on the bulwarks glistened in the moonlight; and like the white ivory tusks of some huge elephant, vast curving icicles depended from the bows.

Lank Bildad, as pilot, headed the first watch, and ever and anon, as the old craft deep dived into the green seas, and sent the shivering frost all over her, and the winds howled, and the cordage rang, his steady notes were heard—

"Sweet fields beyond the swelling flood,
Stand dressed in living green.
So to the Jews old Canaan stood,
While Jordan rolled between."

Never did those sweet words sound more sweetly to me than then. They were full of hope and fruition. Spite of this frigid winter night in the boisterous Atlantic, spite of my wet feet and wetter jacket, there was yet, it then seemed to me, many a pleasant haven in store; and meads and glades so eternally vernal, that the grass shot up by the spring, untrodden, unwilted, remains at midsummer.

At last we gained such an offing, that the two pilots were needed no longer. The stout sail-boat that had accompanied us began ranging alongside.

It was curious and not unpleasing, how Peleg and Bildad were affected at this juncture, especially Captain Bildad. For loath to depart, yet; very loath to leave, for good, a ship bound on so long and perilous a voyage—beyond both stormy Capes; a ship in which some thousands of his hard earned dollars were invested; a ship, in which an old shipmate sailed as captain; a man almost as old as he, once more starting to encounter all the terrors of the pitiless jaw; loath to say good-bye to a thing so every way brimful of every interest to him—poor old Bildad lingered long; paced the deck with anxious strides; ran down into the cabin to speak another farewell word there; again came on deck, and looked to windward; looked towards the wide and endless waters, only bounded by the far-off unseen Eastern Continents; looked towards the land; looked aloft; looked right and left; looked everywhere and nowhere; and at last, mechanically coiling a rope upon its pin, convulsively grasped stout Peleg by the hand, and holding up a lantern, for a moment stood gazing heroically in his face, as much as to say, "Nevertheless, friend Peleg, I can stand it; yes, I can."

As for Peleg himself, he took it more like a philosopher; but for all his philosophy, there was a tear twinkling in his eye, when the lantern came too near. And he, too, did not a little run from the cabin to deck—now a word below, and now a word with Starbuck, the chief mate.

But, at last, he turned to his comrade, with a final sort of look about him—"Captain Bildad—come, old shipmate, we must go. Back the mainyard there! Boat ahoy! Stand by to come close alongside, now! Careful, careful!—come, Bildad, boy—say your last. Luck to ye, Starbuck—luck to ye, Mr. Stubb—luck to ye, Mr. Flask—good-bye and good luck to ye all—and this day three years I'll have a hot supper smoking for ye in old Nantucket. Hurrah and away!"

"God bless ye, and have ye in His holy keeping, men," murmured old Bildad, almost incoherently. "I hope ye'll have fine weather now, so that Captain Ahab may soon be moving among ye—a pleasant sun is all he needs, and ye'll have plenty of them in the tropic voyage ye go. Be careful in the hunt, ye mates. Don't stave the boats needlessly, ye harpooneers; good

white cedar plank is raised full three per
cent. within the year. Don't forget your
prayers, either. Mr. Starbuck, mind that
cooper don't waste the spare staves. Oh!
the sail-needles are in the green locker!
Don't whale it too much a' Lord's day,
men; but don't miss a fair chance either,
that's rejecting Heaven's good gifts. Have
an eye to the molasses tierce, Mr. Stubb; it
was a little leaky, I thought. If ye touch at
the islands, Mr. Flask, beware of fornica-
tion. Good-bye, good-bye! Don't keep that
cheese too long down in the hold, Mr. Star-

buck; it'll spoil. Be careful with the butter
—twenty cents the pound it was, and mind
ye, if—"

"Come, come, Captain Bildad; stop palav-
ering—away!" and with that, Peleg hurried him over the side, and both dropt into
the boat.

Ship and boat diverged; the cold, damp
night breeze blew between; a screaming
gull flew overhead; the two hulls wildly
rolled; we gave three heavy-hearted cheers,
and blindly plunged like fate into the lone
Atlantic.

Horatio Alger, Jr.

HORATIO ALGER can hardly be considered an eminent Victorian or a great writer. However, he was a notable storyteller, and his books sold more than twenty million copies. In many ways, Alger paved the way for the era of the dime novel. Born in Revere, Massachusetts, he attended Harvard College, became a Unitarian minister, and was also a tutor of college students in Cambridge. His travels took him abroad, and he lived in Paris for a time. During his life he wrote more than a hundred books. Although he died in New York in 1899, the vogue for Alger's books lasted until well after World War I. Today, he has been largely forgotten.

Many of his stories were centered around the neighborhood of the old Astor Hotel in New York, where bootblacks and street boys, many of whom had been drummers in the Civil War, had gone to seek their fortunes. He wrote first-hand from his acquaintance with "Ragged Dick," "Tattered Tom," and dozens of others who lived in the Newsboys' Lodging House where he also resided. He organized them into a boy scout group known as "Alger's army of up-and-comings." As Van Wyck Brooke wrote in *New England: Indian Summer,* "For many who began their lives as bootblacks and newsboys, by sweeping out the store and by carrying parcels, and who rose to be captains of industry, the Horatio Alger theme was a joy and a solace . . . He made virtue and purity odious for thousands of the following age, who, having been taught to 'swim,' preferred to 'sink.'"

The Christmas story "Mr. Buffington's Lesson" appeared in *Gleason's Pictorial,* published in Boston, December 24, 1859, seven years before Alger moved to New York and long before he became the "laureate of the self-made man."

MR. BUFFINGTON'S LESSON

O, chime of blessed charity,
　Peal soon that Easter morn
When Christ for all shall risen be,
　And in all hearts new-born!
　　　　　　　　　　—J. R. Lowell.

The Christmas bells were ringing. A joyous chime it was; the bells themselves seemed to enter into the spirit of the happy time. "To-morrow is Christmas day!" This was the burden of their merry peal.

"How little Effie will enjoy it!" thought Arnold Buffington, as he walked briskly along the pavement towards his comfortable home.

Mr. Buffington was a merchant in flourishing circumstances, and little Effie was his only daughter, a graceful child of ten. No wonder the father's heart went out to her on that Christmas eve.

"What shall I get for a Christmas present for little Effie?" he murmured. "It shall be a handsome one, at any rate."

At this instant he was passing a large and brilliantly-lighted jeweller's store. As his eye rested on the windows, with their magnificent display, a thought was suggested to him.

"Yes," said he, half aloud, "I have it. It shall be a watch—a gold watch and a chain. It will cost something, but I can afford it. Nothing too good for little Effie."

Straightway he entered the store, and expressed a wish to examine their stock of gold watches—ladies size. The clerk obeyed his directions with alacrity, for he well knew Mr. Buffington's position and wealth, and that his patronage was worth having.

After a prolonged examination, Mr. Buffington made choice of a handsome watch and chain, and drawing out a well-filled pocket-book paid for them on the spot.

"Anything more, Mr. Buffington?" inquired the clerk, well pleased with the sale.

"Not to-night," was the reply.

Mr. Buffington buttoned up his overcoat,
and went out into the street, the watch being carefully deposited in his pocket. He smiled to himself as he thought of Effie's childish wonder and delight when she found her Christmas present away down at the very bottom of her stocking.

"How astonished she will be!" he thought.

Just then his pleasant reflections were interrupted by a sudden apparition. It was a little girl, who might have been from her size ten or twelve years of age. She had on a short calico dress, over which she wore, tightly folded about her neck, a small ragged shawl. On her head was a cape bonnet, appropriate enough for the summer, but a scanty protection on such a night; for, though I have not mentioned it before, it was a cold night—a very cold night. There was no snow on the ground, but the wind was fierce and inclement; it cut its way through the long streets, and whistled round the corners, nipping the cheeks and noses of those whom it encountered. Well clad as he was, Mr. Buffington felt that it would be a relief to get home, and sit down before the glowing grate.

"Please, sir, a few cents to buy bread for mother."

That was what the little girl said, looking up beseechingly into Mr. Buffington's face.

Mr. Buffington looked down a little impatiently. He did not like to have his pleasant thoughts interrupted; besides, he was in haste to get home. It was not very agreeable, standing there in the cold. Then, in order to gratify the little girl's request, he must be obliged to unbutton his coat, and that would cost him some trouble. So he said, a little gruffly—

"I haven't got anything for you, little girl."

"Only a few cents," she pleaded, her eyes filling with tears.

But Mr. Buffington had made up his

mind to be unreasonable, and so he only hardened his heart the more against the little girl's pleading.

"You'd better go home," said he, impatiently. "I don't think it right to encourage beggars."

His cold manner satisfied the little girl that further entreaties would be quite useless; so, with a look of bitter disappointment, her little heart sinking within her at the harsh repulse, and with a sharp shiver running through her little frame, she walked on.

So did Mr. Buffington.

But somehow this little incident had disturbed him more than might be supposed. He did not feel quite so well satisfied with himself as before. Still, he strove to excuse himself by such thoughts as these:

"It's a pity if one can't walk the streets without being stopped by the importunities of beggars."

Conscience whispered, "But she was very poor."

"How do I know that?"—so continued his reflections—"how do I know but she put it all on?"

"She did not look like an impostor," suggested conscience.

"At any rate," he muttered, querulously, "I can't stop in the street such a cold night as this to relieve a distress—that is, if it was real."

And so he forcibly put away from his mind thoughts of the little girl, and resolutely began to think of Effie and her present. Still an uncomfortable impression remained that he could not get rid of at will.

But all this time he had been nearing his house, and now he stands on the steps. It is a handsome brick house, with a swell front. He opens the door and walks into the hall. The cold finds no entrance here. Thanks to the furnace, the temperature is that of summer, and the brilliant gas chandelier makes it light as noonday. Out from the parlor danced a little girl with bright-red cheeks and flaxen curls.

"Good evening, papa," she exclaimed. "What kept you so long?"

"Business, little Effie. But I am glad to get home to you and mamma. Just run and get my dressing-gown and slippers; I long to have them on, and to sit down by the bright fire."

"Here they are, papa, all ready for you."

Mr. Buffington was soon seated in a comfortable rocking chair, with Effie on his knee.

"Papa," said she, a little slily, "have you seen anything of St. Nicholas to-day?"

"Yes, Effie; at least I had a telegraphic despatch from him."

"And what did he say—that he should come here to-night?"

"He thought it just possible—that is, if he got time," said Mr. Buffington.

"I suppose there are a good many places where he doesn't call at all," said Effie, thoughtfully.

"Yes," said her father, hesitatingly.

"I mean poor people," said Effie.

"No, I suppose not," replied Mr. Buffington, shortly.

Somehow he did not relish the topic which Effie had just introduced. He had for the moment the recollection of the little girl who had stopped him in the street, and now Effie's remark had brought back the uncomfortable feeling.

"I wish," thought he, pettishly, "I had given her a little something. It is just possible that she did stand in need of it."

It was more than just possible, but perhaps the merchant had conceded all that could be expected of him under the circumstances.

"I wonder how I should feel if I was poor, and had no pleasant home and no presents," said Effie, looking thoughtfully into the fire from the cricket on which she sat.

"'Tisn't best to trouble yourself with such thoughts," said her father, a little vexed.

Somehow, all seemed leagued together to bring to his mind the little girl whom he already felt that he had done wrong in slighting.

She was just about Effie's size, too, and

though he did not wish it, the thought would intrude itself how should he like to fancy Effie in her place, thinly clad and exposed, shivering to the inclemency of the winter weather.

It was nearly time for Effie to go to bed. It had been her custom for some time to read a chapter in the Testament to her father before retiring. She did so to-night. Mr. Buffington did not listen very attentively, until his attention was drawn to this passage: "Since ye have done it unto one of these little ones, ye have done it unto me."

Mr. Buffington could not help feeling that this was meant for him; it seemed to suit his case exactly. It needed this to set before him his duty in the proper light.

"After all," he thought, "how little trouble it would have been to comply with that poor little girl's request. And as for the money, it would have been to me a mere nothing. I hope she met with some one more charitable afterwards. If I ever see her again, I will make it up to her."

He felt more comfortable after this resolve, although he felt that it was very doubtful whether he would ever be called upon to carry it out.

It was an unusually cold night. Instead of abating, the wind seemed if anything to increase. However, it mattered little to those who were as comfortably housed and protected in every way as Mr. Buffington's family: rather, the sense of comfort seemed to be increased by the thought of the contrast which it presented to the streets without.

Little Effie slept soundly, but early in the morning she was astir. She crept to the chimney corner, and eagerly ran her hand down the stocking which she had hung up so hopefully the night before. She encountered something hard. Her delight could hardly be restrained within bounds when she found what it was that the benevolent Christmas saint had brought her.

"Just what I have been longing for," she thought.

She eagerly thanked her father at the breakfast-table.

"Then St. Nicholas happened to guess right this time," said he, smiling.

"You must thank him for me, papa— that is, when you see him."

"So I will. I think I can make that promise safely. And now, Effie, you may show your gratitude by going out and bringing in the morning paper."

Effie danced into the hall, and quickly reappeared with the morning paper, yet damp from the press, which the news carrier had just brought.

Mr. Buffington took it from her hands, and was soon absorbed in its contents. First he glanced at the telegraphic news, next at the business department, and then carelessly run his eyes over the local paragraphs. At one of these he started. It was a short paragraph, and may be inserted here:

"Policeman 10 fell in last night with a little girl apparently about ten years of age, crouched in a doorway, and nearly frozen. She was very thinly clad, and her hands and arms were numb with the cold. She reported that she lived with her mother in a basement room in S—— street; that they were miserably poor, and had not tasted food for twenty-four hours. She had come out with the hope of obtaining a few pennies, which she intended to spend for a loaf of bread. She had accosted several persons, but none seemed charitably disposed. It being already late, she was taken to the station-house, where she was comfortably cared for."

"It must be the same one," thought Mr. Buffington. "Poor child!"

"What is it that interests you so much, dear papa?" said Effie.

Her father silently pointed to the paragraph. Effie's heart was touched.

"How much I should like to give something to the little girl and her mother. But then, I have spent all my money. Father," she said, with a sudden thought, "how much did my watch cost?"

"The watch and chain cost a hundred dollars."

"Wouldn't a hundred dollars do the little girl a great deal of good?"

"Yes, Effie."

"Do you think the man would take back the watch, papa?"

"What, Effie, you wouldn't resign the watch? I thought you cared for it!"

"So I do, very much; but it makes me feel uncomfortable to think of this little girl suffering for the want of what I can do without."

"My dear child," said her father, "you have taught me a lesson. What will you say when I tell you that I was one of those to whom this little girl applied for assistance, and I was hard-hearted enough to refuse."

"You, papa!" exclaimed Effie, in astonishment.

"Yes, Effie; but I felt ashamed of it immediately. If you will get my coat and hat, I will go immediately and repair my fault. You shall keep your watch, and I will still spend a hundred dollars for the benefit of this little girl and her mother."

Those to whom poverty and privation are strangers, can hardly conceive the delight of the poor mother on receiving the merchant's well-timed gift, while the latter felt that it was truly more blessed to give than to receive.

Eliza Ripley

ELIZA RIPLEY, born in 1832 in Lexington, Kentucky, was the tenth child of a family of twelve. She grew up on a Louisiana plantation and became a keen observer of the way of life of her native South. In later years, she drew heavily on her vivid memory for the material which appeared in two books of reminiscence, *From Flag to Flag,* published in 1888, and *Social Life in Old New Orleans,* which appeared in 1912, the year she died.

A bride at twenty, for ten years Eliza presided over a large plantation near Baton Rouge. She faced the challenge of the Civil War by traveling with her husband and children, in an open wagon, across Texas and Mexico, hauling Confederate cotton. When Lee surrendered, the Ripley family went to Cuba and operated a sugar plantation.

In *Social Life in Old New Orleans, Being Recollections of My Girlhood,* Mrs. Ripley has left for future generations a dramatic picture of plantation life. Her chapter "The Last Christmas" recounts vividly the mode of life, the manner of travel on land and water, and the spirit of lightheartedness that highlighted this picturesque ante-bellum era, especially at Christmas.

THE LAST CHRISTMAS

CHRISTMAS before the war. There never will be another in any land, with any peoples, like the Christmas of 1859—on the old plantation. Days beforehand preparations were in progress for the wedding at the quarters, and the ball at the "big house." Children coming home for the holidays were both amused and delighted to learn that Nancy Brackenridge was to be the quarter bride. "Nancy a bride! Oh, la!" they exclaimed. "Why Nancy must be forty years old." And she was going to marry Aleck, who, if he would wait a year or two, might marry Nancy's daughter. While the young school-girls were busy "letting out" the white satin balldress that had descended from the parlor dance to the quarter bride, and were picking out and freshening up the wreath and corsage bouquet of lilies of the valley that had been the wedding flowers of the mistress of the big house, and while the boys were ransacking the distant woods for holly branches and magnolia boughs, enough for the ballroom as well as the wedding supper table, the family were busy with the multitudinous preparations for the annual dance, for which Arlington, with its ample parlors and halls, and its proverbial hospitality, was noted far and wide.

The children made molasses gingerbread and sweet potato pies, and one big bride's cake, with a real ring in it. They spread the table in the big quarters nursery, and the boys decorated it with greenery and a lot of cut paper fly catchers, laid on the roast mutton and pig, and hot biscuits from the big house kitchen, and the pies and cakes of the girls' own make. The girls proceeded to dress Nancy Brackenridge, pulling together that refractory satin waist which, though it had been "let out" to its fullest extent, still showed a sad gap, to be concealed by a dextrous arrangement of some discarded hair ribbons. Nancy was black as a crow and had rather a startling look in that dazzling white satin dress and the pure white flowers pinned to her kinks. At length the girls gave a finishing pat to the toilet, and their brothers pronounced her "bully," and called Marthy Ann to see how fine her mammy was.

As was the custom, the whole household went to the quarter to witness the wedding. Lewis, the plantation preacher, in a cast-off swallow-tail coat of Marse Jim's that was uncomfortably tight, especially about the waist line, performed the ceremony. Then my husband advanced and made some remarks, to the effect that this marriage was a solemn tie, and there must be no shirking of its duties; they must behave and be faithful to each other; he would have no foolishness. These remarks, though by no means elegant, fitted the occasion to a fraction. There were no high flights of eloquence which the darky mind could

not reach, it was plain, unvarnished admonition.

The following morning, Christmas Day, the field negroes were summoned to the back porch of the big house, where Marse Jim, after a few preliminary remarks, distributed the presents—a head handkerchief, a pocketknife, a pipe, a dress for the baby, shoes for the growing boy (his first pair, maybe), etc., etc., down the list. Each gift was received with a "Thankee, sir," and, perhaps, also a remark anent its usefulness. Then after Charlotte brought forth the jug of whiskey and the tin cups, and everyone had a comfortable dram, they filed off to the quarters, with a week of holiday before them and a trip to town to do their little buying.

The very last Christmas on the old plantation we had a tree. None of us had ever seen a Christmas tree; there were no cedars or pines, so we finally settled upon a tall althea bush, hung presents on it, for all the house servants, as well as for the family and a few guests. The tree had to be lighted up, so it was postponed till evening. The idea of the house servants having such a celebration quite upset the little negroes. I heard one remark, "All us house niggers is going to be hung on a tree." Before the dawn of another Christmas the negroes had become discontented, demoralized and scattered, freer than the whites, for the blacks recognized no responsibilities whatsoever. The family had already abandoned the old plantation home. We could not stand the changed condition of things any longer, and the Federals had entered into possession and completed the ruin. Very likely some reminiscent darky told new-found friends, "All de house niggers was hung on a tree last Christmas." I have heard from Northern lips even more astonishing stories of maltreated slaves than a wholesale hanging.

Frequently before the holidays some of the negroes were questioned as to what they would like to have, and the planter would make notes and have the order filled in the city. That, I think, was the custom at Whitehall plantation. I was visiting there on one occasion when a woman told Judge Chinn she wanted a mourning veil. "A mourning veil!" he replied. "I thought you were going to marry Tom this Christmas?" "Yis, marster, but you know Jim died last grinding, and I ain't never mourned none for 'im. I want to mourn some 'fore I marries agin." I did not remain to see, but I do not doubt she got the mourning veil and had the melancholy satisfaction of wearing it around the quarter lot a few days before she married Tom.

After the departure of our happy negroes, whose voices and laughter could be heard long after the yard gate was closed and they had vanished out of sight, we rushed around like wild to complete the preparations for the coming ball guests. They began to arrive in the afternoon from down the coast and from the opposite side of the river. Miles and miles some of them drove in carriages, with champagne baskets, capital forerunners of the modern suit case, tied on behind, and, like as not, a dusky maid perched on top of it; poor thing, the carriage being full, she had to travel in this precarious way, holding on for dear life. Those old-time turtle-back vehicles had outside a single seat for the coachman only. Parties came also in skiffs, with their champagne baskets and maids. Long before time for the guests from town to appear, mammas and maids were busy in the bedrooms, dressing their young ladies for the occasion. Meanwhile the plantation musicians were assembling, two violins, a flute, a triangle, and a tambourine. A platform had been erected at one end of the room, with kitchen chairs and cuspidors, for their accommodation. Our own negroes furnished the dance music, but we borrowed Col. Hicky's Washington for the tambourine. He was more expert than any "end man" you ever saw. He kicked it and butted it and struck it with elbow and heel, and rattled it in perfect unison with the other instruments, making more noise, and being himself a more inspiring sight, than all the rest of the band put together. Col. Hicky always said it was the only thing Washington was fit for, and he kept the worthless negro simply because he was the image (in bronze) of Gen. Lafayette. Col. Hicky was an octogenarian, and had seen Gen. Lafayette, so he could not have been mistaken. When Washington flagged, a few drops of whiskey was all he needed to refresh his energies.

The whirl of the dance waxed as the night waned. The tired paterfamiliases sat around the rooms, too true to their mission to retire for a little snooze. They were restored to consciousness at intervals by liberal cups of strong coffee. Black William, our first violin, called out the figures, "Ladies to the right!" "Set to your partners?"— and the young people whirled and swung around in the giddy reel as though they would never have such another opportunity to dance—as, indeed, many of them never did. From the porch and lawn windows black faces gazed on the inspiring scene. They never saw the like again, either.

Laughing, wide-awake girls and tired fathers and mothers started homeward at the first blush of dawn, when they could plainly see their way over the roads. I started too early from a party the year before, and the buggy I was in ran over a dirt-colored cow lying asleep in the road. The nodding maid again perilously perched on top the champagne basket, and skiffs with similar freight plied across the broad river as soon as there was sufficient light to enable them to dodge a passing steamboat.

The last ball was a noble success. We danced on and on, never thinking this was to be our last dance in the big house. Clouds were hovering all about us the following Christmas. No one had the heart to dance then. The negroes had already become restless and discontented. After that the Deluge! The big house long ago slid into the voracious Mississippi. The quarters where the wedding feast was spread have fallen into ruins, the negroes scattered or dead. The children, so happy and so busy then, are now old people—the only ones left to look on this imperfectly drawn picture with any personal interest. We lived, indeed, a life never to be lived again.

Irwin Russell

CHRISTMAS in the Deep South, as enjoyed by the darkies on the old plantations, has been recorded in unforgettable verse by a talented young poet whose short life came to a close in the Christmas season of 1879. Irwin Russell was born at Port Gibson, Mississippi, in 1853, but his boyhood was spent in St. Louis. He was a frail but precocious youngster who read Milton at the age of six. An attack of yellow fever and the loss of an eye left their mark on him at an early age. Having graduated from St. Louis University at sixteen, he proceeded to study law, and was admitted to the bar by a special act of the legislature at the age of nineteen. Like Robert Louis Stevenson, he was by nature a rover and a traveler. He reveled in the rough life associated with the steamboats that plied the Mississippi, and learned to know the captains of these boats, as well as the rough characters who worked on them. He wrote his first poem at sixteen, and some of his verse appeared in *Scribner's* and *St. Nicholas*.

In 1878 he assisted his father, who was a physician, in battling a great epidemic of yellow fever at Port Gibson. Later that year he went to New York to seek his fortune, but did not like the big city and its ways. Early in 1879, after his father had died, he secured a job on the New Orleans *Times*. Broken in health, he died in a cheap boarding house on December 23, 1879.

Irwin Russell was one of the first poets to recognize the literary possibilities of the negro dialect and character, and Joel Chandler Harris and Thomas Nelson Page recognized his talent in this direction. Chandler wrote of him, "No man the South has produced gave higher evidence of genius in a period so short. . . . Had he been spared to letters, all the rest of us would have taken back seats so far as representation of life in the South was concerned."

Inspired in his use of dialect by his devotion to Robert Burns, Russell's Christmas poem has been compared favorably with "Tam O'Shanter." He wrote for his own pleasure and that of his friends, and was seldom concerned about remuneration. He disliked Harriet Beecher Stowe's concept of the negro and felt that the unreconstructed darky was worthy of portrayal. He knew the emotional side of his characters, their aims, hopes, desires, and feelings, and captured the fullness of their spirit. "Christmas Night in the Quarters" contains the essence of the worldly wisdom of the negro, his humor, his superstitions, his feelings.

After his death, his poems were published posthumously, with a preface by Joel Chandler Harris. Again, in 1917, the poems appeared under the title of the piece for which he is best known, "Christmas Night in the Quarters and Other Poems." This charming piece of epic poetry blended with negro dialect paints a memorable picture of ante-bellum days among the negroes of the South, and was first published in *Scribner's Monthly* in 1878. It had been refused by the Editor of the *Port Gibson Réveille* because of its length. The illustrations which accompany it were taken from a scrapbook collection of German colored cutouts which were popular in the 1880's.

CHRISTMAS NIGHT IN THE QUARTERS

WHEN merry Christmas day is done,
And Christmas night is just begun;
While clouds in slow procession drift,
To wish the moon-man "Christmas gift,"
Yet linger overhead, to know
What causes all the stir below;
At Uncle Johnny Booker's ball
The darkies hold high carnival.
From all the country side they throng,
With laughter, shouts, and scraps of song,
Their whole deportment plainly showing
That to the Frolic they are going.
Some take the path with shoes in hand,
To traverse muddy bottom-land;
Aristocrats their steeds bestride;
Four on a mule, behold them ride!
And ten great oxen draw apace
The wagon from "de oder place,"
With forty guests, whose conversation
Betokens glad anticipation.
Not so with him who drives: old Jim
Is sagely solemn, hard, and grim,
And frolics have no joys for him.
He seldom speaks but to condemn—
Or utter some wise apothegm—
Or else, some crabbed thought pursuing,
Talk to his team, as now he's doing:

Come up heah, Star! Yee-bawee!
   You alluz is a-laggin'—
Mus' be you think I's dead,
   An' dis de huss you's draggin'—
You's mos' too lazy to draw yo' bref,
   Let 'lone drawin' de waggin.

Dis team—quit bel'rin, sah!
   De ladies don't submit 'at—
Dis team—you ol' fool ox,
   You heah me tell you quit 'at?
Dis team's des like de 'Nited States;
   Dat's what I's tryin' to git at!

De people rides behin',
   De pollytishners haulin'—
Sh'u'd be a well-bruk ox,
   To foller dat ar callin'—
An' sometimes nuffin won't do dem steers,
   But what dey mus' be stallin'!

Woo bahgh! Buck-kannon! Yes, sah, .
   Sometimes dey will be stickin';
An' den, fus thing dey knows,
   Dey takes a rale good lickin'.
De folks gits down: an' den watch out
   For hommerin' an' kickin'.

Dey blows upon dey hands,
    Den flings 'em wid de nails up,
Jumps up an' cracks dey heels,
    An' pruzently dey sails up,
An' makes dem oxen hump deysef,
    By twistin' all dey tails up!

In this our age of printer's ink
'Tis books that show us how to think—
The rule reversed, and set at naught,
That held that books were born of thought.
We form our minds by pedants' rules,
And all we know is from the schools;
And when we work, or when we play,
We do it in an ordered way—
And Nature's self pronounce a ban on,
Whene'er she dares transgress a canon.
Untrammelled thus the simple race is
That "wuks the craps" on cotton places.
Original in act and thought,
Because unlearnèd and untaught.
Observe them at their Christmas party:
How unrestrained their mirth—how hearty!
How many things they say and do
That never would occur to you!
See Brudder Brown—whose saving grace
Would sanctify a quarter-race—
Out on the crowded floor advance,
To "beg a blessin' on dis dance."

O Mahsr! let dis gath'rin' fin' a blessin'
    in yo' sight,
Don't jedge us hard fur what we does—
    you knows it's Christmas night;
An' all de balunce ob de yeah we does as
    right's we kin.
Ef dancin's wrong, O Mahsr! let de time
    excuse de sin!

We labors in de vineya'd, wukin' hard an'
    wukin' true;
Now, shorely you won't notus, ef we eats
    a grape or two,
An' takes a leetle holiday,—a leetle restin'-
    spell,—
Bekase, nex' week, we'll start in fresh, an'
    labor twicet as well.

Remember, Mahsr,—min' dis, now,—de
    sinfulness ob sin
Is 'pendin' 'pon de sperrit what we goes an'
    does it in:

An' in a righchis frame ob min' we's gwine
    to dance an' sing,
A-feelin' like King David, when he cut
    de pigeon wing.

It seems to me—indeed it do—I mebbe
    mout be wrong—
That people raly *ought* to dance, when
    Chrismus comes along;
Des dance bekase dey's happy—like de
    birds hops in de trees,
De pine-top fiddle soundin' to de bowin' ob
    de breeze.

We has no ark to dance afore, like Isrul's
    prophet king;
We has no harp to soun' de chords, to
    holp us out to sing;
But 'cordin' to de gif's we has we does
    de bes' we knows;
An' folks don't 'spise de vi'let flower be-
    kase it ain't de rose.

You bless us, please, sah, eben ef we's doin'
    wrong tonight;
Kase den we'll need de blessin' more'n ef
    we's doin' right;
An' let de blessin' stay wid us, untel we
    comes to die,
An' goes to keep our Chrismus wid dem
    sheriffs in de sky!

Yes, tell dem preshis anguls we's a-gwine
    to jine 'em soon:
Our voices we's a-trainin' fur to sing de
    glory tune;
We's ready when you wants us, an' it
    ain't no matter when—
O Mahsr! call yo' chillen soon, an' take
    'em home! Amen.

The rev'rend man is scarcely through,
When all the noise begins anew,
And with such force assaults the ears,
That through the din one hardly hears
Old fiddling Josey "sound his A,"
Correct the pitch, begin to play,
Stop, satisfied, then, with the bow,
Rap out the signal dancers know:
Git yo' pardners, fust kwattillion!
Stomp yo' feet, an' raise 'em high;
Tune is: "Oh! dat water-million!
Gwine to git to home bime bye."

S'lute yo' pardners!—scrape perlitely—
Don't be bumpin' 'gin de res'—
Balance all!—now step out rightly;
Alluz dance yo' lebbel bes'.
Fo'wa'd foah!—whoop up, niggers!
Back ag'in!—don't be so slow!—
Swing cornahs!—min' de figgers!
When I hollers, den yo' go.
Top ladies cross ober!
Hol' on, till I takes a dram—
Gemmen solo!—yes, *I's* sober—
Cain't say how de fiddle am.
Hands around!—hol' up yo' faces,
Don't be lookin' at yo' feet!
Swing yo' pardners to yo' places!
Dat's de way—dat's hard to beat.
Sides fo'w'd!—when you's ready—
Make a bow as low's you kin!
Swing acrost wid opp'site lady!
Now we'll let you swap ag'in:
Ladies change!—shet up dat talkin';
Do yo' talkin' arter while!
Right an' lef'!—don't want no walkin'—
Make yo' steps, an' show yo' style!

And so the "set" proceeds—its length
Determined by the dancers' strength;
And all agree to yield the palm
For grace and skill to "Georgy Sam,"
Who stamps so hard, and leaps so high,
"Des watch him!" is the wond'ring cry—
"De nigger mus' be, for a fac',
Own cousin to a jumpin'-jack!"
On, on the restless fiddle sounds,
Still chorused by the curs and hounds;
Dance after dance succeeding fast,
Till supper is announced at last.
That scene—but why attempt to show it?
The most inventive modern poet,
In fine new words whose hope and trust is,
Could form no phrase to do it justice!
When supper ends—that is not soon—
The fiddle strikes the same old tune;
The dancers pound the floor again,
With all they have of might and main;
Old gossips, *almost* turning pale,
Attend Aunt Cassy's grewsome tale
Of conjurers, and ghosts, and devils,
That in the smoke-house hold their revels;
Each drowsy baby droops his head,
Yet scorns the very thought of bed:—

So wears the night, and wears so fast,
All wonder when they find it past,
And hear the signal sound to go
From what few cocks are left to crow.
Then, one and all, you hear them shout:
"Hi! Booker! fotch de banjo out,
An' gib us *one* song 'fore we goes—
One ob de berry bes' you knows!"
Responding to the welcome call,
He takes the banjo from the wall,
And tunes the strings with skill and care,
Then strikes them with a master's air,
And tells, in melody and rhyme,
This legend of the olden time:

Go 'way, fiddle! folks is tired o' hearin' you
 a-squawkin'.
Keep silence fur yo' betters!—don't you
 heah de banjo talkin'?
About de possum's tail she's gwine to
 lecter—ladies, listen!—
About de ha'r whut isn't dar, an' why de
 ha'r is missin':

"Dar's gwine to be a oberflow," said Noah,
 lookin' solemn—
Fur Noah tuk the *Herald,* an' he read de
 ribber column—
An' so he sot his hands to wuk a-cl'arin'
 timber-patches,
An' 'lowed he's gwine to build a boat to
 beat the steamah *Natchez.*

Ol' Noah kep' a-nailin' an' a-chippin' an'
 a-sawin',
An' all de wicked neighbors kep' a-laughin'
 an' a-pshawin';
But Noah didn't min' 'em, knowin' whut
 wuz gwine to happen:
An' forty days an' forty nights de rain it
 kep' a-drappin'.

Now, Noah had done cotched a lot ob ebry
 sort o' beas'es—
Ob all de shows a-trabbelin', it beat 'em all
 to pieces!
He had a Morgan colt an' sebral head o'
 Jarsey cattle—
An' druv 'em 'board de Ark as soon's he
 heered de thunder rattle.

Den sech anoder fall ob rain!—it come so
  awful hebby,
De ribber ris immejitly, an' busted troo de
  lebbee;
De people all wuz drownded out—'cep'
  Noah an' de critters,
An' men he'd hired to work de boat—an'
  one to mix de bitters.

De Ark she kep' a-sailin' an' a-sailin' *an*
  a-sailin';
De lion got his dander up, an' like to bruk
  de palin';
De sarpints hissed; de painters yelled; tell,
  whut wid all de fussin',
You c'u'dn't hardly heah de mate a-bossin'
  'roun an' cussin'.

Now, Ham, de only nigger whut wuz
  runnin' on de packet,
Got lonesome in de barber-shop, an' c'u'dn't
  stan' de racket;
An' so, fur to amuse he-se'f, he steamed
  some wood an' bent it,
An' soon he had a banjo made—de fust
  dat wuz invented.

He wet de ledder, stretched it on; made
  bridge an' screws an' aprin;
An' fitted in a proper neck—'twuz berry
  long an' tap'rin';
He tuk some tin, an' twisted him a thimble
  fur to ring it;
An' den de mighty question riz: how wuz
  he gwine to string it?

De 'possum had as fine a tail as dis dat
  I's a-singin';
De ha'r's so long an' thick an' strong,—
  des fit fur banjo stringin';

Dat nigger shaved 'em off as short as
  wash-day-dinner graces;
An' sorted ob 'em by de size, f'om little
  E's to basses.

He strung her, tuned her, struck a jig,—
  'twuz "Nebber min' de wedder,"—
She soun' like forty-lebben bands a-playin'
  all togedder;
Some went to pattin'; some to dancin':
  Noah called de figgers;
An' Ham he sot an' knocked de tune, de
  happiest ob niggers!

Now, sence dat time—it's mighty strange
  —dere's not de slightes' showin'
Ob any ha'r at all upon de 'possum's tail
  a-growin';
An' curi's, too, dat nigger's ways: his people nebber los' 'em—
Fur whar you finds de nigger—dar's de
  banjo an' de 'possum!

The night is spent; and as the day
Throws up the first faint flash of gray,
The guests pursue their homeward way;
And through the field beyond the gin,
Just as the stars are going in,
See Santa Claus departing—grieving—
His own dear Land of Cotton leaving.
His work is done; he fain would rest
Where people know and love him best.
He pauses, listens, looks about;
But go he must: his pass is out.
So, coughing down the rising tears,
He climbs the fence and disappears.
And thus observes a colored youth
(The common sentiment, in sooth):
"Oh! what a blessin' 'tw'u'd ha' been,
Ef Santy had been born a twin!
We'd hab two Chrismuses a yeah—
Or p'r'aps *one* brudder'd *settle* heah!"

William Gordon McCabe

WILLIAM GORDON McCABE was a full-blooded Virginian. Born in Richmond in 1841, he served as a dedicated soldier in the Confederate Army, became a famous schoolmaster and scholar, and died in his native heath in 1920. Two volumes entitled *Memories and Memorials,* which appeared a few years after his death, pay high tribute to this genial scholar whose portrait and writings reveal a man of great warmth and individuality. "His was a face worth painting for its own sake." He loved Virginia, its history and its people, and pursued the record of achievement of his native state throughout his life.

Young McCabe was a student at the University of Virginia when the ordinance of secession was passed and he immediately "joined up" and became a part of the "Army of the Peninsula." Settled in winter quarters at Yorktown, he began to write verse and essays which he sent frequently to the *Southern Literary Messenger.* Possessed of a romantic temperament with strong imaginative gifts, his war journals are not only vividly picturesque but highly entertaining.

Recalling his first Christmas in camp, he wrote: "This log hut of ours is rather a pleasant place. We built it ourselves, maybe, is the reason we have an affection for it. We call it 'Rebel Hall.' You can read the name in charcoal letters on our door; under the name, a line from Virgil. 'The boys' sing great boisterous songs, and pity the miserable wretches who wear black 'cits' and nightly recline on feather beds and hair mattresses. You should have been here with us at Christmas;—our Fête de Noël. How the rafters quivered with our college songs! Even my sad-looking mess-mate's eye brightened a little as we rang out:

> The wine-cup is sparkling before us
> As we pledge 'round to hearts that are true, boys, true!

My pleasure was a little dashed by the fact that I was cook on that day: Chef de Cuisine, I informed the company. Maybe my temper was a little ruffled, as I stood over the seething kettle. . . . However, I served up a very nice meal . . . We laughed when we thought of how the 'folk at home' were pitying the poor lads on the dreary outposts. And then what a grand smoke we had after our café noir!"

As the war progressed and the fighting became bitter, his contributions became less frequent. His poem "Christmas Night of '62," which appeared in the January 1863, issue of the *Messenger,* is the best known of his writings and was frequently included in anthologies for fifty years or more after it first appeared. The reference to his mother's death in the poem was to him in later years a source of great regret, for he felt that poets should not "lug in their own too obvious persons," into personal poems. At any rate, the sentiment expressed and the picture which the young poet painted speaks for itself.

CHRISTMAS NIGHT OF '62

The wintry blast goes wailing by,
  The snow is falling overhead;
  I hear the lonely sentry's tread,
And distant watch-fires light the sky.

Dim forms go flitting through the gloom;
  The soldiers cluster round the blaze
  To talk of other Christmas days,
And softly speak of home and home.

My sabre swinging overhead,
  Gleams in the watch-fire's fitful glow,
  While fiercely drives the blinding snow,
And memory leads me to the dead.

My thoughts go wandering to and fro,
  Vibrating 'twixt the Now and Then;
  I see the low-browed home agen,
The old hall wreathed with mistletoe.

And sweetly from the far off years
  Comes borne the laughter faint and low,
  The voices of the Long Ago!
My eyes are wet with tender tears.

I feel agen the mother kiss,
  I see agen the glad surprise
  That lighted up the tranquil eyes
And brimmed them o'er with tears of bliss,

As, rushing from the old hall-door,
  She fondly clasped her wayward boy—
  Her face all radiant with the joy
She felt to see him home once more.

My sabre swinging on the bough
  Gleams in the watch-fire's fitful glow,
  While fiercely drives the blinding snow
Aslant upon my saddened brow.

Those cherished faces all are gone!
  Asleep within the quiet graves
  Where lies the snow in drifting waves,—
And I am sitting here alone.

There's not a comrade here to-night
  But knows that loved ones far away
  On bended knees this night will pray:
"God bring our darling from the fight."

But there are none to wish me back,
  For me no yearning prayers arise.
  The lips are mute and closed the eyes—
My home is in the bivouac.

In the Army of Northern Virginia

Henry Wadsworth Longfellow

FEW American poets have ever captivated the public at large in the same manner in which Henry Wadsworth Longfellow charmed his audiences and his readers. Born in 1807 in Portland, Maine, he was graduated from Bowdoin College and became Professor of Modern Languages there at the age of twenty-two. Six years later he was called to Harvard in a similar capacity. He became so well-known on both sides of the Atlantic that Hawthorne wrote in 1855 "no other poet has anything like your vogue."

Longfellow's contribution to the field of narrative poetry was great. Although his best known work is "Evangeline," the colorful *Tales of a Wayside Inn,* which are rich in historical lore, have had continued popularity. So great was the demand for his poetry that he resigned his professorship at Harvard at the age of forty-seven to devote himself entirely to writing. He has been compared to many of the great poets, including Geoffrey Chaucer, for his ability to tell a story in a fascinating manner.

At the time of his death in 1882, Longfellow's name was a household word in America, and England honored him as she had previously honored no other American, by placing his bust in the Poets' Corner at Westminster Abbey.

Among his Christmas poems there are several of long-standing appeal. "The Three Kings" recounts the ageless story of the Wise Men with all the glow and warmth so typical of the Victorian era. His "Christmas Carol," a translation from the French, and "Christmas 1863," written at a time when he was deeply moved by the strife of the Civil War, were warmly received when they were published.

CHRISTMAS—1863

I hear the bells on Christmas Day
The old familiar carols play,
  And wild and sweet,
  The words repeat
Of peace on earth, good-will to men.

Then from each black, accursed mouth
The cannon thundered in the South;
  And with that sound
  The carols drowned
Of peace on earth, good-will to men.

It was as if an earthquake rent
The hearthstones of a continent,
  And made forlorn
  The household born
Of peace on earth, good-will to men.

And in despair I bowed my head,
"There is no peace on earth," I said,
  "For hate is strong
  And mocks the song
Of peace on earth, good-will to men."

Then pealed the bells more loud and deep;
"God is not dead, nor doth He sleep;
  The Wrong shall fail,
  The Right prevail,
With peace on earth, good-will to men."

CHRISTMAS CAROL

When Christ was born in Bethlehem,
'T was night, but seemed the noon of day;
  The stars, whose light
  Was pure and bright,
Shone with unwavering ray;
But one, one glorious star
Guided the Eastern Magi from afar.

Then peace was spread throughout the land;
The lion fed beside the tender lamb;
  And with the kid,
  To pasture led,
  The spotted leopard fed;
In peace, the calf and bear,
The wolf and lamb reposed together there.

As shepherds watched their flocks by night,
An angel, brighter than the sun's own light,
  Appeared in air,
  And gently said,
  Fear not,—be not afraid,
For lo! beneath your eyes,
Earth has become a smiling paradise.

Louisa May Alcott

ON CHRISTMAS 1854, Louisa May Alcott put a copy of her first published book in her mother's stocking with a touching note hoping that the gift would be accepted "as an earnest of what I may yet do . . . for I hope to pass in time from fairies and fables to men and realities." The little book was *Flower Fables,* a series of stories written when she was sixteen to amuse young Ellen Emerson. It sold well locally and earned thirty-two dollars for its author. "Duty's faithful child," as her father called her, lived in the golden age of her beloved Concord.

Louisa became famous as an author at the age of thirty-six, the year *Little Women* was published. For years she had done her bit as seamstress, governess, teacher, and household servant to salvage the economic situation in the "temple of learning" which she called home. Her distinguished philosopher father, Bronson Alcott, was hardly adept at earning a living. Early attempts at writing had prompted the publisher of the *Atlantic* to advise her "to stick to your teaching—you can't write." But Louisa persisted, for she had dreams and ambitions to be fulfilled about "books and publishers and a fortune of my own."

When the call came for the boys from Concord to enlist in the Civil War, Louisa was determined to do her part. First it was sewing blue shirts. Then she was finally accepted for service as a nurse. Ministering to the soldiers at Union Hotel Hospital, in Washington, for a period of four weeks, until she developed typhoid fever, was the great adventure of Louisa's life. Had she not been stricken, she might well have been another Clara Barton. This exposure left its imprint and undoubtedly shortened her life, but with the publication of *Hospital Sketches,* months later, paved the way for the phenomenal success of *Little Women* in 1869. Topsy-turvy Louisa, at the age of thirty, was a big, bashful girl with a yard-and-a-half of brown hair neatly braided at the back of her head. Yet, she was jolly and sentimental as she hovered "like a massive cherubim, in a red rigolette over the slumbering sons of men." Typical of her femininity and her gentle breeding, she pursued the bad odors that permeated the hospital with a bottle of cologne or lavender water in one hand as she made her way among the patients, tidying the beds and adjusting pillows with the other. She joked and played games and recited bits of Dickens as she applied bandages, fed the helpless, and ministered to the every need of the human wrecks that surrounded her. These were harrowing days, but she loved every minute of it. Best of all, she recorded her experiences in a series of letters to her family.

These became the basis for *Hospital Sketches,* which first appeared in the *Commonwealth,* an antislavery paper published in Boston, and won immediate popularity. They were copied by papers all over the North, and letters from writers, surgeons, friends, and the general public poured in. A few months later these vivid word pictures of hospital life appeared in book form, which Louisa noted the townsfolk were "buying, reading, laughing and crying over." Undoubtedly inspired by Louisa's own warm heart, the publisher's advertisement in the book stated: "Besides paying the author the usual copyright, the publisher has resolved to devote at least five cents for each copy sold to the support of orphans made fatherless or homeless by the war . . . Should the sale of the little book be large, the orphan's percentage will be doubled."

In 1870 another edition of *Hospital Sketches* was published, together with *Camp and Fireside Stories.* Two thousand copies were sold within a week. Like the *Sketches,* readers found in *Camp and Fireside Stories* a blend of the tragic and the comic which Louisa discovered first-hand in those few short weeks she served as a nurse at the Union Hotel Hospital. One of the *Stories* was "A Hospital Christmas," which reveals more of the stark drama of suffering and death in that critical year than a hundred of Matthew Brady's remarkable photographs could possibly record.

Louisa wrote about other Christmases in her later books, and told of festive seasons when material gifts were not abundant, but she carried the spirit of Christmas in her heart throughout her life, and it flowed into the lives of many of her characters. Dickens was one of her great heroes, and his philosophy was an inseparable part of her greatness of spirit. She died in Concord in 1888, two days after her father had passed away. Orchard House, where she spent the greater part of her life, has become one of the nation's outstanding literary shrines and copies of *Little Women* in several attractively printed editions, as well as many of her other titles, can be found in almost any well-stocked bookshop today.

A HOSPITAL CHRISTMAS

"MERRY Christmas!" "Merry Christmas!" "Merry Christmas, and lots of 'em, ma'am!" echoed from every side, as Miss Hale entered her ward in the gray December dawn. No wonder the greetings were hearty, that thin faces brightened, and eyes watched for the coming of this small luminary more eagerly than for the rising of the sun; for when they woke that morning, each man found that in the silence of the night some friendly hand had laid a little gift beside his bed. Very humble little gifts they were, but well chosen and thoughtfully bestowed by one who made the blithe anniversary pleasant even in a hospital, and sweetly taught the lesson of the hour—Peace on earth, good-will to man.

"I say, ma'am, these are just splendid. I've dreamt about such for a week, but I never thought I'd get 'em," cried one poor fellow, surveying a fine bunch of grapes with as much satisfaction as if he had found a fortune.

"Thank you kindly, Miss, for the paper and the fixings. I hated to keep borrowing, but I hadn't any money," said another, eying his gift with happy anticipations of the home letters with which the generous pages should be filled.

"They are dreadful soft and pretty, but I don't believe I'll ever wear 'em out; my legs are so wimbly there's no go in 'em," whispered a fever patient, looking sorrowfully at the swollen feet ornamented with a pair of carpet slippers gay with roses, and evidently made for his especial need.

"Please hang my posy basket on the gas-burner in the middle of the room, where all the boys can see it. It's too pretty for one alone."

"But then you can't see it yourself, Joe, and you are fonder of such things than the rest," said Miss Hale, taking both the little basket and the hand of her pet patient, a lad of twenty, dying of rapid consumption.

"That's the reason I can spare it for a while, for I shall feel 'em in the room just the same, and they'll do the boys good. You pick out the one you like best, for me to keep, and hang up the rest till by-and-by, please."

She gave him a sprig of mignonette, and he smiled as he took it, for it reminded him of her in her sad-colored gown, as quiet and unobtrusive, but as grateful to the hearts of those about her as was the fresh scent of the flower to the lonely lad who never had known womanly tenderness and care until he found them in a hospital. Joe's prediction was verified; the flowers did do the boys good, for all welcomed them with approving glances, and all felt their refining influence more or less keenly, from cheery Ben, who paused to fill the cup inside with fresher water, to surly Sam, who stopped growling as his eye rested on a geranium very like the one blooming in his sweetheart's window when they parted a long year ago.

"Now, as this is to be a merry day, let us begin to enjoy it at once. Fling up the windows, Ben, and Barney, go for breakfast while I finish washing faces and settling bed-clothes."

With which directions the little woman fell to work with such infectious energy that in fifteen minutes thirty gentlemen with spandy clean faces and hands were partaking of refreshment with as much appetite as their various conditions would permit. Meantime the sun came up, looking bigger, brighter, jollier than usual, as he is apt to do on Christmas days. Not a snow-flake chilled the air that blew in as blandly as if winter had relented, and wished the "boys" the compliments of the season in his mildest mood; while a festival smell pervaded the whole house, and appetizing rumors of turkey, mince-pie, and oysters for dinner, circulated through the wards. When breakfast was done, the wounds dressed, directions for the day delivered, and as many of the disagreeables as possible well over, the fun began. In any other place that would have been considered a very quiet morning; but to the weary invalids prisoned in that room, it was quite a whirl of excitement. None were dangerously ill but Joe, and all were easily amused, for weakness, homesickness and *ennui* made every trifle a joke or an event.

In came Ben, looking like a "Jack in the Green," with his load of hemlock and holly. Such of the men as could get about and had a hand to lend, lent it, and soon, under Miss Hale's direction, a green bough hung at the head of each bed, depended from the gas-burners, and nodded over the fireplace, while the finishing effect was given by a cross and crown at the top and bottom of the room. Great was the interest, many were the mishaps, and frequent was the laughter which attended this performance; for wounded men, when convalescent, are particularly jovial. When "Daddy Mills," as one venerable volunteer was irreverently christened, expatiated learnedly upon the difference between "sprewce, hemlock and pine," how they all listened, each thinking of some familiar wood still pleasantly haunted by boyish recollections of stolen gunnings, gum-pickings, and bird-nestings. When quiet Hayward amazed the company by coming out strong in a most unexpected direction, and telling with much effect the story of a certain "fine old gentleman" who supped on hemlock tea and died like a hero, what commendations were bestowed upon the immortal heathen in language more hearty than classical, as a twig of the historical tree was passed round like a new style of refreshment, that inquiring parties might satisfy themselves regarding the flavor of the Socratic draught. When Barney, the colored incapable, essayed a grand ornament above the door, and relying upon one insufficient nail, descended to survey his success with the proud exclamation, "Look at de neatness of dat job, gen'l'men,"—at which point the

whole thing tumbled down about his ears,—how they all shouted but Pneumonia Ned, who, having lost his voice, could only make ecstatic demonstrations with his legs. When Barney cast himself and his hammer despairingly upon the floor, and Miss Hale, stepping into a chair, pounded stoutly at the traitorous nail and performed some miracle with a bit of string which made all fast, what a burst of applause arose from the beds. When gruff Dr. Bangs came in to see what all the noise was about, and the same intrepid lady not only boldly explained, but stuck a bit of holly in his buttonhole, and wished him a merry Christmas with such a face full of smiles that the crabbed old doctor felt himself giving in very fast, and bolted out again, calling Christmas a humbug, and exulting over the thirty emetics he would have to prescribe on the morrow, what indignant denials followed him. And when all was done, how everybody agreed with Joe when he said, "I think we are coming Christmas in great style; things look so green and pretty, I feel as I was settin' in a bower."

Pausing to survey her work, Miss Hale saw Sam looking as black as any thundercloud. He bounced over on his bed the moment he caught her eye, but she followed him up, and gently covering the cold shoulder he evidently meant to show her, peeped over it, asking, with unabated gentleness,—

"What can I do for you, Sam? I want to have all the faces in my ward bright ones to-day."

"My box ain't come; they said I should have it two, three days ago; why don't they do it, then?" growled Ursa Major.

"It is a busy time, you know, but it will come if they promised, and patience won't delay it, I assure you."

"My patience is used up, and they are a mean set of slow coaches. I'd get it fast enough if I wore shoulder straps; as I don't, I'll bet I sha'n't see it till the things ain't fit to eat; the news is old, and I don't care a hang about it."

"I'll see what I can do; perhaps before

the hurry of dinner begins some one will have time to go for it."

"Nobody ever does have time here but folks who would give all they are worth to be stirring round. You can't get it, I know; it's my luck, so don't you worry, ma'am."

Miss Hale did not "worry," but worked, and in time a messenger was found, provided with the necessary money, pass and directions, and despatched to hunt up the missing Christmas-box. Then she paused to see what came next, not that it was necessary to look for a task, but to decide which, out of many, was most important to do first.

"Why, Turner, crying again so soon? What is it now? the light head or the heavy feet?"

"It's my bones, ma'am. They ache so I can't lay easy any way, and I'm so tired I just wish I could die and be out of this misery," sobbed the poor ghost of a once strong and cheery fellow, as the kind hand wiped his tears away, and gently rubbed the weary shoulders.

"Don't wish that, Turner, for the worst is over now, and all you need is to get your strength again. Make an effort to sit up a little; it is quite time you tried; a change of posture will help the ache wonderfully, and make this 'dreadful bed,' as you call it, seem very comfortable when you come back to it."

"I can't, ma'am, my legs ain't a bit of use, and I ain't strong enough even to try."

"You never will be if you don't try. Never mind the poor legs, Ben will carry you. I've got the matron's easy-chair all ready, and can make you very cosy by the fire. It's Christmas-day, you know; why not celebrate it by overcoming the despondency which retards your recovery, and prove that illness has not taken all the manhood out of you?"

"It has, though, I'll never be the man I was, and may as well lay here till spring, for I shall be no use if I do get up."

If Sam was a growler this man was a whiner, and few hospital wards are with-

out both. But knowing that much suffering had soured the former and pitifully weakened the latter, their nurse had patience with them, and still hoped to bring them round again. As Turner whimpered out his last dismal speech she bethought herself of something which, in the hurry of the morning, had slipped her mind till now.

"By the way, I've got another present for you. The doctor thought I'd better not give it yet, lest it should excite you too much; but I think you need excitement to make you forget yourself, and that when you find how many blessings you have to be grateful for, you will make an effort to enjoy them."

"Blessings, ma'am? I don't see 'em."

"Don't you see one now?" and drawing a letter from her pocket she held it before his eyes. His listless face brightened a little as he took it, but gloomed over again as he said fretfully,—

"It's from wife, I guess. I like to get her letters, but they are always full of grievings and groanings over me, so they don't do me much good."

"She does not grieve and groan in this one. She is too happy to do that, and so will you be when you read it."

"I don't see why,—hey?—why you don't mean—"

"Yes I do!" cried the little woman, clapping her hands, and laughing so delightedly that the Knight of the Rueful Countenance was betrayed into a broad smile for the first time in many weeks. "Is not a splendid little daughter a present to rejoice over and be grateful for?"

"Hooray! hold on a bit,—it's all right, —I'll be out again in a minute."

After which remarkably spirited burst, Turner vanished under the bed-clothes, letter and all. Whether he read, laughed or cried, in the seclusion of that cotton grotto, was unknown; but his nurse suspected that he did all three, for when he reappeared he looked as if during that pause he had dived into his "sea of troubles," and fished up his old self again.

"What *will* I name her?" was his first remark, delivered with such vivacity that his neighbors·began to think he was getting delirious again.

"What is your wife's name?" asked Miss Hale, gladly entering into the domesticities which were producing such a salutary effect.

"Her name's Ann, but neither of us like it. I'd fixed on George, for I wanted my boy called after me; and now you see I ain't a bit prepared for this young woman." Very proud of the young woman he seemed, nevertheless, and perfectly resigned to the loss of the expected son and heir.

"Why not call her Georgiana then? That combines both her parents' names, and is not a bad one in itself."

"Now that's just the brightest thing I ever heard in my life!" cried Turner, sitting bolt upright in his excitement, though half an hour before he would have considered it an utterly impossible feat. "Georgiana Butterfield Turner,—it's a tip-top name, ma'am, and we can call her Georgie just the same. Ann will like that, it's so genteel. Bless 'em both! don't I wish I was at home." And down he lay again, despairing.

"You can be before long, if you choose. Get your strength up, and off you go. Come, begin at once,—drink your beef-tea, and sit up for a few minutes, just in honor of the good news, you know."

"I will, by George!—no, by Georgiana! That's a good one, ain't it?" and the whole ward was electrified by hearing a genuine giggle from the "Blueing-bag."

Down went the detested beef-tea, and up scrambled the determined drinker with many groans, and a curious jumble of chuckles, staggers, and fragmentary repetitions of his first, last, and only joke. But when fairly settled in the great rocking-chair, with the gray flannel gown comfortably on, and the new slippers getting their inaugural scorch, Turner forgot his bones, and swung to and fro before the fire, feeling amazingly well, and looking very like a trussed fowl being roasted in the primitive fashion. The languid importance of the man, and the irrepressible satisfaction of the parent, were both laughable and touching things to see, for the happy soul could not keep the glad tidings to himself. A hospital ward is often a small republic, beautifully governed by pity, patience, and the mutual sympathy which lessens mutual suffering. Turner was no favorite; but more than one honest fellow felt his heart warm towards him as they saw his dismal face kindle with fatherly pride, and heard the querulous quaver of his voice soften with fatherly affection, as he said, "My little Georgie, sir."

"He'll do now, ma'am; this has given him the boost he needed, and in a week or two he'll be off our hands."

Big Ben made the remark with a beaming countenance, and Big Ben deserves a word of praise, because he never said one for himself. An ex-patient, promoted to an attendant's place, which he filled so well that he was regarded as a model for all the rest to copy. Patient, strong, and tender, he seemed to combine many of the best traits of both man and woman; for he appeared to know by instinct where the soft spot was to be found in every heart, and how best to help sick body or sad soul. No one would have guessed this to have seen him lounging in the hall during one of the short rests he allowed himself. A brawny, six-foot fellow, in red shirt, blue trousers tucked into his boots, an old cap, visor always up, and under it a roughly-bearded, coarsely-featured face, whose prevailing expression was one of great gravity and kindliness, though a humorous twinkle of the eye at times betrayed the man, whose droll sayings often set the boys in a roar. "A good-natured, clumsy body" would have been the verdict passed upon him by a casual observer; but watch him in his ward, and see how great a wrong that hasty judgment would have done him.

Unlike his predecessor, who helped himself generously when the meals came up, and carelessly served out rations for the rest, leaving even the most helpless to bungle for themselves or wait till he was done, shut himself into his pantry, and there,—to borrow a hospital phrase,—gormed, Ben often left nothing for himself, or took cheerfully such cold bits as remained when all the rest were served; so patiently feeding the weak, being hands and feet to the maimed, and a pleasant provider for all that, as one of the boys said,—"It gives a relish to the vittles to have Ben fetch 'em." If one were restless, Ben carried him in his strong arms; if one were undergoing the sharp torture of the surgeon's knife, Ben held him with a touch as firm as kind; if one were homesick, Ben wrote letters for him with great hearty blots and dashes under all the affectionate or important words. More than one poor fellow read his fate in Ben's pitiful eyes, and breathed his last breath away on Ben's broad breast,—always a quiet pillow till its work was done, then it would heave with genuine grief, as his big hand softly closed the tired eyes, and made another comrade ready for the last review. The war shows us many Bens,—for the same power of human pity which makes women brave also makes men tender; and each is the womanlier, the manlier, for these revelations of unsuspected strength and sympathies.

At twelve o'clock dinner was the prevailing idea in ward No. 3, and when the door opened every man sniffed, for savory odors broke loose from the kitchens and went roaming about the house. Now this Christmas dinner had been much talked of; for certain charitable and patriotic persons had endeavored to provide every hospital in Washington with materials for this time-honored feast. Some mistake in the list sent to head-quarters, some unpardonable neglect of orders, or some premeditated robbery, caused the long-expected dinner in the —— Hospital to prove a dead failure; but to which of these causes it was attributable was never known, for the deepest mystery enveloped that sad transaction. The full weight of the dire disap-

pointment was mercifully lightened by premonitions of the impending blow. Barney was often missing; for the attendants were to dine *en masse* after the patients were done, therefore a speedy banquet for the latter parties was ardently desired, and he probably devoted his energies to goading on the cooks. From time to time he appeared in the doorway, flushed and breathless, made some thrilling announcement, and vanished, leaving ever-increasing appetite, impatience and expectation, behind him.

Dinner was to be served at one; at half-past twelve Barney proclaimed, "Dere ain't no vegetables but squash and pitaters." A universal groan arose; and several indignant parties on a short allowance of meat consigned the defaulting cook to a warmer climate than the tropical one he was then enjoying. At twenty minutes to one, Barney increased the excitement by whispering ominously, "I say, de puddins isn't plummy ones."

"Fling a piller at him and shut the door, Ben," roared one irascible being, while several others *not* fond of puddings received the fact with equanimity. At quarter to one Barney piled up the agony by adding the bitter information, "Dere isn't but two turkeys for dis ward, and dey's little fellers."

Anxiety instantly appeared in every countenance, and intricate calculations were made as to how far the two fowls would go when divided among thirty men; also friendly warnings were administered to several of the feebler gentlemen not to indulge too freely, if at all, for fear of relapses. Once more did the bird of evil omen return, for at ten minutes to one Barney croaked through the key-hole, "Only jes half ob de pies has come, gen'l'men." That capped the climax, for the masculine palate has a predilection for pastry, and mince-pie was the sheet-anchor to which all had clung when other hopes went down. Even Ben looked dismayed; not that he expected anything but the perfume and pickings for his share, but he had set his heart on having the dinner an honor to the institution and a memorable feast for the men, so far away from home, and all that usually makes the day a festival among the poorest. He looked pathetically grave as Turner began to fret, Sam began to swear under his breath, Hayward to sigh, Joe to wish it was all over, and the rest began to vent their emotions with a freedom which was anything but inspiring. At that moment Miss Hale came in with a great basket of apples and oranges in one hand, and several convivial-looking bottles in the other.

"Here is our dessert, boys! A kind friend remembered us, and we will drink her health in her own currant wine."

A feeble smile circulated round the room, and in some sanguine bosoms hope revived again. Ben briskly emptied the basket, while Miss Hale whispered to Joe,

"I know you would be glad to get away from the confusion of this next hour, to enjoy a breath of fresh air, and dine quietly with Mrs. Burton round the corner, wouldn't you?"

"Oh, ma'am, so much! the noise, the smells, the fret and flurry, make me sick just to think of! But how can I go? that dreadful ambulance 'most killed me last time, and I'm weaker now."

"My dear boy, I have no thought of trying that again till our ambulances are made fit for the use of weak and wounded men. Mrs. Burton's carriage is at the door, with her motherly self inside, and all you have got to do is to let me bundle you up, and Ben carry you out."

With a long sigh of relief Joe submitted to both these processes, and when his nurse watched his happy face as the carriage slowly rolled away, she felt well repaid for the little sacrifice of rest and pleasure so quietly made; for Mrs. Burton came to carry her, not Joe, away.

"Now, Ben, help me to make this unfortunate dinner go off as well as we can," she whispered. "On many accounts it is a mercy that the men are spared the temptations of a more generous meal; pray don't tell them so, but make the best of it, as you know very well how to do."

"I'll try my best, Miss Hale, but I'm no less disappointed, for some of 'em, being no better than children, have been living on the thoughts of it for a week, and it comes hard to give it up."

If Ben had been an old-time patriarch, and the thirty boys his sons, he could not have spoken with a more paternal regret, or gone to work with a better will. Putting several small tables together in the middle of the room, he left Miss Hale to make a judicious display of plates, knives and forks, while he departed for the banquet. Presently he returned, bearing the youthful turkeys and the vegetables in his tray, followed by Barney, looking unutterable things at a plum-pudding baked in a milk-pan, and six very small pies. Miss Hale played a lively tattoo as the procession approached, and, when the viands were arranged, with the red and yellow fruit prettily heaped up in the middle, it really did look like a dinner.

"Here's richness! here's the delicacies of the season and the comforts of life!" said Ben, falling back to survey the table with as much apparent satisfaction as if it had been a lord mayor's feast.

"Come, hurry up, and give us our dinner, what there is of it!" grumbled Sam.

"Boys," continued Ben, beginning to cut up the turkeys, "these noble birds have been sacrificed for the defenders of their country; they will go as far as ever they can, and, when they can't go any farther, we shall endeavor to supply their deficiencies with soup or ham, oysters having given out unexpectedly. Put it to vote; both have been provided on this joyful occasion, and a word will fetch either."

"Ham! ham!" resounded from all sides. Soup was an every-day affair, and therefore repudiated with scorn; but ham, being a rarity, was accepted as a proper reward of merit and a tacit acknowledgment of their wrongs.

The "noble birds" did go as far as possible, and were handsomely assisted by their fellow martyr. The pudding was not as plummy as could have been desired, but a slight exertion of fancy made the crusty knobs do duty for raisins. The pies were small, yet a laugh added flavor to the mouthful apiece, for, when Miss Hale asked Ben to cut them up, that individual regarded her with an inquiring aspect as he said, in his drollest tone,—

"I wouldn't wish to appear stupid, ma'am, but, when you mention 'pies,' I presume you allude to these trifles. 'Tarts,' or 'patties,' would meet my views better, in speaking of the third course of this lavish dinner. As such I will do my duty by 'em, hoping that the appetites is to match."

Carefully dividing the six pies into twenty-nine diminutive wedges, he placed each in the middle of a large clean plate, and handed them about with the gravity of an undertaker. Dinner had restored good humor to many; this hit at the pies put the finishing touch to it, and from that moment an atmosphere of jollity prevailed. Healths were drunk in currant wine, apples and oranges flew about as an impromptu game of ball was got up, Miss Hale sang a Christmas carol, and Ben gambolled like a sportive giant as he cleared away. Pausing in one of his prances to and fro, he beckoned the nurse out, and, when she followed, handed her a plate heaped up with good things from a better table than she ever sat at now.

"From the matron, ma'am. Come right in here and eat it while it's hot; they are most through in the dining-room, and you'll get nothing half so nice," said Ben, leading the way into his pantry and pointing to a sunny window-seat.

"Are you sure she meant it for me, and not for yourself, Ben?"

"Of course she did! Why, what should I do with it, when I've just been feastin' sumptuous in this very room?"

"I don't exactly see what you have been feasting on," said Miss Hale, glancing round the tidy pantry as she sat down.

"Havin' eat up the food and washed up the dishes, it naturally follows that you don't see, ma'am. But if I go off in a fit by-and-by you'll know what it's owin' to," answered Ben, vainly endeavoring to look like a man suffering from repletion.

"Such kind fibs are not set down against one, Ben, so I will eat your dinner, for if I don't I know you will throw it out of the window to prove that you can't eat it."

"Thankee ma'am, I'm afraid I should; for, at the rate he's going on, Barney wouldn't be equal to it," said Ben, looking very much relieved, as he polished his last pewter fork and hung his towels up to dry.

A pretty general siesta followed the excitement of dinner, but by three o'clock the public mind was ready for amusement, and the arrival of Sam's box provided it. He was asleep when it was brought in and quietly deposited at his bed's foot, ready to surprise him on awaking. The advent of a box was a great event, for the fortunate receiver seldom failed to "stand treat," and next best to getting things from one's own home was the getting them from some other boy's home. This was an unusually large box, and all felt impatient to have it opened, though Sam's exceeding crustiness prevented the indulgence of great expectations. Presently he roused, and the first thing his eye fell upon was the box, with his own name sprawling over it in big black letters. As if it were merely the continuance of his dream, he stared stupidly at it for a moment, then rubbed his eyes and sat up, exclaiming,—

"Hullo! that's mine!"

"Ah! who said it wouldn't come? who hadn't the faith of a grasshopper? and who don't half deserve it for being a Barker by nater as by name?" cried Ben, emphasizing each question with a bang on the box, as he waited, hammer in hand, for the arrival of the ward-master, whose duty it was to oversee the opening of such matters, lest contraband articles should do mischief to the owner or his neighbors.

"Ain't it a jolly big one? Knock it open, and don't wait for anybody or anything!" cried Sam, tumbling off his bed and beating impatiently on the lid with his one hand.

In came the ward-master, off came the cover, and out came a motley collection of apples, socks, dough-nuts, paper, pickles, photographs, pocket-handkerchiefs, ginger-bread, letters, jelly, newspapers, tobacco, and cologne. "All right, glad it's come,— don't kill yourself," said the ward-master, as he took a hasty survey and walked off again. Drawing the box nearer the bed, Ben delicately followed, and Sam was left to brood over his treasures in peace.

At first all the others, following Ben's example, made elaborate pretences of going to sleep, being absorbed in books, or utterly uninterested in the outer world. But very soon curiosity got the better of politeness, and one by one they all turned round and stared. They might have done so from the first, for Sam was perfectly unconscious of everything but his own affairs, and, having read the letters, looked at the pictures, unfolded the bundles, turned everything inside out and upside down, tasted all the eatables and made a spectacle of himself with jelly, he paused to get his breath and find his way out of the confusion he had created. Presently he called out,—

"Miss Hale, will you come and right up my duds for me?" adding, as her woman's hands began to bring matters straight, "I don't know what to do with 'em all, for some won't keep long, and it will take pretty steady eating to get through 'em in time, supposin' appetite holds out."

"How do the others manage with their things?"

"You know they give 'em away; but I'll be hanged if I do, for they are always callin' names and pokin' fun at me. Guess they won't get anything out of me now."

The old morose look came back as he spoke, for it had disappeared while reading the home letters, touching the home gifts. Still busily folding and arranging, Miss Hale asked,—

"You know the story of the Three Cakes; which are you going to be—Harry, Peter, or Billy?"

Sam began to laugh at this sudden application of the nursery legend; and, seeing her advantage, Miss Hale pursued it:

"We all know how much you have suffered, and all respect you for the courage with which you have borne your long confinement and your loss; but don't you think you have given the boys some cause for making fun of you, as you say? You used to be a favorite, and can be again, if

you will only put off these crusty ways, which will grow upon you faster than you think. Better lose both arms than cheerfulness and self-control, Sam."

Pausing to see how her little lecture was received, she saw that Sam's better self was waking up, and added yet another word, hoping to help a mental ailment as she had done so many physical ones. Looking up at him with her kind eyes, she said, in a lowered voice,—

"This day, on which the most perfect life began, is a good day for all of us to set about making ourselves readier to follow that divine example. Troubles are helpers if we take them kindly, and the bitterest may sweeten us for all our lives. Believe and try this, Sam, and when you go away from us let those who love you find that two battles have been fought, two victories won."

Sam made no answer, but sat thoughtfully picking at the half-eaten cookey in his hand. Presently he stole a glance about the room, and, as if all helps were waiting for him, his eye met Joe's. From his solitary corner by the fire and the bed he would seldom leave again until he went into his grave, the boy smiled back at him so heartily, so happily, that something gushed warm across Sam's heart as he looked down upon the faces of mother, sister, sweetheart, scattered round him, and remembered how poor his comrade was in all such tender ties, and yet how rich in that beautiful content, which, "having nothing, yet hath all." The man had no words in which to express this feeling, but it came to him and did him good, as he proved in his own way. "Miss Hale," he said, a little awkwardly, "I wish you'd pick out what you think each would like, and give 'em to the boys."

He got a smile in answer that drove him to his cookey as a refuge, for his lips would tremble, and he felt half proud, half ashamed to have earned such bright approval.

"Let Ben help you,—he knows better than I. But you must give them all yourself, it will so surprise and please the boys;

and then to-morrow we will write a capital letter home, telling what a jubilee we made over their fine box."

At this proposal Sam half repented; but, as Ben came lumbering up at Miss Hale's summons, he laid hold of his new resolution as if it was a sort of shower-bath and he held the string, one pull of which would finish the baptism. Dividing his most cherished possession, which (alas for romance!) was the tobacco, he bundled the larger half into a paper, whispering to Miss Hale,—

"Ben ain't exactly what you'd call a ministerin' angel to look at, but he is amazin' near one in his ways, so I'm goin' to begin with him."

Up came the "ministering angel," in red flannel and cow-hide boots; and Sam tucked the little parcel into his pocket, saying, as he began to rummage violently in the box,—

"Now jest hold your tongue, and lend a hand here about these things."

Ben was so taken aback by this proceeding that he stared blankly, till a look from Miss Hale enlightened him; and, taking his cue, he played his part as well as could be expected on so short a notice. Clapping Sam on the shoulder,—not the bad one, Ben was always thoughtful of those things, —he exclaimed heartily,—

"I always said you'd come round when this poor arm of yours got a good start, and here you are jollier'n ever. Lend a hand! so I will, a pair of 'em. What's to do? Pack these traps up again?"

"No; I want you to tell what *you'd* do with 'em if they were yours. Free, you know,—as free as if they really was."

Ben held on to the box a minute as if this second surprise rather took him off his legs; but another look from the prime mover in this resolution steadied him, and he fell to work as if Sam had been in the habit of being "free."

"Well, let's see. I think I'd put the clothes and sich into this smaller box that the bottles come in, and stan' it under the table, handy. Here's newspapers—pictures in 'em, too! I should make a circulatin' lib'ry of them; they'll be a real treat.

Pickles—well, I guess I should keep them on the winder here as a kind of a relish dinner-times, or to pass along to them as longs for 'em. Cologne—that's a dreadful handsome bottle, ain't it? That, now, would be fust-rate to give away to somebody as was very fond of it,—a kind of a delicate attention, you know,—if you happen to meet such a person anywheres."

Ben nodded towards Miss Hale, who was absorbed in folding pocket-handkerchiefs. Sam winked expressively, and patted the bottle as if congratulating himself that it *was* handsome, and that he *did* know what to do with it. The pantomime was not elegant, but as much real affection and respect went into it as if he had made a set speech, and presented the gift upon his knees.

"The letters and photographs I should probably keep under my piller for a spell; the jelly I'd give to Miss Hale, to use for the sick ones; the cake-stuff and that pot of jam, that's gettin' ready to work, I'd stand treat with for tea, as dinner wasn't all we could have wished. The apples I'd keep to eat, and fling at Joe when he was too bashful to ask for one, and the *tobaccer* I would *not* go lavishin' on folks that have no business to be enjoyin' luxuries when many a poor feller is dyin' of want down to Charlestown. There, sir! that's what *I'd* do if any one was so clever as to send me a jolly box like this."

Sam was enjoying the full glow of his shower-bath by this time. As Ben designated the various articles, he set them apart; and when the inventory ended, he marched away with the first instalment: two of the biggest, rosiest apples for Joe, and all the pictorial papers. Pickles are not usually regarded as tokens of regard, but as Sam dealt them out one at a time,— for he would let nobody help him, and his single hand being the left, was as awkward as it was willing,—the boys' faces brightened; for a friendly word accompanied each, which made the sour gherkins as welcome as sweetmeats. With every trip the donor's spirits rose; for Ben circulated freely between whiles, and, thanks to him, not an allusion to the past marred the satisfaction of the present. Jam, soda-biscuits, and cake, were such welcome additions to the usual bill of fare, that when supper was over a vote of thanks was passed, and speeches were made; for, being true Americans, the ruling passion found vent in the usual "Fellow-citizens!" and allusions to the "Star-spangled Banner." After which Sam subsided, feeling himself a public benefactor, and a man of mark.

A perfectly easy, pleasant day throughout would be almost an impossibility in any hospital, and this one was no exception to the general rule; for, at the usual time, Dr. Bangs went his rounds, leaving the customary amount of discomfort, discontent and dismay behind him. A skilful surgeon and an excellent man was Dr. Bangs, but not a sanguine or conciliatory individual; many cares and crosses caused him to regard the world as one large hospital, and his fellow-beings all more or less dangerously wounded patients in it. He saw life through the bluest of blue spectacles, and seemed to think that the sooner people quitted it the happier for them. He did his duty by the men, but if they recovered he looked half disappointed, and congratulated them with cheerful prophecies that there would come a time when they would wish they hadn't. If one died he seemed relieved, and surveyed him with pensive satisfaction, saying heartily,—

"He's comfortable, now, poor soul, and well out of this miserable world, thank God!"

But for Ben the sanitary influences of the doctor's ward would have been small, and Dante's doleful line might have been written on the threshold of the door,—

"Who enters here leaves hope behind."

Ben and the doctor perfectly understood and liked each other, but never agreed, and always skirmished over the boys as if manful cheerfulness and medical despair were fighting for the soul and body of each one.

"Well," began the doctor, looking at Sam's arm, or, rather, all that was left of that member after two amputations, "we shall be ready for another turn at this in a day or two if it don't mend faster. Tetanus sometimes follows such cases, but that is soon over, and I should not object to a case of it, by way of variety." Sam's hopeful face fell, and he set his teeth as if the fatal symptoms were already felt.

"If one kind of lockjaw was more prevailing than 'tis, it wouldn't be a bad thing for some folks I could mention," observed Ben, covering the well-healed stump as carefully as if it were a sleeping baby; adding, as the doctor walked away, "There's a sanguinary old sawbones for you! Why, bless your buttons, Sam, you are doing splendid, and he goes on that way because there's no chance of his having another cut at you! Now he's squenchin' Turner, jest as we've blowed a spark of spirit into him. If ever there was a born extinguisher its Bangs!"

Ben rushed to the rescue, and not a minute too soon; for Turner, who now labored under the delusion that his recovery depended solely upon his getting out of bed every fifteen minutes, was sitting by the fire, looking up at the doctor, who pleasantly observed, while feeling his pulse,—

"So you are getting ready for another fever, are you? Well, we've grown rather fond of you, and will keep you six weeks longer if you have set your heart on it."

Turner looked nervous, for the doctor's jokes were always grim ones; but Ben took the other hand in his, and gently rocked the chair as he replied, with great politeness,—

"This robust convalescent of ourn would be happy to oblige you, sir, but he has a pressin' engagement up to Jersey for next week, and couldn't stop on no account. You see Miss Turner wants a careful nuss for little Georgie, and he's a goin' to take the place."

Feeling himself on the brink of a laugh as Turner simpered with a ludicrous mixture of pride in his baby and fear for himself, Dr. Bangs said, with unusual sternness and a glance at Ben,—

"You take the responsibility of this step

upon yourself, do you? Very well; then I wash my hands of Turner; only, if that bed is empty in a week, don't lay the blame of it at my door."

"Nothing shall induce me to do it, sir," briskly responded Ben. "Now then, turn in my boy, and sleep your prettiest, for I wouldn't but disappoint that cheerfulest of men for a month's wages; and that's liberal, as I ain't likely to get it."

"How is this young man after the rash dissipations of the day?" asked the doctor, pausing at the bed in the corner, after he had made a lively progress down the room, hotly followed by Ben.

"I'm first-rate, sir," panted Joe, who always said so, though each day found him feebler than the last. Every one was kind to Joe, even the gruff doctor, whose manner softened, and who was forced to frown heavily to hide the pity in his eyes.

"How's the cough?"

"Better, sir; being weaker, I can't fight against it as I used to do, so it comes rather easier."

"Sleep any last night?"

"Not much; but it's very pleasant laying here when the room is still, and no light but the fire. Ben keeps it bright; and, when I fret, he talks to me, and makes the time go telling stories till he gets so sleepy he can hardly speak. Dear old Ben! I hope he'll have some one as kind to him, when he needs it as I do now."

"He will get what he deserves by-and-by, you may be sure of that," said the doctor, as severely as if Ben merited eternal condemnation.

A great drop splashed down upon the hearth as Joe spoke; but Ben put his foot on it, and turned about as if defying any one to say he shed it.

"Of all the perverse and reckless women whom I have known in the course of a forty years' practice, this one is the most perverse and reckless," said the doctor, abruptly addressing Miss Hale, who just then appeared, bringing Joe's "posy-basket" back. "You will oblige me, ma'am, by sitting in this chair with your hands folded for twenty minutes; the clock will then

strike nine, and you will go straight up to your bed."

Miss Hale demurely sat down, and the doctor ponderously departed, sighing regretfully as he went through the room, as if disappointed that the whole thirty were not lying at death's door; but on the threshold he turned about, exclaimed "Goodnight, boys! God bless you!" and vanished as precipitately as if a trap-door had swallowed him up.

Miss Hale was a perverse woman in some things; for, instead of folding her tired hands, she took a rusty-covered volume from the mantel-piece, and, sitting by Joe's bed, began to read aloud. One by one all other sounds grew still; one by one the men composed themselves to listen; and one by one the words of the sweet old Christmas story came to them, as the woman's quiet voice went reading on. If any wounded spirit needed balm, if any hungry heart asked food, if any upright purpose, newborn aspiration, or sincere repentance wavered for want of human strength, all found help, hope, and consolation in the beautiful and blessed influences of the book, the reader, and the hour.

The bells rung nine, the lights grew dim, the day's work was done; but Miss Hale lingered beside Joe's bed, for his face wore a wistful look, and he seemed loath to have her go.

"What is it, dear?" she said; "what can I do for you before I leave you to Ben's care?"

He drew her nearer, and whispered earnestly,—

"It's something that I know you'll do for me, because I can't do it for myself, not as I want it done, and you can. I'm going pretty fast now, ma'am; and when—when some one else is laying here, I want you to tell the boys,—every one, from Ben to Barney,—how much I thanked 'em, how much I loved 'em, and how glad I was that I had known 'em, even for such a little while."

"Yes, Joe, I'll tell them all. What else can I do, my boy?"

"Only let me say to you what no one

else must say for me, that all I want to live for is to try and do something in my poor way to show you how I thank you, ma'am. It isn't what you've said to me, it isn't what you've done for me alone, that makes me grateful; it's because you've learned me many things without knowing it, showed me what I ought to have been before, if I'd had any one to tell me how, and made this such a happy, home-like place, I shall be sorry when I have to go."

Poor Joe! it must have fared hardly with him all those twenty years, if a hospital seemed home-like, and a little sympathy, a little care, could fill him with such earnest gratitude. He stopped a moment to lay his cheek upon the hand he held in both of his, then hurried on as if he felt his breath beginning to give out:

"I dare say many boys have said this to you, ma'am, better than I can, for I don't say half I feel; but I know that none of 'em ever thanked you as I thank you in my heart, or ever loved you as I'll love you all my life. To-day I hadn't anything to give you, I'm so poor; but I wanted to tell you this, on the last Christmas I shall ever see."

It was a very humble kiss he gave that hand; but the fervor of a first love warmed it, and the sincerity of a great gratitude made it both a precious and pathetic gift to one who, half unconsciously, had made this brief and barren life so rich and happy at its close. Always womanly and tender, Miss Hale's face was doubly so as she leaned over him, whispering,—

"I have had my present, now. Good-night, Joe."

Frank A. Burr

In 1888 a big volume of more than 600 pages entitled *Camp-Fire Sketches and Battle-Field Echoes,* compiled by W. C. King and W. P. Derby, of the 27th Massachusetts Regiment, was published in Springfield, Massachusetts. In presenting this book of Civil War reminiscences and stories the authors expressed the hope that it would be welcomed by "the people who cherish the memory of the noble deeds and heroism of the brave hearts who left father and mother, wife and daughter, brother and sister, home and friends, for their country, thousands of whom to-day are peacefully sleeping in the 'City of the Silent,' where no earthly 'bugle call' disturbs their slumber.

"These venerable and heroic men, who, in full vigor of manhood, marched to the cannon's mouth, are now rapidly falling from the ranks, and their burning words will be treasured in memory's bosom, by a grateful nation, which is justly proud of the bravery, heroism, and sacrifices so freely contributed to save the Union.

"A war, so gigantic, continuing through four long, weary years, so costly in blood and treasure, reaching with its sore bereavement into the peaceful quietude of almost every home circle of our land, attaches to this volume an individual and personal interest without a parallel in the whole range of war literature.

"Nowhere in the realm of books is portrayed more vividly the grandeur and heroism of the American soldier, his courage and love for home and country. But the sword has been sheathed, and the gentle breezes waft sweet perfumes over the graves of peaceful warriors as they sleep side by side. Monuments dot hillside and plain where once the battle raged.

"Federal and Confederate chieftains sit side by side in the Senate chamber, and unite in the councils of our chosen ruler.

"Peace and joy have spread their silver wings over the desolations and bereavements of the past, and to-day we are one people, one country, united under one flag."

Among the two hundred or more stories in this collection was the following, written by Frank A. Burr. The title and subtitle as they were originally printed are reproduced here. When this story was published, many of the men who had spent the Christmas of 1863 in Libby were still living. The author listed many of their names at the end of his story. He stated that almost every state in the Union was represented in the crowd. He, too, was a prisoner of war and believed his account was a faithful picture.

CHRISTMAS IN LIBBY PRISON

A Strange Celebration by Prisoners of War
A Banquet Under Difficulty and What It Cost

I. Seeking Santa Claus in Prison Walls

"Mamma, do you know that it's only two weeks till Christmas! I wonder if Nadine will be well then? Oh! if she only was well and papa would come home, what a beautiful Christmas we would have!"

A little twelve-year old girl uttered these words, almost in a breath, and the mother, who sat in another part of the room, by the bedside of a pretty child some four years younger, had no chance to respond. The girl who wished so earnestly for her sister's recovery and for her father's return, stood looking out of the window, watching the fast falling snowflakes that were being piled into great drifts by the driving wind. Her long, dark hair fell carelessly over her shoulders, and a few becoming curls fringed the broad forehead that crowned rather a striking face.

It was near the end of one of the most eventful years of the history of the republic. It was in December, 1863. Vicksburg had fallen. The billows of angry war rolling up from Virginia had been broken at Gettysburg, and turned southward again by the splendid bulwark of Union arms. But the dark clouds of a desperate conflict yet darkened the skies of the land, and the fierce clash of sword and musket still drowned the voices of peace. Thousands of homes were wrapt in sadness and mourning for their absent ones. The approach of Christmas-tide, usually so full of joy and merriment, brought to the hearthstones of the nation, only a vision of the old-time happiness in a troubled dream of war and death.

It was in a quiet, simple home, not far from Syracuse, N. Y., that the scene mentioned in the opening lines of this sketch occurred. It was the counterpart of thousands of others in every part of the land, in which the little ones, unable to understand the strange ways of men, looked forward to the holiday time with wistful longing for the return of the absent. The snow kept on falling, as if it would gladly cover with a spotless mantle all the wounds strife had made. The little girl still stood at the window looking out upon the dreary scene before her, while her mother sat by the bedside of her sick child. Suddenly she left the scene without, and, walking slowly over to her mother, took a seat at her feet. She was silent a moment, as if in deep thought, and then looking up said, almost appealingly:—

"Mamma, why do men go to war?"

"My child, men go to war for great principles. You would not understand if I told you. Your father went to battle for his country because he loved you and me. It was his duty. Don't be sad, darling, he will think of us at Christmas, even if he isn't with us."

"Yes, I know he will, but it is so hard to be without him. But we'll think of him, won't we?" replied the child, and then, as if visited by a sudden inspiration, she said: "Why, mamma, I'll write him a letter and tell him how much we miss him, and in it I'll ask him to come home for Christmas." The little girl stole away from the sick room and wrote the letter. It was a child's message to a father. It told of Nadine's illness and breathed hope for her recovery. It pictured the loneliness of the household, the mother's anxiety, the dreariness of winter, and the longing for the return of papa. The missive was sent on its way to reach the father the day before the child so longed for him to come home.

II. Christmas Eve in Prison

It was Christmas eve, the close of a dreary, desolate day. Even to those who were free to come and go at will, the dull, cloudy sky was gloomy and dispiriting, and cast a shade of melancholy over what ought to be the most joyous festival in all the year. To the nine hundred and fifty Union officers confined in Libby Prison, and the thousands of private soldiers that were huddled together at Belle Isle, on the banks of the James river, just beyond the city of Richmond, the occasion was doubly dismal. The afternoon was fast running on toward the gloaming, when Dick Turner, the keeper of Libby, appeared with the mail, for which every prisoner had been longing for weeks. The letters were quickly distributed, and it was not long before the eager ones who had received them were sitting apart in different parts of the building, greedily reading the news from home. Almost a dead silence prevailed. The time was a solemn one. The realization of having to spend the happiest and holiest of all holidays in a prison pen, remote from the hearthstone and its loved ones, was sharpened and made keener than ever by the arrival of those tender messages from home. An hour went by, and most of the fortunate ones had read their letters, folded them away to be read again to-morrow, and were walking about or engaged in quiet conversation to distract their minds from the thoughts of home and Christmas eve. One jovial spirited fellow, who had helped to cheer scores of gloomy hearts in camp and on the march, and afterward in prison, walking down the long room of the prison, spied a friend sitting, gloomy and silent, apart from every one. His chin rested on his right palm and his elbow was supported by his knee. His head was bowed low, and in his left hand, with outstretched arm, a white letter was clutched. He was the image of sorrow and despair. The merry hearted prisoner approached, slapped him on the back, and exclaimed:—

"Come, Rocky, old boy, don't be so sad. Cheer up. Remember this is Christmas eve." Lieutenant Rockwell, of the 97th New York infantry, looked up at his friend, but for a minute did not speak. Then, with an effort, as if choking back his emotions, he handed him the letter he held in his hand and said:—

"Colonel, read that."

The speaker rose and the two men walked slowly to a window inside of the building overlooking the James river. Twilight was fast approaching, and the shadows were just beginning to settle over the scene. In the distance, a long, low ridge of hills lifted themselves up against the sky, like sentinels guarding the prison from the armed hosts which lay beyond. The two men stood in the window. Just below rolled the James on its way to the sea, and the James river canal almost touched the base of the prison walls. About them murmured the soft winds of evening, breathing suggestions of liberty and peace in distant homes. In the fast fading light of this lonely Christmas eve the lieutenant's friend read the letter. This is what it said:—

December 11, 1863.

Dear, Dear Papa:—It was snowing so hard to-day I couldn't go to school, and so I staid at home with mamma and Nadine. Poor little thing, she has been very sick, but she's getting a little better now. You would hardly know her, papa, she looks so thin and pale. Once this afternoon, when I went over to the bed, she put her little white hands up to my face and looked up to me with her big blue eyes, which look bigger than ever since she has been sick, and said: "I love you, Clara; you look so much like papa. Poor, dear papa, I wonder if he will ever come home?" And then she said: "I wonder why he stays away so long?" I couldn't answer her, papa, and I had to go to the window and look out at the drifting snow to hide my tears. When mamma came in, I sat down by her side and asked her what she meant when she said you were a prisoner of war. She told me,

but I can't understand why they should keep you so long. It's a great while since we have seen you, and it seems so hard that you should be kept away from us. It's almost Christmas, papa. Please do come home by that time. It will make us all so happy, for we love you very dearly. Christmas isn't half so nice without you, papa. Ask them to let you come home, just for Christmas. I know they won't refuse you. I can't write any more now, and the only wish we all have is that you may come home, and you will, won't you? Every night when I kneel down to say my prayers I ask the good Lord to keep you safe and let you come home to us. So does mamma, too; and even Nadine doesn't forget you in her simple prayers. We shall watch and wait for you till Christmas. We all send lots of love, and will be so happy when you come home.

Your loving daughter, Clara.

III. A Christmas Eve Tragedy

The colonel could not repress the tears which filled his eyes as he finished reading the child's simple letter. He folded it, replaced it in its tiny envelope, and handed it back to the lieutenant, who stood silent and motionless beside him. It had just been placed carefully in the owner's pocket, and the two men were standing, looking out upon the scene, neither caring to break the silence first. A cry of terror from beneath relieved them of the suspense, and, looking down, they saw that the fragile ice on the canal had given way beneath the feet of the skaters on its surface, and six of the pleasure seekers, all children, were struggling in its waters. The scene was an appalling one. The cries of the helpless children fighting for life in the dark, icy waters of the canal, and the shouts of the excited throng along the banks, brought to the windows of the prison nearly one thousand brave-hearted men, whose hands would have been quick to save had they been free to act. But the harsh decree of war rose like an impassable barrier between

them and the duty they would gladly have done for humanity, and they stood on the walls helpless, idle and mute, watching the fierce struggle below. An interval of confusion and suspense, and five of the imperiled skaters were safely rescued. The sixth, a fair-haired, manly little fellow, was taken from the water stiff and cold, and laid tenderly upon the bank to await identification. Suddenly a wild cry startled the throng gathered on the banks of the canal, as well as those in the prison, and a woman with flashing eye and disheveled hair, rushed through the crowd crying: "My child! my child! Give me my child!"

The drowned boy was her child. She instinctively ran to the spot where his body lay, and the crowd fell back to let her pass. With one long, low moan, she clutched the rigid form to her breast, speaking to it in endearing words, and trying by all the means known to motherhood, to warm it into life again. As the twilight faded into the gloaming, the dead boy was carried tenderly away to his home, followed by the heartbroken mother, and the lights of Christmas eve began to twinkle in the windows of the city. To the strong men who had been compelled to stand helpless and view it, the scene of death and sorrow just described was almost a torture. After it was all over, they turned to the quiet of the prison, and most of them sat speechless or discussed in low voice the sad occurrence. Each man seemed to have partaken of the sadness of the scene he had witnessed, and the gloom of the hour was made deeper still by the thoughts which it suggested. Hardly a man spoke aloud. The silence was like death. It was painful in its intensity. Unable to endure the terrible monotony any longer, some one finally rose, and, walking hastily across the floor, exclaimed: —

"For God's sake, men, let's do something to break this monotony. It will drive us mad." Then turning to a fellow prisoner he said: "McCauley, sing for us."

McCauley was an assistant engineer in the navy, who had been captured in a naval engagement some months before. He had an excellent voice, and had often whiled away many an hour with his songs, and had done much to sustain the spirits of his companions in prison. A hundred other voices united in the request. He sang for them the first stanza of "Rock Me to Sleep, Mother."

The tender words of the simple old ballad, pouring out upon the quiet air of the night, touched the heart-strings of every man. One verse was enough. The private soldiers confined as prisoners in Pemberton's warehouse, just across the street, had caught the strains of McCauley's voice, and one of them called to the singer:

"Officer, for God's sake, don't sing another line of that song."

The request was seconded by half a thousand others, and the pathetic words of the ballad, which had brought tears to countless eyes that had seen the flash of cannon and the gleam of bayonet without flinching, were left unsung. But the song had broken the spell which hung over the prison, and the men became gay in spite of their gloomy surroundings. A dance was suggested, and soon the orchestra, led by Lieutenant Chandler of a West Virginia regiment, struck up, and the shuffle of a thousand feet beat time to the notes of the quadrille and waltz. A minstrel performance followed later in the evening, given by a company of officers who had organized their musical forces into an excellent orchestra and glee club. When the entertainment was concluded, dancing was resumed, and the fun began anew. It was a stag party, probably the most novel ever given to the world, hundreds of officers dancing the Virginia reel by the dim, flickering lights of a few old lamps in a gloomy prison in a hostile city on Christmas eve. The atmosphere changed easily in the evening, and the dreariness and silence of the twilight gave way to merrymaking, wild enough in its character to contrast strongly with the utter loneliness of its surroundings. Far into the night, old men and young romped, and danced, and sang, and yelled like school boys at play, and then, when time was touching the sands with the wand of a new-born day, an old, grizzled officer appeared among the crowd with a well-worn sock in his hand, and said: "Now, children, it is late, and this is Christmas eve. Hang up your stockings where Santa Claus will find them, and go to bed." The suggestion was adopted, and half a thousand officers hung their stockings along the wall as they had in childhood. Libby Prison was asleep and dreaming of Santa Claus.

The rollicking began with the day. Men did not care to think of serious things. Occasionally, when their thoughts turned toward home and their spirits began to wane, some new game would be proposed and started with a will. When the church bells summoned the citizens who dwelt in the capitol of the Confederacy to divine service, the voice of Chaplain McCabe of a Maryland regiment called the rollicking prisoners to divine service. Morning, afternoon, and evening, the ministers who were

also prisoners gathered their comrades together and invoked the divine blessing on
them and the cause for which they were
suffering. The hours between the service

were filled full of games, pastimes and
songs; to keep away the sad thoughts that
ever and anon would come unbidden.

IV. Christmas Dinner in Libby

The Christmas dinner was the great feature of the day, but, with all but a very
few, there was not much to make it a
meal. No luxuries, and, in many instances,
not enough to satisfy the pangs of hunger,
was at hand. Yet all spread their humble
feast upon the floor, and gathered around
in little knots of three or four, and went
through the form of a Christmas feast.
Apple butter spread on corn bread, occasionally a single potato or a little piece of
bacon, perhaps a scrap of meat, or a chunk
of dried beef, stood in the place of the
bountifully spread table in their homes far
away, over which was spread a shadow, because of the vacant chair at the family
board. With these crude and rude necessities of life, the prisoners served to each
other imaginary dishes of turkey and cranberry sauce, plum pudding and other dain-
ties, and they laughed, joked and frolicked
over the illusion, and got all the comfort
that brave men possibly could out of the
dispiriting surroundings.

Perhaps ten officers out of the one thousand confined there had a full meal that
day. They had been lucky enough to
smuggle in a few dollars before the holidays and to have them exchanged for
Confederate money, with which they in-
duced the prison officials to purchase for
them a few necessities which were luxuries
to them. A description of one little group
in the throng huddled into the tobacco
warehouse called Libby Prison, is essential, as it is the groundwork of my whole
story. The officer who presided over it is
the same who read the letter from Lieutenant Rockwell's little daughter, and who
now, almost twenty years after the event,
recalls the incidents here related.

Many weeks before the holidays, he had
written home, asking that a box of eat-

ables be sent to him. He also wanted
money. But he could not ask for it, nor
could it be sent to him unless concealed
so as to escape the eye of the prison officials. The old United States notes bore the
pictures of Mr. Lincoln. At the end of
his letter he said: "Send me two of Lincoln's pictures."

The letter reached home. An ample box
was quickly prepared for him, and his
mother cast about for two of President
Lincoln's pictures to send to him.

"It isn't pictures he wants," said his
sweetheart, now his wife, "it is money."

She quickly took two $10 notes, crowded
them into a tiny druggists' vial, cut open
one of the four pieces of dried beef that
were in the box, carefully concealed it and
then drew the meat together, and no one
would have ever detected the arts woman
had devised to get money to her lover.

In due time the box and its precious
contents arrived at Libby Prison, and finally
found its way to the owner, after being
carefully inspected by the Confederate au-
thorities. When it came to the officer's
hands he quickly overhauled it, looking
carefully into every possible and impossible
place he could think of for the money he
has so much coveted. He looked in vain
and began to empty the box. He took the
dried beef out, hung it up on the prison
wall, and day by day disposed of it and
the other contents of his box among his
little mess. It was not all gone when the
rumor came that the Union soldiers who
were on Belle Isle were starving. The officers secured a parole for one of their number to go over and investigate. Gen. Neal
Dow of Maine, the noted temperance advocate, was selected. He returned with a
sorrowful story of the sufferings of the
soldiers in the exposed camp on the oppo-

site side of the James. He assembled the one thousand officers and recounted the touching story of what he had seen and heard there, closing his remarks with, "For God's sake, gentlemen, if any of you have anything to spare, send it to those starving men."

Each officer responded nobly. One by one they went to their scanty board, and, taking the lion's share therefrom, gladly contributed it to the soldiers whom Neal Dow had visited. The officer whose story I am writing had consumed all the contents of his box except three pieces of dried beef. Two of these he sent to the camp across the river, keeping one for himself. The next day he began cutting into the last piece. Two days later, and the day before Christmas, he was hacking away at the meat, getting a few chips for his dinner. The knife struck a hard substance. A minute later he pulled out the vial which loving hands had placed in this singular receptacle, and cautiously withdrew the two Lincoln pictures for which he had written. They had finally reached him, almost by a miracle.

"Just in time for a Christmas dinner," was the first thought and exclamation. He sold one of the $10 bills for $150 Confederate money, and got the prison keeper to buy him from the market the materials for his contemplated feast. The next day Col. A. K. Dunklee, now secretary of internal affairs of Pennsylvania, invited Capt. John C. Johnson, 149th Pennsylvania, and Lieutenant Fellows of the same regiment, to enjoy the good cheer with him. Here is the bill of fare and the cost of each item.

One chicken, $12; one dozen eggs, $12; half pound of sugar, $4; a few potatoes, $3; one pound of butter, $12; total, $43.

This spread was the envy of all the prisoners in Libby, and it was divided among them as far as it would go. Not a dozen officers had anything but prison fare. Col. J. M. Sanderson, commissary of subsistence on General Reynolds's staff, who had friends in Richmond, had a turkey sent to him—the only one in the prison. A Massachusetts officer, who had received a ham from home, and in cutting into it had found it stuffed with gold dollars, was also one of the fortunate ones, and had something that resembled a dinner in his New England home. Instances of this kind in this holiday dinner in Libby were not numerous, but they were striking. Columns might be written of the scenes before and after Christmas, but the plain story is the best.

May Christmas Mirth wed New Year Joy

Phillips Brooks

AMONG the greatly cherished Christmas carols of American origin in the Victorian era are several by Bishop Phillips Brooks, founder of Boston's famed Trinity Church in Copley Square. Best known are "O Little Town of Bethlehem" and "The Christmas Carol," usually referred to by its opening line, "Everywhere, Everywhere, Christmas To-night!"

Although a native of Boston and a graduate of Harvard, the young minister was practically unknown when he offered the opening prayer at the commemorative service for the deceased Harvard alumni of the Civil War, held in Cambridge in July 1865. Yet, in company with Julia Ward Howe, Ralph Waldo Emerson, Oliver Wendell Holmes, and James Russell Lowell, all of whom read poems, he made a profound impression on the distinguished audience with his "spontaneous and intimate expression." And, President Eliot summed it up by adding, "A young prophet has risen up in Israel." Later, his brilliant career involved many trips abroad, including five years' residence in Europe, during which time he preached before Queen Victoria. Bishop Brooks became one of the most revered Americans of his generation, both at home and abroad. Among other endeavors, he championed the cause for church unity.

In 1865, at the age of thirty, this noted preacher made a trip to the Holy Land and was deeply moved by what he saw. It is believed by Dr. Raymond W. Albright, his latest biographer, that "O Little Town of Bethlehem" was first written in his notebook in the fields outside Bethlehem on Christmas Eve. All during his life, whenever he was deeply moved, Bishop Brooks was inclined to express his feelings of sadness or joy in verse.

The story of this carol as traditionally told begins with the minister's conversation with his organist in Trinity Church, Philadelphia, during the Advent season of 1868. He was anxious to have the carol for his Christmas Sunday-school service and asked the organist, Lewis Redner, to write a tune for it. As it turned out, the music was written under pressure and in great haste, for the organist was more concerned about the Sunday-school lesson than about the hymn. Neither the minister nor the organist thought that the carol or the music would live beyond that Christmas. In fact, it was nearly twenty years later that it was discovered by the public, when it appeared in a metropolitan newspaper. Since that time, "O Little Town" has taken its place among the classic Christmas hymns.

Everyone who loves Christmas knows a few lines of "Everywhere, Everywhere, Christmas To-night!" yet few are acquainted with the entire five verses as originally written. Less familiar is "The Voice of the Christ Child," which, like all the carols of Phillips Brooks, reflects his great devotion to Christ and his abiding love for children. Christmas, the real children's day, was a very special time for him. His sermons reflected this feeling, as did his letter to his Philadelphia Sunday School. "I do not mind telling you (though of course I should not like to have you speak of it to any of the older people of the church) that I am much afraid the younger part of my congregation has more than its share of my thoughts and interest." His Christmas carols were composed especially for the children he knew and loved, and they were legion.

O LITTLE TOWN OF BETHLEHEM

O little town of Bethlehem,
  How still we see thee lie!
Above thy deep and dreamless sleep
  The silent stars go by.
Yet in thy dark streets shineth
  The everlasting light;
The hopes and fears of all the years
  Are met in thee to-night.

For Christ is born of Mary;
  And, gathered all above,
While mortals sleep, the angels keep
  Their watch of wondering love.
O morning stars, together
  Proclaim the holy birth,
And praises sing to God the King,
  And peace to men on earth;

How silently, how silently,
  The wondrous gift is given!
So God imparts to human hearts
  The blessings of his heaven.
No ear may hear his coming;
  But in this world of sin,
Where meek souls will receive him, still
  The dear Christ enters in.

Where children pure and happy
  Pray to the blessèd Child,
Where misery cries out to thee,
  Son of the mother mild;
Where charity stands watching
  And faith holds wide the door,
The dark night wakes, the glory breaks,
  And Christmas comes once more.

O holy Child of Bethlehem,
  Descend to us, we pray;
Cast out our sin, and enter in,
  Be born in us to-day.
We hear the Christmas Angels
  The great glad tidings tell:
O come to us, abide with us,
  Our Lord Emmanuel.

A CHRISTMAS CAROL

Everywhere, everywhere, Christmas to-
night!
Christmas in lands of the fir-tree and pine,
Christmas in lands of the palm-tree and
vine,
Christmas where snow-peaks stand solemn
and white,
Christmas where corn-fields lie sunny and
bright;
Everywhere, everywhere, Christmas to-
night!

Christmas where children are hopeful and
gay,
Christmas where old men are patient and
gray;
Christmas where peace, like a dove in its
flight,
Broods o'er brave men in the thick of the
fight;
Everywhere, everywhere, Christmas to-
night!

For the Christ-child who comes is the
Master of all,
No palace too great and no cottage too
small;
The Angels who welcome Him sing from
the height,
"In the City of David a King in His
might."
Everywhere, everywhere, Christmas to-
night!

Then let every heart keep its Christmas
within,
Christ's pity for sorrow, Christ's hatred of
sin,
Christ's care for the weakest, Christ's courage for right,
Christ's dread of the darkness, Christ's love
of the light;
Everywhere, everywhere, Christmas to-
night!

So the stars of the midnight which com-
pass us round
Shall see a strange glory, and hear a sweet
sound,
And, cry "Look! the earth is aflame with
delight,
O sons of the morning, rejoice at the
sight."
Everywhere, everywhere, Christmas to-
night!

THE VOICE OF THE CHRIST-CHILD

The earth has grown old with its burden
of care,
But at Christmas it always is young,
The heart of the jewel burns lustrous and
fair,
And its soul full of music breaks forth on
the air,
When the song of the Angels is sung.

It is coming, old earth, it is coming to-
night,
On the snowflakes which cover thy sod,
The feet of the Christ-child fall gently and
white,
And the voice of the Christ-child tells out
with delight
That mankind are the children of God.

On the sad and the lonely, the wretched
and poor,
That voice of the Christ-child shall fall;
And to every blind wanderer opens the
door
Of a hope which he dared not to dream
of before,
With a sunshine of welcome for all.

The feet of the humblest may walk in the
field
Where the feet of the holiest have trod,
This, this is the marvel to mortals revealed,
When the silvery trumpets of Christmas
have pealed,
That mankind are the children of God.

Bret Harte

"The New California Dickens" was the way that Bret Harte was described by more than one literary critic, even during his lifetime. He was, like Dickens, an impressive-looking man, always well groomed and sartorially correct, with dapper manners. Born in Albany, New York, in 1836, his early life was spent in various Eastern cities. His father was a college professor and his mother had a keen interest in literature, so that as a boy Harte had every cultural advantage available. At the age of eighteen he went to California, where he worked as a tutor, an express messenger on stagecoaches, a miner, a printer, and finally a newspaper editor. For six years he served as Secretary of the California Mint.

In 1869 "The Luck of Roaring Camp" appeared in the *Overland Monthly*, of which Harte was Editor. Although California critics were not impressed, this story gave him his literary reputation. Six months later, a poem entitled "Plain Language from Truthful James," or the "Heathen Chinee," as it was popularly referred to, brought him renown. A year later Boston's distinguished Editor of the *Atlantic* offered Harte a contract for all his writing for a year, at the handsome sum of $10,000. Bret Harte produced four stories and five poems to fulfill the contract. Among them was "How Santa Claus Came to Simpson's Bar," generally considered one of the four best tales he ever wrote. The spirit of Dickens permeates this breathless story as it does most of Harte's early writings. Curiously enough, Dickens wrote Harte a letter a few days before he died, asking him to write a story for his magazine, *All the Year Round*.

Few Americans knew their Dickens better than Bret Harte. He had been reading his hero since he was a boy. No wonder he saw the Dickensian traits in the California pioneers of the gold-rush era which he portrayed. He even gave them Dickens-like names. Most of all, Bret Harte gave his readers humor with sentiment that was a blend of reverence and sympathy. It is the very essence of "How Santa Claus Came to Simpson's Bar."

HOW SANTA CLAUS CAME TO SIMPSON'S BAR

IT HAD been raining in the valley of the Sacramento. The North Fork had overflowed its banks, and Rattlesnake Creek was impassable.

The mud lay deep on the mountain road and the way to Simpson's Bar was indicated by broken-down teams and hard swearing. And farther on, cut off and inaccessible, rained upon and bedraggled, smitten by high winds and threatened by high water, Simpson's Bar, on the eve of Christmas Day, 1862, clung like a swallow's nest to the rocky entablature and splintered capitals of Table Mountain, and shook in the blast.

As night shut down on the settlement, a few lights gleamed through the mist from the windows of cabins on either side of the highway now crossed and gullied by lawless streams and swept by marauding winds. Happily most of the population were gathered at Thompson's store, clustered round a red-hot stove, at which they silently spat in some accepted sense of social communion that perhaps rendered conversation unnecessary. Indeed, most methods of diversion had long since been exhausted on Simpson's Bar; high water had suspended the regular occupations on gulch and on river, and a consequent lack of money and whiskey had taken the zest from most illegitimate recreations.

The man who entered was a figure familiar enough to the company, and known in Simpson's Bar as "The Old Man." A man of perhaps fifty years; grizzled and scant of hair, but still fresh and youthful of complexion. He had evidently just left some hilarious companions, and did not at first notice the gravity of the group, but clapped the shoulder of the nearest man jocularly, and threw himself into a vacant chair. "Dismal weather, ain't it?" he said reflectively, after a pause. "Mighty rough papers on the boys, and no show for money this season. And tomorrow's Christmas."

There was a movement among the men at this announcement, but whether of satisfaction or disgust was not plain. "Yes," continued the Old Man, "Yes, Christmas, and tonight's Christmas Eve. Ye see, boys, I kinder thought—that is, I sorter had an idee, jest passin' like, you know—that maybe ye'd all like to come over to my house tonight and have a sort of tear round. But I suppose, now, you wouldn't? Don't feel like it, maybe?" he added with anxious sympathy, peering into the faces of his companions.

"Well, I don't know," responded Tom Flynn with some cheerfulness. "P'r'aps we may. But how about your wife, Old Man? What does she say to it?"

The Old Man hesitated. His conjugal experience had not been a happy one, and the fact was known to Simpson's Bar. His first wife, a delicate, pretty little woman, had suffered keenly and secretly from the jealous suspicions of her husband, until one day he invited the whole Bar to his house to expose her infidelity. On arriving, the party found the shy, petite creature quietly engaged in her household duties, and retired abashed and discomfited. But the sensitive woman did not easily recover from the shock of this extraordinary outrage. It was with difficulty she regained her equanimity sufficiently to release her lover from the closet in which he was concealed, and escape with him. She left a boy of three years to comfort her bereaved husband. The Old Man's present wife had been his cook. She was large, loyal, and aggressive.

"Thar's no trouble about thet," said the Old Man, "it's my own house, built every stick on it myself. Don't you be afeard o'her, boys, she may cut up a trifle rough—ez wimmin do—but she'll come round."

As yet, Dick Bullen, the oracle and leader of Simpson's Bar, had not spoken. He now took his pipe from his lips. "Old

Man, how's that yer Johnny gettin' on? Seems to me he didn't look so peart last time I seed him. Maybe now, we'd be in the way ef he was sick?"

The father hastened to assure him that Johnny was better and that a "little fun might 'liven him up." Whereupon Dick arose, shook himself, and said, "I'm ready. Lead the way, Old Man: here goes."

Their way led up Pine-Tree Canyon, at the head of which a broad, low, bark-thatched cabin burrowed in the mountainside. It was the home of the Old Man, and the entrance to the tunnel in which he worked when he worked at all. Here the crowd paused for a moment, out of delicate deference to their host, who came up panting in the rear.

"P'r'aps ye'd better hold on a second out yer, whilst I go in and see that things is all right," said the Old Man, with an indifference he was far from feeling. The suggestion was graciously accepted, the door opened and closed on the host, and the crowd, leaning their backs against the wall and cowering under the eaves, waited and listened.

For a few moments there was no sound but the dripping of water from the eaves, and the stir and rustle of wrestling boughs above them. Then the men became uneasy, and whispered suggestion and suspicion passed from the one to the other. "Reckon she's caved in his head the first lick!" "Decoyed him inter the tunnel and barred him up, likely." "Got him down and sittin' on him." "Prob'ly biling suthin' to heave on us: stand clear the door, boys!" For just then the latch clicked, the door slowly opened, and a voice said: "Come in out o' the wet."

The voice was neither that of the Old Man nor of his wife. It was the voice of a small boy, its weak treble broken by that preternatural hoarseness which only vagabondage and the habit of premature self-assertion can give. It was the face of a small boy that looked up at theirs—a face that might have been pretty, and even refined, but that it was darkened by evil

knowledge from within, and dirt and hard experience from without. He had a blanket around his shoulders, and had evidently just risen from his bed. "Come in," he repeated, "and don't make no noise." The men, entering quietly, ranged themselves around a long table of rough boards which occupied the centre of the room. Johnny then gravely proceeded to a cupboard and brought out several articles, which he deposited on the table. "Thar's whisky. And crackers. And red herons. And cheese." He took a bite of the latter on his way to the table. "And sugar." He scooped up a mouthful *en route* with a small and very dirty hand. "Thar's dried appils too on the shelf, but I don't admire 'em. Appils is swellin'! Thar," he concluded, "now wade in, and don't be afeard. I don't mind the old woman. She don't b'long to me. S'long."

He had stepped to the threshold of a small room, scarcely larger than a closet, partitioned off from the main apartment, and holding in its dim recess a small bed. He stood there a moment looking at the company, his bare feet peeping from the blanket, and nodded.

"Hallo, Johnny! You ain't goin' to turn in agin, are ye?" said Dick.

"Yes, I are," responded Johnny decidedly.

"Why, wat's up, old fellow?"

"I'm sick."

"How sick?"

"I've got a fevier. And childblains. And roomatiz," returned Johnny, and vanished within. After a moment's pause, he added in the dark, apparently from under the bed-clothes—"And biles!"

There was an embarrassing silence. The men looked at each other and at the fire. Even with the appetizing banquet before them, it seemed as if they might again fall into the despondency of Thompson's grocery, when the voice of the Old Man, incautiously lifted, came deprecatingly from the kitchen.

"Certainly! Thet's so. In course they is. A gang o' lazy, drunken loafers, and that ar Dick Bullen's the ornariest of all. Didn't hev no more *sabe* than to come round yar with sickness in the house and no provision. Thet's what I said: 'Bullen,' sez I, 'it's crazy drunk you are, or a fool,' sez I, 'to think o' such a thing. Staples,' I sez, 'be you a man, Staples, and 'spect to raise hell under my roof and invalids yin' round?' But they would come—they would. Thet's wot you must 'spect o' such trash as lays around the Bar."

A burst of laughter from the men followed this unfortunate exposure. Whether it was overheard in the kitchen, or whether the Old Man's irate companion had just then exhausted all other modes of expressing her contemptuous indignation, I cannot say, but a back door was suddenly slammed with great violence. A moment later and the Old Man reappeared, haply unconscious of the cause of the late hilarious outburst, and smiled blandly.

"The old woman thought she'd just run over to Mrs. McFadden's for a sociable call," he explained, with jaunty indifference, as he took a seat at the board.

Oddly enough it needed this untoward incident to relieve the embarrassment that was beginning to be felt by the party, and their natural audacity returned with their host.

It was nearly midnight when the festivities were interrupted. "Hush," said Dick Bullen, holding up his hand. It was the querulous voice of Johnny from his adjacent closet: "Oh, dad!"

The Old Man arose hurriedly and disappeared in the closet. Presently he reappeared. "His rheumatiz is coming on agin bad," he explained, "and he wanted rubbin'." He lifted the demijohn of whisky from the table and shook it. It was empty. Dick Bullen put down his tin cup with an embarrassed laugh. So did the others. The Old Man examined their contents and said hopefully, "I reckon that's enough; he don't need much. You hold on all o' you for a spell, and I'll be back"; and vanished in the closet with an old flannel shirt and the whisky. The door closed but imperfectly, and the following dialogue was distinctly audible:

"Now, sonny, whar does she ache worst?"

"Sometimes over yar and sometimes under yer; but it's most powerful from yer to yer. Rub yer, dad."

A silence seemed to indicate a brisk rubbing. Then Johnny:

"Hevin' a good time out yer, dad?"

"Yes, sonny."

"To-morrer's Chrismiss—ain't it?"

"Yes, sonny. How does she feel now?"

"Better. Rub a little furder down. Wot's Chrismiss, anyway? Wot's it all about?"

"Oh, it's a day."

This exhaustive definition was apparently satisfactory, for there was a silent interval of rubbing. Presently Johnny again:

"Mar sez that everywhere else but yer everybody gives things to everybody Chrismiss, and then she jist waded inter you. She sez thar's a man they call Sandy Claws, not a white man, you know, but a kind o' Chinemin, comes down the chimbley night afore Chrismiss and gives things to chillern—boys like me. Puts 'em in their butes! Thet's what she tried to play upon me. Easy now, pop. Whar are you rubbin' to—thet's a mile from the place. She jest made that up, didn't she, jest to aggrewate me and you? Don't rub thar . . . Why, dad! Thar, that'll do, dad. I don't ache near so bad as I did. Now wrap me tight in this yer blanket. So. Now," he added in a muffled whisper, "sit down by me till I go asleep." To assure himself of obedience, he disengaged one hand from the blanket and, grasping his father's sleeve, again composed himself to rest.

For some moments the Old Man waited patiently. Then the unwonted stillness of the house excited his curiosity, and without moving from the bed he cautiously opened the door with his disengaged hand, and looked into the main room. To his infinite surprise it was dark and deserted. The Old Man would have followed the men but for the hand that still unconsciously grasped his sleeve. He could have easily disengaged it; it *was* small, weak and emaciated. But perhaps because it was small, weak, and emaciated, he changed his mind, and drawing his chair closer to the bed, rested his head upon it. In this defenseless attitude the potency of his earlier potations surprised him. The room flickered and faded before his eyes, reappeared, faded again, went out, and left him —asleep.

Meantime Dick Bullen confronted his companions. "Are you ready?" said Staples. "Ready," said Dick; "what's the time?" "Past twelve," was the reply; "can you make it?—it's nigh on fifty miles, the round trip hither and yon." "I reckon," returned Dick shortly. "Whar's the mare?" "Bill and Jack's holdin' her at the crossin'."

Sing, O Muse, the ride of Richard Bullen! Sing, O Muse, of chivalrous men! the sacred quest, the doughty deeds, the battery of low churls, the fearsome ride and gruesome peril, of the Flower of Simpson's Bar!

It was one o'clock and yet he had only gained Rattlesnake Hill. For in that time Jovita had rehearsed to him all her imperfections and practised all her vices. Thrice had she stumbled. Twice had she thrown up her Roman nose in a straight line with the reins, and, resisting bit and spur, struck out madly across country. Twice had she reared, and rearing, fallen backward; and twice had the agile Dick, unharmed, regained his seat before she found her vicious legs again. And a mile beyond them, at the foot of a long hill, was Rattlesnake Creek. Dick knew that here was the crucial test of his ability to perform his enterprise, set his teeth grimly, put his knees well into her flanks, and changed his defensive tactics to brisk aggression. Bullied and maddened, Jovita began the descent of the hill. Here the artful Richard pretended to hold her in with ostentatious objurgation and well-feigned cries of alarm. It is unnecessary to add that Jovita instantly ran away. Nor need I state the time made in the descent; it is written in the chronicles of Simpson's Bar. Enough that in another moment, as it seemed to Dick, she was

splashing on the overflowed banks of Rattlesnake Creek. As Dick expected, the momentum she had acquired carried her beyond the point of balking, and holding her well together for a mighty leap, they dashed into the middle of the swiftly flowing current. A few moments of kicking, wading, and swimming, and Dick drew a long breath on the opposite bank.

The road from Rattlesnake Creek to Red Mountain was tolerably level. At half-past two Dick rose in his stirrups with a great shout. Stars were glittering through the rifted clouds, and beyond him, out of the plain, rose two spires, a flag-staff, and a straggling line of black objects. Dick jingled his spurs and swung his riata, Jovita bounded forward, and in another moment they swept into Tuttleville, and drew up before the wooden piazza of "The Hotel of All Nations."

After Jovita had been handed over to a sleepy ostler, whom she at once kicked into unpleasant consciousness, Dick sallied out with the bar-keeper for a tour of the sleeping town. Lights still gleamed from a few saloons and gambling-houses; but, avoiding these, they stopped before several closed shops, and by persistent tapping and judicious outcry roused the proprietors from their beds, and made them unbar the doors of their magazines and expose their wares. Sometimes they were met by curses, but oftener by interest and some concern in their needs, and the interview was invariably concluded by a drink. It was three o'clock before this pleasantry was given over, and with a small waterproof bag of India rubber strapped on his shoulders Dick returned to the hotel, sprang to the saddle and dashed down the lonely street and out into the lonelier plain.

It was five before Dick reached the long level that led to Rattlesnake Creek. Another half-hour would bring him to the creek. He threw the reins lightly upon the neck of the mare, chirruped to her, and began to sing.

Suddenly Jovita shied with a bound that would have unseated a less practised rider.

Hanging to her rein was a figure that had leaped from the bank, and at the same time from the road before her arose a shadowy horse and rider. "Throw up your hands," commanded the second apparition, with an oath.

Dick felt the mare tremble, quiver, and apparently sink under him. He knew what it meant and was prepared.

"Stand aside, Jack Simpson, I know you, you d—d thief! Let me pass, or—"

He did not finish the sentence. Jovita rose straight in the air with a terrific bound, throwing the figure from her bit with a single shake of her vicious head, and charged with deadly malevolence down on the impediment before her. An oath, a pistol-shot, horse and highwayman rolled over in the road, and the next moment Jovita was a hundred yards away. But the good right arm of her rider, shattered by a bullet, dropped helplessly at his side.

Without slackening his speed he shifted the reins to his left hand. He had no fear of pursuit, but looking up he saw that the eastern stars were already paling, and that the distant peaks had lost their ghostly whiteness, and now stood out blackly against a lighter sky. Day was upon him. Then completely absorbed in a single idea, he forgot the pain of his wound, and mounting again dashed on toward Rattlesnake Creek. But now Jovita's breath came broken by gasps, Dick reeled in his saddle, and brighter and brighter grew the sky.

For the last few rods there was a roaring in his ears. Was it exhaustion from loss of blood, or what? He was dazed and giddy as he swept down the hill, and did not recognize his surroundings. Had he taken the wrong road, or was this Rattlesnake Creek? It was. But the brawling creek he had swum a few hours before had risen, more than doubled its volume, and now rolled a swift and resistless river between him and Rattlesnake Hill. He cast off his coat, pistol, boots, and saddle, bound his precious pack tightly to his shoulders, grasped the bare flanks of Jovita with his bared knees, and with a shout dashed into the yellow water. A cry rose from the opposite bank as the head of a man and horse struggled for a few moments against the battling current, and then were swept away amidst uprooted trees and whirling driftwood.—

The Old Man started and woke. The fire on the hearth was dead, the candle in the outer room flickering in its socket, and somebody was rapping at the door. He opened it, but fell back with a cry before the dripping, half-naked figure that reeled against the doorpost.

"Dick?"

"Hush! Is he awake yet?"

"No—but, Dick—?"

"Dry up, you old fool! Get me some whisky, quick!" The Old Man flew and returned with—an empty bottle! Dick would have sworn, but his strength was not equal to the occasion. He staggered, caught at the handle of the door, and motioned to the Old Man.

"Thar's suthin' in my pack yer for Johnny. Take it off. I can't."

The Old Man unstrapped the pack, and laid it before the exhausted man.

"Open it, quick!"

He did so with trembling fingers. It contained only a few poor toys—cheap and barbaric enough, goodness knows, but bright with paint and tinsel. One of them was broken; another, I fear, was irretrievably ruined by water, and on the third— ah me! there was a cruel spot.

"It don't look like much, that's a fact," said Dick ruefully. "But it's the best we could do . . . Take 'em, Old Man, and put 'em in his stocking, and tell him—tell him, you know—hold me, Old Man—" The Old Man caught at his sinking figure. "Tell him," said Dick, with a weak little laugh—"tell him Sandy Claus has come."

And even so, bedraggled, ragged, unshaven, and unshorn, with one arm hanging helplessly at his side, Santa Claus came to Simpson's Bar and fell fainting on the first threshold. The Christmas dawn came slowly after, touching the remoter peaks with the rosy warmth of ineffable love. And it looked so tenderly on Simpson's Bar that the whole mountain, as if caught in a generous action, blushed to the skies.

Harriet Beecher Stowe

NEXT to Dickens, Harriet Beecher Stowe was the most widely read author of her day. The phenomenal success story of *Uncle Tom's Cabin,* published in 1852, by the "little lady who started the big war," as Lincoln dubbed her, is still talked about in publishing circles. Mrs. Stowe was born in Connecticut in 1832 and died in her native state in 1896. In a letter to a friend she described herself, saying: "I am a little bit of a woman, somewhat more than forty, about as thin and dry as a pinch of snuff; never very much to look at in my best days, and looking like a used-up article now." Her writings included ten long novels and countless short stories.

Of her ten pieces of fiction, which are divided into three groups, two are concerned with antislavery, four are novels of old New England in which she established a pattern followed by Mary E. Wilkins Freeman, Sarah Orne Jewett, and other writers who succeeded her. She also wrote three society novels, and one of historical interest called *Agnes of Sorrento.*

She was the daughter of a preacher, as well as the wife and the mother of one, and the sister of seven clergymen. As Edward Wagenknecht has expressed it, "She understood that breed only too well. But the insight of a Christian mother—all that is the norm by which she tests everything." She made strong use of powerful preachers in several of her characters and was a stanch advocate of decent Christian thinking in all her writing. This was evidenced particularly in one of her lesser known stories, "Elder Brewster's Christmas Sermon," which appeared in 1876 in a book entitled *Betty's Bright Idea.* There were three truly didactic stories in this small volume, which included two on Christmas and one on Thanksgiving. In presenting the first Christmas in New England, she wrote the kind of message which she knew only too well, having been born and bred in it.

ELDER BREWSTER'S CHRISTMAS SERMON

SUNDAY morning found the little company gathered once more on the ship, with nothing to do but rest and remember their homes, temporal and spiritual—homes backward, in old England, and forward, in Heaven. They were, every man and woman of them, English to the back-bone. From Captain Jones who commanded the ship to Elder Brewster who ruled and guided in spiritual affairs, all alike were of that stock and breeding which made the Englishman of the days of Bacon and Shakespeare, and in those days Christmas was knit into the heart of every one of them by a thousand threads, which no after years could untie.

Christmas carols had been sung to them by nurses and mothers and grandmothers; the Christmas holly spoke to them from every berry and prickly leaf, full of dearest household memories. Some of them had been men of substance among the English gentry and in their prosperous days had held high festival in ancestral halls in the season of good cheer. Elder Brewster himself had been a rising young diplomat in the court of Elizabeth, in the days when the Lord Keeper of the Seals led the revels of Christmas as Lord of Misrule.

So that, though this Sunday morning arose gray and lowering, with snow-flakes hovering through the air, there was Christmas in the thoughts of every man and woman among them—albeit it was the Christmas of wanderers and exiles in a wilderness looking back to bright home-fires across stormy waters.

The men had come back from their work on shore with branches of green pine and holly, and the women had stuck them about the ship, not without tearful thoughts of old home-places, where their childhood fathers and mothers did the same.

Bits and snatches of Christmas carols were floating all around the ship, like land-birds blown far out to sea. In the forecastle Master Coppin was singing:

"Come, bring with a noise,
My merry boys,
    The Christmas log to the firing;
While my good dame, she
Bids ye all be free,
    And drink to your hearts' desiring.
Drink now the strong beer,
Cut the white loaf here.
    The while the meat is shredding
For the rare minced pie,
And the plums stand by
    To fill the paste that's a-kneading."

"Ah, well-a-day, Master Jones, it is dull cheer to sing Christmas songs here in the woods, with only the owls and the bears for choristers. I wish I could hear the bells of merry England once more."

And down in the cabin Rose Standish was hushing little Peregrine, the first American-born baby, with a Christmas lullaby:

"This winter's night
I saw a sight—
    A star as bright as day;
And ever among
A maiden sung,
    Lullay, by-by, lullay!

"This lovely laydie sat and sung,
    And to her child she said,
My son, my brother, and my father dear,
    Why lyest thou thus in hayd?
My sweet bird,
Tho' it betide
    Thou be not king veray;
But nevertheless
I will not cease
    To sing, by-by, lullay!

"The child then spake in his talking,
    And to his mother he said,
It happeneth, mother, I am a king,
    In crib though I be laid,
For angels bright
Did down alight,
    Thou knowest it is no nay;
And of that sight
Thou may'st be light
    To sing, by-by, lullay!

"Now, sweet son, since thou art a
    king,
Why art thou laid in stall?
Why not ordain thy bedding
    In some great king his hall?
We thinketh 'tis right
    That king or knight
Should be in good array;
    And them among,
It were no wrong
    To sing, by-by, lullay!

"Mary, mother, I am thy child,
    Tho' I be laid in stall;
Lords and dukes shall worship me,
    And so shall kinges all.
And ye shall see
    That kinges three
Shall come on the twelfth day;
    For this behest
Give me thy breast,
    And sing, by-by, lullay!"

"See here," quoth Miles Standish, "when
my Rose singeth, the children gather round
her like bees round a flower. Come, let us
all strike up a goodly carol together. Sing
one, sing all, girls and boys, and get a bit
of Old England's Christmas before to-
morrow, when we must to our work on
shore."

Thereat Rose struck up a familiar ballad-
meter of a catching rhythm, and every
voice of young and old was soon joining
in it:

"Behold a silly,* tender Babe,
    In freezing winter night,
In homely manger trembling lies;
    Alas! a piteous sight,
The inns are full, no man will yield
    This little Pilgrim bed;
But forced He is, with silly beasts
    In crib to shroud His head.
Despise Him not for lying there,
    First what He is inquire:
An orient pearl is often found
    In depth of dirty mire.

* Old English—simple.

Weigh not His crib, His wooden dish,
    Nor beasts that by Him feed;
Weigh not His mother's poor attire,
    Nor Joseph's simple weed.
This stable is a Prince's court,
    The crib His chair of state,
The beasts are parcel of His pomp,
    The wooden dish His plate.
The persons in that poor attire
    His royal liveries wear;
The Prince Himself is come from Heaven,
    This pomp is prized there.
With joy approach, O Christian wight,
    Do homage to thy King;
And highly praise His humble pomp,
    Which He from Heaven doth bring."

The cheerful sounds spread themselves
through the ship like the flavor of some
rare perfume, bringing softness of heart
through a thousand tender memories.

Anon, the hour of Sabbath morning
worship drew on, and Elder Brewster read
from the New Testament the whole story
of the Nativity, and then gave a sort of
Christmas homily from the words of St.
Paul, in the eighth chapter of Romans, the
sixth and seventh verses, which the Geneva
version thus renders:

"For the wisdom of the flesh is death,
but the wisdom of the spirit is life and
peace.

"For the wisdom of the flesh is enmity
against God, for it is not subject to the
law of God, neither indeed can be."

"Ye know full well, dear brethren, what
the wisdom of the flesh sayeth. The wisdom of the flesh sayeth to each one, 'Take
care of thyself; look after thyself, to get
and to have and to hold and to enjoy.'
The wisdom of the flesh sayeth, 'So thou
art warm, full, and in good liking, take
thine ease, eat, drink, and be merry, and
care not how many go empty and be lacking.' But ye have seen in the Gospel this
morning that this was not the wisdom of
our Lord Jesus Christ, who, though he
was Lord of all, became poorer than any,
that we, through His poverty, might become rich. When our Lord Jesus Christ

came, the wisdom of the flesh despised Him; the wisdom of the flesh had no room for Him at the inn.

"There was room enough always for Herod and his concubines, for the wisdom of the flesh set great store by them; but a poor man and woman were thrust out to a stable; and *there* was a poor baby born whom the wisdom of the flesh knew not, because the wisdom of the flesh is enmity against God.

"The wisdom of the flesh, brethren, ever despiseth the wisdom of God, because it knoweth it not. The wisdom of the flesh looketh at the thing that is great and strong and high; it looketh at riches, at kings' courts, at fine clothes and fine jewels and fine feastings, and it despiseth the little and the poor and the weak.

"But the wisdom of the Spirit goeth to worship the poor babe in the manger, and layeth gold and myrrh and frankincense at his feet while he lieth in weakness and poverty, as did the wise men who were taught of God.

"Now, forasmuch as our Saviour Christ left His riches and throne in glory and came in weakness and poverty to this world, that he might work out a mighty salvation that shall be to all people, how can we better keep Christmas than to follow in his steps? We be a little company who have forsaken houses and lands and possessions, and come here unto the wilderness that we may prepare a resting-place whereto others shall come to reap what we shall sow. And to-morrow we shall keep our first Christmas, not in flesh-pleasing and in reveling and in fullness of bread, but in small beginning and great weakness, as our Lord Christ kept it when He was born in a stable and lay in a manger.

"To-morrow, God willing, we will all go forth to do good, honest Christian work, and begin the first house-building in this our New England—it may be roughly fashioned, but as good a house, I'll warrant me, as our Lord Christ had on the Christmas Day we wot of. And let us

not faint in heart because the wisdom of the world despiseth what we do. Though Sanballat the Horonite, and Tobias the Ammonite, and Geshem the Arabian make scorn of us, and say, 'What do these weak Jews?. If a fox go up, he shall break down their stone wall;' yet the Lord our God is with us, and He can cause our work to prosper.

"The wisdom of the Spirit seeth the grain of mustard-seed, that is the least of all seeds, how it shall become a great tree, and the fowls of heaven shall lodge in its branches. Let us, then, lift up the hands that hang down and the feeble knees, and let us hope that, like as great salvation to all people came out of small beginnings of Bethlehem, so the work which we shall begin to-morrow shall be for the good of many nations.

"It is a custom on this Christmas Day to give love-presents. What love-gift giveth our Lord Jesus on this day? Brethren, it is a great one and a precious; as St. Paul said to the Philippians: 'For unto you it is given for Christ, not only that ye should believe on Him, but also that ye should *suffer* for His sake;' and St. Peter also saith, 'Behold, we count them blessed which endure.' And the holy Apostles rejoiced that they were counted worthy to suffer rebuke for the name of Jesus.

"Our Lord Christ giveth us of His cup and His baptism; He giveth of the manger and the straw; He giveth of persecutions and afflictions; He giveth of the crown of thorns, and right dear unto us be these gifts.

"And now will I tell these children a story, which a cunning playwright, whom I once knew in our Queen's court, hath made concerning gifts:

"A great king would marry his daughter worthily, and so he caused three caskets to be made, in one of which he hid her picture. The one casket was of gold set with diamonds, the second of silver set with pearls, and the third a poor casket of lead.

"Now it was given out that each comer

should have but one choice, and if he chose the one with the picture he should have the lady to wife.

"Divers kings, knights, and gentlemen came from far, but they never won, because they always snatched at the gold and the silver caskets, with the pearls and diamonds. So, when they opened these, they found only a grinning death's-head or a fool's cap.

"But anon cometh a true, brave knight and gentleman, who chooseth for love alone the old leaden casket; and, behold, within is the picture of her he loveth! and they were married with great feasting and content.

"So our Lord Jesus doth not offer himself to us in silver and gold and jewels, but in poverty and hardness and want; but whoso chooseth them for His love's sake shall find Him therein whom his soul loveth, and shall enter with joy to the marriage supper of the Lamb.

"And when the Lord shall come again in his glory, then he shall bring worthy gifts with him, for he saith: 'Be thou faithful unto death, and I will give thee a crown of life; to him that overcometh I will give to eat of the hidden manna, and I will give him a white stone with a new name that no man knoweth save he that receiveth it. He that overcometh and keepeth my words, I will give power over the nations and I will give him the morning star.'

"Let us then take joyfully Christ's Christmas gifts of labors and adversities and crosses to-day, that when he shall appear we may have these great and wonderful gifts at his coming; for if we suffer with him we shall also reign; but if we deny him, he also will deny us."

And so it happens that the only record of Christmas Day in the pilgrims' journal is this:

"Monday, the 25th, being Christmas Day, we went ashore, some to fell timber, some to saw, some to rive, and some to carry; and so no man rested all that day. But towards night some, as they were at work, heard a noise of Indians, which caused us all to go to our muskets; but we heard no further, so we came aboard again, leaving some to keep guard. That night we had a sore storm of wind and rain. But at night the ship-master caused us to have some beer aboard."

So worthily kept they the first Christmas, from which comes all the Christmas cheer of New England to-day. There is no record how Mary Winslow and Rose Standish and others, with women and children, came ashore and walked about encouraging the builders; and how little Love gathered stores of bright checker-berries and partridge plums, and was made merry in seeing squirrels and wild rabbits; nor how old Margery roasted certain wild geese to a turn at a woodland fire, and conserved wild cranberries with honey for sauce. In their journals the good pilgrims say they found bushels of strawberries in the meadows in December. But we, knowing the nature of things, know that these must have been cranberries, which grow still abundantly around Plymouth harbor.

And at the very time that all this was doing in the wilderness, and the men were working yeomanly to build a new nation, in King James's court the ambassadors of the French King were being entertained with maskings and mummerings, wherein the staple subject of merriment was the Puritans!

So goes the wisdom of the world and its ways—and so goes the wisdom of God!

Blanche Howard

THE state of Maine produced its share of writers in the 19th century, and one of them was the novelist Blanche Willis Howard. She was born in 1847, grew up in Bangor, and finally became associated with the *Boston Transcript*. At the age of twenty-eight her first book, a novel entitled *One Summer,* was published and brought her considerable fame. That same year she went to Stuttgart, Germany, and served as a correspondent for Boston's best-known paper.

A woman of considerable talent and ability, she taught school in Germany, wrote articles and edited a magazine published in English in Stuttgart. Miss Howard was also a pianist of great ability and her playing won the praise of both Wagner and Liszt. In 1890 she married Baron Julius von Teuffel, physician to the King of Württemberg. Life filled with excitement and gracious living created for her a pleasant atmosphere for writing. Her novels about European peasant life were notably popular and her portrayal of life in the Tyrol and among the Breton peasants won the approbation of both critics and readers.

In 1877 she wrote *A Year Abroad,* in which she described her travels vividly. Her account of Christmas provided American readers with the kind of delightful word pictures of European Christmases which they loved. It was an era when globe-trotting spinsters and sometimes whole families were traveling and writing about what they saw. There are many delightful accounts of German Christmases to be found in the travel books and reminiscences of Victorian writers, and Blanche Howard's account has its own kind of charm.

SOME CHRISTMAS PICTURES

A FEW days before Christmas the three kings from the Orient came stealing up our stairs in the gloaming. They wore cheap white cotton raiment over their ordinary work-a-day clothes, and gilt-paper crowns on their heads. They were small, thin kings. Melchior's crown was awry, Kaspar felt very timid, and was continually stumbling over his train; but Balthazar was brave as a lion, and nudged his royal brothers,—one of whom was a girl, by the way,—putting courage into them with his elbows; and the dear little souls sang their songs and got their pennies, and their white robes vanished in the twilight as their majesties trudged on towards the next house. There they would again stand in an uncertain, tremulous row, and sing more or sing less, according to the reception they met with, and put more or less pennies—generally less, poor dears!—into their pockets. Poor, dear, shabby little wise men,—including the one who was a girl,—you were potentates whom it was a pleasure to see, and we trust you earned such an affluence of Christmas pennies that you were in a state of ineffable bliss when, at last, freed from the restraint of crowns and royal robes, you stood in your poor home before your Christmas-tree. It may have been a barren thing, but to your happy child-eyes no doubt it shone as the morning star and blossomed as the rose.

Other apparitions foretelling the approach of Christmas visited us. One was an old woman with cakes. Her prominent characteristic is staying where she is put, or rather where she puts herself, which is usually where she is not wanted. Buy a cake of this amiable old person, whose breath (with all the respect due to age let it be said) smells unquestionably of *schnapps,* and she will bless you with astounding volubility. Her tongue whirls like a mill-wheel as she tearfully assures us, "God will reward us," —and *how* she stays! Men may come and

men may go, but the old woman is still there, blessing away indefatigably. She must possess, to a remarkable degree, those clinging qualities men praise in woman. Indeed, her tendrils twine all over the house; and when, through deep plots against a dear friend, we manage to lead her out of our own apartment, it is not long before, through our dear friend's counter-plots, the old woman stands again in our doorway with her great basket on her head, smiling and weeping and bobbing and blessing as she offers her wares. Queer old woman, rare old plant!—though you cannot be said to beautify, yet, twining and clinging and staying forever like the ivy-green, you were not so attractive as the little shadowy kings, but you, too, heralded Christmas; and may you have had a comfortable time somewhere with sausage and whatever is nearest your heart in these your latter days! That she is not a poetical figure in the Christmas picture is neither her fault nor mine. She may, ages ago, have had a thrilling story, now completely drowned in *schnapps,* but that she exists, and sells cakes according to the manner described, is all we ever shall know of her.

Then the cakes themselves—"genuine Nurembergers," she called them—were strange things to behold. Solid and brown, of manifold shapes and sizes, wrapped in silver-paper, they looked impenetrable and mysterious. The friends in council each seized a huge round one with an air as of sailing off on a voyage of discovery, or of storming a fortress, and nibbled away at it. As a massive whole it was strange and foreign, but familiar things were gradually evolved. There was now and then a trace of honey, a bit of an almond, a slice of citron, a flavor of vanilla, a soupcon of orange.

Gazing out from behind her cake, one young woman remarks, sententiously,—

"It's gingerbread with things in it."
Another stops in her investigations with,—

"It is as hard as a brownstone front."

"It's delightful not to know in the least what's coming next," says another. "I've just reached a stratum of jelly and am going deeper. Farewell."

"Echt Nürnberger, echt Nürnberger!" croaked the old dame, still nodding, still blessing; and so, meditatively eating her cakes, we gazed at her and wondered if any one could possibly be as old as she looked, and if she too were a product of "Nuremberg the ancient," to which "quaint old town of toil and traffic" we wandered off through the medium of Longfellow's poem, as every conscientious American in Europe is in duty bound to do. It is always a comfort to go where he has led the way. We are sure of experiencing the proper emotions. They are gently and quietly instilled into us, and we never know they do not come of themselves, until we happen to realize that some verse of his, familiar to our childhood, has been haunting us all the time. What a pity he never has written a poetical guide-book!

These unusual objects penetrating our quiet study hours told us Christmas was coming, and the aspect of the Stuttgart streets also proclaimed the glad tidings. They were a charming, merry sight. The Christmas fair extended its huge length of booths and tables through the narrow, quaint streets by the old *Stiftskirche,* reaching even up to the *Königstrasse,* where great piles of furniture rose by the pavements, threatening destruction to the passer-by. Thronging about the tables, where everything in the world was for sale and all the world was buying, could be seen many a dainty little lady in a costume fresh from Paris; many a ruddy peasant-girl with braids and bodice, short gown and bright stockings; many types of feature, and much confusion of tongues; and you are crowded and jostled: but you like it all, for every face wears the happy Christmas look that says so much.

These fairs are curious places, and have a benumbing effect upon the brain. People come home with the most unheard-of purchases, which they never seriously intended to buy. Perhaps a similar impulse to that which makes one grasp a common inkstand in a burning house, and run and deposit it far away in a place of safety, leads ladies to come from the "Messe" with a wooden comb and a string of yellow-glass beads. In both cases the intellect is temporarily absent, it would seem. Buy you must, of course. What you buy, whether it be a white wooden chair, or a child's toy, or a broom, or a lace barbe, or a blue-glass breastpin, seems to be pure chance. The country people, who come into the city especially to buy, know what they want, and no doubt make judicious purchases. But we, who go to gaze, to wonder, and to be amused, never know why we buy anything, and, when we come home and recover our senses, look at one another in amazement over our motley collections.

At this last fair a kind fate led us to a photograph table, where old French beauties smiled at us, and all of Henry the Eighth's hapless wives gazed at us from their ruffs, and the old Greek philosophers looked as if they could tell us a thing or two if they only would. The discovery of this haven in the sea of incongruous things around us was a fortunate accident. The photograph-man was henceforth our magnet. To him our little family, individually and collectively, drifted, and day by day the stock of Louise de la Vallieres, and Maintenons, and Heloises, and Anne Boleyns, and Pompadours, and Sapphos, and Socrates, and Diogenes, etc.,—(perfect likenesses of all of them, I am sure!)—increased in our *pension,* where we compared purchases between the courses at dinner, and made Archimedes and the duchess of Lamballe stand amicably side by side against the soup-tureen. Halcyon, but, alas! fleeting days, when we could buy these desirable works of art for ten *pfennig,* which, I mention with satisfaction, is two and one half cents!

But, of all the Christmas sights, the Christmas-trees and' the dolls were the most striking. The trees marched about like Birnam Wood coming to Dunsinane. There were solid family men going off with solid, respectable trees, and servants in livery condescending to stalk away with trees of the most lofty and aristocratic stature; and many a poor woman dragging along a sickly, stunted child with one hand and a sickly, stunted tree with the other.

As to the doll-world into which I have recently been permitted to penetrate, all language, even aided by a generous use of exclamation-points, fails to express its wondrous charm. A doll kindergarten, with desks and models and blackboards, had a competent, amiable, and elderly doll-instructress with spectacles. The younger members were occupied with toys and diversions that would not fatigue their infant minds, while the older ones pored over their books. They had white pinafores, flaxen hair, plump cheeks. I think they were all alive.

Then there were dolls who looked as if they lay on the sofa all day and read French novels, and dolls that looked as if they were up with the birds, hard-working, merry, and wise,—elegant, aristocratic countess dolls, with trunks of fine raiment; and jolly little peasant dolls, with long yellow braids hanging down their backs, and stout shoes, and a general look of having trudged in from the Black Forest to see the great city-world at Christmas. Such variety of expression, so many phases of doll-nature, —for nature they have in Germany! And in front of two especially alluring windows, where bright lights streamed upon fanciful decorations, toys, and a wonderful world of dolls, was always a great group of children. Once, in the early evening, they fairly blockaded the pavement and reached far into the street, wide-eyed, open-mouthed, not talking much, merely devouring those enchanted windows with their eager eyes; some wishing, some not daring to wish, but worshipping only, like pale, rapt devotees. And we others, who labor under the disadvantage of being "grown up," looked at the pretty doll-world within the windows and the lovely child-world without, and wished that old Christmas might bring to each of us the doll we want, and never, never let us know that it is stuffed with sawdust.

A Portfolio of

HOLIDAY
DECORATIONS

(Drawings by Lucy Ellen Merrill
in the Nineteenth Century)

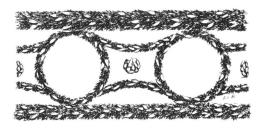

WHEN the December issue of *Godey's Lady's Book* appeared in 1850, that old German custom, the Christmas tree, became a conversation piece all across America. Sarah Josepha Hale, the editor, had "borrowed" a picture from *The Illustrated London News* and entitled it "The Christmas tree—a new American custom." In the years that followed, churches and homes were decorated lavishly with colorful trees and greens of every description, accentuated with red berries, cones, and dried seed pods. "Bringing home Christmas" meant gathering greens with all the family participating. Charles Dickens, with his "Christmas Carol" and other holiday stories, had been largely responsible for the revival of this feast of the heart and the home. Even in Puritan New England, Christmas was observed with great warmth and enthusiasm, highlighted by the most elaborate kinds of decorations.

In the historic town of Newburyport, Massachusetts, Miss Lucy Ellen Merrill, who made a career for herself painting the portraits of local dignitaries, sketching scenes of the area, and giving drawing lessons, has left to posterity a vivid record of the fancy decor of the period. It is believed that the drawings were made about 1870 to illustrate a book entitled "Merry Christmas," which had been planned by Anna Gardner Hale, a local poetess, but the volume was apparently never published. The portfolio of pen-and-ink drawings, delineated in careful detail, contained notes identifying all the greens used. In 1958 the folder containing these sketches, owned by the Historical Society of Old Newbury, was used as the inspiration for the Christmas decorations at the Society's headquarters. The photographs tell this part of the story.

At a time when tinsel, glitter, and baubles were unknown, laurel leaves, sprigs of pine, cedar and hemlock, bittersweet berries, trailing stems of ground pine, ferns, thistle heads, clematis plumes and other wildings were used to make elaborate patterns and tracery around doorways, on mantles, dadoes, and window frames, and wherever space was available for adornment. A number of the original drawings and the decorations adapted from them appear in the following pages. Others are scattered at intervals throughout the book.

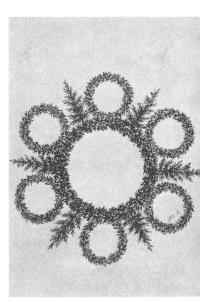

Lucretia Peabody Hale

LUCRETIA PEABODY HALE was one of those extraordinary Boston spinsters who was born in the Athens of America, lived eighty years, and died in the city of her birth. The number eighty has a magical significance in her life story. *The Peterkin Papers,* which made all America laugh when they were published and continued to be favorites for several generations, were first published in the year 1880. Eighty years after the publication of the first of *The Peterkin Papers* they were brought out in complete form by her great-niece, Nancy Hale.

Miss Hale was a member of a distinguished New England family, and counted among her brothers and sisters several celebrated personages. Her brother, Edward Everett Hale, became a noted Unitarian minister and editor and author. Best known of his books was *A Man Without a Country.* He also wrote many Christmas stories, but they have little appeal for present-day readers. Another brother, Charles Hale, served as Consul-General to Egypt at the time of the opening of the Suez Canal. Both Lucretia and her spinster sister Susan, who was also a noted writer, made a trip to Egypt to see their brother. This was probably the only extended trip Miss Hale ever made, for there was no point in going beyond the boundaries of Boston, since everything important in the world was centered there—the Hub of the Universe.

Miss Hale's inimitable stories appeared first as a series in a magazine known as *Our Young Folks,* which later became the famous *St. Nicholas.* The Peterkins were known to children and grownups all over America in their day. In fact, the name "Peterkin" became a household word. As Nancy Hale puts it, "They were funny—it is probable that their saga constituted the first nonsense writing done for children in America—and they seemed, in some odd way, universal. In laughing at them, America was somehow laughing at itself."

Like many another writer of her day, Miss Hale was ever aware of some of the more amusing aspects of Victorian primness. The desire of parents to dominate every member of the family often stifled the ambitions of the younger set. To quote Nancy Hale again, "There were those even in good Victoria's golden days who felt their talents being dissolved and their individuality foundering in the swamp of nineteenth century togetherness." Lucretia may well have experienced some of this frustration. At any rate, she has written a fascinating account of the amusing idiosyncrasies of the Victorian way of doing things. Not the least of the inimitable tales was "The Peterkins' Christmas Tree," a charming story to read aloud.

THE PETERKINS' CHRISTMAS TREE

EARLY in autumn the Peterkins began to prepare for their Christmas tree. Everything was done in great privacy, as it was to be a surprise to the neighbors, as well as to the rest of the family. Mr. Peterkin had been up to Mr. Bromwick's woodlot, and, with his consent, selected the tree. Agamemnon went to look at it occasionally after dark, and Solomon John made frequent visits to it mornings, just after sunrise. Mr. Peterkin drove Elizabeth Eliza and her mother that way, and pointed furtively to it with his whip; but none of them ever spoke of it to each other. It was suspected that the little boys had been to see it Wednesday and Saturday afternoons. But they came home with their pockets full of chestnuts, and said nothing about it.

At length Mr. Peterkin had it cut down and brought secretly into the Larkins' barn. A week or two before Christmas a measurement was made of it with Elizabeth Eliza's yard-measure. To Mr. Peterkin's great dismay it was discovered that it was too high to stand in the back parlor.

This fact was brought out at a secret council of Mr. and Mrs. Peterkin, Elizabeth Eliza, and Agamemnon.

Agamemnon suggested that it might be set up slanting; but Mrs. Peterkin was very sure it would make her dizzy, and the candles would drip.

But a brilliant idea came to Mr. Peterkin. He proposed that the ceiling of the parlor should be raised to make room for the top of the tree.

Elizabeth Eliza thought the space would need to be quite large. It must not be like a small box, or you could not see the tree.

"Yes," said Mr. Peterkin, "I should have the ceiling lifted all across the room; the effect would be finer."

Elizabeth Eliza objected to having the whole ceiling raised, because her room was over the back parlor, and she would have no floor while the alteration was going on, which would be very awkward. Besides, her room was not very high now, and, if the floor were raised, perhaps she could not walk in it upright.

Mr. Peterkin explained that he didn't propose altering the whole ceiling, but to lift up a ridge across the room at the back part where the tree was to stand. This would make a hump, to be sure, in Elizabeth Eliza's room; but it would go across the whole room.

Elizabeth Eliza said she would not mind that. It would be like the cuddy thing that comes up on the deck of a ship, that you sit against, only here you would not have the sea-sickness. She thought she should like it, for a rarity. She might use it for a divan.

Mrs. Peterkin thought it would come in the worn place of the carpet, and might be a convenience in making the carpet over.

Agamemnon was afraid there would be

trouble in keeping the matter secret, for it would be a long piece of work for a carpenter; but Mr. Peterkin proposed having the carpenter for a day or two, for a number of other jobs.

One of them was to make all the chairs in the house of the same height, for Mrs. Peterkin had nearly broken her spine by sitting down in a chair that she had supposed was her own rocking chair, and it had proved to be two inches lower. The little boys were now large enough to sit in any chair; so a medium was fixed upon to satisfy all the family, and the chairs were made uniformly of the same height.

On consulting the carpenter, however, he insisted that the tree could be cut off at the lower end to suit the height of the parlor, and demurred at so great a change as altering the ceiling. But Mr. Peterkin had set his mind upon the improvement, and Elizabeth Eliza had cut her carpet in preparation for it.

So the folding-doors into the back parlor were closed, and for nearly a fortnight before Christmas there was great litter of fallen plastering, and laths, and chips, and shavings; and Elizabeth Eliza's carpet was taken up, and the furniture had to be changed, and one night she had to sleep at the Bromwicks', for there was a long hole in her floor that might be dangerous.

All this delighted the little boys. They could not understand what was going on. Perhaps they suspected a Christmas tree, but they did not know why a Christmas tree should have so many chips, and were still more astonished at the hump that appeared in Elizabeth Eliza's room. It must be a Christmas present, or else the tree in a box.

Some aunts and uncles, too, arrived a day or two before Christmas, with some small cousins. These cousins occupied the attention of the little boys, and there was a great deal of whispering and mystery, behind doors, and under the stairs, and in the corners of the entry.

Solomon John was busy, privately making some candles for the tree. He had been collecting some bayberries, as he understood they made very nice candles, so that it would not be necessary to buy any.

The elders of the family never all went into the back parlor together, and all tried not to see what was going on. Mrs. Peterkin would go in with Solomon John, or Mr. Peterkin with Elizabeth Eliza, or Elizabeth Eliza and Agamemnon and Solomon John. The little boys and the small cousins were never allowed even to look inside the room.

Elizabeth Eliza meanwhile went into town a number of times. She wanted to consult Amanda as to how much ice cream they should need, and whether they could make it at home, as they had cream and ice. She was pretty busy in her own room; the furniture had to be changed, and the carpet altered. The "hump" was higher than she expected. There was danger of bumping her own head whenever she crossed it. She had to nail some padding on the ceiling for fear of accidents.

The afternoon before Christmas, Elizabeth Eliza, Solomon John, and their father collected in the back parlor for a council. The carpenters had done their work, and the tree stood at its full height at the back of the room, the top stretching up into the space arranged for it. All the chips and shavings were cleared away, and it stood on a neat box.

But what were they to put upon the tree?

Solomon John had brought in his supply of candles; but they proved to be very "stringy" and very few of them. It was strange how many bayberries it took to make a few candles! The little boys had helped him, and he had gathered as much as a bushel of bayberries. He had put them in water, and skimmed off the wax, according to the directions; but there was so little wax!

Solomon John had given the little boys some of the bits sawed off from the legs of the chairs. He had suggested that they should cover them with gilt paper, to answer for gilt apples, without telling them what they were for.

These apples, a little blunt at the end, and the candles, were all they had for the tree!

After all her trips into town Elizabeth Eliza had forgotten to bring anything for it.

"I thought of candies and sugar plums," she said; "but I concluded if we made caramels ourselves we should not need them. But, then, we have not made caramels. The fact is, that day my head was full of my carpet. I had bumped it pretty badly, too."

Mr. Peterkin wished he had taken, instead of a fir tree, an apple tree he had seen in October, full of red fruit.

"But the leaves would have fallen off by this time," said Elizabeth Eliza.

"And the apples, too," said Solomon John.

"It is odd I should have forgotten, that day I went in on purpose to get the things," said Elizabeth Eliza, musingly. "But I went from shop to shop, and didn't know exactly what to get. I saw a great many gilt things for Christmas trees; but I knew the little boys were making the gilt apples; there were plenty of candles in the shops, but I knew Solomon John was making the candles."

Mr. Peterkin thought it was quite natural.

Solomon John wondered if it were too late for them to go into town now.

Elizabeth Eliza could not go in the next morning, for there was to be a grand Christmas dinner, and Mr. Peterkin could not be spared, and Solomon John was sure he and Agamemnon would not know what to buy. Besides, they would want to try the candles tonight.

Mr. Peterkin asked if the presents everybody had been preparing would not answer. But Elizabeth Eliza knew they would be too heavy.

A gloom came over the room. There was only a flickering gleam from one of Solomon John's candles that he had lighted by way of trial.

Solomon John again proposed going into town. He lighted a match to examine the newspaper about the trains. There were plenty of trains coming out at that hour, but none going in except a very late one. That would not leave time to do anything and come back.

"We could go in, Elizabeth Eliza and I," said Solomon John, "but we should not have time to buy anything."

Agamemnon was summoned in. Mrs. Peterkin was entertaining the uncles and aunts in the front parlor. Agamemnon wished there was time to study up something about electric lights. If they could only have a calcium light! Solomon John's candle sputtered and went out.

At this moment there was a loud knocking at the front door. The little boys, and the small cousins, and the uncles and aunts, and Mrs. Peterkin, hastened to see what was the matter.

The uncles and aunts thought somebody's house must be on fire. The door was opened, and there was a man, white with flakes, for it was beginning to snow, and he was pulling in a large box.

Mrs. Peterkin supposed it contained some of Elizabeth Eliza's purchases, so she ordered it to be pushed into the back parlor, and hastily called back her guests and the little boys into the other room. The little boys and the small cousins were sure they had seen Santa Claus himself.

Mr. Peterkin lighted the gas. The box was addressed to Elizabeth Eliza. It was from the lady from Philadelphia! She had gathered a hint from Elizabeth Eliza's letters that there was to be a Christmas tree, and had filled this box with all that would be needed.

It was opened directly. There was every kind of gilt hanging-thing, from gilt peapods to butterflies on springs. There were shining flags and lanterns, and bird-cages, and nests with birds sitting on them, baskets of fruit, gilt apples and bunches of grapes, and, at the bottom of the whole, a large box of candles and a box of Philadelphia bonbons!

Elizabeth Eliza and Solomon John could scarcely keep from screaming. The little boys and the small cousins knocked on the folding-doors to ask what was the matter.

Hastily Mr. Peterkin and the rest took out the things and hung them on the tree, and put on the candles.

When all was done, it looked so well that Mr. Peterkin exclaimed:

"Let us light the candles now, and send to invite all the neighbors tonight, and have the tree on Christmas Eve!"

And so it was that the Peterkins had their Christmas tree the day before, and on Christmas night could go and visit their neighbors.

Laura E. Richards

LAURA E. Richards was born in 1850 and died in 1943. At the age of ninety-three, she had written over ninety books, most of them for children. Her father was Samuel Gridley Howe, noted philanthropist who founded Perkins Institution for the Blind, and pioneered in helping handicapped children. Her mother was Julia Ward Howe, whose writings were widely known, among them "The Battle Hymn of the Republic," written during the Civil War.

Laura was named for Laura Bridgman, a child who was deaf and blind and was brought into contact with the world through the efforts of Mr. Howe. From the beginning, Laura Richards had a background destined to be great in its influence over the minds and hearts of children. Through all the years of her rich and stimulating life, she never lost the spirit of youth. She loved books, and knew only too well their value in molding the thoughts of young people.

It was in *Four Feet, Two Feet and No Feet,* published in 1885, that "A Letter from a Christmas Turkey" appeared. This was "a venture into the realm of natural history, where I did not really belong," she wrote. However, she depended on her husband's knowledge of the wonders of nature, and her gift of telling what she knew with childish delight made her a model of what she believed was the aim of life. Her philosophy at the age of ninety was "to learn, to teach, to serve, to enjoy."

Three generations of children and their parents knew her name, and read her delightful stories and equally delightful books of nonsense. Laura E. Richards was one of those fabulous Victorians whose knowledge was even more varied than the things she wrote about, and her vital creative spirit burned a long, long time.

A LETTER FROM A CHRISTMAS TURKEY

DEAR Little Ones:—

A very suspicious-looking man came into the barn-yard the other day. He looked all around among my brothers and cousins. Then he pointed at me and said I was a nice, big fellow. This made me feel very proud.

When he put his hand into his pocket I supposed he was going to give me some corn. Instead of that he counted out money to my master. Then I knew he would take me away, and I began gobbling good-by to my relatives and friends of the barn-yard.

Now I am alone in the little pen he brought me to. I have been thinking of all this fuss over me, and having so many good things to eat must mean something.

I gobbled to some other fowls running about in a yard, and found out from them that it was almost Christmas-time.

Now let me ease your tender little hearts about my career being so suddenly cut short. I want to tell you that in Turkeydom it is considered a great glory to be the centre of attraction at a Christmas dinner-table; to be dressed up in a nice brown coat; to be surrounded by sparkling jellies, rich cranberry sauce, and all the other good things; to hear the children cry, "Oh! Oh!" and the papas and mamas say, "What a fine turkey!" This is what we live for, my little dears. So, when I have gobbled my last gobble, don't be sorry for

Yours, when fat,

TURKEY GOBBLER

William Dean Howells

OFTEN referred to as "the father of American realism," William Dean Howells was an outstanding literary figure in the last half of the 19th century. Author, editor, poet, he was born in Ohio in 1837, and went to Boston at an early age, where he spent more than twenty years. His novels, his critical works, his verse, and his drama brought him great distinction during his lifetime. He had strong opinions about style in writing and the young writers who attempted to express their thoughts with vigor and enthusiasm. He always succeeded in making his own characters real. One of his best-known books was *The Rise of Silas Lapham*.

As an Editor of *Atlantic* he was intimately associated with Thomas Bailey Aldrich, and they shared many pleasant associations with the literary fraternity in Boston. Later he became associated with *Harper's Monthly* in New York. The author of forty novels, Howells also wrote short stories, drama, verse, travel books, literary criticisms, and an autobiography. His influence on Mark Twain and other leading writers of the period was considerable.

That he should have written the delightful story "Christmas Every Day" for *St. Nicholas*, "the magazine that for generations gladdened the hearts of children," is indicated by his versatility as a writer and his genial personality. It was largely autobiographical and, in a broad measure, is typical of the kind of amusement which parents used to think essential to provide for their children. The art of storytelling came into full flower in Victorian days in the midst of a great flood of books and magazines published for everyone old enough to hold a book or curious enough to listen to a tale being told.

CHRISTMAS EVERY DAY

THE little girl came into her papa's study, as she always did Saturday morning before breakfast, and asked for a story. He tried to beg off that morning, for he was very busy, but she would not let him. So he began:

"Well, once there was a little pig—"

She put her hand over his mouth and stopped him at the word. She said she had heard little pig stories till she was perfectly sick of them.

"Well, what kind of story *shall* I tell, then?"

"About Christmas. It's getting to be the season. It's past Thanksgiving already."

"It seems to me," argued her papa, "that I've told as often about Christmas as I have about little pigs."

"No difference! Christmas is more interesting."

"Well!" Her papa roused himself from his writing by a great effort. "Well, then, I'll tell you about the little girl that wanted it Christmas every day in the year. How would you like that?"

"First-rate!" said the little girl; and she nestled into comfortable shape in his lap, ready for listening.

"Very well, then, this little pig,—Oh, what are you pounding me for?"

"Because you said little pig instead of little girl."

"I should like to know what's the difference between a little pig and a little girl that wanted it Christmas every day!"

"Papa," said the little girl, warningly, "if you don't go on, I'll *give* it to you!" And at this her papa darted off like lightning, and began to tell the story as fast as he could.

Well, once there was a little girl who liked Christmas so much that she wanted it to be Christmas every day in the year; and as soon as Thanksgiving was over she began to send postal cards to the old Christmas Fairy to ask if she mightn't

have it. But the old Fairy never answered any of the postals; and, after a while, the little girl found out that the Fairy was pretty particular, and wouldn't notice anything but letters, not even correspondence cards in envelopes; but real letters on sheets of paper, and sealed outside with a monogram,—or your initial, any way. So, then, she began to send her letters; and in about three weeks—or just the day before Christmas, it was—she got a letter from the Fairy, saying she might have it Christmas every day for a year, and then they would see about having it longer.

The little girl was a good deal excited already, preparing for the old-fashioned, once-a-year Christmas that was coming the next day, and perhaps the Fairy's promise didn't make such an impression on her as it would have made at some other time. She just resolved to keep it to herself, and surprise everybody with it as it kept coming true; and then it slipped out of her mind altogether.

She had a splendid Christmas. She went to bed early, so as to let Santa Claus have a chance at the stockings, and in the morning she was up the first of anybody and went and felt them, and found hers all lumpy with packages of candy, and oranges and grapes, and pocket-books and rubber balls and all kinds of small presents, and her big brother's with nothing but the tongs in them, and her young lady sister's with a new silk umbrella, and her papa's and mama's with potatoes and pieces of coal wrapped up in tissue paper, just as they always had every Christmas. Then she waited around till the rest of the family were up, and she was the first to burst into the library, when the doors were opened, and look at the large presents laid out on the library-table—books, and portfolios, and boxes of stationery, and breast-pins, and dolls, and little stoves, and dozens of handkerchiefs, and ink-stands, and skates, and snow-shovels, and photograph-frames, and little easels, and boxes of water-colors, and Turkish paste, and nougat, and candied cherries, and dolls' houses, and waterproofs,—and the big Christmas-tree, lighted and standing in a waste-basket in the middle.

She had a splendid Christmas all day. She ate so much candy that she did not want any breakfast; and the whole forenoon the presents kept pouring in that the expressman had not had time to deliver the night before; and she went 'round giving the presents she had got for other people, and came home and ate turkey and cranberry for dinner, and plum-pudding and nuts and raisins and oranges and more candy, and then went out and coasted and came in with a stomach-ache, crying; and her papa said he would see if his house was turned into that sort of fool's paradise another year; and they had a light supper, and pretty early everybody went to bed cross.

Here the little girl pounded her papa in the back, again.

"Well, what now? Did I say pigs?"

"You made them *act* like pigs."

"Well, didn't they?"

"No matter; you oughtn't to put it into a story."

"Very well, then, I'll take it all out."

Her father went on:

The little girl slept very heavily, and she slept very late, but she was wakened at last by the other children dancing 'round her bed with their stockings full of presents in their hands.

"What is it?" said the little girl. and she rubbed her eyes and tried to rise up in bed.

"Christmas! Christmas! Christmas!" they all shouted, and waved their stockings.

"Nonsense! It was Christmas yesterday."

Her brothers and sisters just laughed. "We don't know about that. It's Christmas to-day, any way. You come into the library and see."

Then all at once it flashed on the little girl that the Fairy was keeping her promise, and her year of Christmases was beginning.

She was dreadfully sleepy, but she sprang up like a lark—a lark that had overeaten itself and gone to bed cross—and darted into the library. There it was again! Books, and portfolios, and boxes of stationery, and breast-pins—

"You needn't go over it all, Papa; I guess I can remember just what was there," said the little girl.

Well, and there was the Christmas-tree blazing away, and the family picking out their presents, but looking pretty sleepy, and her father perfectly puzzled, and her mother ready to cry. "I'm sure I don't see how I'm to dispose of all these things," said her mother, and her father said it seemed to him they had had something just like it the day before, but he supposed he must have dreamed it. This struck the little girl as the best kind of a joke; and so she ate so much candy she didn't want any breakfast, and went 'round carrying presents, and had turkey and cranberry for dinner, and then went out and coasted, and came in with a—

"Papa!"

"Well, what now?"

"What did you promise, you forgetful thing?"

"Oh! oh, yes!"

Well, the next day, it was just the same thing over again, but everybody getting crosser; and at the end of a week's time so many people had lost their tempers that you could pick up lost tempers anywhere; they perfectly strewed the ground. Even when people tried to recover their tempers they usually got somebody else's, and it made the most dreadful mix.

The little girl began to get frightened, keeping the secret all to herself; she wanted to tell her mother, but she didn't dare to; and she was ashamed to ask the Fairy to take back her gift, it seemed ungrateful and ill-bred, and she thought she would try to stand it, but she hardly knew how she could, for a whole year. So it went on and on, and it was Christmas on St. Valentine's Day, and Washington's Birthday just the same as any day, and it didn't skip even the First of April, though everything was counterfeit that day, and that was some *little* relief.

After a while, coal and potatoes began to be awfully scarce, so many had been wrapped up in tissue paper to fool papas and mammas with. Turkeys got to be about a thousand dollars apiece—

"Papa!"

"Well, what?"

"You're beginning to fib."

"Well, *two* thousand, then."

And they got to passing off almost anything for turkeys,—half-grown humming-birds, and even rocs out of the "Arabian Nights,"— the real turkeys were so scarce. And cranberries—well, they asked a diamond apiece for cranberries. All the woods and orchards were cut down for Christmas-trees, and where the woods and orchards used to be, it looked just like a stubble-field, with the stumps. After a while they had to make Christmas-trees out of rags, and stuff them with bran, like old-fashioned dolls; but there were plenty of rags, because people got so poor, buying presents for one another, that they couldn't get any new clothes, and they just wore their old ones to tatters. They got so poor that everybody had to go to the poor-house, except the confectioners, and the fancy store-keepers, and the picture-booksellers, and the expressmen; and *they* all got so rich and proud that they would hardly wait upon a person when he came to buy; it was perfectly shameful!

Well, after it had gone on about three or four months, the little girl, whenever she came into the room in the morning and saw those great ugly lumpy stockings dangling at the fire-place, and the disgusting presents around everywhere, used to just sit down and burst out crying. In six months she was perfectly exhausted; she couldn't even cry any more; she just lay on the lounge and rolled her eyes and panted. About the beginning of October she took to sitting down on dolls, wherever she found them, —French dolls, or any kind,—she hated the sight of them so; and by Thanksgiving she was crazy, and just slammed her presents across the room.

By that time people didn't carry presents around nicely any more. They flung them over the fence, or through the window, or anything; and, instead of running their tongues out and taking great pains to write "For dear · Papa," or "Mamma," or "Brother," or "Sister," or "Susie," or "Sammie," or "Billie," or "Bobby," or "Jimmie," or "Jennie," or whoever it was, and troubling to get the spelling right, and then signing their names, and "Xmas, 188–," they used to write in the gift-books, "Take it, you horrid old thing!" and then go and bang it against the front door. Nearly everybody had built barns to hold their presents, but pretty soon the barns overflowed, and then they used to let them lie out in the rain, or anywhere. Sometimes the police used to come and tell them to shovel their presents off the sidewalk, or they would arrest them.

"I thought you said everybody had gone to the poor-house," interrupted the little girl.

"They did go, at first," said her papa; "but after a while the poor-houses got so full that they had to send the people back to their own houses. They tried to cry, when they got back, but they couldn't make the least sound."

"Why couldn't they?"

"Because they had lost their voices, saying 'Merry Christmas' so much. Did I tell you how it was on the Fourth of July?"

"No; how was it?" And the little girl nestled closer, in expectation of something uncommon.

Well, the night before, the boys staid up to celebrate, as they always do, and fell asleep before twelve o'clock, as usual, expecting to be wakened by the bells and cannon. But it was nearly eight o'clock before the first boy in the United States woke up, and then he found out what the trouble was. As soon as he could get his clothes on, he ran out of the house and smashed a big cannon-torpedo down on the pavement; but it didn't make any more noise than a damp wad of paper, and, after he tried about twenty or thirty more, he began to pick them up and look at them.

Every single torpedo was a big raisin! Then he just streaked it upstairs, and examined his fire-crackers and toy-pistol and two-dollar collection of fireworks, and found that they were nothing but sugar and candy painted up to look like fireworks! Before ten o'clock, every boy in the United States found out that his Fourth of July things had turned into Christmas things; and then they just sat down and cried,— they were so mad. There are about twenty million boys in the United States, and so you can imagine what a noise they made. Some men got together before night, with a little powder that hadn't turned into purple sugar yet, and they said they would fire off *one* cannon, any way. But the cannon burst into a thousand pieces, for it was nothing but rock-candy, and some of the men nearly got killed. The Fourth of July orations all turned into Christmas carols, and when anybody tried to read the Declaration, instead of saying, "When in the course of human events it becomes necessary," he was sure to sing, "God rest you, merry gentlemen." It was awful.

The little girl drew a deep sigh of satisfaction.

"And how was it at Thanksgiving?" she asked.

Her papa hesitated. "Well, I'm almost afraid to tell you. I'm afraid you'll think it's wicked."

"Well, tell, any way," said the little girl.

Well, before it came Thanksgiving, it had leaked out who had caused all these Christmases. The little girl had suffered so much that she had talked about it in her sleep; and after that, hardly anybody would play with her. People just perfectly despised her, because if it had not been for her greediness, it wouldn't have happened; and now, when it came Thanksgiving, and she wanted them to go to church, and have squash-pie and turkey, and show their gratitude, they said that all the turkeys had been eaten up for her old Christmas dinners, and if she would stop the Christmases, they would see about the gratitude. Wasn't it dreadful? And the very next day the

little girl began to send letters to the Christmas Fairy, and then telegrams, to stop it. But it didn't do any good; and then she got to calling at the Fairy's house, but the girl that came to the door always said "Not at home," or "Engaged," or "At dinner," or something like that; and so it went on till it came to the old once-a-year Christmas Eve. The little girl fell asleep, and when she woke up in the morning—

"She found it was all nothing but a dream," suggested the little girl.

"No, indeed!" said her papa. "It was all every bit true!"

"Well, what *did* she find out then?"

"Why, that it wasn't Christmas at last, and wasn't ever going to be, any more. Now it's time for breakfast."

The little girl held her papa fast around the neck.

"You sha'n't go if you're going to leave it *so!*"

"How do you want it left?"

"Christmas once a year."

"All right," said her papa; and he went on again.

Well, there was the greatest rejoicing all over the country, and it extended clear up into Canada. The people met together everywhere, and kissed and cried for joy. The city carts went around and gathered up all the candy and raisins and nuts, and dumped them into the river; and it made the fish perfectly sick; and the whole United States, as far out as Alaska, was one blaze of bonfires, where the children were burning up their gift-books and presents. They had the greatest *time!*

The little girl went to thank the old Fairy because she had stopped its being Christmas, and she said she hoped she would keep her promise, and see that Christmas never, never came again. Then the Fairy frowned, and asked her if she was sure she knew what she meant; and the little girl asked her, why not? and the old Fairy said that now she was behaving just as greedily as ever, and she'd better look out. This made the little girl think it all over carefully again, and she said she would be willing to have it Christmas about once in a thousand years; and then she said a hundred, and then she said ten, and at last she got down to one. Then the Fairy said that was the good old way that had pleased people ever since Christmas began, and she was agreed. Then the little girl said, "What're your shoes made of?" And the Fairy said, "Leather." And the little girl said, "Bargain's done forever," and skipped off, and hippity-hopped the whole way home, she was so glad.

"How will that do?" asked the papa.

"First-rate!" said the little girl; but she hated to have the story stop, and was rather sober. However, her mamma put her head in at the door, and asked her papa:

"Are you never coming to breakfast? What have you been telling that child?"

"Oh, just a moral tale."

The little girl caught him around the neck again.

"*We* know! Don't you tell *what,* Papa! Don't you tell *what!*"

Kate Douglas Wiggin

CHARLES DICKENS had been dead for sixteen years when Kate Douglas Wiggin wrote "The Birds' Christmas Carol." What joy he would have had reading this heart-warming story by the little girl he had chatted with on the train on that March day in 1868 when he was traveling to Boston from Portland, Maine, where he had given a lecture the night before. Kate told the story with great gusto in her biography, *My Garden of Memory,* and in a little book, *A Child's Journey with Dickens.* She spoke of Dickens as "the Adored One" and she knew him at once when she glimpsed him on the platform, with his hands plunged deep in his pockets. What she remembered was "the smiling, genial, mobile face, rather highly colored, the brilliant eyes, the watch-chain, the red carnation in the buttonhole, and the expressive hands much given to gesture."

On that memorable trip little Kate managed to sit next to Dickens, who put his arm around her and even held her hand. She deigned to tell him of how well she knew his books and how she had read *David Copperfield* six times. She spoke of those she liked best, and confessed that she skipped some of the dull passages as she read.

They talked of dogs and reading and Mr. Dickens' own characters as the train sped to Boston. In fact, they discussed those passages which brought tears to their eyes, and Kate learned that Dickens cried when he wrote *The Christmas Carol* and every time he read it in public. Kate's own story has had a similar effect on readers ever since it was published in 1888. Charles Dickens left his imprint on her very soul in "The Birds' Christmas Carol," for she too wrote a classic.

Kate Douglas Wiggin was born in Philadelphia in 1859 and spent her girlhood in Maine, then traveled to San Francisco, where she organized the first free kindergarten for poor children west of the Rockies. One of the great pioneers in kindergarten work, her writings in that field were considered authoritative. After writing "The Birds' Christmas Carol," she went on to do such books as *Rebecca of Sunny-*

brook Farm, The Old Peabody Pew, Mother Carey's Chickens, and many others, which were widely read and greatly loved. Even more important was her influence and inspiration with other writers of juveniles in her day and for years to follow.

At the age of seventeen, Mrs. Wiggin wrote her first story for *St. Nicholas* magazine, and was paid one hundred and fifty dollars. She was naturally elated and encouraged. However, she soon became engrossed in establishing a kindergarten in a section of San Francisco known as Tar Flat. Recalling the experience in later years, she wrote: "I was too busy with living to think of writing. I was happy in my woman's way (I fear at first it was but a girl's way) to do my share of the world's work, and it absorbed all my energies of body, mind and soul. But though the public was generous, there was never money enough! Fifty children under school age, between four and six years, were enrolled, but the procession of waiting mothers daily grew longer. Patrick's mother, Henri's, Levi's, Angelo's, Leo's, Katrina's, Selma's, Alexandrina's, stood outside the door asking when there would be room for more children.

"On a certain October day I wondered to myself if I could write a story, publish it in paper covers, and sell it here and there for a modest price, the profits to help toward the establishment of a second kindergarten. Preparations for Christmas were already in the air, and as I sat down at my desk in a holiday spirit I wrote in a few days my first real book, 'The Birds' Christmas Carol.'

"It was the simplest of all possible tales: the record of a lame child's life; a child born on Christmas Day, and named Carol by Mr. and Mrs. Bird, her father and mother. The dark ages in which I wrote were full of literary Herods who put to death all the young children in their vicinity, and I was no exception with my fragile little heroine. What saved me finally was a rudimentary sense of humor that flourished even in the life I was giving, a life in which I saw pain, cruelty and wickedness, struggling against the powers for good that lifted their heads here and there, battling courageously and often overcoming. If Carol Bird and her family were inclined to sentimentality (as I have reason to fear) the Ruggles brood, who lived in the rear, were perhaps a wholesome antidote. Mrs. Ruggles and the nine big, medium-sized and little Ruggleses who inhabited a small house in an alley that backed the Bird mansion—these furnished a study in contrast and gave a certain amount of fun to counteract my somewhat juvenile tendency to tears."

The story was privately printed in San Francisco in 1886, bound in paper covers and sold for the benefit of the Silver Street Kindergarten. Out of "languid curiosity," Kate sent her little paper-bound "Carol" to Houghton Mifflin Company in Boston. Mr. Henry O. Houghton, the senior member of the firm, took it home and read it to his family, whom he had assembled on a piazza on a summer day in 1888. He then took it to his office and declared he would publish it on his own if his associates didn't happen to like the story. They did like it, and "The Birds' Christmas Carol," which was published later that year, went through many, many editions. It was translated into several foreign languages, including Japanese, but nothing pleased the author more than its appearance in Braille. Because the "Carol" was frequently adapted for amateur theatricals, Mrs. Wiggin finally arranged it in dramatic form in 1914, and it has become a perennial favorite among adults and children.

In writing an introduction to a new edition of her book many years after it was first published, Mrs. Wiggin said: "You have been a good friend to me, my book —none better! It was you who eased my shoulder from the burden, who delivered my hands from making the pots. At the very first, you earned the wherewithal to take a group of children out of the confusion and danger of squalid streets, and transport them into a place of sunshine, safety and gladness. Then you took my hand and led me into the bigger crowded world where the public lives."

THE BIRDS' CHRISTMAS CAROL

IT WAS very early Christmas morning, and in the stillness of the dawn, with the soft snow falling on the housetops, a little child was born in the Bird household. They had intended to name the baby Lucy, if it were a girl; but they had not expected her on Christmas morning, and a real Christmas baby was not to be lightly named—the whole family agreed in that.

They were consulting about it in the nursery. Mr. Bird said that he had assisted in naming the three boys, and that he should leave this matter entirely to Mrs. Bird; Donald wanted the child called "Dorothy," after a pretty, curly-haired girl who sat next him in school; Paul chose "Luella," for Luella was the nurse who had been with him during his whole babyhood, up to the time of his first trousers, and the name suggested all sorts of comfortable things. Uncle Jack said that the first girl should always be named for her mother, no matter how hideous the name happened to be.

Grandma said that she would prefer not to take any part in the discussion, and everybody suddenly remembered that Mrs. Bird had thought of naming the baby Lucy, for Grandma herself; and, while it would be indelicate for her to favor that name, it would be against human nature for her to suggest any other, under the circumstances.

Hugh, the "hitherto baby," if that is a possible term, sat in one corner and said nothing, but felt, in some mysterious way, that his nose was out of joint; for there was a newer baby now, a possibility he had never taken into consideration; and the "first girl," too—a still higher development of treason, which made him actually green with jealousy.

But it was too profound a subject to be settled then and there, on the spot; besides, Mamma had not been asked, and everybody felt it rather absurd, after all, to forestall a decree that was certain to be absolutely wise, just, and perfect.

The reason that the subject had been brought up at all so early in the day lay in the fact that Mrs. Bird never allowed her babies to go over night unnamed. She was a person of so great decision of character that she would have blushed at such a thing; she said that to let blessed babies go dangling and dawdling about without names, for months and months, was enough to ruin them for life. She also said that if one could not make up one's mind in twenty-four hours it was a sign that— But I will not repeat the rest, as it might prejudice you against the most charming woman in the world.

So Donald took his new velocipede and went out to ride up and down the stone pavement and notch the shins of innocent people as they passed by, while Paul spun his musical top on the front steps.

But Hugh refused to leave the scene of

action. He seated himself on the top stair in the hall, banged his head against the railing a few times, just by way of uncorking the vials of his wrath, and then subsided into gloomy silence, waiting to declare war if more "first girl babies" were thrust upon a family already surfeited with that unnecessary article.

Meanwhile dear Mrs. Bird lay in her room, weak, but safe and happy, with her sweet girl baby by her side and the heaven of motherhood opening again before her. Nurse was making gruel in the kitchen, and the room was dim and quiet. There was a cheerful open fire in the grate, but though the shutters were closed, the side windows that looked out on the Church of Our Saviour, next door, were a little open.

Suddenly a sound of music poured out into the bright air and drifted into the chamber. It was the boy choir singing Christmas anthems. Higher and higher rose the clear, fresh voices, full of hope and cheer, as children's voices always are. Fuller and fuller grew the burst of melody as one glad strain fell upon another in joyful harmony:

"Carol, brothers, carol,
    Carol joyfully,
Carol the good tidings,
    Carol merrily!
And pray a gladsome Christmas
    For all your fellow-men:
Carol, brothers, carol,
    Christmas Day again."

One verse followed another, always with the same sweet refrain:

"And pray a gladsome Christmas
    For all your fellow-men:
Carol, brothers, carol,
    Christmas Day again."

Mrs. Bird thought, as the music floated in upon her gentle sleep, that she had slipped into heaven with her new baby, and that the angels were bidding them welcome. But the tiny bundle by her side stirred a little, and though it was scarcely more than the ruffling of a feather, she awoke; for the mother-ear is so close to the heart that it can hear the faintest whisper of a child.

She opened her eyes and drew the baby closer. It looked like a rose dipped in milk, she thought, this pink and white blossom of girlhood, or like a pink cherub, with its halo of pale yellow hair, finer than floss silk.

"Carol, brothers, carol,
    Carol joyfully,
Carol the good tidings,
    Carol merrily!"

The voices were brimming over with joy.

"Why, my baby," whispered Mrs. Bird in soft surprise, "I had forgotten what day it was. You are a little Christmas child, and we will name you 'Carol'—mother's Christmas Carol!"

"What!" said Mr. Bird, coming in softly and closing the door behind him.

"Why, Donald, don't you think 'Carol' is a sweet name for a Christmas baby? It came to me just a moment ago in the singing, as I was lying here half asleep and half awake."

"I think it is a charming name, dear heart, and sounds just like you, and I hope that, being a girl, this baby has some chance of being as lovely as her mother";— at which speech from the baby's papa, Mrs. Bird, though she was as weak and tired as she could be, blushed with happiness.

And so Carol came by her name.

Of course, it was thought foolish by many people, though Uncle Jack declared laughingly that it was very strange if a whole family of Birds could not be indulged in a single Carol; and Grandma, who adored the child, thought the name much more appropriate than Lucy, but was glad that people would probably think it short for Caroline.

Perhaps because she was born in holiday time, Carol was a very happy baby. Of course, she was too tiny to understand the joy of Christmas-tide, but people say there is everything in a good beginning, and she may have breathed in unconsciously the fragrance of evergreens and holiday dinners; while the peals of sleigh-bells and the laughter of happy children .may have fallen upon her baby ears and wakened in them a glad surprise at the merry world she had come to live in.

Her cheeks and lips were as red as holly-berries; her hair was for all the world the color of a Christmas candle-flame; her eyes were bright as stars; her laugh like a chime of Christmas-bells, and her tiny hands forever outstretched in giving.

Such a generous little creature you never saw! A spoonful of bread and milk had always to be taken by Mamma or nurse before Carol could enjoy her supper; what-ever bit of cake or sweetmeat found its way into her pretty fingers was straightway broken in half to be shared with Donald, Paul, or Hugh; and when they made be-lieve nibble the morsel with affected en-joyment, she would clap her hands and crow with delight.

"Why does she do it?" asked Donald thoughtfully. "None of us boys ever did."

"I hardly know," said Mamma, catch-ing her darling to her heart, "except that she is a little Christmas child, and so she has a tiny share of the blessedest birthday the world ever knew!"

II: Drooping Wings

It was December, ten years later. Carol had seen nine Christmas trees lighted on her birthdays, one after another; nine times she had assisted in the holiday festivities of the household, though in her babyhood her share of the gayeties was somewhat limited.

For five years, certainly, she had hidden presents for Mamma and Papa in their own bureau drawers, and harbored a num-ber of secrets sufficiently large to burst a baby brain, had it not been for the relief gained by whispering them all to Mamma, at night, when she was in her crib, a pro-ceeding which did not in the least lessen the value of a secret in her innocent mind.

For five years she had heard " 'Twas the night before Christmas," and hung up a scarlet stocking many sizes too large for her, and pinned a sprig of holly on her little white nightgown, to show Santa Claus that she was a "truly" Christmas child, and dreamed of fur-coated saints and toy-packs and reindeer, and wished everybody a "Merry Christmas" before it was light in the morning, and lent every one of her new toys to the neighbors' chil-dren before noon, and eaten turkey and plum-pudding, and gone to bed at night in a trance of happiness at the day's pleasures.

Donald was away at college now. Paul and Hugh were great manly fellows, taller than their mother. Papa Bird had gray hairs in his whiskers; and Grandma, God bless her, had been four Christmases in heaven.

But Christmas in the Birds' Nest was scarcely as merry now as it used to be in the bygone years, for the little child, that once brought such an added blessing to the day, lay month after month a patient, helpless invalid, in the room where she was born. She had never been very strong in body, and it was with a pang of terror her mother and father noticed, soon after she was five years old, that she began to limp, ever so slightly; to complain too often of weariness, and to nestle close to her mother, saying she "would rather not go out to play, please." The illness was slight at first, and hope was always stirring in Mrs. Bird's heart. "Carol would feel stronger in the summer-time"; or, "She would be better when she had spent a year in the coun-try"; or, "She would outgrow it"; or, "They would try a new physician"; but by and by it came to be all too sure that no physician save One could make Carol strong again, and that no "summer-time" nor "country air," unless it were the everlasting summer-time in a heavenly country, could bring back the little girl to health.

The cheeks and lips that were once as red as holly-berries faded to faint pink; the star-like eyes grew softer, for they often gleamed through tears; and the gay child-laugh, that had been like a chime of

Christmas bells, gave place to a smile so lovely, so touching, so tender and patient, that it filled every corner of the house with a gentle radiance that might have come from the face of the Christ-child himself.

Love could do nothing; and when we have said that we have said all, for it is stronger than anything else in the whole wide world. Mr. and Mrs. Bird were talking it over one evening, when all the children were asleep. A famous physician had visited them that day, and told them that some time, it might be in one year, it might be in more, Carol would slip quietly off into heaven, whence she came.

"It is no use to close our eyes to it any longer," said Mr. Bird, as he paced up and down the library floor; "Carol will never be well again. It almost seems as if I could not bear it when I think of that loveliest child doomed to lie there day after day, and, what is still more, to suffer pain that we are helpless to keep away from her. Merry Christmas, indeed; it gets to be the saddest day in the year to me!" and poor Mr. Bird sank into a chair by the table, and buried his face in his hands to keep his wife from seeing the tears that would come in spite of all his efforts.

"But, Donald, dear," said sweet Mrs. Bird, with trembling voice, "Christmas Day may not be so merry with us as it used, but it is very happy, and that is better, and very blessed, and that is better yet. I suffer chiefly for Carol's sake, but I have almost given up being sorrowful for my own. I am too happy in the child, and I see too clearly what she has done for us and the other children. Donald and Paul and Hugh were three strong, willful, boisterous boys, but now you seldom see such tenderness, devotion, thought for others, and self-denial in lads of their years. A quarrel or a hot word is almost unknown in this house, and why? Carol would hear it, and it would distress her, she is so full of love and goodness. The boys study with all their might and main. Why? Partly, at least, because they like to teach Carol, and amuse her by telling her what they read. When the seamstress comes, she likes to sew in Miss Carol's room, because there she forgets her own troubles, which, heaven knows, are sore enough! And as for me, Donald, I am a better woman every day for Carol's sake; I have to be her eyes, ears, feet, hands—her strength, her hope; and she, my own little child, is my example!"

"I was wrong, dear heart," said Mr. Bird more cheerfully; "we will try not to repine, but to rejoice instead, that we have an 'angel of the house.' "

"And as for her future," Mrs. Bird went on, "I think we need not be overanxious. I feel as if she did not belong altogether to us, but that when she has done what God sent her for, He will take her back to Himself—and it may not be very long!" Here it was poor Mrs. Bird's turn to break down, and Mr. Bird's turn to comfort her.

III: The Birds' Nest

Carol herself knew nothing of motherly tears and fatherly anxieties; she lived on peacefully in the room where she was born.

But you never would have known that room; for Mr. Bird had a great deal of money, and though he felt sometimes as if he wanted to throw it all in the sea, since it could not buy a strong body for his little girl, yet he was glad to make the place she lived in just as beautiful as it could be.

The room had been extended by the building of a large addition that hung out over the garden below, and was so filled with windows that it might have been a conservatory. The ones on the side were thus still nearer the Church of Our Saviour than they used to be; those in front looked out on the beautiful harbor, and those in the back commanded a view of nothing in particular but a narrow alley; nevertheless, they were pleasantest of all to Carol, for the Ruggles family lived in the alley, and the nine little, middle-sized, and big Ruggles children were a source of inexhaustible interest.

The shutters could all be opened and Carol could take a real sunbath in this lovely glass house, or they could all be closed when the dear head ached or the dear eyes were tired. The carpet was of soft gray, with clusters of green bay and holly leaves. The furniture was of white wood, on which an artist had painted snow scenes and Christmas trees and groups of merry children ringing bells and singing carols.

Donald had made a pretty, polished shelf, and screwed it on the outside of the foot-board, and the boys kept this full of blooming plants, which they changed from time to time; the head-board, too, had a bracket on either side, where there were pots of maiden-hair ferns.

Love-birds and canaries hung in their golden houses in the windows, and they, poor caged things, could hop as far from their wooden perches as Carol could venture from her little white bed.

On one side of the room was a bookcase filled with hundreds—yes, I mean it—with hundreds and hundreds of books; books with gay-colored pictures, books without; books with black and white outline sketches, books with none at all; books with verses, books with stories; books that made children laugh, and some, only a few, that made them cry; books with words of one syllable for tiny boys and girls, and books with words of fearful length to puzzle wise ones. This was Carol's "Circulating Library." Every Saturday she chose ten books, jotting their names down in a diary; into these she slipped cards that said:

"Please keep this book two weeks and read it. With love,

CAROL BIRD."

Then Mrs. Bird stepped into her carriage and took the ten books to the Children's Hospital, and brought home ten others that she had left there the fortnight before.

This was a source of great happiness; for some of the Hospital children that were old enough to print or write, and were strong enough to do it, wrote Carol sweet little letters about the books, and she answered them, and they grew to be friends. (It is very funny, but you do not always have to see people to love them. Just think about it, and tell me if it isn't so.)

There was a high wainscoting of wood about the room, and on top of this, in a narrow gilt framework, ran a row of illuminated pictures, illustrating fairy tales, all in dull blue and gold and scarlet and silver. From the door to the closet there was the story of "The Fair One with Golden Locks"; from closet to bookcase, ran "Puss in Boots"; from bookcase to fireplace, was "Jack the Giant-killer"; and on the other side of the room were "Hop o' my Thumb," "The Sleeping Beauty," and "Cinderella."

Then there was a great closet full of beautiful things to wear, but they were all dressing-gowns and slippers and shawls; and there were drawers full of toys and games, but they were such as you could play with on your lap. There were no ninepins, nor balls, nor bows and arrows, nor bean bags, nor tennis rackets; but, after all, other children needed these more than Carol Bird, for she was always happy and contented, whatever she had or whatever she lacked; and after the room had been made so lovely for her, on her eighth Christmas, she always called herself, in fun, a "Bird of Paradise."

On these particular December days she was happier than usual, for Uncle Jack was coming from England to spend the holidays. Dear, funny, jolly, loving, wise Uncle Jack, who came every two or three years, and brought so much joy with him that the world looked as black as a thundercloud for a week after he went away again.

The mail had brought this letter:

London, November 28, 188–.

Wish you merry Christmas, you dearest birdlings in America! Preen your feathers, and stretch the Birds' nest a trifle, if you please, and let Uncle Jack in for the holidays. I am coming with such a trunk full of treasures that you'll have to borrow the stockings of Barnum's Giant and Giantess;

I am coming to squeeze a certain little lady-bird until she cries for mercy; I am coming to see if I can find a boy to take care of a black pony that I bought lately. It's the strangest thing I ever knew; I've hunted all over Europe, and can't find a boy to suit me! I'll tell you why. I've set my heart on finding one with a dimple in his chin, because this pony particularly likes dimples! ("Hurrah!" cried Hugh; "bless my dear dimple; I'll never be ashamed of it again.")

Please drop a note to the clerk of the weather, and have a good, rousing snow-storm—say on the twenty-second. None of your meek, gentle, nonsensical, shilly-shallying snow-storms; not the sort where the flakes float lazily down from the sky as if they didn't care whether they ever got here or not and then melt away as soon as they touch the earth, but a regular business-like whizzing, whirring, blurring, cutting snow-storm, warranted to freeze and stay on!

I should like rather a LARGE Christmas tree, if it's convenient: not one of those "sprigs," five or six feet high, that you used to have three or four years ago, when the birdlings were not fairly feathered out; but a tree of some size. Set it up in the garret, if necessary, and then we can cut a hole in the roof if the tree chances to be too high for the room.

Tell Bridget to begin to fatten a turkey. Tell her that by the twentieth of December that turkey must not be able to stand on its legs for fat, and then on the next three days she must allow it to recline easily on its side, and stuff it to bursting. (One ounce of stuffing beforehand is worth a pound afterwards.)

The pudding must be unusually huge, and darkly, deeply, lugubriously blue in color. It must be stuck so full of plums that the pudding itself will ooze out into the pan and not be brought on to the table at all. I expect to be there by the twentieth, to manage these little things myself—remembering it is the early Bird that catches the worm—but give you the instructions in case I should be delayed.

And Carol must decide on the size of the tree—she knows best, she was a Christmas child; and she must plead for the snow-storm—the "clerk of the weather" may pay some attention to her; and she must look up the boy with the dimple for me—she's likelier to find him than I am, this minute. She must advise about the turkey, and Bridget must bring the pudding to her bedside and let her drop every separate plum into it and stir it once for luck, or I'll not eat a single slice—for Carol is the dearest part of Christmas to Uncle Jack, and he'll have none of it without her. She is better than all the turkeys and puddings and apples and spare-ribs and wreaths and garlands and mistletoe and stockings and chimneys and sleigh-bells in Christendom! She is the very sweetest Christmas Carol that was ever written, said, sung, or chanted, and I am coming as fast as ships and railway trains can carry me, to tell her so.

Carol's joy knew no bounds. Mr. and Mrs. Bird laughed like children and kissed each other for sheer delight, and when the boys heard it they simply whooped like wild Indians; until the Ruggles family, whose back yard joined their garden, gathered at the door and wondered what was "up" in the big house.

IV: "Birds of a Feather Flock Together"

Uncle Jack did really come on the twentieth. He was not detained by business, nor did he get left behind nor snowed up, as frequently happens in stories, and in real life too, I am afraid. The snow-storm came also; and the turkey nearly died a natural and premature death from overeating.

Donald came, too; Donald, with a line of down upon his upper lip, and Greek and Latin on his tongue, and stores of knowledge in his handsome head, and stories—bless me, you couldn't turn over a chip without reminding Donald of something that happened "at College." One or the other was always at Carol's bedside, for they fancied her paler than she used to be, and they could not bear her out of sight. It was Uncle Jack, though, who sat beside her in the winter twilights. The room was quiet, and almost dark, save for the snow-light outside, and the flickering flame of the fire, that danced over the "Sleeping Beauty's" face and touched the Fair One's golden locks with ruddier glory. Carol's hand (all too thin and white these latter days) lay close clasped in Uncle Jack's, and they talked together quietly of many, many things.

"I want to tell you all about my plans for Christmas this year, Uncle Jack," said Carol, on the first evening of his visit, "because it will be the loveliest one I ever had. The boys laugh at me for caring so much about it; but it isn't altogether because it is Christmas, nor because it is my birthday; but long, long ago, when I first began to be ill, I used to think, the first thing when I waked on Christmas morning, 'To-day is Christ's birthday—*and mine!*' I did not put the words close together, you know, because that made it seem too bold; but I first said, 'Christ's birthday,' out loud, and then, in a minute, softly to myself—'*and mine!*' 'Christ's birthday—*and mine!*' And so I do not quite feel about Christmas as other girls do. Mamma says she supposes that ever so many other children have been born on that day. I often wonder where they are, Uncle Jack, and whether it is a dear thought to them, too, or whether I am so much in bed, and so often alone, that it means more to me. Oh, I do hope that none of them are poor, or cold, or hungry; and I wish—I wish they were all as happy as I, because they are really my little brothers and sisters. Now, Uncle Jack dear, I am going to try and make somebody happy every single Christmas that I live, and this year it is to be the 'Ruggleses in the rear.'"

"That large and interesting brood of children in the little house at the end of the back garden?"

"Yes; isn't it nice to see so many to-gether?—and, Uncle Jack, why do the big

families always live in the small houses, and the small families in the big houses? We ought to call them the Ruggles children, of course; but Donald began talking of them as the 'Ruggleses in the rear,' and Papa and Mamma took it up, and now we cannot seem to help it. The house was built for Mr. Carter's coachman, but Mr. Carter lives in Europe, and the gentleman who rents his place for him doesn't care what happens to it, and so this poor family came to live there. When they first moved in, I used to sit in my window and watch them play in their back yard; they are so strong, and jolly, and good-natured—and then, one day, I had a terrible headache, and Donald asked them if they would please not scream quite so loud, and they explained that they were having a game of circus, but that they would change and play 'Deaf and Dumb Asylum' all the afternoon."

"Ha, ha, ha!" laughed Uncle Jack, "what an obliging family, to be sure!"

"Yes, we all thought it very funny, and I smiled at them from the window when I was well enough to be up again. Now, Sarah Maud comes to her door when the children come home from school, and if Mamma nods her head, 'Yes,' that means 'Carol is very well,' and then you ought to hear the little Ruggleses yell—I believe they try to see how much noise they can make; but if Mamma shakes her head, 'No,' they always play at quiet games. Then, one day, 'Cary,' my pet canary, flew out of her cage, and Peter Ruggles caught her and brought her back, and I had him up here in my room to thank him."

"Is Peter the oldest?"

"No; Sarah Maud is the oldest—she helps do the washing; and Peter is the next. He is a dressmaker's boy."

"And which is the pretty little red-haired girl?"

"That's Kitty."

"And the fat youngster?"

"Baby Larry."

"And that—most freckled one?"

"Now, don't laugh—that's Peoria."

"Carol, you are joking."

"No, really, Uncle dear. She was born in Peoria; that's all."

"And is the next boy Oshkosh?"

"No," laughed Carol, "the others are Susan, and Clement, and Eily, and Cornelius; they all look exactly alike, except that some of them have more freckles than the others."

"How did you ever learn all their names?"

"Why, I have what I call a 'window-school.' It is too cold now; but in warm weather I am wheeled out on my balcony, and the Ruggleses climb up and walk along our garden fence, and sit on the roof of our carriage-house. That brings them quite near, and I tell them stories. On Thanksgiving Day they came up for a few minutes—it was quite warm at eleven o'clock—and we told each other what we had to be thankful for; but they gave such queer answers that Papa had to run away for fear of laughing; and I couldn't understand them very well. Susan was thankful for *'trunks,'* of all things in the world; Cornelius, for 'horse-cars'; Kitty, for 'pork steak'; while Clem, who is very quiet, brightened up when I came to him, and said he was thankful for *'his lame puppy.'* Wasn't that pretty?"

"It might teach some of us a lesson, mightn't it, little girl?"

"That's what Mamma said. Now I'm going to give this whole Christmas to the Ruggleses; and, Uncle Jack, I earned part of the money myself."

"You, my bird; how?"

"Well, you see, it could not be my own, own Christmas if Papa gave me all the money, and I thought to really keep Christ's birthday I ought to do something of my very own; and so I talked with Mamma. Of course she thought of something lovely; she always does: Mamma's head is just brimming over with lovely thoughts—all I have to do is ask, and out pops the very one I want. This thought was to let her write down, just as I told her, a description of how a child lived in her own room for three years, and what she did to amuse herself; and we sent it to a magazine and got twenty-five dollars for it. Just think!"

"Well, well," cried Uncle Jack, "my little girl a real author! And what are you going to do with this wonderful 'own' money of yours?"

"I shall give the nine Ruggleses a grand Christmas dinner here in this very room—that will be Papa's contribution—and afterwards a beautiful Christmas tree, fairly blooming with presents—that will be my part; for I have another way of adding to my twenty-five dollars, so that I can buy nearly anything I choose. I should like it very much if you would sit at the head of the table, Uncle Jack, for nobody could ever be frightened of you, you dearest, dearest, dearest thing that ever was! Mamma is going to help us, but Papa and the boys are going to eat together downstairs for fear of making the little Ruggleses shy; and after we've had a merry time with the tree we can open my window and all listen together to the music at the evening church-service, if it comes before the children go. I have written a letter to the organist, and asked him if I might have the two songs I like best. Will you see if it is all right?"

Birds' Nest, December 21, 188–.
Dear Mr. Wilkie—I am the little girl who lives next door to the church, and, as I seldom go out, the music on practice days and Sundays is one of my greatest pleasures.

I want to know if you can have "Carol, brothers, carol," on Christmas night, and if the boy who sings "My ain countree" so beautifully may please sing that too. I think it is the loveliest thing in the world, but it always makes me cry; doesn't it you?

If it isn't too much trouble, I hope they can sing them both quite early, as after ten o'clock I may be asleep.

Yours respectfully,
Carol Bird.

P.S.—The reason I like "Carol, brothers, carol," is because the choir-boys sang it eleven years ago, the morning I was born, and put it into Mamma's head to call me

Carol. She didn't remember then that my other name would be Bird, because she was half asleep, and could only think of one thing at a time. Donald says if I had been born on the Fourth of July they would have named me "Independence," or if on the twenty-second of February, "Georgina," or even "Cherry," like Cherry in "Martin Chuzzlewit"; but I like my own name and birthday best.   Yours truly,
                             Carol Bird.

Uncle Jack thought the letter quite right, and did not even smile at her telling the organist so many family items.

The days flew by as they always fly in holiday time, and it was Christmas Eve before anybody knew it. The family festival was quiet and very pleasant, but almost overshadowed by the grander preparations for the next day. Carol and Elfrida, her pretty German nurse, had ransacked books, and introduced so many plans, and plays, and customs, and merry-makings from Germany, and Holland, and England, and a dozen other countries, that you would scarcely have known how or where you were keeping Christmas. Even the dog and the cat had enjoyed their celebration under Carol's direction. Each had a tiny table with a lighted candle in the centre, and a bit of Bologna sausage placed very near it; and everybody laughed till the tears stood in their eyes to see Villikins and Dinah struggle to nibble the sausages, and at the same time to evade the candle flame. Villikins barked, and sniffed, and howled in impatience, and after many vain attempts suc-

ceeded in dragging off the prize, though he singed his nose in doing it. Dinah, meanwhile, watched him placidly, her delicate nostrils quivering with expectation, and, after all excitement had subsided, walked with dignity to the table, her beautiful gray satin trail sweeping behind her, and, calmly putting up one velvet paw, drew the sausage gently down, and walked out of the room without turning a hair, so to speak. Elfrida had scattered handfuls of seed over the snow in the garden, that the wild birds might have a comfortable breakfast next morning, and had stuffed bundles of dry grasses in the fireplaces, so that the reindeer of Santa Claus could refresh themselves after their long gallops across country. This was really only done for fun, but it pleased Carol.

And when, after dinner, the whole family had gone to the church to see the Christmas decorations, Carol limped out on her slender crutches, and with Elfrida's help, placed all the family boots in a row in the upper hall. That was to keep the dear ones from quarreling all through the year. There were Papa's stout top boots; Mamma's pretty buttoned shoes next; then Uncle Jack's, Donald's, Paul's, and Hugh's; and at the end of the line her own little white worsted slippers. Last, and sweetest of all, like the children in Austria, she put a lighted candle in her window to guide the dear Christchild, lest he should stumble in the dark night as he passed up the deserted street. This done, she dropped into bed, a rather tired, but very happy Christmas fairy.

V: "Some Other Birds Are Taught to Fly"

Before the earliest Ruggles could wake and toot his five-cent tin horn, Mrs. Ruggles was up and stirring about the house, for it was a gala day in the family. Gala day! I should think so! Were not her nine "childern" invited to a dinner-party at the great house, and weren't they going to sit down free and equal with the mightiest in the land? She had been preparing for this grand occasion ever since the receipt of

Carol Bird's invitation, which, by the way, had been speedily enshrined in an old photograph frame and hung under the looking-glass in the most prominent place in the kitchen, where it stared the occasional visitor directly in the eye, and made him livid with envy:

Birds' Nest, December 17, 188–.

Dear Mrs. Ruggles—I am going to have a dinner-party on Christmas Day, and would like to have all your children come. I want them every one, please, from Sarah Maud to Baby Larry. Mamma says dinner will be at half past five, and the Christmas tree at seven; so you may expect them home at nine o'clock. Wishing you a Merry Christmas and a Happy New Year, I am

Yours truly,
Carol Bird.

Breakfast was on the table promptly at seven o'clock, and there was very little of it, too; for it was an excellent day for short rations, though Mrs. Ruggles heaved a sigh as she reflected that the boys, with their India-rubber stomachs, would be just as hungry the day after the dinner-party as if they had never had any at all. As soon as the scanty meal was over, she announced the plan of the campaign: "Now, Susan, you an' Kitty wash up the dishes; an' Peter, can't yer spread up the beds, so 't I can git ter cuttin' out Larry's new suit? I ain't satisfied with his clo'es, an' I thought in the night of a way to make him a dress out o' my old red plaid shawl—kind o' Scotch style, yer know, with the fringe 't the bottom.—Eily, you go find the comb and take the snarls out the fringe, that's a lady! You little young ones clear out from under foot! Clem, you and Con hop into bed with Larry while I wash yer underflannins; 't won't take long to dry 'em.—Yes, I know it's bothersome, but yer can't go int' s'ciety 'thout takin' some trouble, 'n' anyhow I couldn't git round to 'em last night.—Sarah Maud, I think 't would be perfeckly han'som' if you ripped them brass buttons off yer uncle's police-man's coat 'n' sewed 'em in a row up the front o' yer green skirt. Susan, you must iron out yours 'n' Kitty's apurns; 'n' there, I come mighty near forgettin' Peory's stockin's! I counted the whole lot last night when I was washin' of 'em, 'n' there ain't but nineteen anyhow yer fix 'em, 'n' no nine pairs mates nohow; 'n' I ain't goin' ter have my childern wear odd stockin's to a dinner-comp'ny, fetched up as I was!—Eily, can't you run out and ask Mis' Cullen ter lend me a pair o' stockin's for Peory, 'n' tell her if she will, Peory'll give

Jim half her candy when she gets home. Won't yer, Peory?"

Peoria was young and greedy, and thought the remedy so out of all proportion to the disease, that she set up a deafening howl at the projected bergain—a howl so rebellious and so entirely out of season that her mother started in her direction with flashing eye and uplifted hand; but she let it fall suddenly, saying, "No, I vow I won't lick ye Christmas Day, if yer drive me crazy; but speak up smart, now, 'n' say whether yer'd ruther give Jim Cullen half yer candy or go bare-legged ter the party?" The matter being put so plainly, Peoria collected her faculties, dried her tears, and chose the lesser evil, Clem having hastened the decision by an affectionate wink, that meant he'd go halves with her on his candy.

"That's a lady!" cried her mother. "Now, you young ones that ain't doin' nothin', play all yer want ter before noontime, for after ye git through eatin' at twelve o'clock me 'n' Sarah Maud's goin' ter give yer sech a washin' 'n' combin' 'n' dressin' as yer never had before 'n' never will agin likely, 'n' then I'm goin' to set yer down 'n' give yer two solid hours trainin' in manners; 'n' 't won't be no foolin' neither."

"All we've got ter do's go eat!" grumbled Peter.

"Well, that's enough," responded his mother; "there's more 'n one way of eatin', let me tell yer, 'n' you've got a heap ter learn about it, Peter Ruggles. Land sakes, I wish you childern could see the way I was fetched up to eat. I never took a meal o' vittles in the kitchen before I married Ruggles; but yer can't keep up that style with nine young ones 'n' yer Pa always off ter sea."

The big Ruggleses worked so well, and the little Ruggleses kept from "under foot" so successfully, that by one o'clock nine complete toilets were laid out in solemn grandeur on the beds. I say, "complete"; but I do not know whether they would be called so in the best society. The law of compensation had been well applied: he that had necktie had no cuffs; she that had sash had no handkerchief, and vice versa; but they all had shoes and a certain amount of clothing, such as it was, the outside layer being in every case quite above criticism.

"Now, Sarah Maud," said Mrs. Ruggles, her face shining with excitement, "everything's red up an' we can begin. I've got a boiler 'n' a kettle 'n' a pot o' hot water. Peter, you go into the back bedroom, 'n' I'll take Susan, Kitty, Peory, 'n' Cornelius; 'n' Sarah Maud, you take Clem, 'n' Eily, 'n' Larry, one to a time. Scrub 'em 'n' rinse 'em, or 't any rate git's fur's yer can with 'em, and then I'll finish 'em off while you do yerself."

Sarah Maud couldn't have scrubbed with any more decision and force if she had been doing floors, and the little Ruggleses bore it bravely, not from natural heroism, but for the joy that was set before them. Not being satisfied, however, with the "tone" of their complexions, and feeling that the number of freckles to the square inch was too many to be tolerated in the highest social circles, she wound up operations by applying a little Bristol brick from the knife-board, which served as the proverbial "last straw," from under which the little Ruggleses issued rather red and raw and out of temper. When the clock struck four they were all clothed, and most of them in their right minds, ready for those last touches that always take the most time.

Kitty's red hair was curled in thirty-four ringlets, Sarah Maud's was braided in one pig-tail, and Susan's and Eily's in two braids apiece, while Peoria's resisted all advances in the shape of hair oils and stuck out straight on all sides, like that of the Circassian girl of the circus—so Clem said; and he was sent into the bedroom for it, too, from whence he was dragged out forgivingly, by Peoria herself, five minutes later. Then, exciting moment, came linen collars for some and neckties and bows for others—a magnificent green glass breastpin was sewed into Peter's purple necktie, —and Eureka! the Ruggleses were dressed, and Solomon in all his glory was not arrayed like one of these!

A row of seats was then formed directly through the middle of the kitchen. Of course, there were not quite chairs enough for ten, since the family had rarely wanted to sit down all at once, somebody always being out or in bed, or otherwise engaged, but the wood-box and the coal-hod finished out the line nicely, and nobody thought of grumbling. The children took their places according to age, Sarah Maud at the head and Larry on the coal-hod, and Mrs. Ruggles seated herself in front, surveying them proudly as she wiped the sweat of honest toil from her brow.

"Well," she exclaimed, "if I do say so as shouldn't, I never see a cleaner, more stylish mess o' childern in my life! I do wish Ruggles could look at ye for a minute! —Larry Ruggles, how many times have I got ter tell yer not ter keep pullin' at yer sash? Haven't I told yer if it comes ontied, yer waist 'n' skirt'll part comp'ny in the middle, 'n' then where'll yer be?—Now look me in the eye, all of yer! I've of'en told yer what kind of a family the McGrills was. I've got reason to be proud, goodness knows! Your uncle is on the police force o' New York City; you can take up the paper most any day an' see his name printed right out—James McGrill—'n' I can't have my childern fetched up common, like some folks'; when they go out they've got to have clo'es, and learn to act decent! Now I want ter see how yer goin' to behave when yer git there to-night. 'Tain't so awful easy as you think 't is. Let's start in at the beginnin' 'n' act out the whole business. Pile into the bedroom, there, every last one o' ye, 'n' show me how yer goin' to go int' the parlor. This'll be the parlor, 'n' I'll be Mis' Bird."

The youngsters hustled into the next room in high glee, and Mrs. Ruggles drew herself up in the chair with an infinitely haughty and purse-proud expression that much better suited a descendant of the McGrills than modest Mrs. Bird.

The bedroom was small, and there presently ensued such a clatter that you would have thought a herd of wild cattle had broken loose. The door opened, and they straggled in, all the younger ones giggling, with Sarah Maud at the head, looking as if she had been caught in the act of stealing sheep; while Larry, being last in line, seemed to think the door a sort of gate of heaven which would be shut in his face if he didn't get there in time; accordingly he struggled ahead of his elders and disgraced himself by tumbling in head foremost.

Mrs. Ruggles looked severe. "There, I knew yer'd do it in some sech fool way! Now go in there and try it over again, every last one o' ye, 'n' if Larry can't come in on two legs he can stay ter home—d' yer hear?"

The matter began to assume a graver aspect; the little Ruggleses stopped giggling and backed into the bedroom, issuing presently with lock step, Indian file, a scared and hunted expression on every countenance.

"No, no, no!" cried Mrs. Ruggles, in despair. "That's worse yet; yer look for all the world like a gang o' pris'ners! There ain't no style ter that: spread out more, can't yer, 'n' act kind o' careless-like— nobody's goin' ter kill ye! That ain't what a dinner-party is!"

The third time brought deserved success, and the pupils took their seats in the row. "Now, yer know," said Mrs. Ruggles impressively, "there ain't enough decent hats to go round, 'n' if there was I don' know's I'd let yer wear 'em, for the boys would never think to take 'em off when they got inside, for they never do—but anyhow, there ain't enough good ones. Now, look me in the eye. You're only goin' jest round the corner; you needn't wear no hats, none of yer, 'n' when yer get int' the parlor, 'n' they ask yer ter lay off yer hats, Sarah Maud must speak up 'n' say it was sech a pleasant evenin' 'n' sech a short walk that yer left yer hats to home. Now, can yer remember?"

All the little Ruggleses shouted, "Yes, marm!" in chorus.

"What have you got ter do with it?" demanded their mother; "did I tell you

to say it? Warn't I talkin' to Sarah Maud?"

The little Ruggleses hung their diminished heads. "Yes, marm," they piped, more discreetly.

"Now we won't leave nothin' to chance; get up, all of ye, an' try it. Speak up, Sarah Maud."

Sarah Maud's tongue clove to the roof of her mouth.

"Quick!"

"Ma thought—it was—sech a pleasant hat that we'd—we'd better leave our short walk to home," recited Sarah Maud, in an agony of mental effort.

This was too much for the boys. An earthquake of suppressed giggles swept all along the line.

"Oh, whatever shall I do with yer?" moaned the unhappy mother. "I s'pose I've got to learn it to yer!"—which she did, word for word, until Sarah Maud thought she could stand on her head and say it backwards.

"Now, Cornelius, what are you goin' ter say ter make yerself good comp'ny?"

"Do? Me? Dunno!" said Cornelius, turning pale, with unexpected responsibility.

"Well, ye ain't goin' to set there like a bump on a log 'thout sayin' a word ter pay for yer vittles, air ye? Ask Mis' Bird how she's feelin' this evenin', or if Mr. Bird's hevin' a busy season, or how this kind o' weather agrees with him, or somethin' like that. Now we'll make b'lieve we've got ter the dinner—that won't be so hard, 'cause yer'll have somethin' to do—it's awful bothersome to stan' round an' act stylish. If they have napkins, Sarah Maud down to Peory may put 'em in their laps, 'n' the rest of ye can tuck 'em in yer necks. Don't eat with yer fingers—don't grab no vittles off one 'nother's plates; don't reach out for nothin', but wait till yer asked, 'n' if you never *git* asked don't git up and grab it.— Don't spill nothin' on the tablecloth, or like's not Mis' Bird'll send yer away from the table—'n' I hope she will if yer do! (Susan! keep yer handkerchief in yer lap where Peory can borry it if she needs it, 'n' I hope she'll know when she does need it, though I don't expect it.) Now we'll try a few things ter see how they'll go! Mr. Clement, do you eat cramb'ry sarse?"

"Bet yer life!" cried Clem, who in the excitement of the moment had not taken in the idea exactly and had mistaken this for an ordinary bosom-of-the-family question.

"Clement McGrill Ruggles, do you mean to tell me that you'd say that to a dinner-party? I'll give ye one more chance. Mr. Clement, will you take some of the cramb'ry?"

"Yes, marm, thank ye kindly, if you happen ter have any handy."

"Very good, indeed! But they won't give yer two tries tonight—yer just remember that! Miss Peory, do you speak for white or dark meat?"

"I ain't perticler as ter color—anything that nobody else wants will suit me," answered Peory with her best air.

"First-rate! Nobody could speak more genteel than that. Miss Kitty, will you have hard or soft sarse with your pudden?"

"Hard or soft? Oh! A little of both, if you please, an' I'm much obliged," said Kitty, bowing with decided ease and grace; at which all the other Ruggleses pointed the finger of shame at her, and Peter *grunted* expressively, that their meaning might not be mistaken.

"You just stop your gruntin', Peter Ruggles; that warn't greedy, that was all right. I wish I could git it inter your heads that it ain't so much what yer say, as the way you say it. And don't keep starin' crosseyed at your necktie pin, or I'll take it out 'n' sew it on to Clem or Cornelius: Sarah Maud'll keep her eye on it, 'n' if it turns broken side out she'll tell yer. Gracious! I shouldn't think you'd ever seen nor worn no jool'ry in your life. Eily, you an' Larry's too little to train, so you' just look at the rest an' do's they do, 'n' the Lord

have mercy on ye 'n' help ye to act decent! Now, is there anything more ye'd like to practice?"

"If yer tell me one more thing, I can't set up an' eat," said Peter gloomily; "I'm so cram full o' manners now I'm ready ter bust, 'thout no dinner at all."

"Me too," chimed in Cornelius.

"Well, I'm sorry for yer both," rejoined Mrs. Ruggles sarcastically; "if the 'mount o' manners yer've got on hand now troubles ye, you're dreadful easy hurt! Now, Sarah Maud, after dinner, about once in so often, you must git up 'n' say, 'I guess we'd better be goin''; 'n' if they say, 'Oh, no, set a while longer,' yer can set; but if they don't say nothin' you've got ter get up 'n' go. Now hev yer got that int' yer head?"

"*About once in so often!*" Could any words in the language be fraught with more terrible and wearing uncertainty?

"Well," answered Sarah Maud mournfully, "seems as if this whole dinner-party set right square on top o' me! Mebbe I could manage my own manners, but to manage nine mannerses is worse 'n staying to home!"

"Oh, don't fret," said her mother, good-naturedly, now that the lesson was over; "I guess you'll git along. I wouldn't mind if folks would only say, 'Oh, childern will be childern'; but they won't. They'll say, 'Land o' Goodness, who fetched them childern up?' It's quarter past five, 'n' yer can go now—remember 'bout the hats—don't all talk ter once—Susan, lend yer han'k'chief ter Peory—Peter, don't keep screwin' yer scarf-pin—Cornelius, hold yer head up straight—Sarah Maud, don't take yer eyes off o' Larry, 'n' Larry, you keep holt o' Sarah Maud 'n' do jest as she says—'n' whatever you do, all of yer, never forgit for one second that yer mother was a McGrill."

VI: "When the Pie Was Opened, the Birds Began to Sing!"

The children went out of the back door quietly, and were presently lost to sight, Sarah Maud slipping and stumbling along

absent-mindedly, as she recited rapidly under her breath, "Itwassuchapleasantevenin'n' suchashortwalk,thatwethoughtwe'dleaveour hatstohome — itwassuchapleasantevenin'n' suchashortwalk,thatwethoughtwe'dleaveour hatstohome."

Peter rang the doorbell, and presently a servant admitted them, and, whispering something in Sarah's ear, drew her downstairs into the kitchen. The other Ruggleses stood in horror-stricken groups as the door closed behind their commanding officer; but there was no time for reflection, for a voice from above was heard, saying, "Come right upstairs, please!"

> "Theirs not to make reply,
> Theirs not to reason why,
> Theirs but to do or die."

Accordingly they walked upstairs, and Elfrida, the nurse, ushered them into a room more splendid than anything they had ever seen. But, oh woe! where was Sarah Maud! and was it Fate that Mrs. Bird should say, at once, "Did you lay your hats in the hall?" Peter felt himself elected by circumstance the head of the family, and, casting one imploring look at tongue-tied Susan, standing next him, said huskily, "It was so very pleasant—that—that—" "That we hadn't good hats enough to go 'round," put in little Susan, bravely, to help him out, and then froze with horror that the ill-fated words had slipped off her tongue.

However, Mrs. Bird said, pleasantly, "Of course you wouldn't wear hats such a short distance—I forgot when I asked. Now will you come right in to Miss Carol's room? She is so anxious to see you."

Just then Sarah Maud came up the back stairs, so radiant with joy from her secret interview with the cook that Peter could have pinched her with a clear conscience; and Carol gave them a joyful welcome. "But where is Baby Larry?" she cried, looking over the group with searching eye. "Didn't he come?"

"Larry! Larry!" Good gracious, where was Larry? They were all sure that he had come in with them, for Susan remembered scolding him for tripping over the door-mat. Uncle Jack went into convulsions of laughter. "Are you sure there were nine of you?" he asked, merrily.

"I think so, sir," said Peoria, timidly; "but anyhow, there was Larry." And she showed signs of weeping.

"Oh, well, cheer up!" cried Uncle Jack. "Probably he's not lost—only mislaid. I'll go and find him before you can say Jack Robinson!"

"I'll go, too, if you please, sir," said Sarah Maud, "for it was my place to mind him, an' if he's lost I can't relish my vittles!"

The other Ruggleses stood rooted to the floor. Was this a dinner-party, forsooth; and if so, why were such things ever spoken of as festive occasions?

Sarah Maud went out through the hall, calling, "Larry! Larry!" and without any interval of suspense a thin voice piped up from below, "Here I be!"

The truth was that Larry, being deserted by his natural guardian, dropped behind the rest, and wriggled into the hat-tree to wait for her, having no notion of walking unprotected into the jaws of a fashionable entertainment. Finding that she did not come, he tried to crawl from his refuge and call somebody, when—dark and dreadful ending to a tragic day—he found that he was too much intertwined with umbrellas and canes to move a single step. He was afraid to yell (when I have said this of Larry Ruggles I have pictured a state of helpless terror that ought to wring tears from every eye); and the sound of Sarah Maud's beloved voice, some seconds later, was like a strain of angel music in his ears. Uncle Jack dried his tears, carried him upstairs, and soon had him in breathless fits of laughter, while Carol so made the other Ruggleses forget themselves that they were presently talking like accomplished diners-out.

Carol's bed had been moved into the farthest corner of the room, and she was lying on the outside, dressed in a wonderful dressing-gown that looked like a fleecy cloud. Her golden hair fell in fluffy curls over her white forehead and neck, her cheeks flushed delicately, her eyes beamed with joy, and the children told their mother, afterwards, that she looked as beautiful as the angels in the picture books.

There was a great bustle behind a huge screen in another part of the room, and at half past five this was taken away, and the Christmas dinner-table stood revealed. What a wonderful sight it was to the poor little Ruggles children, who ate their sometimes scanty meals on the kitchen table! It blazed with tall colored candles, it gleamed with glass and silver, it blushed with flowers, it groaned with good things to eat; so it was not strange that the Ruggleses, forgetting altogether that their mother was a McGrill, shrieked in admiration of the fairy spectacle. But Larry's behavior was the most disgraceful, for he stood not upon the order of his going, but went at once for a high chair that pointed unmistakably to him, climbed up like a squirrel, gave a comprehensive look at the turkey, clapped his hands in ecstasy, rested his fat arms on the table, and cried with joy, "I beat the hull lot o' yer!" Carol laughed until she cried, giving orders, meanwhile—"Uncle Jack, please sit at the head, Sarah Maud at the foot, and that will leave four on each side; Mamma is going to help Elfrida, so that the children need not look after each other, but just have a good time."

A sprig of holly lay by each plate, and nothing would do but each little Ruggles must leave his seat and have it pinned on by Carol, and as each course was served, one of them pleaded to take something to her. There was hurrying to and fro, I can assure you, for it is quite a difficult matter to serve a Christmas dinner on the third floor of a great city house; but if it had been necessary to carry every dish up a rope ladder the servants would gladly have done so. There were turkey and chicken, with delicious gravy and stuffing, and there were half a dozen vegetables, with cranberry jelly, and celery, and pickles; and as for the way these delicacies were served, the Ruggleses never forgot it as long as they lived.

Peter nudged Kitty, who sat next to him, and said, "Look, will yer, ev'ry feller's got his own partic'lar butter; I s'pose that's to show you can eat that 'n' no more. No, it ain't either, for that pig of a Peory's just gettin' another helpin'!"

"Yes," whispered Kitty, "an' the napkins is marked with big red letters! I wonder if that's so nobody'll nip 'em; an' oh, Peter, look at the pictures stickin' right on ter the dishes! Did yer ever?"

"The plums is all took out o' my cramb'ry sarse an' it's friz to a stiff jell'!" whispered Peoria, in wild excitement.

"Hi—yah! I got a wish-bone!" sang Larry, regardless of Sarah Maud's frown; after which she asked to have his seat changed, giving as excuse that he "gen'ally set beside her, an' would feel strange"; the true reason being that she desired to kick him gently, under the table, whenever he passed what might be termed "the McGrill line."

"I declare to goodness," murmured Susan, on the other side, "there's so much to look at I can't scarcely eat nothin'!"

"Bet yer life I can!" said Peter, who had kept one servant busily employed ever since he sat down; for, luckily, no one was asked by Uncle Jack whether he would have a second helping, but the dishes were quietly passed under their noses, and not a single Ruggles refused anything that was offered him, even unto the seventh time.

Then, when Carol and Uncle Jack perceived that more turkey was a physical impossibility, the meats were taken off and the dessert was brought in—a dessert that would have frightened a strong man after such a dinner as had preceded it. Not so the Ruggleses—for a strong man is nothing to a small boy—and they kindled to the dessert as if the turkey had been a dream and the six vegetables an optical delusion. There were plum-pudding, mince-pie, and ice-cream; and there were nuts, and raisins, and oranges. Kitty chose ice-cream, explaining that she knew it "by sight, though she hadn't never tasted none;" but all the rest took the entire variety, without any regard to consequences.

"My dear child," whispered Uncle Jack, as he took Carol an orange, "there is no doubt about the necessity of this feast, but I do advise you after this to have them twice a year, or quarterly perhaps, for the way these children eat is positively dangerous;

I assure you I tremble for that terrible Peoria. I'm going to run races with her after dinner."

"Never mind," laughed Carol; "let them have enough for once; it does my heart good to see them, and they shall come oftener next year."

The feast being over, the Ruggleses lay back in their chairs languidly, like little gorged boa-constrictors, and the table was cleared in a trice. Then a door was opened into the next room, and there, in a corner facing Carol's bed, which had been wheeled as close as possible, stood the brilliantly lighted Christmas tree, glittering with gilded walnuts and tiny silver balloons, and wreathed with snowy chains of pop-corn. The presents had been bought mostly with Carol's story-money, and were selected after long consultations with Mrs. Bird. Each girl had a blue knitted hood, and each boy a red crocheted comforter, all made by Mamma, Carol, and Elfrida. ("Because if you buy everything, it doesn't show so much love," said Carol.) Then every girl had a pretty plaid dress of a different color, and every boy a warm coat of the right size. Here the useful presents stopped, and they were quite enough; but Carol had pleaded to give them something "for fun." "I know they need the clothes," she had said, when they were talking over the matter just after Thanksgiving, "but they don't care much for them, after all. Now, Papa, won't you please let me go without part of my presents this year, and give me the money they would cost, to buy something to amuse the Ruggleses?"

"You can have both," said Mr. Bird, promptly; "is there any need of my little girl's going without her own Christmas, I should like to know? Spend all the money you like."

"But that isn't the thing," objected Carol, nestling close to her father; "it wouldn't be mine. What is the use? Haven't I almost everything already, and am I not the happiest girl in the world this year, with Uncle Jack and Donald at home? You know very well it is more blessed to give than to receive; so why won't you

let me do it? You never look half as happy when you are getting your presents as when you are giving us ours. Now, Papa, submit, or I shall have to be very firm and disagreeable with you!"

"Very well, your Highness, I surrender."

"That's a dear Papa! Now what were you going to give me? Confess!"

"A bronze figure of Santa Claus; and in the 'little round belly that shakes when he laughs like a bowlful of jelly,' is a wonderful clock—oh, you would never give it up if you could see it!"

"Nonsense," laughed Carol; "as I never have to get up to breakfast, nor go to bed, nor catch trains, I think my old clock will do very well! Now, Mamma, what were you going to give me?"

"Oh, I hadn't decided. A few more books, and a gold thimble, and a smelling-bottle, and a music-box, perhaps."

"Poor Carol," laughed the child, merrily, "she can afford to give up these lovely things, for there will still be left Uncle Jack, and Donald, and Paul, and Hugh, and Uncle Rob, and Aunt Elsie, and a dozen other people to fill her Christmas stocking!"

So Carol had her way, as she generally did; but it was usually a good way, which was fortunate, under the circumstances; and Sarah Maud had a set of Miss Alcott's books, and Peter a modest silver watch, Cornelius a tool-chest, Clement a dog-house for his lame puppy, Larry a magnificent Noah's ark, and each of the younger girls a beautiful doll.

You can well believe that everybody was very merry and very thankful. All the family, from Mr. Bird down to the cook, said that they had never seen so much happiness in the space of three hours; but it had to end, as all things do. The candles flickered and went out, the tree was left alone with its gilded ornaments, and Mrs. Bird sent the children downstairs at half past eight, thinking that Carol looked tired.

"Now, my darling, you have done quite enough for one day," said Mrs. Bird, getting Carol into her little nightgown. "I'm afraid you will feel worse tomorrow, and that would be a sad ending to such a charming evening."

"Oh, wasn't it a lovely, lovely time," sighed Carol. "From first to last, everything was just right. I shall never forget Larry's face when he looked at the turkey; nor Peter's when he saw his watch; nor that sweet, sweet Kitty's smile when she kissed her dolly; nor the tears in poor, dull Sarah Maud's eyes when she thanked me for her books; nor—"

"But we mustn't talk any longer about it to-night," said Mrs. Bird, anxiously; "you are too tired, dear."

"I am not so very tired, Mamma. I have felt well all day; not a bit of pain anywhere. Perhaps this has done me good."

"Perhaps; I hope so. There was no noise or confusion; it was just a merry time. Now, may I close the door and leave you alone, dear? Papa and I will steal in softly by and by to see if you are all right; but I think you need to be very quiet."

"Oh, I'm willing to stay by myself; but I am not sleepy yet, and I am going to hear the music, you know."

"Yes, I have opened the window a little, and put the screen in front of it, so that you won't feel the air."

"Can I have the shutters open? And won't you turn my bed, please? This morning I woke ever so early, and one bright, beautiful star shone in that eastern window. I never noticed it before, and I thought of the Star in the East, that guided the Wise Men to the place where the baby Jesus was. Good-night, Mamma. Such a happy, happy day!"

"Good-night, my precious Christmas Carol—mother's blessed Christmas child."

"Bend your head a minute, mother dear," whispered Carol, calling her mother back. "Mamma, dear, I do think that we have kept Christ's birthday this time just as He would like it. Don't you?"

"I am sure of it," said Mrs. Bird, softly.

VII: *The Birdling Flies Away*

The Ruggleses had finished a last romp in the library with Paul and Hugh, and Uncle Jack had taken them home and stayed awhile to chat with Mrs. Ruggles, who opened the door for them, her face all aglow with excitement and delight. When Kitty and Clem showed her the oranges and nuts that they had kept for her, she astonished them by saying that at six o'clock Mrs. Bird had sent her in the finest dinner she had ever seen in her life; and not only that, but a piece of dress-goods that must have cost a dollar a yard if it cost a cent.

As Uncle Jack went down the rickety steps he looked back into the window for a last glimpse of the family, as the children gathered about their mother, showing their beautiful presents again and again— and then upward to a window in the great house yonder. "A little child shall lead them," he thought. "Well, if—if anything ever happens to Carol, I will take the Ruggleses under my wing."

"Softly, Uncle Jack," whispered the boys, as he walked into the library awhile later. "We are listening to the music in the church. The choir has sung 'Carol, brothers, carol,' and now we think the organist is beginning to play 'My ain countree' for Carol."

"I hope she hears it," said Mrs. Bird; "but they are very late tonight, and I dare not speak to her lest she should be asleep. It is almost ten o'clock."

The boy soprano, clad in white surplice, stood in the organ loft. The light shone full upon his crown of fair hair, and his pale face, with its serious blue eyes, looked paler than usual. Perhaps it was something in the tender thrill of the voice, or in the sweet words, but there were tears in many eyes, both in the church and in the great house next door.

"I am far frae my hame,
    I am weary aften whiles
For the langed-for hame-bringin',
    An' my Faether's welcome smiles;

An' I'll ne'er be fu' content,
Until my e'en do see
The gowden gates o' heaven
In my ain countree.

"The earth is decked wi' flow'rs,
Mony tinted, fresh an' gay,
An' the birdies warble blythely,
For my Faether made them sae;
But these sights an' these soun's
Will as naething be to me,
When I hear the angels singin'
In my ain countree.

"Like a bairn to its mither,
A wee birdie to its nest,
I fain would be gangin' noo
Unto my Faether's breast;
For He gathers in His arms
Helpless, worthless lambs like me,
An' carries them Himsel'
To His ain countree."

There were tears in many eyes, but not in Carol's. The loving heart had quietly ceased to beat, and the "wee birdie" in the great house had flown to its "home nest." Carol had fallen asleep! But as to the song, I think perhaps, she heard it after all!

So sad an ending to a happy day! Perhaps—to those who were left; and yet Carol's mother, even in the freshness of her grief, was glad that her darling had slipped away on the loveliest day of her life, out of its glad content, into everlasting peace.

She was glad that she had gone as she had come, on the wings of song, when all the world was brimming over with joy; glad of every grateful smile, of every joyous burst of laughter, of every loving thought and word and deed the dear last day had brought.

Sadness reigned, it is true, in the little house behind the garden; and one day poor Sarah Maud, with a courage born of despair, threw on her hood and shawl, walked straight to a certain house a mile away, up the marble steps into good Dr. Bartol's office, falling at his feet as she cried, "Oh, sir, it was me an' our children that went to Miss Carol's last dinner-party, an' if we made her worse we can't never be happy again!" Then the kind old gentleman took her rough hand in his and told her to dry her tears, for neither she nor any of her flock had hastened Carol's flight; indeed, he said that had it not been for the strong hopes and wishes that filled her tired heart, she could not have stayed long enough to keep that last merry Christmas with her dear ones.

And so the old years, fraught with memories, die, one after another, and the new years, bright with hopes, are born to take their places; but Carol lives again in every chime of Christmas bells that peal glad tidings, and in every Christmas anthem sung by childish voices.

Sarah Orne Jewett

AT THE close of the Civil War, city folk started going to small towns in Maine for their summer vacations. Many of these visitors were highly amused at the peculiarities of the inhabitants, and used to ridicule them. Sarah Orne Jewett was a mere girl at the time, but she was determined to "teach the world that country people were not the awkward, ignorant set," as commonly described. Her charming story, "The Empty Purse," portrays Miss Debby Gaines, who had seen better days just as South Berwick had, and was making the best of it.

This cultivated Maine spinster, daughter of the village doctor, was inspired by the novels of Harriet Beecher Stowe and William Dean Howells, and her writing has been compared with the "exquisite freshness of feeling" which no one since Hawthorne had achieved in portraying New England. Born in South Berwick in 1849, she died there in 1909. She was nineteen when her first story appeared in the *Atlantic,* and a few years later a collection of her character sketches in book form, entitled *Deephaven,* established her reputation. She is best known today for two later collections of stories, *A White Heron* and *The Country of the Pointed Firs.*

Miss Jewett also wrote novels, children's stories, and a book of verse. She was a polished writer who could etch with carefully chosen words in a few precise sentences the fading glory of that region of New England which she loved. However frustrated or confused her dear old ladies became, she treated them with dignity and warm humanity. She counted among her friends many of the renowned literary people of a notable age of cultural achievement, and was the first woman to be given the honorary degree of Doctor of Literature at Bowdoin College.

She spent considerable time with her sister, Mrs. James T. Fields, wife of the famous publisher, whose Boston home was known as "the temple of literary piety." In one of her memoirs, Laura E. Richards described this treasure house filled with wonderful books and manuscripts. "Over the fireplace was the life-sized portrait of Dickens in his youth, pen in hand, looking full at the fortunate guest, with his luminous, questioning smile." The radiance of that smile shone in a variety of ways in the writing of many American authors, and not the least of them was Sarah Orne Jewett.

AN EMPTY PURSE

LITTLE Miss Debby Gaines was counting the days to Christmas; there were only three, and the weather was bright and warm for the time of year. "I've got to step fast to carry out all my plans," she said to herself. "It seems to me as if it were going to be a beautiful Christmas; it won't be like any I've spent lately, either. I shouldn't wonder if it turned out for the best, my losing that money I always call my Christmas money; anyway I'll do the best I can to make up for it."

Miss Debby was sitting by the window sewing as fast as she could, for the light of the short winter day was going, mending a warm old petticoat and humming a psalm-tune. Suddenly she heard a knock at the door; she lived in two upstairs rooms, and could not see the street.

"Come in!" she said cheerfully, and dropped her lapful of work.

"Why, if it isn't Mrs. Rivers!" she exclaimed with much pleasure.

The guest was a large woman, fashionably dressed. You would have thought that a very elegant blue-jay had come to make a late afternoon call upon such a brown chippy-sparrow as Miss Debby Gaines. Miss Debby felt much honored, and brought forward her best rocking-chair; and Mrs. Rivers seated herself and began to rock. Her stiff silk gown creaked as if she were a ship at sea.

"What are you doing—something pretty for Christmas?" she asked.

"It may be for Christmas, but it isn't very pretty," answered Miss Debby with a little laugh and shake of the head. "Tell you the truth, I was mending up a nice warm petticoat that I don't have much use for; I thought I'd give it to old Mrs. Bean, at the poorhouse. She's a complaining, cold old creatur', an' she's got poor eyesight and can't sew, and I thought this would make her real comfortable. It's rather more heavy than I need to wear."

"I've been down town all the afternoon, and it's so tiresome trying to get anything in the stores," complained Mrs. Rivers. "They push you right away from what you want time to look over. I like to consider what I buy. It's a great burden to me trying to get ready for Christmas, and I thought I shouldn't do anything this year on account of my health. I've had large expenses this autumn. I had to buy new carpets and a new outside garment. I do like to see the pretty things in the stores, but they were so full of people and so hot and disagreeable this afternoon."

Miss Debby had picked up her petticoat and was holding it close to the window while she sewed on the button with firm linen stitches.

"I haven't been down the street for two or three days," she said. "You'll excuse me for goin' on with my work; it's most dark, and I'll be done in a moment; then we can sit an' talk."

"It does me good to come and see you once in a while," said Mrs. Rivers plaintively. "I thought I'd stop on my way home. Last year you had so many pretty little things that you'd been making."

"There aren't any at all this year," answered Miss Debby bravely. "It wasn't convenient, so I thought I'd just try having another kind of a merry Christmas."

"Sometimes I wish I had no more responsibilities than you have. My large house is such a care. Mr. Rivers is very particular about everything, and so am I." She gave a great sigh, and creaked louder than before, but Miss Debby did not find the right sort of consolation to offer, and kept silence. "You enjoy having your pretty house," she ventured to say after a few moments; "you wouldn't like to do with as little as some,"—and Mrs. Rivers shook her head in the dusk, and went on rocking.

"Presents aren't nothing unless the heart goes with them," said Miss Debby boldly at last, "and I think we can show good feelin' in other ways than by bestowing little pin-cushions. Anyway, I've got to find those ways for me this year. 'Tis a day when we New England folks can speak right out to each other, and that does us some good. Somethin' gets in the air. I expect now to enjoy this Christmas myself, though I felt dreadful bad last week, sayin' to myself 'twas the first time I couldn't buy Christmas presents. I didn't know how interested I was goin' to get; you see I've made my little plans."

Then they talked about other things, and Mrs. Rivers grew more cheerful and at last went away. She always found Christmas a melancholy season. She did not like the trouble of giving presents then, or at any other time; but she had her good points, as Miss Debby Gaines always bravely insisted.

Early on Christmas morning Miss Debby waked up with a feeling of happy expectation, and could hardly wait to make her cup of tea and eat her little breakfast on the corner of the table before she got out her best bonnet and Sunday cloak to begin her Christmas errands. It was cloudy and dark, but the sunlight came at last, pale and radiant, into the little brown room; and Miss Debby's face matched it with a quiet smile and happy look of eagerness.

"Take neither purse nor scrip," she said to herself as she went downstairs into the street. There was nobody else stirring in the house, but she knew that the poorhouse would be open and its early breakfast past by the time she could get there. It was a mile or so out of town. She hugged a large package under her shawl, and shivered a little at the beginning of her walk. There was no snow, but the heavy hoar-frost glistened on the sidewalks, and the air was sharp.

Old Mrs. Bean was coming out of the great kitchen, and when her friend wished her a merry Christmas she shook her head.

"There ain't anybody to make it merry for me," she said.

"I wish you a happy Christmas!" said Miss Debby again; "I've come on purpose to be your first caller, an' I'm going to make you the only present I shall give this year. 'Tis somethin' useful, Mis' Bean; a warm petticoat I've fixed up nice, so's you can put it right on and feel the comfort of it."

The old woman's face brightened. "Why, you are real kind," she said eagerly. "It is the one thing I've been wantin'. Oh yes, *dear sakes!* ain't it a beautiful warm one—one o' the real old-fashioned quilted kind. I always used to have 'em when I was better off. Well, that *is* a present!"

"Now I'm goin', because I can come an' set an' talk with you any day, and today I've got Christmas work," and off Miss Debby went to the heart of the town again.

Christmas was on Tuesday that year, and she opened the door of a little house where a tired-looking young woman stood by an ironing-table and looked at her with surprise. "Why, Miss Gaines!" she exclaimed; "where are you going so early?"

"I wish you a happy Christmas!" said Miss Debby. "I've come to spend the mornin' with you. Just through breakfast? No; the little girls are eatin' away yet. Why, you're late!"

"I didn't mean to be," said the young mother; "but I felt so tired this morning, and pretty sad, too, thinking of last year an' all. So I just let the children sleep. Nelly's got cold and was coughing most all night, and I couldn't bear to get up and begin the day. Mother sent for me to come over to spend Christmas, but I couldn't get the courage to start. She said she'd have some little presents ready for the little girls, and now I'm most sorry I disappointed her."

"That's just why I'm here," said Miss Debby gayly, and with double her usual decision. "No, Nelly's not fit to go out, I can see; and you leave her here with me, an' you just get ready and take Susy and go. Your mother'll think everything of it, and I'll see to things here. Ironin'? Why, 'twill do me good. I feel a little chilly, and Nelly and I can have a grand time. Now you go right off an' get ready, and catch the quarter-to-nine train. I won't hear no words about it."

So presently the pale, hard-worked young mother put on her widow's bonnet and started off down the street, leading bright-faced little Susy by the hand; and Miss Debby and her favorite, Nelly, watched them go, from the window. The breakfast dishes were washed and put away in such fashion that Nelly thought it quite as good as doll's housekeeping; and then, while Miss Debby ironed, she sat in a warm corner by the stove and listened to stories and to Miss Debby's old-fashioned ballads, which, though sung in a slightly cracked voice, were most delightful to childish ears. What a Christmas morning it was! And after the small ironing was done, what pleasant things there seemed to be to do! Miss Debby rummaged until she found some little aprons cut for the children; and first she basted one for Nelly to sew, and then she took the other herself, and they sat down together and sewed until dinnertime. The aprons were pink and added to the gayety of the occasion; and they were ready at last to surprise Nelly's mother by being put back

in their place in the same roll—all done even to the buttons and buttonholes, for Miss Debby found time to finish Nelly's as well as her own. And they had bread and milk for dinner, and Miss Debby told stories of when she was a little girl. Altogether there never was a happier Christmas Day, and the spirit of Christmas, of peace and good-will, shone brightly in Miss Debby's face. Her quick eyes saw many chances to lend a helping hand to the poor defenceless household. When Nelly's mother came home at night, heartened and cheered by her visit, she found the ironing and mending done; and a day or two later the pink aprons turned up all ready to be put on. And Nelly's tiresome cough, which sounded like the whooping-cough, was quite stilled by some good old-fashioned dose which Miss Debby mixed agreeably with molasses and put to simmer on the stove. There seemed to be no end to the kind and thoughtful things Miss Debby did that day in a neighbor's house.

She had started for home at dusk, just before it was time for young Mrs. Prender to get back, and was walking along the street, a little tired, but very happy.

"Why, it's only half past four o'clock now!" she exclaimed, as she passed the watchmaker's window. "I mean to go and see Mrs. Wallis a little while," and she quickened her steps.

Presently Miss Debby Gaines came to a fine large house, very different from the one she had just left, and took pains to straighten her little black bonnet as she went up the long flight of handsome stone steps. An elderly man-servant opened the door.

"I wish you a happy Christmas!" said Miss Debby. "Can I see Mrs. Wallis, do you suppose, Mr. Johnson?"

"Oh, yes'm," said Johnson with feeling. "I was wishing somebody'd come in, Miss Gaines, now it's beginning to get dark. The young ladies was here this morning, and brought their presents, but they'd made a promise to go out into the country with some young friends, so they aren't coming to dinner, and Mrs. Wallis has been alone all day. She was pleased to have 'em go, though."

By this time Miss Debby had crossed the wide hall to the library, where the kind mistress of the house was sitting alone. She hesitated a moment before she could speak.

"I wish you a happy Christmas!" she said. "It's only me, Mrs. Wallis—Debby Gaines."

"Why, Miss Debby!" and there was something in the tone of this hostess which told at once that she was glad to see a friend. "Why, dear Miss Debby! Come and sit down in this chair by me! I don't doubt you have been trotting about all day," and Mrs. Wallis held out a warm, affectionate hand.

"No, I've been keepin' house for Mis' Prender, so she could go and see her mother," explained Miss Debby quite simply. "I had a nice time with her little girl that's just getting over a cold and couldn't go with the others. I was just on my way home. I thought I'd stop and see if there was anything I could do for you."

"Nothing except to stay a little while and keep me company," said Mrs. Wallis. "My granddaughters are usually here, but they had a very pleasant plan made for them, and I was very glad to have them go. A skating party and a dinner at the Ashtons' country house, and a dance."

"Young folks will be young folks," said Miss Debby. "I should like to hear all about it when they come and tell. Everybody seemed to be goin' somewhere today; 'twas the nice clear weather."

"There are all my pretty presents on the table," said Mrs. Wallis. "Somehow they haven't been very good company; this is the first Christmas in all my life that I have happened to spend quite alone."

Miss Debby might not have done so much without thinking, by daylight, but she drew a little nearer and took hold of Mrs. Wallis's hand.

"You must have had a great many lovely things to remember," she said softly. "But anybody can't help feeling lonesome; I

know how 'tis. Everybody misses somebody the world over. There was all of us together once at home, and now I'm a kind of sparrow on the housetops. But I've had a beautiful day so far. I own I was afraid you'd have a sight of company an' I should have to miss askin' to see you."

"I'm glad somebody wanted to see me," said Mrs. Wallis more cheerfully, "and one of the friends I've known longest"; then they went on with much pleasant talk of the old days, and Mrs. Wallis gave Miss Debby an excellent cup of tea, and they had a happy little feast together there in the library before the humble, loving-hearted guest went away, leaving peace and good-will once more in a lonely and troubled heart.

She stopped here and there at the houses of other friends, forgetting in her happiness that she was empty-handed on Christmas Day, and everywhere she left a new feeling of friendliness and pleasant kindness. At one house she comforted a crying child by mending his broken top, and at another she knew just how to help a pretty girl to get ready for her Christmas party, and sat down and took off her big woollen gloves to alter the refractory dress, which had seemed impossible to be worn. She was like a good angel as she sat there, sewing and smiling and putting everybody's mind at ease.

It was late in the evening when this was finished, and she had had a long day; but she stopped, with great bravery, and asked to see the minister, just to tell him how thankful she was for his sermon on Sunday and wish him a happy Christmas. The minister had been a little discouraged for some reason, as ministers often are, and even Christmas kindnesses in the shape of welcome presents from his friends did not cheer him half so much as the sincerity and affection of Miss Debby's visit. He watched the little figure go down the steps with tears in his eyes. So few persons could forget themselves to remember others as this dear parishioner could; it was worth living for, if one could sometimes help and refresh those who are the true helpers; and he went back to his work in the study feeling like a better and busier man than when he had left it.

So Miss Debby came back to her little home again. The fire was out and it was all dark, but she went straight to her small rocking-chair by the window and sat down to rest, and to thank the Lord for such a happy day. Though her purse was empty her heart was full, and she had left pleasure and comfort behind her all along the way.

Presently she lighted her lamp, and then she saw on the table a great package with a note beside it; the note was from Mrs. Rivers.

"Something you said the other day," Miss Debby read, "made me feel differently about Christmas from the way I have before, and I am going right to work to try to make as many people happy as I can. And you must feel that my heart goes with these presents that I send you first. They are some of my own things that I liked, and I send them with love."

Miss Debby's face shone with joy. She had always liked Mrs. Rivers, but she had often pitied her a little; and now the note made her feel as if she had found a new friend in an old one. This was the way that Miss Debby's Christmas came to its happy end.

Charles Egbert Craddock

UNIQUE among the women writers of her day, this slightly crippled little lady from Murfreesboro, Tennessee, who was born and died in the community named for her family, was a most exceptional storyteller. Born in 1851, she was educated in Philadelphia and Nashville, and also lived in St. Louis. This talented woman had a rich cultural background which included music. Her family suffered heavily as a result of the Civil War, and she turned to writing as a profession. She spent her summers in the Tennessee Mountains and learned to love the natives. Their customs, traditions, and old-world speech fascinated her and she portrayed them vividly. As a novelist and writer of short stories she paved the way for later writers like John Fox, Jr., and others.

Partially paralyzed from a childhood illness, she was lame all her life and slight of stature. Fearing that her writings would not be well received if she used her own name, she chose as a pen name that of one of her earliest heroes. Her forthright, vigorous style, which was virile and robust, and her bold, heavily shaded handwriting obviously impressed the gentle, mild-mannered Thomas Bailey Aldrich, Editor of *The Atlantic Monthly.* He once wrote, "I wonder if Craddock has laid in his winter's ink yet, so that I can get a serial out of him." A year later Mr. Aldrich could hardly believe his eyes when Miss Murfree arrived in Boston and announced herself as Charles Egbert Craddock. This meeting occurred in connection with the publication of a collection of her short stories, *In the Tennessee Mountains,* which brought its author great fame. The year 1884 became known as the "climactic year in the history of the short story," and Charles Egbert Craddock became as well known as Oliver Wendell Holmes. Her literary output was sizable. Including both novels and short stories, it totaled twenty-five volumes. "Christmas Day on Old Windy Mountain" was published in a book of short stories, *The Young Mountaineers,* which appeared in 1897.

CHRISTMAS DAY ON OLD WINDY MOUNTAIN

THE sun had barely shown the rim of his great red disk above the sombre woods and snow-crowned crags of the opposite ridge, when Rick Herne, his rifle in his hand, stepped out of his father's log cabin, perched high among the precipices of Old Windy Mountain. He waited motionless for a moment, and all the family trooped to the door to assist at the time-honored ceremony of firing a salute to the day.

Suddenly the whole landscape catches a rosy glow, Rick whips up his rifle, a jet of flame darts swiftly out, a sharp report rings all around the world, and the sun goes grandly up—while the little tow-headed mountaineers hurrah shrilly for "Chris'mus!"

As he began to re-load his gun, the small boys clustered around him, their hands in the pockets of their baggy jeans trousers, their heads inquiringly askew.

"They air a-goin' ter hev a pea-fow*el* fur dinner down yander ter Birk's Mill," Rick remarked.

The smallest boy smacked his lips,—not that he knew how pea-fowl tastes, but he imagined unutterable things.

"Somehows I hates fur ye ter go ter eat at Birk's Mill, they air sech a set o' drinkin' men down thar ter Malviny's house," said Rick's mother, as she stood in the doorway, and looked anxiously at him.

For his older sister was Birk's wife, and to this great feast he was invited as a representative of the family, his father being disabled by "rheumatics," and his mother kept at home by the necessity of providing dinner for those four small boys.

"Hain't I done promised ye not ter tech a drap o' liquor this Chris'mus day?" asked Rick.

"That's a fac'," his mother admitted. "But boys, an' men-folks ginerally, air scandalous easy ter break a promise whar whiskey is in it."

"I'll hev ye ter know that when I gin my word, I keeps it!" cried Rick pridefully.

He little dreamed how that promise was to be assailed before the sun should go down.

He was a tall, sinewy boy, deft of foot as all these mountaineers are, and a seven-mile walk in the snow to Birk's Mill he considered a mere trifle. He tramped along cheerily enough through the silent solitudes of the dense forest. Only at long intervals the stillness was broken by the cracking of a bough under the weight of snow, or the whistling of a gust of wind through the narrow valley far below.

All at once—it was a terrible shock of surprise—he was sinking! Was there nothing beneath his feet but the vague depths of air to the base of the mountain? He realized with a quiver of dismay that he had mistaken a huge drift-filled fissure, between a jutting crag and the wall of the ridge, for the solid, snow-covered ground. He tossed his arms about wildly in his effort to grasp something firm. The motion only dislodged the drift. He felt that it was falling, and he was going down—down—down with it. He saw the trees on the summit of Old Windy disappear. He caught one glimpse of the neighboring ridges. Then he was blinded and enveloped in this cruel whiteness. He had a wild idea that he had been delivered to it forever; even in the first thaw it would curl up into a wreath of vapor, and rise from the mountain's side, and take him soaring with it—whither? How they would search these bleak wintry fastnesses for him,—while he was gone sailing with the mist! What would they say at home and at Birk's Mill? One last thought of the "pea-fow*el*," and he seemed to slide swiftly away from the world with the snow.

He was unconscious probably only for a few minutes. When he came to himself, he found that he was lying, half-submerged in the great drift, on the slope of the mountain, and the dark, icicle-begirt cliff towered high above. He stretched his limbs —no bones broken! He could hardly believe that he had fallen unhurt from those heights. He did not appreciate how gradually the snow had slidden down. Being so densely packed, too, it had buoyed him up, and kept him from dashing against the sharp, jagged edges of the rock. He had lost consciousness in the jar when the moving mass was abruptly arrested by a transverse elevation of the ground. He was still a little dizzy and faint, but otherwise uninjured.

Now a great perplexity took hold on him. How was he to make his way back up the mountain, he asked himself, as he looked at the inaccessible cliffs looming high into the air. All the world around him was unfamiliar. Even his wide wanderings had never brought him into this vast, snowy, trackless wilderness, that stretched out on every side. He would be half the day in finding the valley road that led to Birk's Mill. He rose to his feet, and gazed about him in painful indecision. The next moment a thrill shot through him, to which he was unaccustomed. He had never before shaken except with the cold,—but this was fear.

For he heard voices! Not from the cliffs above,—but from below! Not from the dense growth of young pines on the slope of the mountain,—but from the depths of the earth beneath! He stood motionless, listening intently, his eyes distended, and his heart beating fast.

All silence! Not even the wind stirred in the pine thicket. The snow lay heavy among the dark green branches, and every slender needle was encased in ice. Rick rubbed his eyes. It was no dream. There was the thicket; but whose were the voices that had rung out faintly from beneath it?

A crowd of superstitions surged upon him. He cast an affrighted glance at the ghastly snow-covered woods and sheeted earth. He was remembering fireside legends, horrible enough to raise the hair on a so-

phisticated, educated boy's head; much more horrible, then, to a young backwoodsman like Rick. On this, the most benign day that ever dawns upon the world, was he led into these endless wastes of forest to be terrified by the "harnts"?

Suddenly those voices from the earth again! One was singing a drunken catch,— it broke into falsetto, and ended with an unmistakable hiccup.

Rick's blood came back with a rush.

"I hev never hearn tell o' the hoobies gittin' boozy!" he said with a laugh. "That's whar they hev got the upper-hand o' humans."

As he gazed again at the thicket, he saw now something that he had been too much agitated to observe before,—a column of dense smoke that rose from far down the declivity, and seemed to make haste to hide itself among the low-hanging boughs of a clump of fir-trees.

"It's somebody's house down thar," was Rick's conclusion. "I kin find out the way to Birk's Mill from the folkses."

When he neared the smoke, he paused abruptly, staring once more.

There was no house! The smoke rose from among low pine bushes. Above were the snow-laden branches of the fir.

"Ef thar war a house hyar, I reckon I could see it!" said Rick doubtfully, infinitely mystified.

There was a continual drip, drip of moisture all around. Yet a thaw had not set in. Rick looked up at the gigantic icicles that hung to the crags and glittered in the sun,—not a drop trickled from them. But this fir-tree was dripping, dripping, and the snow had melted away from the nearest pine bushes that clustered about the smoke. There was heat below certainly, a strong heat, and somebody was keeping the fire up steadily.

"An' air it folkses ez live underground like foxes an' sech!" Rick exclaimed, astonished, as he came upon a large, irregularly shaped rift in the rocks, and heard the same reeling voice from within, beginning to sing once more. But for this bacchanalian melody, the noise of Rick's entrance might have given notice of his approach. As it was, the inhabitants of this strange place were even more surprised than he, when, after groping through a dark, low passage, an abrupt turn brought him into a lofty, vaulted subterranean apartment. There was a great flare of light, which revealed six or seven muscular men grouped about a large copper vessel built into a rude stone furnace, and all the air was pervaded by an incomparably strong alcoholic odor. The boy started back with a look of terror. That pale terror was reflected on each man's face, as on a mirror. At the sight of the young stranger they all sprang up with the same gesture,—each instinctively laid his hand upon the pistol that he wore.

Poor Rick understood it all at last. He had stumbled upon a nest of distillers, only too common among these mountains, who were hiding from the officers of the Government, running their still in defiance of the law and eluding the whiskey-tax. He realized that in discovering their stronghold he had learned a secret that was by no means a safe one for him to know. And he was in their power; at their mercy!

"Don't shoot!" he faltered. "I jes' want ter ax the folkses ter tell me the way ter Birk's Mill."

What would he have given to be on the bleak mountain outside!

One of the men caught him as if anticipating an attempt to run. Two or three, after a low-toned colloquy, took their rifles, and crept cautiously outside to reconnoitre the situation. Rick comprehended their suspicion with new quakings. They imagined that he was a spy, and had been sent among them to discover them plying their forbidden vocation. This threatened a long imprisonment for them. His heart sank as he thought of it; they would never let him go.

After a time the reconnoitring party came back.

"Nothin' stirrin'," said the leader tersely.

"I misdoubts," muttered another, cast-ing a look of deep suspicion on Rick. "Thar air men out thar, I'm a-thinkin', hid some-whar."

"They air furder 'n a mile off, enny-how," returned the first speaker. "We never lef' so much ez a bush 'thout sarchin' of it."

"The off'cers can't find this place no-ways 'thout that thar chap fur a guide," said a third, with a surly nod of his head at Rick.

"We're safe enough, boys, safe enough!" cried a stout-built, red-faced, red-bearded man, evidently very drunk, and with a voice that rose into quavering falsetto as he spoke. "This chap can't do nothin'. We hev got him bound hand an' foot. Hyar air the captive of our bow an' spear, boys! Mighty little captive, though! hi!" He tried to point jeeringly at Rick, and forgot what he had intended to do before he could fairly extend his hand. Then his rollicking head sank on his breast, and he began to sing sleepily again.

One of the more sober of the men had extinguished the fire in order that they should not be betrayed by the smoke out-side to the revenue officers who might be seeking them. The place, chilly enough at best, was growing bitter cold. The strange subterranean beauty of the surroundings, the limestone wall and arches, scintillating wherever they caught the light; the shad-owy, mysterious vaulted roof; the white stalactites that hung down thence to touch the stalagmites as they rose up from the floor, and formed with them endless vistas of stately colonnades, all were oddly in-congruous with the drunken, bloated faces of the distillers. Rick could not have put his thought into words, but it seemed to him that when men had degraded them-selves like this, even inanimate nature is something higher and nobler. "Sermons in stones" were not far to seek.

He observed that they were making preparations for flight, and once more the fear of what they would do with him clutched at his heart. He was something of a problem to them.

"This hyar cub will go blab," was the first suggestion.

"He will keep mum," said the vocalist, glancing at the boy with a jovially tipsy combination of leer and wink. "Hyar is the persuader!" He rapped sharply on the muzzle of his pistol. "This'll scotch his wheel."

"Hold yer own jaw, ye drunken 'possum!" retorted another of the group. "Ef ye fire off that pistol in hyar, we'll hev all these hyar rocks"—he pointed at the walls and the long colonnades—"answerin' back an' yelpin' like a pack o' hounds on a hot scent. Ef thar air folks outside, the noise would fotch 'em down on us fur true!"

Rick breathed more freely. The rocks would speak up for him! He could not be harmed with all these tell-tale witnesses at hand. So silent now, but with a latent voice strong enough for the dread of it to save his life!

The man who had put out the fire, who had led the reconnoitring party, who had made all the active preparations for departure, who seemed, in short, to be an executive committee of one,—a 'long, lazy-looking mountaineer, with a decision of action in startling contrast to his whole aspect,—now took this matter in hand.

"Nothin' easier," he said tersely. "Fill him up. Make him ez drunk ez a fraish b'iled ow*el*. Then lead him to the t'other eend o' the cave, an' blindfold him, an' lug him off five mile in the woods, an' leave him thar. He'll never know what he hev seen nor done."

"That's the dinctum!" cried the red-bearded man, in delighted approval, breaking into a wild, hiccupping laugh, inexpressibly odious to the boy. Rick had an extreme loathing for them all that showed itself with impolitic frankness upon his face. He realized as he had never done before the depths to which strong drink will reduce men. But that the very rocks would cry out upon them, they would have murdered him.

In the preparations for departure all the lights had been extinguished, except a single lantern, and a multitude of shadows had come thronging from the deeper recesses of the cave. In the faint glimmer the figures of the men loomed up, indistinct, gigantic, distorted. They hardly seemed men at all to Rick; rather some evil underground creatures, neither beast nor human.

And he was to be made equally besotted, and even more helpless than they, in order that his senses might be sapped away, and he should remember no story to tell. Perhaps if he had not had before him so vivid an illustration of the malign power that swayed them, he might not have experienced so strong an aversion to it. Now, to be made like them seemed a high price to pay for his life. And there was his promise to his mother! As the long, lank, lazy-looking mountaineer pressed the whiskey upon him, Rick dashed it aside with a gesture so unexpected and vehement that the cracked jug fell to the floor, and was shivered to fragments.

Rick lifted an appealing face to the man, who seized him with a strong grip. "I can't—I won't," the boy cried wildly. "I—I—promised my mother!"

He looked around the circle deprecatingly. He expected first a guffaw and then a blow, and he dreaded the ridicule more than the pain.

But there were neither blows nor ridicule. They all gazed at him, astounded. Then a change, which Rick hardly comprehended, flitted across the face of the man who had grasped him. The moonshiner turned away abruptly, with a bitter laugh that startled all the echoes.

"I—I promised *my* mother, too!" he cried. "It air good that in her grave whar she is she can't know how I hev kep' my word."

And then there was a sudden silence. It seemed to Rick, strangely enough, like the sudden silence that comes after prayer. He was reminded, as one of the men rose at length and the keg on which he had been sitting creaked with the motion, of the creaking benches in the little mountain church when the congregation started from their knees. And had some feeble, groping sinner's prayer filled the silence and the moral darkness!

The "executive committee" promptly recovered himself. But he made no further attempt to force the whiskey upon the boy. Under some whispered instructions which he gave the others, Rick was half-led, half-dragged through immensely long black halls of the cave, while one of the men went before, carrying the feeble lantern. When the first glimmer of daylight appeared in the distance, Rick understood that the cave had an outlet other than the one by which he had entered, and evidently miles distant from it. Thus it was that the distillers were well enabled to baffle the law that sought them.

They stopped here and blindfolded the boy. How far and where they dragged him through the snowy mountain wilderness outside, Rick never knew. He was exhausted when at length they allowed him to pause. As he heard their steps dying away in the distance, he tore the bandage from his eyes, and found that they had left him in the midst of the wagon road to make his way to Birk's Mill as best he might. When he reached it, the wintry sun was low in the western sky, and the very bones of the "pea-fowel" were picked.

On the whole, it seemed a sorry Christmas Day, as Rick could not know then—indeed, he never knew—what good results it brought forth. For among those who took the benefit of the "amnesty" extended by the Government to the moonshiners of this region, on condition that they discontinue illicit distilling for the future, was a certain long, lank, lazy-looking mountaineer, who suddenly became sober and steady and a law-abiding citizen. He had been reminded, this Christmas Day, of a broken promise to a dead mother, and this by the unflinching moral courage of a mere boy in a moment of mortal peril. Such wise, sweet, uncovenanted uses has duty, blessing alike the unconscious exemplar and him who profits by the example.

* I WISH YOU A JOYFUL CHRISTMAS *

* A bone of contention well removed. *

Hezekiah Butterworth

HEZEKIAH BUTTERWORTH was born in Warren, Rhode Island, in 1839, and became a well-known journalist. As a young man, Butterworth was in poor health and was prevented from having the complete education that had been planned for him at Brown University. He attracted the attention of the editor of the *Youth's Companion* with a series of articles which he had prepared on self-education, based on his own experience. For twenty-five years he was a frequent contributor to the magazine. During a ten-year period the circulation increased from 140,000 to 400,000, due largely to his travel stories, which achieved wide popularity among young folks of the seventies and eighties.

"My Grandmother's Grandmother's Christmas Candle," a fanciful story based on an actual happening in Rhode Island in the days when the early settlers had occasional encounters with the Indians, has given Hezekiah Butterworth a permanent place in American Christmas lore. Like many of his stories, it was written for a juvenile audience. It has been included in many anthologies since it was first published in 1894, together with "The Parson's Miracle."

THE PARSON'S MIRACLE

FOR fifty years Parson Pool had faithfully served the little parish among the New Hampshire hills. There was not a house in the village in which he had not prayed; there was hardly a little red cottage on the road that wound through the intervale in which he had not at least "married one and preached the funeral sermon of two," as he expressed himself in a discourse at the close of the half-century of his ministry.

There had been but few episodes in the parson's life. He had seldom travelled so far as to lose sight of Mount Washington, or not to hear on Sunday the ringing of his own church bell. Week by week on Friday evening and Sunday morning, his strong form was seen passing through the wicket gate that led to the church, whether the breath of June was in the air, or Chocorua's triple peaks were obscured by a scowling sky, or rose in silence, covered with snow. But in his old age there happened to him a *miracle*. I myself saw it, though I was then a child.

Parson Pool was my grandfather. I was his pet. He used to take me with him to his parishioners whenever he went. I well remember his gig and poor old Dolly, the mare, with her harness all tied up with tow strings and toggles,—a faithful animal who bore her lashings with resignation, and has long been free from her woes.

Parson Pool was a very tender-hearted man, and next to his love of children was that of animals, notwithstanding the whacks that old Dolly received.

There used to be a season in the village which was called "killing-time,"—a few weeks in December when the fatted cattle, hogs, and poultry were killed. The neighbors used to gather from house to house on the occasion of such annual slaughters, but the parson was never seen among them. He usually shut himself up in the garret on the morning that his own pig was killed, and did not appear below stairs until the defunct animal's "liver and lights" were frying for the butcher's dinner. If he were riding at this season and heard one of his neighbor's pigs squeal on being run down by the butcher, he would give old Dolly an extra whack, put the reins between his knees, and clap both hands over his ears, and hold them there tightly.

"Mary," I once heard him say, after such an experience, "it does seem to me that there is something wrong in the make-up of this world; but then," he added, "I ought not to say anything,—I like a piece of fresh pork myself sometimes."

The people generally remembered the parson at "killing-time," and generously sent him spare-ribs, turkeys, and geese. He was so well provided for with poultry at this season by others, that he was never known to kill any of his own.

"I wouldn't kill a chicken," he used to say, "if I had to live on corn bread all the year. I sell all my poultry to the hen-cart."

Just what the hen-cart man did with the parson's poultry, the good man never cared to investigate. The hen-cart always went outside of the mountain hemlocks that bordered the quiet town.

Grandmother Pool was a person of different fibre. At "killing-time" at the parsonage, she went round with her sleeves rolled up, ready for the fray. When she mounted the gig, and said "Go lang," old Dolly put back her ears, and her stiffened legs flew like drum-sticks. Grandfather used to have to speak to me about the same thing often, but I very distinctly remember that grandmother, after giving me one or two very impressive lessons, never had to speak to me in that way but once. Grandmother was *not* a popular woman in the parish.

Parson Pool liked to raise poultry. He would often bring up a large brood of chickens by hand, and his flock of hens would follow him about the farm whenever he went out to walk. In the summer afternoons we used to go up on a hill together, which commanded almost as fine a view of the green mountain walls and the bald summits of Washington and Lafayette as does the Bald Mountain itself. Then we would sit down and watch the shadows of the clouds on the pine-covered mountain sides, as they sailed along like ghosts of the air. When Grandmother Pool asked us where we were going, as we set out for these excursions, he would often answer, "Hens' nesting."

A mania had spread over the country. It was called the "hen fever." It reached at last our village. Several people became the possessors of Cochin China and Shanghai hens, and among them was a brisk young farmer by the name of Campbell.

Just after Thanksgiving this young man summoned Parson Pool to marry him. He paid the old man two dollars in money, and promised to make him a present of a Christmas dinner, which he assured him should be "a surprise."

On the day before Christmas young Campbell called at the parsonage, and fulfilled his promise. It was a surprise indeed,

—a Shanghai chicken of astonishing weight, and seemingly fabulous length of neck and legs.

"Here, parson," said he, setting the pullet down on the kitchen floor, "I've brought you something for your Christmas dinner. Big as a turkey, ain't it? Legs almost as long as yours, parson, and a neck like as it was going to peek over the meetin' hus' into the graveyard. Did you ever see the like of that?"

The chicken ruffled its feathers, and walked about the kitchen very calmly, lifting high its feet in a very dignified way.

" 'When this you see, remember me,' parson," said the lively young man, quoting provincial poetry. "You will have *him* on the table to-morrow, won't you, parson?"

"Yes; but, but—"

The old man held out a piece of bread. The pullet walked up to it like a child, and swallowed it so fast that it choked desperately.

"But what, parson?"

The pullet wiped her bill on grandfather's dressing-gown, which seemed to please him greatly.

"But I would kind o' hate to cut her head off."

"Is that so, parson? Well, I'll save you the trouble. You just let me take your hatchet, and I'll—"

"No, no," said grandfather, with a distressed look, "I'll attend to the matter. I'll attend to the matter. I always was kind o' chicken-hearted, myself."

After the young man left, grandmother came upon the scene, with a resolute look in her face and her cap borders flying.

"Samuel!"

"Well?"

"I want you to cut that chicken's head right off, right off now, so that I can have it to bake for breakfast to-morrow. Who do you think is coming to spend Christmas with us? Sophia,—Sophia Van Buren, from Boston. She spent the summer at the Crawford House, and came to the mountains again in October. But now that the hotels are closed, she is coming here."

"What is *she* coming for?" asked grandfather, with a distressed look at the chicken.

"To see Mount Washington covered with snow. She is an artist; she exhibits pictures in the art rooms in Boston. She is my second cousin."

"When is she coming?"

"This very afternoon, in the Ossipee stage. So just take that great fat chicken, and off with its head just as quick as you can, and I will get the feathers out of the way in half an hour."

"But I never killed a chicken in my life, and I would rather hate to hack the head off of such a fine-looking bird as that."

"Won't she *brown* up well?" said grandmother.

"Rebecca, that fowl loves to live just as well as you do. Just think of it, when the day-star rises to-morrow and the cocks crow, she—"

"Will be dead and baked in the larder," said Grandmother Pool.

"And when the sun rises and the other fowls are enjoying the sunlight—"

"You will be eating one of the best roast chickens you ever tasted. Here she is," added grandmother, catching up the plump pullet and handing her to Grandfather Pool, who looked as though he had been called upon to execute a child.

Grandfather Pool went out with the pullet, which did not seem to manifest any concern. I followed. He went to the woodhouse where the chopping-block was, and sat down in an old armchair, in the sun. The woodhouse was open in front, and the chopping-block stood in the opening.

"Are you really going to do it?" said I.

"I wish one of those Old Testament miracles would turn that pullet into a chopping-block, for *she* has said it must be done, and nothing but a miracle will ever save the poor thing from the *gallows*."

Grandfather Pool rose up and laid the chicken on the block. He measured the distance with the hatchet.

"Oh, let me run," said I.

"I am not going to do it yet," said he. "When I do, I shall measure the distance *so,* with my eyes open; then I shall shut my eyes tight, chop her head off quick, and throw her away, and shall not open my eyes until she is as dead as a stone. Now you run away, and write the epitaph," he added, with a grim smile.

I ran to my room. It looked out on the woodhouse. I drew the curtain so as not to see the awful sight. I began to think of the epitaph.

There was a nice fat pullet that sat upon
    a roost;
Death came along and gave her a *boost.*

That did not seem quite correct.

There was a nice plump pullet that lay
    beneath the brier;
Death came along and caused her to expire.

This seemed to me perfectly lovely, and I felt willing that the pullet should die, that she might be honored by such an epitaph. Parson Pool was famous as a writer of epitaphs, and I now felt sure I had inherited his genius.

I thought I would just open the curtain to see if the deed was done, when a most remarkable sight met my eyes. Grandfather Pool stood by the block on which the pullet was laid, measuring the distance to strike. He then shut his eyes, brought down the hatchet strongly, and threw the pullet away. What was my astonishment to see the fowl jump up and run across the meadow into the hemlocks.

Grandfather stood like a statue, with closed eyes, waiting for the pullet to expire. I think he stood in this position some five minutes, when he ventured to look slowly round.

There was nothing to be seen but the chopping-block.

He walked round it, and then surveyed the yard. I never saw such a look of astonishment as came into his face.

Presently I heard a shrill voice cry,—

"Samuel, ain't that chicken ready yet?"

Then I heard him say,—

"Rebecca, come here."

"Where is the pullet, Samuel?"

"I chopped her head off, when she vanished right into the chopping-block. It is a punishment for my sins. I never thought it quite right to kill innocent animals for food."

"Samuel, have you lost your senses? I am not a fool. You never cut that pullet's head off in this world. It stands to reason you didn't; there isn't a drop of blood on the block."

"Rebecca, I have never told a lie since I entered the ministry. I tell you the truth: I cut that pullet's head off; the hatchet went clean through her neck, when she vanished head and all,—went right into the chopping-block!"

"Split open the block and you will find her, then."

Grandfather took up the broad-axe, severed the chopping-block in the middle, and examined it carefully as it fell apart.

"There is no pullet there," said he. "I feel like Balaam. I've read of such things in books,—they happened to Samuel Wesley, and he was a good man; and to Elder John Leland, and he was a good man."

"What things?"

"Supernatural things,—miracles, like."

"Well, I don't believe in them."

"What's come of that pullet, then?"

"Didn't you fall asleep over the chopping-block, and some one steal her?"

"Rebecca, you know that there isn't a person in this whole town who would steal a hen from me in the night, to say nothing of broad daylight. What's the use of arguing against the supernatural? Just as soon as I had cut her head off, I let go of her, and expected she would flutter and leap up into the air, just as pullets do when other folks kill them. Instead of that she never made a sound, but turned right into that there chopping-block, and never left so much as a drop of blood or a feather behind."

"It is very mysterious."

"Very."

"Where's Jamie?"

"He's hid so as not to see the *murder.*"

Just then the sound of wheels was heard,

and the Ossipee stage stopped before the little red cottage, and Miss Van Buren, all fluffs and furbelows, appeared. As soon as I was alone with grandfather he said,—

"Jamie, you know what has happened; don't tell your grandmother that rash wish of mine."

"What wish?"

"What I said to you before the pullet vanished,—that she might turn into a chopping-block."

I had intended to tell him what I had seen, but a mystery had a charm for me even in childhood. I disliked to spoil such a famous story as this was sure to become, and when my conscience began to trouble me, I stifled it by reflecting that to explain the matter too soon would cause the capture and death of the pullet.

The next day, a wonderfully mild Christmas in that region, grandfather, Miss Van Buren, and myself, went up the high hill to get a view of the mountains. The sharp peaks of Chocorua seemed to cut the air, and grandfather told Miss Van Buren as we slowly went along the awful story of Chocorua's curse. Had I not known the true explanation to the pullet story, this story of the old Conway farms would have chilled me, for the Conway farmers believe that Chocorua's curse causes the cattle to die. The air was very still, only a low murmur at times in the tops of the pines.

There were hunters in the woods below us, and from time to time the crack of a rifle would cause us to stop to listen to the echoes. As we returned, I hurried ahead of grandfather and Miss Van Buren, and gained the highway some minutes before them.

A wagon was passing, full of hunters and game. Out of one of the game bags hung the head of a noble bird; my eyes recognized it with astonishment,—it was Parson Pool's Christmas pullet.

John Fox, Jr.

KENTUCKY-BORN storyteller John Fox, Jr., was one of Teddy Roosevelt's spirited Rough Riders. A Civil War baby, he was born in Stony Point, Bourbon County, Kentucky, in 1863, and attended both the University of Kentucky and Harvard. Like many another writer of his day, he pursued law at first, but abandoned it for writing.

He is best remembered for *The Little Shepherd of Kingdom Come,* a Civil War romance with a Kentucky setting, and *The Trail of the Lonesome Pine,* which were dramatized and later made into movies. Fox had been a reporter in the Spanish-American war and wrote first-hand of it from Cuba. A romancer by nature, he became a devotee of Mary N. Murfree, who wrote under the pen name Charles Egbert Craddock, and championed the folk of the Cumberland Mountain region, telling their stories to an admiring public. As a young man, he organized a voluntary police force to make his beloved mountains safe for travelers.

Fox has been called a confectioner of words, because his stories, full of the atmosphere of cowhide and homespun, moonshine makers, poke bonnets and rhododendrons, were of the sweet, sentimental type. Yet, he was exceedingly popular, for he knew at first hand the folk he wrote about and brought to the American reading public of his day a fascinating new world about which they knew little. The folk ways and customs, as well as the spirit of an earlier era, proved to be good reading at the turn of the century. His story, "Christmas Eve on Lonesome," is one of those touching tales that rings with the spirit of Christmas. It served as the title for a book of short stories published in 1904.

CHRISTMAS EVE ON LONESOME

IT WAS Christmas Eve on Lonesome. But nobody on Lonesome knew that it was Christmas Eve, although a child of the outer world could have guessed it, even out in those wilds where Lonesome slipped from one lone log-cabin high up the steeps, down through a stretch of jungled darkness to another lone cabin at the mouth of the stream.

There was the holy hush in the gray twilight that comes only on Christmas Eve. There were the big flakes of snow that fell as they never fall except on Christmas Eve. There was a snowy man on horseback in a big coat, and with saddle-pockets that might have been bursting with toys for children in the little cabin at the head of the stream.

But not even he knew that it was Christmas Eve. He was thinking of Christmas Eve, but it was of Christmas Eve of the year before, when he sat in prison with a hundred other men in stripes, and listened to the chaplain talk of peace and good-will to all men upon earth, when he had forgotten all men upon earth but one, and had only hatred in his heart for him.

"Vengeance is mine!" saith the Lord.

That was what the chaplain had thundered at him. And then, as now, he thought of the enemy who had betrayed him to the law, and had sworn away his liberty, and had robbed him of everything in life except a fierce longing for the day when he could strike back and strike to kill. And then, while he looked back hard into the chaplain's eyes, and now, while he splashed through the yellow mud thinking of that Christmas Eve, Buck shook his head; and then, as now, his sullen heart answered:

"Mine!"

The big flakes drifted to crotch and twig and limb. They gathered on the brim of Buck's slouch hat, filled out the wrinkles in his big coat, whitened his hair and his long mustache, and sifted into the yellow, twisting path that guided his horse's feet.

High above he could see through the whirling snow now and then the gleam of a red star. He knew it was the light from his enemy's window; but somehow the chaplain's voice kept ringing in his ears, and every time he saw the light he couldn't help thinking of the story of the Star that the chaplain told that Christmas Eve, and he dropped his eyes by and by, so as not to see it again, and rode on until the light shone in his face.

Then he led his horse up a little ravine and hitched it among the snowy holly and rhododendrons, and slipped toward the light. There was a dog somewhere, of course; and like a thief he climbed over the low rail-fence and stole through the tall snow-wet grass until he leaned against an apple-tree with the sill of the window two feet above the level of his eyes.

Reaching above him, he caught a stout limb and dragged himself up to a crotch of the tree. A mass of snow slipped softly to the earth. The branch creaked above the light wind; around the corner of the house a dog growled and he sat still.

He had waited three long years and he had ridden two hard nights and lain out two cold days in the woods for this.

And presently he reached out very carefully, and noiselessly broke leaf and branch and twig until a passage was cleared for his eye and for the point of the pistol that was gripped in his right hand.

A woman was just disappearing through the kitchen door, and he peered cautiously and saw nothing but darting shadows. From one corner a shadow loomed suddenly out in human shape. Buck saw the shadowed gesture of an arm, and he cocked his pistol. That shadow was his man, and in a moment he would be in a chair in the chimney-corner to smoke his pipe, maybe—his last pipe.

Buck smiled—pure hatred made him smile—but it was mean, a mean and sorry thing to shoot this man in the back, dog though he was; and now that the moment had come a wave of sickening shame ran through Buck. No one of his name had ever done that before; but this man and his people had, and with their own lips they had framed palliation for him. What was fair for one was fair for the other, they always said. A poor man couldn't fight money in the courts; and so they had shot from the brush, and that was why they were rich now and Buck was poor—why his enemy was safe at home, and he was out here, homeless, in the apple-tree.

Buck thought of all this, but it was no use. The shadow slouched suddenly and disappeared; and Buck was glad. With a gritting oath between his chattering teeth he pulled his pistol in and thrust one leg down to swing from the tree—he would meet him face to face next day and kill him like a man—and there he hung as rigid as though the cold had suddenly turned him, blood, bones, and marrow, into ice.

The door had opened, and full in the firelight stood the girl who he had heard was dead. He knew now how and why that word was sent him. And now she who had been his sweetheart stood before him—the wife of the man he meant to kill. Her lips moved—he thought he could tell what she said: "Git up, Jim, git up!" Then she went back.

A flame flared up within him now that must have come straight from the devil's forge. Again the shadows played over the ceiling. His teeth grated as he cocked his pistol, and pointed it down the beam of light that shot into the heart of the apple-tree, and waited.

The shadow of a head shot along the rafters and over the fireplace. It was a madman clutching the butt of the pistol now, and as his eye caught the glinting sight and his heart thumped, there stepped into the square light of the window—a child!

It was a boy with yellow tumbled hair, and he had a puppy in his arms. In front of the fire the little fellow dropped the dog, and they began to play.

"Yap! yap! yap!"

Buck could hear the shrill barking of the fat little dog, and the joyous shrieks of the child as he made his playfellow chase his tail round and round or tumbled him head over heels on the floor. It was the first child Buck had seen for three years; it was *his* child and *hers;* and, in the apple-tree, Buck watched fixedly.

They were down on the floor now, rolling over and over together; and he watched them until the child grew tired and turned his face to the fire and lay still—looking into it. Buck could see his eyes close presently, and then the puppy crept closer, put his head on his playmate's chest, and the two lay thus asleep.

And still Buck looked—his clasp loosening on his pistol and his lips loosening under his stiff mustache—and kept looking until the door opened again and the woman crossed the floor. A flood of light flashed suddenly on the snow, barely touching the snow-hung tips of the apple-tree, and he saw her in the doorway—saw her look anxiously into the darkness—look and listen a long while.

Buck dropped noiselessly to the snow when she closed the door. He wondered what they would think when they saw his tracks in the snow next morning; and then he realized that they would be covered before morning.

As he started up the ravine where his horse was he heard the clink of metal down the road and the splash of a horse's hoofs in the soft mud, and he sank down behind a holly-bush.

Again the light from the cabin flashed out on the snow.

"That you, Jim?"

"Yep!"

And then the child's voice: "Has oo dot thum tandy?"

"Yep!"

The cheery answer rang out almost at Buck's ear, and Jim passed death waiting for him behind the bush which his left foot brushed, shaking the snow from the red berries down on the crouching figure beneath.

Once only, far down the dark jungled way, with the underlying streak of yellow that was leading him whither, God only knew—once only Buck looked back. There was the red light gleaming faintly through the moonlit flakes of snow. Once more he thought of the Star, and once more the chaplain's voice came back to him.

"Mine!" saith the Lord.

Just how, Buck could not see with himself in the snow and *him* back there for life with her and the child, but some strange impulse made him bare his head.

"Yourn," said Buck grimly.

But nobody on Lonesome—not even Buck—knew that it was Christmas Eve.

Thomas Bailey Aldrich

KNOWN for his polished writing, delicate and fanciful, yet at times sentimental, Thomas Bailey Aldrich described himself as "Boston plated." And such he was. As a distinguished Editor of the *Atlantic Monthly*, he knew all the promising writers of his day, and was particularly charmed by Dickens, who called on him during his second visit to America in 1867.

Aldrich is best remembered by a novel based on his own boyhood, *The Story of a Bad Boy*. "Kriss Kringle," the poem chosen for this album, is one of those lacey, imaginative drawing-room bits as appropriate to the time in which it was written as were the antimacassars that adorned the chairs in his Beacon Hill home, where he entertained Dickens, Longfellow, Lowell, and practically all the other great literary figures of his time.

KRISS KRINGLE

Just as the moon was fading amid her misty rings,
And every stocking was stuffed with childhood's precious things,
Old Kriss Kringle looked round, and saw on an elm-tree bough,
High-hung, an oriole's nest, silent and empty now.

"Quite like a stocking," he laughed, "pinned up there on the tree!
Little I thought the birds expected a present from me!"
Then old Kriss Kringle, who loves a joke as well as the best,
Dropped a handful of flakes in the oriole's empty nest.

Eugene Field

ALTHOUGH born in St. Louis in 1850, Eugene Field spent his youth in Amherst, Massachusetts. His college education was begun in the East, transferred to the Midwest, and ended with a trip to Europe. After serving on several newspapers in the Midwest, Field became Editor of a humorous column of the *Chicago News,* which he called "Flats and Sharps." To him it was his melting pot for every sort of written expression from poetry to parodies, and practically everything he wrote appeared in it at one time or another. In 1887 he wrote "Little Boy Blue," which attracted considerable attention in the literary world. Two other books followed to make him even better known. Then his readers learned of his untimely death in 1895, at the age of forty-five.

Field remained popular and was even more greatly admired after his death for his high-spirited, warm-hearted humor. A maker of brilliant trifles, his was the ability to paraphrase, to parody and to adapt, or to blend seriousness and humor. Yet, in many ways, he had all the marks of a boy who never grew up. His task was to write for the moment, the kind of timely things people enjoyed in newspapers, and he drew on all kinds of literary and popular sources for his material. This easygoing versifier helped greatly to pave the way for popularizing literature in the daily newspapers. "Jest 'Fore Christmas" and "The Three Kings" are two examples of his inimitable style, which he varied according to the mood of his subject.

JEST 'FORE CHRISTMAS

Father calls me William, sister calls me
    Will,
Mother calls me Willie, but the fellers call
    me Bill!
Mighty glad I ain't a girl—ruther be a boy,
Without them sashes, curls, an' things
    that's worn by Fauntleroy!
Love to chawnk green apples an' go swim-
    min' in the lake—
Hate to take the castor-ile they give for
    belly-ache!
'Most all the time, the whole year round,
    there ain't no flies on me,
But jest 'fore Christmas I'm good as I
    kin be!

Got a yeller dog named Sport, sic him on
    the cat;
First thing she knows she doesn't know
    where she is at!
Got a clipper sled, an' when us kids goes
    out to slide,
'Long comes the grocery cart, an' we all
    hook a ride!
But sometimes when the grocery man is
    worried an' cross,
He reaches at us with his whip, an' larrups
    up his hoss,
An' then I laff an' holler, "Oh, ye never
    teched *me!*"
But jest 'fore Christmas I'm good as I kin
    be!

Gran'ma says she hopes that when I git
    to be a man,
I'll be a missionarer like her oldest brother,
    Dan,
As was et up by the cannibuls that lives in
    Ceylon's Isle,
Where every prospeck pleases, an' only man
    is vile!
But gran'ma she has never been to see a
    Wild West show,
Nor read the Life of Daniel Boone, or else
    I guess she'd know
That Buff'lo Bill and cow-boys is good
    enough for me!
Except, jest 'fore Christmas, when I'm
    good as I kin be!

And when old Sport he hangs around, so
    solemn-like an' still,
His eyes they keep a-sayin': "What's the
    matter, little Bill?"
The old cat sneaks down off her perch an'
    wonders what's become
Of them two enemies of hern that used to
    make things hum!
But I am so perlite an' tend so earnestly to
    biz,
That mother says to father: "How im-
    proved our Willie is!"
But father, havin' been a boy hisself, sus-
    picions me
When jest 'fore Christmas, I'm as good as
    I kin be!

For Christmas, with its lots an' lots of
    candies, cakes an' toys,
Was made, they say, for proper kids an'
    not for naughty boys;
So wash yer face an' bresh yer hair, an'
    mind yer p's and q's,
An' don't bust out yer pantaloons, an' don't
    wear out yer shoes;
Say "Yessum" to the ladies, an' "Yessur"
    to the men,
An' when they's company, don't pass yer
    plate for pie again;
But, thinking of the things yer'd like to
    see upon that tree,
Jest 'fore Christmas be as good as yer kin
    be!

THE THREE KINGS

From out Cologne there came three kings
  To worship Jesus Christ, their King;
To him they sought fine herbs they brought
  And many a beauteous golden thing;
  They brought their gifts to Bethlehem
    town
  And in that manger set them down.

Then spake the first king, and he said:
  "O Child, most heavenly bright and fair,
I bring this crown to Bethlehem town
  For Thee, and only Thee, to wear;
  So give a heavenly crown to me
  When I shall come at last to Thee."

The second then: "I bring thee here
  This royal robe, O Child!" he cried;
"Of silk 'tis spun and such an one
  There is not in the world beside!
  So in the day of doom requite
  Me with a heavenly robe of white!"

The third king gave his gift, and quoth:
  "Spikenard and myrrh to Thee I bring,
And with these twain would I most fain
  Anoint the body of my King.
  So may their incense some time rise
  To plead for me in yonder skies."

Thus spake the three kings of Cologne
  That gave their gifts and went their way;
And now kneel I in prayer hard-by
  The cradle of the Child to-day;
  Nor crown, nor robe, nor spice I bring
  As offering unto Christ my King.

Yet have I brought a gift the Child
  May not despise, however small;
For here I lay my heart to-day,
  And it is full of love to all!
  Take Thou the poor, but loyal thing,
  My only tribute, Christ, my King.

Francis P. Church

FEW letters written by children ever attracted more attention than a brief "letter to the Editor," addressed to the *New York Sun* in the autumn of 1897. The writer was eight-year-old Virginia O'Hanlon, of New York City, who was puzzled about the existence of Santa Claus. She was seeking the answer to a question which many children had asked previously. The responses given by parents were obviously not adequate. It remained for Francis P. Church, one of the *Sun's* editorial writers, to furnish the classic reply. Millions of parents have dim recollections of this letter. They may not recall how or when it was written, nor does it matter. The sentiment expressed in the belief so dear to the heart of childhood has sufficed to provide the answer to the eternal question asked in a thousand different ways each year at Christmas. And no schoolteacher in America in the 20th century has been better fitted to tell her classes a better Christmas story than Virginia O'Hanlon who retired recently from the public school system of New York City.

Within four generations after the introduction of Saint Nicholas, more familiarly known as Santa Claus, a new facet of Christmas lore had become one of the most deeply rooted of all American traditions.

Dr. Clement Moore, with his "Visit from St. Nicholas" written in 1822, had unwittingly launched an ageless celebrity in the classless society of childhood. Forty years later, Thomas Nast publicized him in the most flattering of all media —pencil-and-ink drawings. These lively sketches brought a blithe touch to *Harper's Weekly* in the midst of the impending gloom of the Civil War. Virginia O'Hanlon raised the question that settled the existing doubt that had crept into children's minds all over the land. Before the dawn of the 20th century Santa Claus had been enshrined as an idol.

IS THERE A SANTA CLAUS?

AN EDITORIAL reprinted from the *New York Sun,* Sept. 21, 1897:

We take pleasure in answering at once and thus prominently the communication below, expressing at the same time our great gratification that its faithful author is numbered among the friends of The Sun:

Dear Editor:

I am 8 years old. Some of my little friends say there is no Santa Claus. Papa says "If you see it in The Sun it's so." Please tell me the truth, is there a Santa Claus?

Virginia O'Hanlon,
115 West 95th Street,
New York City

Virginia, your little friends are *wrong.* They have been affected by the skepticism of a skeptical age. They do not *believe* except they *see.* They think that nothing can be which is not comprehensible by their little minds. All minds, Virginia, whether they be men's or children's are little. In this great universe of ours man is a mere insect, an ant, in his intellect, as compared with the boundless world about him, as measured by the intelligence capable of grasping the whole of truth and knowledge.

Yes, Virginia, there *is* a Santa Claus. He exists as certainly as love, and generosity and devotion exist, and you know that they abound and give to your life its highest beauty and joy. Alas! how dreary would be the world if there were no Santa Claus! It would be as dreary as if there were no Virginias. There would be no childlike faith, then, no poetry, no romance to make tolerable this existence. We should have no enjoyment, except in sense and sight. The eternal light with which childhood fills the world would be extinguished.

Not believe in *Santa Claus!* You might as well not believe in fairies! You might get your papa to hire men to watch in all the chimneys on Christmas Eve to catch Santa Claus, but even if they did not see Santa Claus coming down what would that prove? Nobody sees Santa Claus, but that is no sign that there is no Santa Claus. The most real things in the world are those that neither children nor men can see. Did you ever see fairies dancing on the lawn? Of course not, but that's no proof that they are not there. Nobody can conceive or imagine all the wonders there are unseen and unseeable in the world.

You tear apart the baby's rattle and see what makes the noise inside, but there is a veil covering the unseen world which not the strongest man, nor even the united strength of all the strongest men that ever lived, could tear apart. Only faith, fancy, poetry, love, romance, can push aside that curtain and view—and picture the supernal beauty and glory beyond. Is it all real? Ah, Virginia, in all this world there is nothing else real and abiding.

No Santa Claus! Thank God he lives, and he lives forever. A thousand years from now, Virginia, nay, ten times ten thousand years from now, he will continue to make glad the heart of childhood.

Jacob A. Riis

FEW men in late 19th-century America lived the spirit of Christmas more meaningfully than Jacob A. Riis. At the age of thirteen he began his great humanitarian work in a modest way in his native Denmark, and later became known all over America as the emancipator of the slums. His tremendous energy and vividly written stories attracted the attention of the entire country, and President Theodore Roosevelt dubbed him "the nation's most useful citizen." Jacob Riis was offered positions of high honor in the government, but declined because he was too busy writing, lecturing, and accomplishing his cherished ideals.

Through his work as a journalist, first as police reporter of the *New York Tribune* and later with the *Evening Sun,* he gathered first-hand information about the deplorable conditions of immigrants in New York City. He wrote with vigor, tenderness, and sympathy of the plight of the tenement dwellers. Through his efforts for social betterment, he pioneered programs for slum clearance, child labor laws, playgrounds and neighborhood clubs and the clean-up of conditions that aided crime and juvenile delinquency.

His books, which included more than a dozen titles and innumerable columns in newspapers and magazines, were widely read, quoted and praised. He is probably best known for *The Making of An American,* but all his writing had a lively quality and the beat of a warm heart could be felt in his every utterance. Often he reminisced about his childhood in his writings and no season of the year evoked a brighter glow than Christmas. His vivid portrayal of *Christmas in the Tenements* first appeared in book form in 1897.

In *The Making of An American,* Jacob Riis recorded the incident which fashioned his career as a great social reformer. It has all the earmarks of a good Christmas story: "Rag Hall displeased me very much . . . An open gutter that was full of rats led under the house to the likewise open gutter of the street. My energies spent themselves in unending warfare with those rats, whose nests choked the gutter. I could hardly have been over twelve or thirteen when Rag Hall challenged my resentment . . . I had received a 'mark,' which was a coin like our silver quarter, on Christmas Eve, and I hied myself to Rag Hall at once to divide it with the poorest family there, on the express condition that they should tidy up things, especially those children, and generally change their way of living. The man took the money—I have a vague recollection of seeing a stunned look on his face—and, I believe, brought it back to our house to see if it was all right, thereby giving me great offence. But he did the best for himself that way, for so Rag Hall came under the notice of my mother too. And there really was some whitewashing done, and the children were cleaned up for a season. So that the eight skilling were, if not wisely, yet well invested, after all.

"No doubt Christmas had something to do with it. Poverty and misery always seem to jar more at the time when the whole world makes merry . . . I am a believer in organized, systematic charity upon the evidence of my senses; but—I am glad we have that one season in which we can forget our principles and err on the side of mercy, that little corner in the days of the dying year for sentiment and no questions asked. No need to be afraid. It is safe. Christmas charity never corrupts. Love keeps it sweet and good—the love He brought into the world at Christmas to temper the hard reason of man. Let it loose for that little spell. January comes soon enough with its long cold. Always it seems to me the longest month in the year. It is so far to another Christmas!"

MERRY CHRISTMAS IN THE TENEMENTS

IT WAS just a sprig of holly, with scarlet berries showing against the green, stuck in, by one of the office boys probably, behind the sign that pointed the way up to the editorial rooms. There was no reason why it should have made me start when I came suddenly upon it at the turn of the stairs; but it did. Perhaps it was because that dingy hall, given over to dust and draughts all the days of the year, was the last place in which I expected to meet with any sign of Christmas; perhaps it was because I myself had nearly forgotten the holiday. Whatever the cause, it gave me quite a turn.

I stood, and stared at it. It looked dry, almost withered. Probably it had come a long way. Not much holly grows about Printing-House Square, except in the colored supplements, and that is scarcely of a kind to stir tender memories. Withered

and dry, this did. I thought, with a twinge of conscience, of secret little conclaves of my children, of private views of things hidden from mamma at the bottom of drawers, of wild flights when papa appeared unbidden in the door, which I had allowed for once to pass unheeded. Absorbed in the business of the office, I had hardly thought of Christmas coming on, until now it was here. And this sprig of holly on the wall that had come to remind me,—come nobody knew how far,—did it grow yet in the beech-wood clearings, as it did when I gathered it as a boy, tracking through the snow? "Christ-thorn" we called it in our Danish tongue. The red berries, to our simple faith, were the drops of blood that fell from the Saviour's brow as it drooped under its cruel crown upon the cross.

Back to the long ago wandered my

thoughts: to the moss-grown beech in which I cut my name and that of a little girl with yellow curls, of blessed memory, with the first jack-knife I ever owned; to the story-book with the little fir-tree that pined because it was small, and because the hare jumped over it, and would not be content though the wind and the sun kissed it, and the dews wept over it and told it to rejoice in its young life; and that was so proud when, in the second year, the hare had to go round it, because then it knew it was getting big,—Hans Christian Andersen's story that we loved above all the rest; for we knew the tree right well, and the hare; even the tracks it left in the snow we had seen. Ah, those were the Yule-tide seasons, when the old Domkirke shone with a thousand wax candles on Christmas eve; when all business was laid aside to let the world make merry one whole week; when big red apples were roasted on the stove, and bigger doughnuts were baked within it for the long feast! Never such had been known since. Christmas to-day is but a name, a memory.

A door slammed below, and let in the noises of the street. The holly rustled in the draft. Someone going out said, "A Merry Christmas to you all!" in a big, hearty voice. I awoke from my reverie to find myself back in New York with a glad glow at the heart. It was not true. I had only forgotten. It was myself that had changed, not Christmas. That was here, with the old cheer, the old message of good-will, the old royal road to the heart of mankind. How often had I seen its blessed charity, that never corrupts, make light in the hovels of darkness and despair! how often watched its spirit of self sacrifice and devotion in those who had, besides themselves, nothing to give! and as often the sight had made whole my faith in human nature. No! Christmas was not of the past, its spirit not dead. The lad who fixed the sprig of holly on the stairs knew it; my reporter's note-book bore witness to it.

The lights of the Bowery glow like a myriad twinkling stars upon the ceaseless flood of humanity that surges ever through the great highway of the homeless. They shine upon long rows of lodging-houses, in which hundreds of young men, cast helpless upon the reef of the strange city, are learning their first lessons of utter loneliness; for what desolation is there like that of the careless crowd when all the world rejoices? They shine upon the tempter setting his snares there, and upon the missionary and the Salvation Army lass, disputing his catch with him; upon the police detective going his rounds with coldly observant eye intent upon the outcome of the contest; upon the wreck that is past hope, and upon the youth passing on the verge of the pit in which the other has long ceased to struggle. Sights and sounds of Christmas there are in plenty in the Bowery. Balsam and hemlock and fir stand in groves along the busy thoroughfare, and garlands of green embower mission and dive impartially. Once a year the old street recalls its youth with an effort. It is true that it is largely a commercial effort; that the evergreen, with an instinct that is not of its native hills, haunts saloon-corners by preference; but the smell of the pine woods is in the air, and—Christmas is not too critical—one is grateful for the effort. It varies with the opportunity. At "Beefsteak John's" it is content with artistically embalming crullers and mince-pies in green cabbage under the window lamp. Over yonder, where the mile-post of the old lane still stands,—in its unhonored old age become the vehicle of publishing the latest "sure cure" to the world,—a florist, whose undenominational zeal for the holiday and trade outstrips alike distinction of creed and property, has transformed the sidewalk and the ugly railroad structure into a veritable bower, spanning it with a canopy of green, under which dwell with him, in neighborly good-will, the Young Men's Christian Association and the Jewish tailor next door. . . .

Down at the foot of the Bowery is the "panhandlers' beat," where the saloons elbow one another at every step, crowding out all other business than that of keeping lodgers to support them. Within call of it, across the square, stands a church which, in the memory of men yet living, was built to shelter the fashionable Baptist audiences of a day when Madison Square was out in the fields, and Harlem had a foreign sound. The fashionable audiences are gone long since. To-day the church, fallen into premature decay, but still handsome in its strong and noble lines, stands as a missionary outpost in the land of the enemy, its builders would have said, doing a greater work than they planned. To-night is the Christmas festival of its English-speaking Sunday-school, and the pews are filled. The banners of United Italy, of modern Hellas, of France and Germany and England, hang side by side with the Chinese dragon and the starry flag-signs of the cosmopolitan character of the congregation. Greek and Roman Catholics, Jews and joss-worshippers, go there; few Protestants, and no Baptists. It is easy to pick out the children in their seats by nationality, and as easy to read the story of poverty and suffering that stands written in more than one mother's haggard face, now beaming with pleasure at the little ones' glee. A gayly decorated Christmas tree has taken the place of the pulpit. At its foot is stacked a mountain of bundles, Santa Claus's gifts to the school. A self-conscious young man with soap-locks had just been allowed to retire, amid tumultuous applause, after blowing "Nearer, my God, to Thee" on his horn until his cheeks swelled almost to bursting. A trumpet ever takes the Fourth Ward by storm. A class of little girls is climbing upon the platform. Each wears a capital letter on her breast, and together they spell its lesson. There is momentary consternation: one is missing. As the discovery is made, a child pushes past the doorkeeper, hot and breathless. "I am in 'Boundless Love,'" she says, and makes for the platform, where her arrival restores confidence and the language.

In the audience the befrocked visitor from up-town sits cheek by jowl with the pigtailed Chinaman and the dark-browed Italian. Up in the gallery, farthest from the preacher's desk and the tree, sits a Jewish mother with three boys, almost in rags. A dingy and threadbare shawl partly hides her poor calico wrap and patched apron. The woman shrinks in the pew, fearful of being seen; her boys stand upon the benches, and applaud with the rest. She endeavors vainly to restrain them. "Tick, tick!" goes the old clock over the door through which wealth and fashion went out long years ago, and poverty came in. . . .

Within hail of the Sullivan Street school camps a scattered little band, the Christmas customs of which I had been trying for years to surprise. They are Indians, a handful of Mohawks and Iroquois, whom some ill wind has blown down from their Canadian reservation, and left in these West Side tenements to eke out such a living as they can, weaving mats and baskets, and threading glass pearls on slippers and pin-cushions, until one after another they have died off and gone to happier hunting-grounds than Thompson Street. There were as many families as one could count on the fingers of both hands when I first came upon them, at the death of old Tamenund, the basket maker. Last Christmas there were seven. I had about made up my mind that the only real Americans in New York did not keep the holiday at all, when one Christmas eve they showed me how. Just as dark was setting in, old Mrs. Benoit came from her Hudson Street attic —where she was known among the neighbors, as old and poor as she, as Mrs. Ben Wah, and was believed to be the relict of a warrior of the name of Benjamin Wah— to the office of the Charity Organization Society, with a bundle for a friend who had helped her over a rough spot—the rent, I suppose. The bundle was done up elaborately in blue cheese-cloth, and contained a lot of little garments which she had made out of the remnants of blankets and cloth of her own from a younger and better day. "For those," she said, in her

French patois, "who are poorer than my self;" and hobbled away. I found out, a few days later, when I took her picture weaving mats in the attic room, that Christmas day and not the car fare to take her to church! Walking was bad, and her old limbs were stiff. She sat by the window through the winter evening and watched the sun go down behind the western hills, comforted by her pipe. Mrs. Ben Wah, to give her her local name, is not really an Indian; but her husband was one, and she lived all her life with the tribe till she came here. She is a philosopher in her own quaint way. "It is no disgrace to be poor," said she to me, regarding her empty tobacco-pouch; "but it is sometimes a great inconvenience." Not even the recollection of the vote of censure that was passed upon me once by the ladies of the Charitable Ten for surreptitiously supplying an aged couple, the special object of their charity, with army plug, could have deterred me from taking the hint. . . .

In a hundred places all over the city, when Christmas comes, as many open-air fairs spring suddenly into life. A kind of Gentile Feast of Tabernacles possesses the tenement districts especially. Green-embowered booths stand in rows at the curb, and the voice of the tin trumpet is heard in the land. The common source of all the show is down by the North River, in the district known as "the Farm." Down there Santa Claus establishes headquarters early in December and until past New Year. The broad quay looks then more like a clearing in a pine forest than a busy section of the metropolis. The steamers discharge their loads of fir trees at the piers until they stand stacked mountain high, with foot-hills of holly and ground-ivy trailing off toward the land side. An army train of wagons is engaged in carting them away ʼfrom early morning till late at night; but the green forest grows, in spite of it all, until in places it shuts the shipping out of sight altogether. The air is redolent with the smell of balsam and pine. After night-

fall, when the lights are burning in the busy market, and the homeward-bound crowds with baskets and heavy burdens of Christmas greens jostle one another with good-natured banter,—nobody is ever cross down here in the holiday season,—it is good to take a stroll through the Farm, if one has a spot in his heart faithful yet to the hills and the woods in spite of the latter-day city. But it is when the moonlight is upon the water and upon the dark phantom forest, when the heavy breathing of some passing steamer is the only sound that breaks the stillness of the night, and the watchman smokes his only pipe on the bulwark, that the Farm has a mood and an atmosphere all its own, full of poetry which some day a painter's brush will catch and hold. . . .

Farthest down town, where the island narrows toward the Battery, and warehouses crowd the few remaining tenements, the sombre-hued colony of Syrians is astir with preparation for the holiday. How comes it that in the only settlement of the real Christmas people in New York the corner saloon appropriates to itself all the outward signs of it? Even the floral cross that is nailed over the door of the Orthodox church is long withered and dead; it has been there since Easter, and it is yet twelve days to Christmas by the belated reckoning of the Greek Church. But if the houses show no sign of the holiday, within there is nothing lacking. The whole colony is gone a-visiting. There are enough of the unorthodox to set the fashion, and the rest follow the custom of the country. The men go from house to house, laugh, shake hands, and kiss one another on both cheeks, with the salutation, "Kol am va antom Salimoon." "Every year and you are safe," the Syrian guide renders it into English; and a non-professional interpreter amends it: "May you grow happier year by year." Arrack made from grapes and flavored with anise-seed, and candy baked in little white balls like marbles, are served with the indispensable cigarette; for long callers, the pipe. . . .

The bells in old Trinity chime the midnight hour. From dark hallways men and women pour forth and hasten to the Maronite church. In the loft of the dingy old warehouse wax candles burn before an altar of brass. The priest, in a white robe with a huge gold cross worked on the back, chants the ritual. The people respond. The women kneel in the aisles, shrouding their heads in their shawls; a surpliced acolyte swings his censer; the heavy perfume of burning incense fills the hall.

The band at the anarchists' ball is tuning up for the last dance. Young and old float to the happy strains, forgetting injustice, oppression, hatred. Children slide upon the waxed floor, weaving fearlessly in and out between couples—between fierce, bearded men and short-haired women with crimson-bordered kerchiefs. A Punch-and-Judy show in the corner evokes shouts of laughter.

Outside the snow is falling. It sifts silently into each nook and corner, softens all the hard and ugly lines, and throws the spotless mantle of charity over the blemishes, the shortcomings. Christmas morning will dawn pure and white.

Henry Augustus Shute

"Plupy" Shute was the chummy name for a remarkable man who was born in Exeter, New Hampshire, in 1856 and died there eighty-seven years later. He was inordinately proud of his home town, of Phillips Exeter Academy and Harvard College, from which he was graduated, and the town brass band, of which he was a member. In addition to practicing law, he served as judge of the police court and at the age of forty began to write. Judge Shute counted among his intimate friends the publisher of the town paper. On one occasion the publisher asked him to write a column, which eventually developed into "The Real Diary of a Real Boy." It was published in book form in 1902 by a Boston publisher who was attracted by the articles he had read in the *Exeter News Letter*.

The book is still in print, for its whimsical author quickly earned a reputation for humor and was frequently compared with Mark Twain and Booth Tarkington. However, Judge Shute never took these compliments seriously, or, for that matter, any of the honors that came to him. He gave his own account of how the "Diary" originated, and it could be a true story. At any rate, *Me and Pewt and Beany* was largely autobiographical. So, too, was practically all that he wrote in the twenty volumes that appeared following the "Diary." Among the titles of his other books were *Sequil, The Country Lawyer, Farming It,* and *The Real Diary of the Worst Farmer*. The last two are considered minor classics in their field.

In the preface to the "Diary," printed in the original edition, its discovery was given as follows: "In the winter of 1901-02, while rummaging an old closet in the shed-chamber of my father's house, I unearthed a salt-box which had been equipped with leather hinges at the expense of considerable ingenuity, and at a very remote period. In addition to this, a hasp of the same material, firmly fastened by carpet-tacks and a catch of bent wire, bade defiance to burglars, midnight marauders, and safe-breakers.

"With the aid of a tack-hammer the combination was readily solved, and an eager examination of the contents of the box disclosed:—

"1. Fish-line of braided shoemaker's thread, with perch hook, to which adhered the mummied remains of a worm that lived and flourished many, many years ago.

"2. Popgun of pith elder and hoop-skirt wire.

"3. Horse-chestnut bolas, calculated to revolve in opposite directions with great velocity, by an up-and-down motion of the holder's wrist; also extensively used for the adornment of telegraph-wires—there were no telephones in those days— and the cause of great profanity amongst linemen.

"4. More fish-hooks of the ring variety, now obsolete.

"5. One blood alley, two chinees, a parti-colored glass agate, three peewees, and unnumbered drab-colored marbles.

"6. Small bow of whalebone, with two arrows.

"7. Six-inch bean-blower, for school use—a weapon of considerable range and great precision when used with judgment behind a Guyot's Common School Geography.

"8. Unexpended ammunition for same, consisting of putty pellets.

"9. Frog's hind leg, extra dry.

"10. Wing of bluejay, very ditto.

"11. Letter from 'Beany,' postmarked 'Biddeford, Me.,' and expressing great indignation because 'Pewt' 'hasent wrote.'

"12. Copy-book inscribed 'Diry.'

"The examination of this copy-book lasted the rest of the day, and it was read with the peculiar pleasure one experiences in reviewing some of the events of a happy boyhood.

"With the earnest hope that others may experience a little of the pleasure I gained from the reading, I submit the 'Diry' to the public."

The picture recorded of the Christmas season and the antics of the boys in a New Hampshire town in the period following the Civil War is told with the plainest kind of humor and affection. When Judge Shute died in 1943, all the business establishments were closed during his funeral, and the *Boston Post* editorialized, "Judge Henry A. ·Shute of Exeter is dead, but Plupy, the hero of the genial jurist's book, 'The Real Diary of a Real Boy,' will go on living in American hearts eternally, like Huck Finn and Tom Sawyer."

THE REAL DIARY OF A REAL BOY

FATHER thot i aught to keep a diry, but i sed i dident want to, because i coodent wright well enuf, but he sed he wood give $1000 dolars if he had kept a diry when he was a boy.

Mother said she gessed nobody wood dass to read it, but father said everybody would tumble over each other to read it, anyhow he would give $1000 dolars if he had kept it. I told him i would keep one regular if he would give me a quarter of a dolar a week, but he said I had got to keep it anyhow and i woodent get no quarter for it neither, but he woodent ask to read it for a year, and i know he will forget it before that, so i am going to wright just what i want to in it. Father always forgets everything but my lickins. he remembers them every time you bet.

So i have got to keep it, but it seems to me that my diry is worth a quarter of a dolar a week if fathers is worth $1000 dolars, everybody says father was a buster when he was a boy and went round with Gim Melcher and Charles Talor. my grandmother says i am the best boy she ever see, if i didn't go with Beany Watson and Pewter Purinton, it was Beany and Pewt made me tuf.

there dos'nt seem to be much to put into a diry only fites and who got licked at school and if it ranes or snows, so i will begin to-day.

December 1, 186– brite and fair, late to brekfast, but mother dident say nothing. father goes to boston and works in the custum house so i can get up as late as i want to. father says he works like time, but i went to boston once and father dident do anything but tell stories about what he and Gim Melcher usted to do when he was a boy. once or twice when a man came in they would all be wrighting fast, when the man came in again i sed why do you all wright so fast when he comes in and stop when he goes out, and the man sort

of laffed and went out laffing, and the men were mad and told father not to bring that dam little fool again.

December 2. Skinny Bruce got licked in school today. I told my granmother about it and she said she was glad i dident do enything to get punnished for and she felt sure i never wood. i dident tell her i had to stay in the wood box all the morning with the cover down. i dident tell father either you bet.

December 2. rany. i forgot to say it raned yesterday too. i got cold and have a red rag round my gozzle.

December 2. pretty near had a fite in schol today. Skinny Bruce and Frank Elliot got rite up with there fists up when the bell rung. it was two bad, it wood have been a buly fite. i bet on Skinny.

December 3, 186– brite and fair. went to church today. Me and Pewt and Beany go to the Unitarial church. we all joined sunday school to get into the Crismas festerval. they have it in the town hall and have two trees and supper and presents for the scholars . . . so we are going to stay til after crismas anyway the unitarials have jest built a new church. Pewt and Beany's fathers painted it and so they go there. i don't know why we go there xcept because they don't have any church in the afternoon. Nipper Brown and Micky Gould go there. we all went into the same class. our teacher is Mister Winsor a student. we call them stewdcats. after we had said our lesson we all skinned out with Mr. Winsor. when we went down Maple street we saw 2 roosters fiting in Dany Wingates yard, and we stoped to see it. I knew more about fiting roosters than any of the fellers, because me and Ed Towle had fit roosters lots. Mr. Winsor said i was a sport, well while the roosters were fiting, sunday school let out and he skipped acros the street and walked off with one of the girls and we hollered for him to come and see the fite out, and he turned red and looked mad. the leghorn squorked and stuck his head into a corner. when a rooster squorks he wont fite any more.

December 5. snowed today and school let out at noon. this afternoon went down to the library to plug stewdcats. there was me and Beany and Pewt, and Whacker and Pozzy Chadwick and Pricilla Hobbs. Pricilla is a feller you know, and Pheby Talor, Pheby is a feller too, and Lubbin Smith and Nigger Bell, he isn't a nigger only we call him Nigger, and Tommy Tompson and Dutchey Seamans and Chick Chickering, and Tady Finton and Chitter Robinson.

December 6. Gim Wingate has got a new bobtail coat.

December 7, 186– Got sent to bed last nite for smoking hayseed cigars and can't go with Beany enny more. It is funny, my father wont let me go with Beany becaus he is tuf, and Pewts father wont let Pewt go with me becaus im tuf, and Beanys father says if he catches me or Pewt in his yard he will lick time out of us. Rany today.

December 8. Skinny Bruce got licked in school today. Skipy Moses was in the wood box all the morning.

December 9. brite and fair, speakin day today. missed in Horatius at the brige.

December 10. Clowdy but no rane. went to church. lots of new fellers in sunday school. me and Beany and Pewt and Pile Woods and Billy Folsom and Jimmy Gad and lots of others. Mister Winsor dident teach today, gess they woodent let him on account of the rooster fite.

December 11. My new boots from Tommy Gads came today. i tell you they are clumpers. no snow yet.

December 12. Crismas is pretty near, dont know wether i shall get ennything. father says i dont desirve ennything. you can get goozeberrys down to Si Smiths 1 dozen for 5 cents.

December 15. Fite at recess today, Gran Miller and Ben Rundlet. Ben licked him easy. the fellers got to stumping each other to fite. Micky Gould said he cood lick me and i said he want man enuf and he said if i wood come out behind the school house after school he wood show me and i said i wood and all the fellers hollered and said they wood be there. But after school i thaught i aught to go home and split my kindlings and so i went home. a feller aught to do something for his family ennyway. i cood have licked him if i had wanted to.

December 16. Tady Finton got licked in school today. snowed today a little.

December 17. rained in the nite and then snowed a little. it was auful slipery and coming out of church Squire Lane fell down whak and Mr. Burley cought hold of the fence and his feet went so fast that they seemed all fuzzy, i tell you if he cood run as fast as that he cood run a mile a minite.

December 18. brite and fair. nothing particilar. o yes, Skinny Bruce got licked in school.

December 19. Cold as time. Went to a sosiable tonite at the Unitarial vestry. cant go again because Keene told mother i was impident to the people. i want impident. you see they was making poetry and all sitting around the vestry. they wanted to play copenhagin and post office and clap in and clap out, but Mister Erl woodent let them because it was in church. so they had to play poetry. one person wood give a word and then the oppisite person would give a word that rimed with it. it was auful silly. a girl would give the word direxion and then a stewdcat would say affexion and waul his eyes towards the girl. and then another wood say miss, and another stewdcat wood say kiss and then he wood waul his eyes, and when it came my turn i said what rimes with jellycake, and the girls turned red and the stewdcats looked funny, and Mister Burley said if i coodent behave i had better go home. Keene needent have told mother anyway. You jest wait Keene, and see what will happen some day.

December 20. Bully skating. went after school and skated way up to the eddy, was going to skate with Lucy Watson but Pewt and Beany hollered so that i dident dass to. Johnny Toomey got hit with a hocky block rite in the snoot and broke his nose.

December 21. Brite and fair. nothing particular to-day. nobody got licked. old Francis had his hand done up in a sling. he said he had a bile on it. i tell you the fellers were glad.

December 22. Warm and rany and spoiled the skating. coodent do anything but think of Crismas.

December 23. Saturday and no skating. went down to the library to get a book for sunday. me and Beany were sticking pins into the fellers and making them holler and Jo Parsons the libarian jumped rite over the counter and chased us way down to Mr. Hams coffin shop. he dident catch us either. then we went down town and Billy Swett lent me a dime novel to read sunday. it was named Billy Bolegs a sequil

to Nat Tod the traper. sequil means the things in Nat Tod that was not finished.

December 24. Brite and fair. Crismas tomorrow. went to sunday school. Mr. Lovel is our teacher now.

December 25. Crismas. got a new nife, a red and white scarf and a bag of Si Smiths goozeberies. pretty good for me.

December 26. Crismas tree at the town hall. had supper and got a bag of candy and a long string of pop corn. Mr. Lovel took off the presents and his whiskers caught fire, and he hollered o hell right out. that was pretty good for a sunday school teacher, wasent it. Jimmy Gad et too much and was sick.

December 27. Beany has got a new striped shirt not a false bosom but a whole shirt. Beany wont speak to me now. Lucy Watson has got a new blew hat with a fether. she wont speak to Keene and Cele. you jest wait Beany and Lucy and see.

O. Henry

WHILE serving as a prescription clerk in his uncle's drugstore in Greensboro, North Carolina, Will Porter first began to write and draw cartoons. He was born in this town in 1862 and grew up under the tutelage of a maiden aunt who kept a private school. His mother had died when Will was three years old, and his father, who was known as a successful physician, turned his attention to various impractical inventions, neglected his patients, and paid little attention to his son. Miss Evelina Porter spent considerable time reading to her pupils, and on Friday nights many of them gathered at her house for an evening of fun and storytelling. Both she and her nephew were reputed to be adept at telling tales.

At the age of twenty Will Porter went to Texas and lived on a ranch. He secured a position in a bank in Austin, fell in love with a local schoolgirl and eloped with her. Through a curious set of circumstances he was accused of embezzling funds from the bank in which he worked, and finally fled to Central America, where he remained until summoned home by his wife's illness. Following her death he served part of a term in a Federal penitentiary, during which time he wrote some of his short stories. The last eight years of his life were spent in New York City, where he died in 1910. The pen name O. Henry originated when Porter was in prison. Several accounts of its origin have been given by his associates. The prince of storytellers has been the subject of even more tales than flowed from his fertile mind in the thirteen years of his writing career.

Sixteen volumes containing 251 stories were his contribution to the millions of readers who read and loved his stories. Most of them were written hurriedly, often under pressure of deadlines or other circumstances. A few of them are of little merit, others are fair, but most of Will Porter's output was excellent. He had a magic formula which others tried to imitate but failed to achieve. His genius has been discussed by many critics, both here and abroad, and his devotees have their favorites among his stories.

"The Gift of the Magi" was undoubtedly the most popular Christmas story he ever wrote, and the account of its creation is as warm and glowing as the tale itself. He wrote it in a period of three hours at a single sitting in his apartment at 55 Irving Place, New York, in late November 1905. The portrait he painted of Della in the story was that of his first wife, Athol Estes, who had died eight years earlier. In his lively biography, *The Caliph of Bagdad,* by Robert H. Davis and Arthur B. Maurice, we read: "'She had a habit of saying little silent prayers about the simplest everyday thing,' wrote O. Henry of Della. In the trying days of the life of Athol Estes Porter, no sacrifice was too great, no weariness of the spirit too demanding, that Athol was not always ready for her husband with a smile and a word of cheer. The habit of 'little silent prayers' was always with her. There was one sad Christmas season that she sold a lace handkerchief that she had made for twenty-five dollars. She was almost penniless herself, but like Della, she devoted the money to a Christmas box for Will, an exile far away in Honduras. She packed the box running a temperature of one hundred and five."

There is more to the making of this story. During the three years O. Henry had lived in New York, his stories published in the *World* had been warmly received. Naturally enough, the Editor requested a story for the magazine section of the Christmas number, to be illustrated in color, and Dan Smith, the paper's leading illustrator, was directed to make the drawings. He knew only too well that O. Henry was famous for procrastinating in carrying out his assignments. His biographers, Davis and Maurice, have recorded this cherished story: "There was the usual desperation when time grew short and no copy was forthcoming from O. Henry. Finally Dan Smith started out on a hunt for the delinquent. Cornering him in his rooms, he extracted the confession that not a line had been written, nor had the author the faintest idea of what the story was to be about. Smith urged the seriousness of the situation. 'I must get to work at once. Can't you tell me something to draw and then fit your story to it?' For a time O. Henry sat in silence. Then in his slow Southern drawl he said: 'I'll tell you what you do, Colonel. Just draw a picture of a poorly furnished room, the kind you find in a boarding house or rooming house over on the West Side. In the room there is only a chair or two, a chest of drawers, a bed, and a trunk. On the bed a man and a girl are sitting side by side. They are talking about Christmas. The man has a watch fob in his hand. He is playing with it while he is thinking. The girl's principal feature is the long, beautiful hair that is hanging down her back. That's all I can think of now. But the story is coming.'

"Paraphrasing O. Henry, the story of that story should end here. But hardly had Dan Smith descended the flight of brownstone steps from Number 55 to the sidewalk of Irving Place than Lindsey Denison received an urgent, imperative telephone call to 'come right over.' Complying, Denison found his host seated at his writing table, penciling sheets of the familiar yellow copy paper. But the story on which he was working was not the one that had been promised to Dan Smith. "With Lindsey Denison's arrival O. Henry pushed aside his manuscript, rose, locked the door of the apartment, produced from a cupboard material entertainment, and pointed to the sofa in the corner of the room. 'Lie down there,' he said, 'I've got to forget this story and write another one. Have to have it done this afternoon and not a line written. I've thought of an idea for it but I need a living model. You are that model. I'm going to write a story about you and your wife. I've never met your wife, but I think that you two are the kind that would make sacrifices for each other. Now stay on the sofa and don't interrupt.' Three hours later O. Henry had written the last lines of 'The Gift of the Magi.'"

THE GIFT OF THE MAGI

ONE dollar and eighty-seven cents. That was all. And sixty cents of it was in pennies. Pennies saved one and two at a time by bulldozing the grocer and the vegetable man and the butcher until one's cheeks burned with the silent imputation of parsimony that such close dealing implied. Three times Della counted it. One dollar and eighty-seven cents. And the next day would be Christmas.

There was clearly nothing to do but flop down on the shabby little couch and howl. So Della did it. Which instigates the moral reflection that life is made up of sobs, sniffles, and smiles, with sniffles predominating.

While the mistress of the home is gradually subsiding from the first stage to the second, take a look at the home. A furnished flat at eight dollars per week. It did not exactly beggar description, but it certainly had that word on the lookout for the mendicancy squad.

In the vestibule below was a letter-box into which no letter would go, and an electric button from which no mortal finger could coax a ring. Also appertaining thereunto was a card bearing the name "Mr. James Dillingham Young."

The "Dillingham" had been flung to the breeze during a former period of prosperity when its possessor was being paid thirty dollars per week. Now, when the income was shrunk to twenty dollars, the letters of "Dillingham" looked blurred, as though they were thinking seriously of contracting to a modest and unassuming D. But whenever Mr. James Dillingham Young came home and reached his flat above he was called "Jim" and greatly hugged by Mrs. James Dillingham Young, already introduced to you as Della. Which is all very good.

Della finished her cry and attended to her cheeks with a powder-puff. She stood by the window and looked out dully at a gray cat walking a gray fence in a gray back yard. Tomorrow would be Christmas Day, and she had only $1.87 with which to buy Jim a present. She had been saving every penny she could for months, with this result. Twenty dollars a week doesn't go far. Expenses had been greater than she had calculated. They always are. Only $1.87 to buy a present for Jim. Her Jim. Many a happy hour she had spent planning for something nice for him. Something fine and rare and sterling—something just a little bit near to being worthy of the honor of being owned by Jim.

There was a pier-glass between the windows of the room. Perhaps you have seen a pier-glass in an eight-dollar flat. A very thin and very agile person may, by observing his reflection in a rapid sequence of longitudinal strips, obtain a fairly accurate conception of his looks. Della, being slender, had mastered the art.

Suddenly she whirled from the window and stood before the glass. Her eyes were shining brilliantly, but her face had lost its color within twenty seconds. Rapidly she pulled down her hair and let it fall to its full length.

Now, there were two possessions of the James Dillingham Youngs in which they both took a mighty pride. One was Jim's gold watch that had been his father's and his grandfather's. The other was Della's hair. Had the Queen of Sheba lived in the flat across the airshaft, Della would have let her hair hang out the window some day to dry just to depreciate Her Majesty's jewels and gifts. Had King Solomon been the janitor, with all his treasures piled up in the basement, Jim would have pulled out his watch every time he passed, just to see him pluck at his beard from envy.

So now Della's beautiful hair fell about her, rippling and shining like a cascade of brown waters. She did it up again nervously and quickly. Once she faltered for a minute and stood still while a tear or two splashed on the worn red carpet.

On went her old brown jacket; on went her old brown hat. With a whirl of skirts and with the brilliant sparkle still in her eyes, she fluttered out the door and down the stairs to the street.

Where she stopped the sign read: "Mme. Sofronie. Hair Goods of All Kinds." One flight up Della ran, and collected herself, panting. Madame, large, too white, chilly, hardly looked the "Sofronie."

"Will you buy my hair?" asked Della.

"I buy hair," said Madame. "Take yer hat off and let's have a sight at the looks of it."

Down rippled the brown cascade.

"Twenty dollars," said Madame, lifting the mass with a practiced hand.

"Give it to me quick," said Della.

Oh, and the next two hours tripped by on rosy wings. Forget the hashed meta-phor. She was ransacking the stores for Jim's present.

She found it at last. It surely had been made for Jim and no one else. There was no other like it in any of the stores, and she had turned all of them inside out. It was a platinum watch-chain, simple and chaste in design, properly proclaiming its value by substance alone and not by meretricious ornamentation—as all good things should do. It was even worthy of The Watch. As soon as she saw it she knew that it must be Jim's. It was like him. Quietness and value—the description applied to both. Twenty-one dollars they took from her for it, and she hurried home with the eighty-seven cents. With that chain on his watch Jim might be properly anxious about the time in any company. Grand as the watch was, he sometimes looked at it on the sly on account of the old leather strap that he used in place of a chain.

When Della reached home her intoxication gave way a little to prudence and reason. She got out her curling-irons and lighted the gas and went to work repairing the ravages made by generosity added to love. Which is always a tremendous task, dear friends—a mammoth task.

Within forty minutes her head was covered with tiny close-lying curls that made her look wonderfully like a truant school-boy. She looked at her reflection in the mirror long, carefully, and critically.

"If Jim doesn't kill me," she said to herself, "before he takes a second look at me, he'll say I look like a Coney Island chorus girl. But what could I do—oh! what could I do with a dollar and eighty-seven cents?"

At seven o'clock the coffee was made and the frying-pan was on the back of the stove, hot and ready to cook the chops.

Jim was never late. Della doubled the watch-chain in her hand and sat on the corner of the table near the door that he always entered. Then she heard his step on the stair away down on the first flight, and she turned white for just a moment. She had a habit of saying little silent prayers about the simplest everyday things, and now she whispered: "Please, God, make him think I am still pretty."

The door opened and Jim stepped in and closed it. He looked thin and very serious. Poor fellow, he was only twenty-two—and to be burdened with a family! He needed a new overcoat and he was without gloves.

Jim stepped inside the door, as immovable as a setter at the scent of quail. His eyes were fixed upon Della, and there was an expression in them that she could not read, and it terrified her. It was not anger, nor surprise, nor disapproval, nor horror, nor any of the sentiments that she had been prepared for. He simply stared at her fixedly with that peculiar expression on his face.

Della wriggled off the table and went for him.

"Jim, darling," she cried, "don't look at me that way. I had my hair cut off and sold it because I couldn't have lived through Christmas without giving you a present. It'll grow out again—you won't mind, will you? I just had to do it. My hair grows awfully fast. Say 'Merry Christmas!' Jim, and let's be happy. You don't know what a nice—what a beautiful, nice gift I've got for you."

"You've cut off your hair?" asked Jim, laboriously, as if he had not arrived at that patent fact yet even after the hardest mental labor.

"Cut it off and sold it," said Della. "Don't you like me just as well, anyhow? I'm me without my hair, ain't I?"

Jim looked about the room curiously.

"You say your hair is gone?" he said, with an air almost of idiocy.

"You needn't look for it," said Della. "It's sold, I tell you—sold and gone, too. It's Christmas Eve, boy. Be good to me, for it went for you. Maybe the hairs of my head were numbered," she went on with a sudden serious sweetness, "but nobody could ever count my love for you. Shall I put the chops on, Jim?"

Out of his trance Jim seemed to quickly wake. He enfolded his Della. For ten seconds let us regard with discreet scrutiny some inconsequential object in the other direction. Eight dollars a week or a million a year— what is the difference? A mathematician or a wit would give you the wrong answer. The Magi brought valuable gifts, but that was not among them. This dark assertion will be illuminated later on.

Jim drew a package from his overcoat pocket and threw it upon the table.

"Don't make any mistake, Dell," he said, "about me. I don't think there's anything in the way of a haircut or a shave or a shampoo that could make me like my girl any less. But if you'll unwrap that package you may see why you had me going awhile at first."

White fingers and nimble tore at the string and paper. And then an ecstatic scream of joy; and then, alas! a quick feminine change to hysterical tears and wails, necessitating the immediate employment of all the comforting powers of the lord of the flat.

For there lay The Combs—the set of combs that Della had worshiped for long in a Broadway window. Beautiful combs, pure tortoise shell, with jeweled rims—just the shade to wear in the beautiful vanished hair. They were expensive combs, she knew, and her heart had simply craved and yearned over them without the least hope of possession. And now they were hers, but the tresses that should have adorned the coveted adornments were gone.

But she hugged them to her bosom, and at length she was able to look up with dim eyes and a smile and say: "My hair grows so fast, Jim!"

And then Della leaped up like a little singed cat and cried, "Oh, oh!"

Jim had not yet seen his beautiful present. She held it out to him eagerly upon her open palm. The dull precious metal seemed to flash with a reflection of her bright and ardent spirit.

"Isn't it a dandy, Jim? I hunted all over town to find it. You'll have to look at the time a hundred times a day now. Give me your watch. I want to see how it looks on it."

Instead of obeying, Jim tumbled down on the couch and put his hands under the back of his head and smiled.

"Dell," he said, "let's put our Christmas presents away and keep 'em awhile. They're too nice to use just at present. I sold the watch to get the money to buy your combs. And now suppose you put the chops on."

The Magi, as you know, were wise men —wonderfully wise men—who brought gifts to the Babe in the manger. They in-vented the art of giving Christmas pres-ents. Being wise, their gifts were no doubt wise ones, possibly bearing the privilege of exchange in case of duplication. And here I have lamely related to you the un-eventful chronicle of two foolish children in a flat who most unwisely sacrificed for each other the greatest treasures of their house. But in a last word to the wise of these days let it be said that of all who give gifts these two were the wisest. Of all who give and receive gifts, such as they are wisest. Everywhere they are wisest. They are the Magi.

Bibliography

ALCOTT, LOUISA MAY, "Hospital Sketches." Boston: Redpath, 1863

ALCOTT, LOUISA MAY, "Hospital Sketches (Edited by Bessie Z. Jones)." Cambridge: Harvard University Press, 1960

ALCOTT, LOUISA MAY, "Life, Letters, and Journals, Edited by Ednah D. Cheney." 1889

ALDRICH, MRS. THOMAS BAILEY, "Crowding Memories." Boston: Houghton Mifflin, 1920

ANDERSEN, HANS CHRISTIAN, "Christmas Story Book." New York: Leavitt & Allen Bros., 1871

ANDERSEN, HANS CHRISTIAN, "Stories and Tales." New York: Hurd & Houghton, 1871

ANDERSEN, HANS CHRISTIAN, "The Story of My Life." Boston: Houghton Mifflin, 1871

ANONYMOUS, "Casual Essays of the Sun." New York: Robert Grier Cooke, 1905

ANONYMOUS, "Christmas in Art and Song: A Collection of Songs, Carols and Descriptive Poems, Relating to the Festival of Christmas." New York: Arundel Publishing & Printing Co., 1880

ANONYMOUS, "Christmas Eve, and Other Stories (From the German)." Boston: Crosby Nichols, 18—

ANTHONY, KATHARINE, "Louisa May Alcott." New York: Knopf, 1938

AULD, WILLIAM MUIR, "Christmas Traditions." New York: Macmillan, 1931

BARNETT, JAMES H., "The American Christmas." New York: Macmillan, 1954

BARTON, WILLIAM E., "The Life of Clara Barton, 2 Vols." 1922

BECKER, MAY LAMBERTON, "Golden Tales of the Old South." New York: Dodd, Mead, 1930

BLANCK, JACOB, "Peter Parley to Penrod." New York: R. R. Bowker, 1938

BOTKIN, B. A., "A Treasury of New England Folklore." New York: Crown Publishing Co., 1947

BROOKS, VAN WYCK, "The Confident Years: 1885-1915." New York: E. P. Dutton, 1952

BROWN, FRANCES, "The Chirstmas Annual." Cleveland: E. Cowles, 1860

BUDAY, GEORGE, "The History of the Christmas Carol." London: Rockliff, 1954

BUTTERWORTH, HEZEKIAH, "The Parson's Miracle and My Grandmother's Grandmother's Christmas Candle (Christmas in America)." Boston: Dana Estes & Co., 1894.

CATTON, BRUCE, "This Hallowed Ground." New York: Doubleday, 1956

CHASE, ERNEST D., "The Romance of Greeting Cards." Boston: Cambridge University Press, 1926

CHENEY, EDNAH D., "Louisa May Alcott, Her Life, Letters and Journals." Boston: Roberts Bros., 1889

CHESNUT, MARY BOYKIN, "A Diary from Dixie, Edited by Ben Ames Williams." Boston: Houghton Mifflin, 1949

CHESTERTON, G. K., "Charles Dickens." New York: Dodd, Mead, 1917

CLARKE, J. ERSKINE, Editor, "Chatterbox." Boston: Dana Estes, 1878-1905

CLISSOLD, STEPHEN, "Denmark, the Land of Hans Andersen." London: Hutchinson, 1955

COMMANGER, HENRY STEELE, Editor, "The St. Nicholas Anthology." New York: Random House, 1948

CRADDOCK, CHARLES E. (Pseudonym of Mary M. Murfree), "The Young Mountaineers." Boston: Houghton Mifflin, 1897

CRIPPEN, T. G., "Christmas and Christmas Lore." London: Blackie, 1923

DAVIS, ROBERT H., and MAURICE, ARTHUR B., "The Caliph of Bagdad." New York: D. Appleton & Co., 1931

DICKENS, CHARLES, "The Holly Tree and Other Christmas Stories." New York: Scribner's

DOWDEY, CLIFFORD, "The Land They Fought For." New York: Doubleday, 1955

ELLSWORTH, WILLIAM W., "A Golden Age of Authors." Boston: Houghton Mifflin, 1919

FINLEY, RUTH E., "The Lady of Godey's, Sarah Josepha Hale." Philadelphia: J. B. Lippincott, 1931

FOSTER, CHARLES H., "The Rungless Ladder, Harriet Beecher Stowe and New England Puritanism." Durham, N. C.: Duke University Press, 1954

FOX, JOHN, JR., "Christmas Eve on Lonesome and Other Stories." New York: Charles Scribner's Sons, 1904

FREEMAN, RUTH and LARRY, "Cavalcade of Toys." New York: Century House, 1942

GASKELL, MRS., "Cranford." New York: Macmillan, 1892

GODDEN, RUMER, "Hans Christian Andersen." New York: A. A. Knopf, 1955

GODEY'S LADY'S BOOK AND MAGAZINE, Edited by Mrs. Sarah J. Hale and Louis A. Godey. Philadelphia: Louis A. Godey

GORDON, ARMISTEAD C., "Memories and Memorials of William Gordon McCabe, 2 Vols." Richmond, Va.: Old Dominion Press, 1925

GREENSLET, FERRIS, "The Life of Thomas Bailey Aldrich." Boston: Houghton Mifflin, 1908

HALE, E. E., and SUSAN A., "A Family Flight Through France, Germany, Norway and Switzerland." Boston: Lothrop, 1881

HALE, EDWARD E., "Christmas Eve and Christmas Day." Boston: Roberts Bros., 1873

HALE, LUCRETIA P., "The Complete Peterkin Papers." (With the Original Illustrations and an Introduction by Nancy Hale.) Boston: Houghton Mifflin, 1960

HALE, LUCRETIA P., "The Peterkin Papers." New York: Looking Glass Library

HARRISON, MICHAEL, "The Story of Christmas." London: Odhams Press

HARTE, GEOFFREY BRET, "The Letters of Bret Harte." Boston: Houghton Mifflin, 1926

HAUGAN, RALPH E., "Christmas, An American Annual of Christmas Literature and Art." Vols. 1-31. Minneapolis: Augsburg Publishing House, 1959

HONIG, DONALD, Editor, "The Blue and Gray." New York: Avon, 1961

HOTTES, ALFRED CARL, "1001 Christmas Facts and Fancies." New York: De la Mare, 1937

HOUSE, HUMPHRY, "The Dickens World." London: Oxford University Press, 1942

HOWARD, BLANCHE, "One Year Abroad." Boston: Osgood, 1877

HUGHES, WILLIAM R., "A Week's Tramp in Dickens-Land." London: Chapman and Hall, 1891

IRVING, WASHINGTON, "Old Christmas." (From The Sketch Book, Illustrated by R. Caldecott.) London: Macmillan, 1876

JONES, J. B., "A Rebel War Clerk's Diary." Philadelphia: Lippincott, 1866

JONES, KATHARINE M., "Heroines of Dixie (Confederate Women Tell Their Story of the War)." New York: Bobbs-Merrill, 1955

JORDAN, ALICE M., "From Rollo to Tom Sawyer." Boston: The Horn Book, 1948

KANE, HARTNETT T., "The Southern Christmas Book." New York: David McKay, Inc., 1958

KELLEHER, D. L., "An Anthology of Christmas Prose and Verse." London: Cresset Press, 1928

KELSEY, D. M., "Deeds of Daring by the American Soldier, North and South." New York: Saalfield, 1907

KEYES, FRANCIS P., "Roses in December." New York: Doubleday, 1960

KING, W. C., and DERBY, W. P. (Compilers), "Camp Fire Sketches and Battlefield Echoes." Springfield, Mass.: 1888

KRYTHE, MAYMIE R., "All About Christmas." New York: Harper & Bros., 1954

LANGTON, ROBERT, "The Childhood and Youth of Charles Dickens." New York: Charles Scribner's Sons, 1811

LAVER, JAMES, "Victorian Vista." London: Hulton Press, 1954

LAWRENCE, WILLIAM, "Life of Phillips Brooks." New York: Harper & Bros., 1930

LEACOCK, STEPHEN, "Charles Dickens." New York: Doubleday Doran, 1934

LEECH, MARGARET, "Reveille in Washington 1860-1865." New York: Harper & Bros., 1941

LEISY, ERNEST E., "The American Historical Novel." Norman, Oklahoma: University of Oklahoma Press, 1950

LEWIS, D. B. W., and HASELTINE, G. C., "A Christmas Book." London: J. M. Dent, 1928

LICHTEN, FRANCES, "Decorative Arts of Victoria's Era." New York: Scribner, 1950

LONGLEY, MARJORIE; SILVERSTEIN, LOUIS; and TOWER, SAMUEL A., "America's Taste 1851-1959." New York: Simon and Schuster, 1960

LORANT, STEPHAN, "The Life of Abraham Lincoln." New York: Mentor, 1961

MABIE, HAMILTON W., "The Book of Christmas." New York: Macmillan, 1909

McCOSKEY, J. P., "Christmas in Song, Sketch and Story." New York: Harper & Bros., 1891

McGINNIS, R. J., "The Good Old Days." New York: Harper, 1960

McGUIRE, JUDITH W., "Diary of a Southern Refugee, During the War, by A Lady of Virginia." Richmond, Va.: Randolph & English, 1889

MASON, MIRIAM E., "Yours With Love, Kate." Boston: Houghton Mifflin, 1952

MEIGS, CORNELIA, "Invincible Louisa (The Story of the Author of Little Women)." Boston: Little, Brown, 1933

MERWIN, HENRY C., "The Life of Bret Harte." Boston: Houghton Mifflin, 1911

MILES, CLEMENT A., "Christmas in Ritual and Tradition, Christian and Pagan." London: Unwin, 1912

MIMS, EDWIN, and PAYNE, BRUCE R., "Southern Prose and Poetry for Schools." New York: Charles Scribner's Sons, 1910

MITCHELL, EDWARD P., "Memoirs of an Editor." New York: Charles Scribner's Sons, 1910

MORRIS, CHARLES, "The Life of Queen Victoria and the Story of Her Reign." New York: Scull, 1901

MOSES, MONTROSE J., "The Literature of the South." New York: Crowell, 1910

MUIR, PERCY H., "Children's Books of Yesterday." London: National Book League, 1946

MURPHY, WILLIAM H., "Kriss Kringle's Raree Show for Good Boys and Girls." New York: Murphy, 1847

MURRAY, W. H. H., "Adirondack Tales." Burlington, Vt.: Murray Lyceum Bureau, 1886

MURRAY, W. H. H., "How John Norton the Trapper Kept His Christmas." Boston: DeWolfe, Fiske, 1891

NINDE, EDWARD S., "The Story of the American Hymn." New York: Abingdon, 1921

NORTON, CHARLES E., "Henry Wadsworth Longfellow." Boston: Houghton Mifflin, 1907

PAINE, ALBERT B., "Th(omas) Nast: His Period and His Pictures." New York: Macmillan, 1904

PATTEE, FRED L., "A History of American Literature." New York: Century, 1915

PAYNE, EDWARD F., "Dickens' Days in Boston." Boston: Houghton Mifflin, 1927

PERRY, BLISS, "Park-Street Papers." Boston: Houghton Mifflin, 1908

PIERCE, GILBERT A., "The Dickens Dictionary." Boston: Houghton Mifflin, 1872

PRYOR, MRS. ROGER A., "My Day: Reminiscences of a Long Life." New York: Macmillan, 1909

PRYOR, MRS. ROGER A., "Reminiscences of Peace and War." New York: Macmillan, 1905

REESE, LIZETTE WOODWORTH, "A Victorian Village." New York: Farrar & Rinehart, 1929

RICHARDS, KATHERINE L., "How Christmas Came to the Sunday Schools." New York: Dodd, Mead & Co., 1934

RICHARDS, LAURA E., "Four Feet, Two Feet, and No Feet; or Furry and Feathery Pets, and How They Live." Boston: Page, 1886

RICHARDS, LAURA E., "Stepping Westward." New York: D. Appleton, 1931

RICHARDS, LAURA E., "When I Was Your Age." Boston: Page, 1893

RICHMOND, GRACE S., "On Christmas Day in the Morning, On Christmas Day in the Evening." New York: Doubleday, Page, 1905

RIIS, JACOB A., "Out of Mulberry Street." New York: Century Co., 1898

RIIS, JACOB A., "The Children of the Tenements." New York: Macmillan, 1904

RIIS, JACOB A., "The Old Town." New York: Macmillan, 1909

SAFFORD, MARY J., "The Christmas Country and Other Tales." New York: Crowell, 1886

SANDBURG, CARL, "Abraham Lincoln, The Prairie Years and the War Years." 3 Vols. New York: Harcourt, Brace, 1939

SETON, ANYA, "Washington Irving." Boston: Houghton Mifflin, 1960

SHOEMAKER, ALFRED L., "Christmas in Pennsylvania." Kutztown, Pennsylvania: Pennsylvania Folklife Society, 1959

SHUTE, HENRY A., "The Real Diary of a Real Boy." Chicago: Reilly & Lee

SIDGWICK, ALFRED (MRS.), "Home Life in Germany." New York: Macmillan, 1908

SMITH, NORA A., "Kate Douglas Wiggin, as Her Sister Knew Her." Boston: Houghton Mifflin, 1925

STEBBINS, LUCY P., "A Victorian Album." New York: Columbia University Press, 1946

STEDMAN, CLARENCE E., "A Victorian Anthology." Boston: Houghton Mifflin, 1895

STEPHENS, C. A., "A Great Year of Our Lives at the Old Squire's." Norway, Maine: The Old Squire's Bookshop, 1912

STERN, MADELINE B., "Louisa May Alcott." Norman, Oklahoma: University of Oklahoma Press, 1950

STOWE, HARRIET BEECHER, "Betty's Bright Idea, also, Deacon Pitkin's Farm and The First Christmas of New England." New York: J. B. Ford, 1876

STOWE, HARRIET BEECHER, "Oldtown Folks." Boston: Fields, Osgood, 1869

THARP, LOUISE H., "Adventurous Alliance, the Story of the Agassiz Family of Boston." Boston: Little, Brown, 1959

THARP, LOUISE H., "The Peabody Sisters of Salem." Boston: Little, Brown, 1950

THARP, LOUISE H., "Three Saints and a Sinner." Boston: Little, Brown, 1956

THARP, LOUISE H., "Until Victory: Horace Mann and Mary Peabody." Boston: Little, Brown, 1953

TICKNOR, CAROLINE, "Glimpses of Authors." Boston: Houghton Mifflin, 1922

TUER, ANDREW W., "Forgotten Children's Books." London: Leadenhall Press, 1898

VAN DYKE, HENRY, "The First Christmas Tree." New York: Scribner, 1897

WAGENKNECHT, EDWARD, "A Fireside Book of Yuletide Tales." New York: Bobbs Merrill, 1948

WAGENKNECHT, EDWARD, "Cavalcade of the American Novel." New York: Holt, 1952

WAGENKNECHT, EDWARD, "Longfellow, A Full-Length Portrait." New York: Longmans, Green, 1955

WEISER, FRANCIS X., "Handbook of Christian Feasts and Customs." New York: Harcourt, Brace, 1952

WEISER, FRANCIS X., "The Christmas Book." New York: Harcourt, Brace, 1952

WERNECKE, HERBERT H., "Christmas Customs Around the World." Philadelphia: Westminster Press, 1959

WIGGIN, KATE DOUGLAS, "My Garden of Memory, An Autobiography." Boston: Houghton, Mifflin, 1923

WIGGIN, KATE DOUGLAS, "The Birds' Christmas Carol." Boston: Houghton Mifflin, 1895

WITHAM, W. WOSKER, "Panorama of American Literature." New York: Stephen Daye Press, 1947

WOOLSON, CONSTANCE F., "The Front Yard and Other Italian Stories." New York: Harper, 1895

WORTHINGTON, MARJORIE, "Miss Alcott of Concord." New York: Doubleday, 1958

WYNN, WILLIAM T., "Southern Literature, Selections and Biographies." New York: Prentice-Hall, 1932

YOUNG, AGATHA, "The Women and the Crisis, Women of the North in the Civil War." New York: McDowell, Obolensky, 1959

ZABEL, MORTON D., "Charles Dickens' Best Stories." New York: Hanover House, 1959

Index